BEASTS
OF THE
FR⊘ZEN
SUN

BEASTS
OF THE
FRZEN
SUN

JILL CRISWELL

**BLACK
STONE**
PUBLISHING

Copyright © 2019 by Jill Criswell
Published in 2019 by Blackstone Publishing
Cover and book design by Kurt Jones

Printed in the United States of America

First edition: 2019
ISBN 978-1-9825-5627-3
Young Adult Fiction / Fantasy / General

1 3 5 7 9 10 8 6 4 2

CIP data for this book is available
from the Library of Congress

Blackstone Publishing
31 Mistletoe Rd.
Ashland, OR 97520

www.BlackstonePublishing.com

For Brock, for everything

Softly fell the final words of Aillira,
once-beloved mortal, mistress of the Great Betrayer:
"Burn brightly. Love fiercely. For all else is dust."
Thus she breathed her last,
relinquishing her spirit to the god of death's final judgment.
Thus did her children light the fire of her cleansing,
carrying forth through the ashes of her destruction.
—The Immortal Scriptures

PART ONE
GIANTS AND GODS

PROLOGUE

The enemy's small army was spread out before him, waving their weapons, shouting, beating in wild fury upon their shields. They looked more like fishermen than fighters. Reyker would have pitied them if there had been any room left for pity in his decaying heart.

Behind him came the snarls of his fellow warriors; the Dragonmen stared down the fishermen, awaiting his signal.

Reyker squeezed the sword in his right hand, the axe in his left, closing his eyes.

Inside him, the black river stirred—sloshing, boiling, churning. A river of blood and fire, the darkest part of his soul. *Let me out,* it begged.

When his eyes opened, every fisherman bore the loathsome face of the warlord. Reyker arched his neck skyward, roaring at the lambent stars. The Dragonmen howled, joining their animal songs to his.

Let me out.

So he did.

He barely felt the splash of blood, the jolt of axe and sword slicing through flesh. He forgot who these men were as he cut them down—fathers, brothers, husbands, sons. He obeyed the black river's call: slash, strike, stab. It flowed through his limbs, foaming, frothing. It was darkness. It was death.

With every kill, its hunger grew.

With every kill, he was reborn.

—◆—

Around him, fires burned. Corpses sprawled in the dirt. His weapons dripped blood. The battle was finished, the black river sated. All were dead.

All save one. A boy of thirteen, a skilled archer who'd felled three Dragonmen before he was captured. Looking at the boy—young, ferocious, brave to the point of stupidity—Reyker saw himself as he'd once been. He couldn't kill the boy; even monsters like him had limits.

The idea came on a whim. Set the boy free to spread the tale: those who defied the Dragonmen would witness their homes burned, their women stolen, their sons slain.

Reyker steered the boy toward the rowboat, pointing with his sword. "Go."

The boy stared, brown eyes shadowed with hate. He shouted threats of murder, vows of vengeance. Things Reyker had heard before. Things Reyker had said himself as a boy, sitting in the blood-painted snow, his father dying in his arms.

Reyker raised the sword higher. "Go!"

The boy pushed the boat into the cold grip of the sea and toppled in. Grabbing the oars, he rowed away from the island, yelling all the while. Reyker watched until he disappeared.

It didn't matter that Reyker had spared him. He'd killed the boy's people, torched his village. Reyker knew he deserved to die for it.

Someday he would.

When he returned, the warlord stood atop the ruins of the village, addressing the Dragonmen. Tall, imposing, glowing like a golden god. Draki's eyes—an odd hue, green and yellow and gold all at once—missed nothing; they watched Reyker, narrowing.

"You fought well, my brothers," Draki said. "The Rocky Isles now belong to us. But this is only the beginning. When we take the Green Isle, we will show them what a warrior is—a man made of ice and steel." The warlord pounded a fist against his torso, scanning the Dragonmen's eager faces. "Many will kneel before us in awe. The rest will fall to their knees as we cut their legs from beneath them!"

This was met with laughter and howls.

"We have bided our time, strengthening our forces, learning our enemies' weaknesses. We have allowed them to grow fat with riches as we waited on the gods to command us. And the gods have finally spoken!" Draki raised his sword, pointing it at the sky. "Now we strike! The dogs of the east will learn that we are their rightful masters. In the name of the sea god Sjaf, father of our kind, all will bow. In the name of Ildja, eater of souls, all will submit. The era of dogs is over. The Age of the Dragon is upon us!"

The warriors erupted, a riot of celebration. Ale belonging to the dead islanders was brought forth. War chants were sung. Captured women were dragged out, and the men selected which ones they would take to their beds this night.

Draki smiled. This was what he preached: The Dragon and his men were endowed by the gods. The world, and everything in it, existed to be conquered. All was theirs for the taking.

Reyker observed in silence, the lone dissenter.

The warlord approached. "You disapprove of the festivities?"

"I am Sjaf's disciple, servant of Iseneld, a blade to be wielded for the glory of my gods and homeland," Reyker answered flatly, quoting the Dragonmen's code. "If my liege approves, so must I."

Chuckling, Draki slapped Reyker's shoulder. "Ah, Reyker, the reluctant Sword of the Dragon. At last you wear the mask of a dutiful Dragonman. But we both know a rebel's heart still beats beneath it." Draki punched his fist into Reyker's sternum, grabbing Reyker by the neck as he doubled over. "Conquer the Green Isle's north harbor," Draki said, "and perhaps I'll let you keep your heart in your body and live to thwart me a little longer."

The warlord released him. Reyker straightened, ignoring the spikes of pain in his chest.

"I know why you let that young archer go. You can hide nothing from me." Draki shook his head. "After all this time, you continue to cling to your shattered honor. It makes you weak."

"It makes me human."

"Humans are weak. You should wish to be like the gods. You should beg Ildja's forgiveness for not delivering every last one of your enemies to the Mist." Draki laughed again, deep and grating. "Do you remember our scouting expedition to the north harbor, all those years ago? You must be wondering about that sweet little creature we caught in the forest. Such a shame she *escaped*."

Reyker drew a shallow breath. From his memories of a time when he'd still had hope, before he'd become the bastard he was now, came an image—a girl with green eyes full of fire. Another soul he'd snatched from Ildja's waiting jaws.

"I've commanded your legion to find the girl and bring her to me," the warlord said. "Should you try to stop them, their orders are to chop off your sword hand. If you continue to deny Ildja the souls that are rightfully hers to consume, the goddess will seek retribution. And so will I." Draki's smile was as sharp as a blade.

When the warlord turned to leave, Reyker's fingers twitched toward his dagger, aching to bury it in Draki's back. If he'd thought it would change anything, Reyker would not have hesitated, but he knew it would only make things worse.

There was no defeating the Dragon.

Reyker stood in the longship's stem, gazing past the horned dragon figurehead, out at the rolling sea. The Green Isle's north harbor came into view, a blurred shadow on the horizon.

He couldn't say why he'd done it, but before climbing into the ship the previous morning, he'd taken the pendant from where he always kept it, tied to his sword's sheath. He'd cut a length of rope from a fishing net and fit it through the loop, knotting it around his neck. The pendant was tucked beneath his tunic, a cold circle of metal resting against his chest.

If he'd had any hope left inside him, Reyker would have used it on the green-eyed girl from the forest, hoping that she no longer lived in the village he was about to attack. Hoping that she was far from the Dragon's reach, and from his own. As the ship drew closer, he could feel her presence growing stronger, like sparks in the air before a storm. It was the blood magic, awakening the connection he'd forged between them. He wondered if she felt it too.

The shadow took shape. He could make out cliffs and hills, the forest beyond.

Another island. Another ambush. An endless stretch of blood and fire.

Do you watch me from the afterworlds, Mother? Do you loathe what your son has become? The thought sickened him.

A sudden movement in the water caught Reyker's attention. A large creature breached alongside the longship—there, then gone.

Cold dread chilled him. This was no shark or whale. It surfaced again, closer.

A giant black sea-beast, rushing straight for them.

"Spears! Arrows!" Reyker shouted, drawing his weapons. The creature reared its head. It was a demon from the bowels of some dark nether-realm. Reyker hurled his spear, and the point sank into the demon's flesh just as it smashed into the hull. The ship shuddered beneath Reyker's feet, water flooding in.

"Bail!" Reyker called, but it was too late. They were sinking fast.

The sea was merciless, white waves curling around the longship as it foundered. Every man went into the water.

Someone screamed.

A warrior vanished beneath the waves, a rose-colored cloud efflorescing in his wake. Then another man was sucked under. And another. Reyker's comrades—men he respected and reviled, men he'd fought beside and bled with. They were snatched so fast it seemed the demon was in two places at once. Blood tinted the sea red.

He clung to a piece of wreckage, struggling to keep his head above the whitecaps, and watched numbly as every man was taken and devoured.

The demon came for Reyker last.

He stared into the quivering black globes of its eyes, inhaled the sour stench from its gaping mouth. Was this one of Ildja's Destroyers—demons she sent to fetch evil men to her lair? Or was it Ildja herself beneath the monster's scales? Had the serpent-goddess finally come for her retribution: to swallow him, body and soul?

The demon's jaws snapped around him, teeth digging into his flesh, dragging him down into the abyss. It was only instinct that made him kick and fight until his breath was gone.

When that dark womb of stillness engulfed him, he embraced it with a flood of relief. Reyker welcomed whatever torments awaited him on the other side of this world, knowing it was nothing less than he deserved.

CHAPTER 1

It was no small thing to touch a man's soul. To trace the essence of his being, know him as no one—not his mother, brother, or lover—ever could.

Each soul I'd touched was different. They could be dark or light, warm or cold, sharp-edged or smooth. They contained colors and shapes that didn't exist in our world. Some hummed, sang, or screamed. Some smelled of metal, others tasted like salt. Often, I saw scattered images of things the person loved, hated, or feared.

No matter what a soul was like, I sensed its burdens. The weight of guilt was distinct.

The prisoner standing before me, the cord of his life tangling fatefully with mine, was a herdsman named Dyfed. His ankles and wrists were shackled, but my brothers and uncle still held him as Father ushered me forward.

"I done nothing wrong, milady," Dyfed said.

I placed my palm inside his tunic, against his chest. His heart drummed nervously beneath my hand. I closed my eyes, searching.

Around me, the great hall disappeared. I floated in the gauzy realms of the intangible. This man's soul was sharp and light, spread out before me. A warm sphere in its center held an imprint of his family. I waded through pride, love, disappointment—each emotion had its own texture and consistency. I caught a glimpse of what I sought, appearing as if from a fog: the outline of swords, poleaxes, bows. A cartload of weapons, shrouded in cold guilt.

I let go and took a step back.

"Well, Lira?" Father asked. "Did he steal from the armory?"

This was my role in our clan. I'd been touched by the gods, born with the ability to read souls. While other god-gifted women of my island—the Daughters of Aillira, as we were called—were adept at healing, story-telling, navigation, and foretelling foul weather, my gift was different. As a soul-reader, I could steal a man's secrets, reveal his darkest sins.

Father trusted me. I could not lie. "He is guilty, as suspected."

"You're wrong!" Dyfed cried. With a quick jerk, he pulled free from the other men, grabbing my arms. His red-rimmed eyes bored into mine. "There's more. Look again, soul-reader, and you will see—"

My uncle, Madoc, tackled Dyfed, slamming his head against the ground, and Dyfed's eyes rolled up until only the whites showed. My older brother, Garreth, kicked the prone herdsman for good measure, cursing him beneath his breath. When Garreth turned, we shared the briefest of looks, but much was said. *Father is wrong to use you this way*, he seethed in a silent language only siblings could share. *Mother would never have allowed this.*

Mother would want our clan to be safe, I responded. *I want to help, however I can.*

We'd quarreled over this point many times. Was it right for me to be a man's judge? Was it right for Father to ask it of me? I knew Garreth's feelings on the matter. I'd yet to find answers that satisfied my own conscience.

My younger brother, Rhys, clasped my elbow, offering what comfort he could.

"Ready the gallows," Father said to Madoc, "and inform the chieftain and the villagers that there's to be an execution."

My throat tightened at the word. I'd condemned men before, but they had been whipped, imprisoned, or exiled. Never executed.

Madoc's spine stiffened at being given an order by his younger brother. His mouth was an angry slit in his hardened face, but he grabbed Dyfed by the chains on his wrists and dragged him away.

When they were gone, Father sighed and bent over the grand table that took up a corner of the room, palms pressing against the tabletop. On the back of his right hand was the warrior-mark of the Sons of Stone, my clan's legion of warriors: three swords in the shape of a triangle, inked onto the back of the sword hand, so any man foolish enough to cross blades with any one of them would know which clan was about to send him to his grave.

Between Father's hands lay a map of Glasnith, detailing all the village names and the clans who controlled them. I could see Stony Harbor depicted at the very top of the map—the seat of clan Stone, ruled by Lord Aengus, my grandfather. Our village was reduced to a name and the triad of swords that was our clan's symbol. I'd often watched my father study this map, seeing the keen way his mind sorted through lists of landholdings and goods produced, access to ports and trade routes, quality and quantity of combat forces. He was always looking for opportunities to strengthen our clan's position within the convoluted web of alliances.

My brothers and I had been taught to be silent and still when our father conducted clan business. We stood like statues, waiting for him to address us.

"Garreth." Father's voice cut through the air like a lash. My brother straightened his spine even further, pulling his shoulders back. "You cannot allow your anger to get the best of you. Beating an unconscious prisoner is unseemly and beneath your station."

Garreth stepped forward. "The thief went after Lira, Commander. I should have done worse." He spoke with quiet respect, but rage simmered beneath the surface.

"If you wish to be commander one day, you must conduct yourself as a highborn warrior rather than a witless barbarian." Father stood eye-to-eye with his eldest child, regarding him with deep-seated frustration. The resemblance between them was so strong they looked like different-aged versions of the same man. "You'll be mucking out the hog sties this week instead of patrolling. That ought to cool your temper."

Garreth's face reddened. "But, Father—"

"*Commander*," he corrected. "And that was an order, not a request. You are dismissed." For a moment, I thought Garreth would argue, but then his mouth clicked shut. His steps, as he departed, were louder than necessary.

Father had always been hard on Garreth, grooming him to be a commander, possibly a chieftain. I knew he feared Garreth's dark moods and quick temper might turn him into a man more like Madoc than himself.

"Are you all right, daughter?" Father turned to me. When I nodded, he sighed again and ran a hand across his jaw. "What your brother did was wrong, but I cannot say the prisoner didn't deserve it."

"Father." I approached the table. "Please. Don't execute him. Dyfed is not an evil man. I saw—"

"Lira. As always, I thank you for your help, but you must leave decisions regarding men's punishments to me." He kissed the top of my head, a doting gesture left over from when I was small. Sadness glinted in his gaze. With each passing year, I looked more like my mother. I had the same long hair, a deep shade of burgundy. I had her same eyes too, a color Father called springtime grass. It must have hurt him to look at me, a constant reminder of what he'd lost. What we'd all lost.

"Rhys?" At the sound of his name, my younger brother's face lit up, eager for our father's attention. "Escort your sister home."

"Aye, Commander."

"No," I said. "I condemned Dyfed to death. I must bear witness to his execution." When Father started to protest, I overruled him with the logic he used on his own warriors. "How can I understand the consequences of my actions if I do not see them through to the end?"

Father regarded me. "Condemning a man is very different than watching him die. I'd prefer to spare you this, but if it's what you wish, I'll allow it."

"It is."

"Very well. Rhys, escort your sister to the gallows."

My brother led me out of the great hall, past the block of stone cells reserved for holding prisoners until their punishments were decided. We stopped at the back of the crowd that was already gathering around the gallows. The grim tidings had spread quickly.

"Why are you doing this?" Rhys asked.

"You know why." I loved both of my brothers dearly, but they filled very different spaces within my life. Garreth was my self-appointed mentor and protector, and Rhys was my friend. He understood me, as I did him.

"It's not your fault, Lir. Dyfed stole from our clan. That makes him a traitor. He earned his death sentence." These were Father's declarations, coming from my brother's mouth.

"You believe that no more than I do."

"It doesn't matter what we believe. Grandfather is chieftain. Father and Madoc are commanders, as Garreth will be one day. But you and I are followers. I'm a second-born son and a terrible warrior. You're god-gifted and smart, but you're still only a girl to them. Our place is to do as we're told. We've no other worth."

"Father's a second son."

"I'm not Torin." Rhys had the same nut-brown hair and eyes as Father and Garreth, but the similarities ended there—they were born warriors, but Rhys was a quiet, gentle soul. "You should leave Stony Harbor, Lir. You should go to Aillira's Temple. At least there you'll be allowed to make your own choices."

There were two diverging paths my life could take. As a god-gifted Daughter of Aillira, I could pledge myself to Aillira's Temple, a sanctuary in the center of Glasnith where girls like me went to study with priest-esses, learning how to hone their abilities and use them to serve the gods. Or I could marry a highborn lord from an allied clan and sire children to continue the traditions of our clans and country. Both were lifelong commitments. My father had left it for me to decide, but there was little time left. It was only half a year until my eighteenth birthday, when I would have to give an answer. I'd not yet chosen. The notion that I must choose one, and that there were no options but these, rankled me.

"What, and leave my wee brother to care for himself?" I spoke in jest, but it was the truth. How could I leave Rhys? Or Garreth or Father? How could I ever choose to be parted from my family? "You're more than a second son and a lousy warrior to me, you know."

"Aye, I'm the sap who helps you sneak around and defy Father's orders all the time." Rhys's tone was light, but his grip on my arm tightened. The crowd around us had grown. Dyfed's son Ennis was here, pale and frightened, glaring when he saw me.

I was the soul-reader, the one who judged men's guilt. The one who'd damned his father.

Would the other Daughters of Aillira at the temple hate or fear me as the villagers did?

Garreth spotted us, pushing his way through the crowd. "What are you doing here?" He stepped to my side, taking my other arm. "We're going home, Lira. I won't let you watch this."

"No." I held firm. "This is my choice. I'm staying."

Besides, it was too late. Father and Madoc were already steering Dyfed toward the scaffolding steps, his wrists and ankles still chained. Lord Aengus was with them. The chieftain was an older man, his hair and beard gray, his face wrinkled, but he still carried himself like the great warrior he'd once been.

Father threw the rope over the gallows' crossbeam. Madoc knotted the noose.

I could hardly bear to look at Dyfed as he was made to stand upon a crate beneath the gallows. He shook with terror.

"Dyfed of Stone," Aengus called loudly, "you have been found guilty of stealing weapons from your own clan. For this crime, you are sentenced to hang. May the god of death have mercy on your sinful soul."

"Look away, Lira," Garreth said.

I didn't. Madoc kicked the crate out from under Dyfed's feet. The herdsman thrashed, swinging from the noose. His son cried out, but others cheered.

Rhys and Garreth stood on either side of me, as if their presence could protect me from the sight, the awful consequences of using my gift.

I swallowed hard to keep from retching and clenched my fists, digging my nails into my palms.

I had done this. I helped kill this man.

I watched until it was over, until Dyfed dangled motionless. The rope creaked in the wind. Only then did I let my brothers lead me away.

When we neared the stables, I pulled free from them. "I want to ride."

My brothers followed me as I entered the stables, breathing in the scent of straw and manure. Winter stuck her head out, whickering. I scratched between her ears and she pressed her muzzle against my chest. The beautiful white mare had been a gift from Father.

Garreth shook his head. "You're going home."

"Don't you have pig shite to shovel?" I ignored him and looked to my younger brother. "Please, Rhys. I need to get away. Just for a little while."

"No," Garreth said again.

Rhys hugged me. "Go on," he said. "Just be careful."

"Always." Through my skirts, I patted the knife sheathed to my thigh. I was on Winter's back and out of the stables in a flash, leaving Rhys to deal with Garreth's ire.

Our village was surrounded by the Tangled Forest, where trees warred, trunks and branches coiling together, competing for soil and sun—what appeared at first glance to be single, colossal trees were actually many plants knotted in strangleholds. I rode until the trees ended and the land dropped away in sheer bluffs that loomed over the crashing waters below.

The sea had turned angry, foam coating its surface like sugared icing. Anad, the god of wind, was fighting with his jealous wife, Faerran, goddess of the sea. Their passionate clashes flooded villages and sank ships.

The bluffs were the northernmost part of our island. I'd never left Glasnith, but Father and Garreth had taught me, through maps and stories, about the lands beyond. To the east were the Auk Isles, an archipelago of forests and farmlands, their people similar to my own. Sanddune and Savanna were arid landmasses to the south, ruled by strandlopers and bushmen. The rocky northern isles of Skerrey were populated with hardy fishermen and whalers who kept to themselves. And if you sailed far enough west, you might find the elusive lands of the Frozen Sun.

The legends of the Westlanders were far-fetched: stories about frost giants with hearts of ice and souls of fire. I wondered how it would feel to touch a soul made of fire. Would it hurt? Could it burn me?

I glanced down at my wrist, at the strange, small scar there—slim white lines that curved at the ends and came together into a shape that resembled a small flame. A wound from a long-ago dream. A dream I still didn't understand.

I looked back at the sea.

Here, in this beloved place, I could let myself imagine a third option for my life. Not to be tied to a husband or a temple, but to explore the world. To cross the oceans spread out before me. To trek across hills of red sand, summit mountains made of blue ice, speak exotic languages, treat with mysterious tribes from other lands. This was the life my heart yearned for. A life I could never have because girls were considered too fragile to be explorers, and a chieftain's granddaughter—a Daughter of Aillira, no less—was too valuable to set free.

Above, clouds scraped across firmament, torn asunder by Anad's breath. The water swallowed the sun, and Nesper, god of the heavens, split the sky into flecks of blue, orange, and gold. The stars were Nesper's children, appearing loyally to flicker and shine.

The scar on my wrist tightened suddenly, a warm flutter inside my skin—a thing it had never done before. I shook my hand and the sensation ceased. It must have been my nerves running riot.

Back in the village, they would cut Dyfed's body down from the gallows. The priest would read verses from the Immortal Scriptures and set fire to his body. Dyfed's family would pray and weep as it burned.

Quiet, humble Dyfed. Guilty but not evil.

I pushed the thoughts away. Rhys was right—we were followers, with no say in the laws of our people. I could do nothing for Dyfed now except beseech mighty Gwylor, the god of death, to be merciful and accept the herdsman into his Eternal Palace.

My dreams of adventure were useless, selfish. I should care more about what I could do for the people of my clan and my island. I owed it to my mother to make my life mean something, to make myself worthy of the sacrifice she had made for me.

I kneeled at the edge of the bluffs, head bowed, offering prayers to the gods for Dyfed's soul, and my own, until my knees and head ached. *Please,* I begged, fingers digging into the earth, *let me use my gift for healing instead of hurting, for helping instead of damning.*

A gust of wind tore at my hair, whistled in my ear.

Wait, it promised.

CHAPTER 2

Had I not been burdened by the herdsman's death, I might not have lain awake that night. I might not have decided to sneak from my family's cottage to walk along the harbor.

How different my life might have been.

The sky was a black shroud. By the gleam of moon and stars, I crossed the hills of our village, where they sloped down to meet the pebble-strewn shore. Gray water funneled around the massive sea-worn boulders Stony Harbor was named for. The harbor was placid, its waters protected by arms of rocky cliffs stretching out on either side, ragged, like they'd been chiseled haphazardly by a drunken god. Fishing vessels were tied along the wooden pier, buoyed on the swells rolling in. Just beyond the harbor lay the Shattered Sea, full of jagged stone pillars rising like teeth from beneath the wild waves.

Barefoot, I dug my feet into wet sand. Under my breath I sang an old sea ballad my mother had taught me:

> *When will my love return to me?*
> *Each day, each night, I watch the sea.*
> *A cold wind sighs, a lone gull cries.*
> *My love, my love, return to me.*

I lifted my skirt to my knees and edged into the water, letting the waves tug at my ankles. I picked up a thin stone and skipped it across the water's surface.

Oh has my love forgotten me?
The days pass by, storms ravage the sea.
I toss in my sleep, as he calls from the deep.
My love, my love, return to me.

There were shapes bobbing on the swells. I squinted, trying to make out what they were. Distracted, I kept singing, my voice little more than a whisper.

How could my love be lost to me?
His ship was swallowed by the sea.
I feel him close, but it's only his ghost.
My love, my love, return to me.

Splintered pieces of wood washed in on the waves. I plucked one from the water, running my thumb over the smooth lines of a carving; the design looked like scales. The next piece I grabbed was covered in swirling knots.

This was wreckage from a ship, but I'd heard nothing of missing vessels or fishermen.

Something splashed in the water. It looked like a floating pile of rags, but then it moved. I could just make out the shape of a man struggling toward shore. I waded out to help him, taking hold of his flailing arms and dragging him onto the sand.

"Are you—" The sentence died on my lips. The man flopped onto his back, and I saw what was left of his body. His right leg was missing below the knee. His left foot, too, was gone. The sharks had made a meal of him.

"*Mordir*," he said. His eyes were open, but he didn't see me. He stared at the sky, mumbling the same incomprehensible word. "*Mordir*."

I leaned in, studying his weathered face. Black markings decorated the skin of his right eyelid, stretching up to his brow and down to the corners of his eye—reptilian scales, like the design on the ship's wreckage. Likely the warrior-mark of his clan, but it was no clan I knew of. I doubted he was even from our island. His accent was heavy and rough, and the word he repeated was nonsense.

Mordir.

Could it mean …

"Mother," I said with sudden understanding.

That's what he kept saying in his strange language. He was crying out for his mother. I'd heard tales of bloody battles, of men holding their injured comrades. Dying warriors often called for their mothers as the end came.

There was no point fetching a healer; the man would die before we returned. His hand reached out for something unseen. I clasped it and held on.

"*Mordir*," he cried, tears streaming down his cheeks.

"It's all right," I told him. "It will be over soon."

His eyes dulled moments later. His cries fell silent.

"The god of death has claimed you." I set his limp hand on top of his chest. "May Gwylor accept you into his palace."

Up ahead, the harbor curved around a rocky cliff edge, hiding the shore on the other side. There could be survivors. I let go of the dead man and splashed around the barrier.

My stomach sank like a stone.

The harbor was littered with broken planks from a ship. And bodies … so many bodies, lying on the sand, bobbing on the waves.

Dead. Every last man.

I made my way from one shredded corpse to the next. They were nothing more than husks, faces bleak and withered, all of them bearing the same black scale marks around their eyes. These men were ripped apart, every body missing arms or legs. Some were headless. Others had chunks torn from their torsos, their guts spilling onto the sand. Whatever attacked them had left wide, deep bite marks from teeth far bigger than any shark's.

Only one monster caused such carnage.

"The Brine Beast." I fell to my knees. My fingers went to my ankle, tracing the ring of scars where the Beast attacked me all those years ago.

I glanced at the cliffs above, at the stone watchtower that was manned at all times to keep an eye on the harbor. Where was the sentry? The Beast could be out there now, waiting to attack the next Glasnithian ship to cross its path. And who were these dead men—were there more of them out there, other ships that hadn't sunk? I had to alert Father.

On my way back to the village, a flapping of wings startled me. A massive raptor glided over my head, alighting upon the broken section of a spar stuck in the sand. The raptor had feathers of black, gold, and crimson, and eyes that were bloodred. It was a lammergeier, the largest bird in Glasnith; they were vicious, known for knocking lambs, goats, even men, off sea cliffs to the rocks below so they could feast upon the broken bodies. Because the Immortal Scriptures said the Great Betrayer used to transform into a lammergeier to spy on the dealings of mortals, the raptors were feared as harbingers of ill fortune.

The lammergeier lowered its head. As if compelled, I followed its gaze.

Sprawled across the spar was another body.

I moved toward the corpse, the lammergeier's inquisitive eyes following me. It opened its curved beak and unleashed a poignant shriek.

The man lay on his stomach, water lapping at his legs. His hands clutched the spar, as if it would ferry him to the otherworlds. I knelt beside him and let out a slow breath.

A shock of golden hair, smooth skin—he was young. From what I could see, the Beast hadn't touched him. He must have drowned and washed ashore.

The scar on my wrist tingled.

There was a sweet boyishness to his features. Grief tugged at me. I pushed a wet mesh of hair out of his face. "I'll make sure your body is burned, your spirit cleansed," I promised.

His lashes fluttered. Blue-gray eyes stared back.

I yelped, scrambling away. The dead man watched me.

Not dead. The man is not dead.

Looking into his eyes was like gazing at the ocean—swirling shades of deep cobalt and steel gray. Fathomless.

Familiar.

"You?" I choked, wondering briefly if I was actually asleep in my bed and this was all a dream. Because, as impossible as it was, I knew this man.

I'd seen him once before.

It happened when I was twelve, on the third anniversary of my mother's death. Every year, when that hateful day came, I snuck away in the night, took a horse from the stables, and rode to the northern bluffs. Alone on the bluffs, I prayed and wept and let myself remember her, releasing all the pain I tried to bottle up and smother the rest of the year.

On this night, I heard something as I rode home from the bluffs. I'd grown up in these woods, and I knew them as well as my own skin. The strange sound that slunk across the land was not one that belonged. I dismounted and crept nearer, searching. Several shadowy figures gathered, speaking with grunts and snarls that barely resembled language.

I felt the man watching me, like his eyes could burn holes in my flesh.

He was behind me. Before I could turn, his arm closed around my chest, his hand covered my mouth. My nerves crackled where his skin touched mine. I couldn't see his face, but his breath was hot against my neck, his voice a purr in my ear, making threats I couldn't understand.

I kicked and struggled, and he shushed me, reaching for something. The tip of a blade slid behind my ear.

Another voice spoke—younger, gentler. The blade stilled. The two voices seemed to argue, and then a rag was stuffed in my mouth, a sack slipped over my head. My wrists were bound behind my back, and I was thrown over someone's shoulder. I thrashed, drawing grunts of annoyance from whoever carried me.

The slap of waves told me I'd been brought down to the shore. I was tossed into what must have been the hull of a boat, wood scraping my arms. I flailed, trying to stand, but hands pushed me down. The younger voice murmured softly. The hood was pulled from my head.

My captor was tall and leanly muscled, but he was only a boy, not much older than me. Golden hair brushed his shoulders. His face was far too grave for his age, as if the world was a millstone worn about his neck.

We were in the stern of a small boat, bobbing just offshore. There were three other prisoners lying on their stomachs in the bow, tied up as I was, with sacks over their heads. In the dim moonlight, I could see the men bore no warrior-marks on their hands; they were not from Stony Harbor.

I scrambled to my feet and spit out the rag. "Don't touch me."

The boy stared at me curiously. His eyes were ocean blue. There were strange black markings around one of his eyelids.

From his belt, he drew a knife.

My foot caught on something as I tried to back away, and I tripped, toppling onto my side. The boy hovered above me, too big for me to fight. Maybe if I'd had my own knife, I'd have stood a chance, but it was strapped beneath my skirts, out of reach.

"Go on then," I said. "Kill me."

He grabbed my wrists, kneeling behind me. There was a long pause, and then the blade bit into me, slicing into the underside of my wrist as I cried out. It went on for a full minute before his palm brushed across the stinging cuts and an almost-pleasant heat simmered under my skin. He picked up the rag I'd spit out, and I felt him wrap it around my bleeding wrist. A moment later, the rope that bound me fell away. The boy hauled me to my feet.

"What did you do to me?" I motioned to the bloody rag on my wrist.

His eyes drifted over me again, but he remained silent.

"Whatever you want from me, you won't get it."

The boy looked up toward the forest, like he heard someone coming. He mumbled something. When I didn't reply, he jostled me and spoke again, more insistent. "*Svim?*" he asked, gesturing at the water.

Did he mean *swim*, as in, *Can you swim?* Confused, I nodded.

He shoved me off the boat.

I hit the water, cold seeping into me instantly. I swam hard, staying under as long as I could, aiming for one of the sea caves carved along the cliffs. Once I was inside the cave, I dug my fingers into the sloping rock wall and climbed onto a ledge. I waited there, shivering, until daylight seeped in.

By the time I made my way through the forest and back home, I was feverish. Father ordered sentries to scour the woods, but no trace was found of any intruders. It was assumed that I'd taken ill, fallen asleep on the bluffs, and dreamed it all. With no proof otherwise, I'd begun to believe it myself. No proof, except the mark on my wrist that could not be explained. Father suspected I'd cut myself out of grief, but I didn't think so.

And each year since, on the anniversary of my mother's death, when I crawled into bed after returning from my prayers at the bluffs, I dreamed of eyes the color of oceans.

Now, after all this time, here he was. Not a dream at all.

The ocean-eyed warrior coughed, water trickling from his mouth. No longer a boy, but a young man, exhausted and half-drowned, freezing in the harbor's cold waters. He was blue enough that I'd thought him dead already. If I did nothing, he would die where he lay.

If I summoned a healer, Father would know. The man would be sent to the cells. He might be tortured for information or hanged as a spy.

What if he *was* a spy? I knew nothing about him. Just because he'd let me go that night didn't mean he wasn't a brute. He'd been creeping about in the forest in the company of other dangerous men; he'd cut me with a knife for no apparent reason.

The warrior clasped my wrist with what little strength he had left. "*Hjalp mir*," he whispered through cracked, bleeding lips. I didn't need to speak his language to understand. He'd suffered. He was no older than Garreth, and I thought of my brothers washing up on a foreign shore— how I hoped someone would take pity on them.

His thumb stroked the inside of my wrist, over the scar he'd left, and it pulsed with warmth in response, as if springing to life at his touch.

My choice would seal his fate, and I already had one man's death on my conscience. There was only one way to decide.

Men could lie. Souls could not.

Carefully, I began to roll him over. When he gagged, I held him on his side as he retched up seawater. There were tears in his jerkin, traces of blood seeping through from injuries hidden beneath his clothes. Like the corpses on the beach, a warrior-mark adorned his right eye, but his was different. Instead of scales, black tendrils of fire curled across his eyelid—the markings I'd been unable to see clearly that night years ago. Its shape was oddly similar to the scar on my wrist.

I unfastened the collar of his tunic. There, resting in the hollow of his broad chest, lay a silver medallion. *My* medallion, attached to a loop of rope around his neck. The medallion was once my mother's; I'd lost it that night when I was caught by his people in the forest. How had he gotten it? Why was he wearing it?

None too gently, I pulled the rope from around his neck and slipped it over my own. "This is mine, you bloody thief."

Brushing salt and sand from his chest, I pressed my palm against his heart, opening my mind, seeking the core of his true self.

I did not touch his soul. I fell into it—like I'd been shoved off a cliff. It was all around me, submerging me in its wilderness. Images flickered, rippling like reflections on water; as I tried to grasp them, they trickled through my fingers. His soul was darkness and light, jagged and smooth, smoldering fire and crackling ice. It screamed and whispered. It was every shape, every color. Laden with guilt, buoyant with innocence. It was all things, all at once, and I was lost in it.

The strangest part was that I sensed him—his consciousness—floating there beside me. Watching me drown in him. Feeling everything I felt.

As I sank deeper, he pushed back, expelling me. Pain shot through my arms and I followed it, returning to my own mind. Gasping, I opened my eyes and met the man's furious glare. His hands gripped my forearms, hard enough to bruise.

No soul felt like his—it defied their very nature. No one had ever been able to shove me out of their soul from within. "Who are you?" I demanded. "Where did you come from?"

He spit out words I couldn't comprehend, and then he released me, his head falling back, eyes closed.

"All right." I sighed. "You aided me once, so I'll return the favor. At least until I figure out who in the bloody fates you are."

I'd nearly forgotten the lammergeier perched on the spar. As if satisfied, the raptor burbled and took flight, circling high above us, soaring over the living and the dead.

I steered clear of the sentries, circling the village by way of the forest, over to the stables to fetch Winter, creeping with her back along the same route to the harbor. Motioning for Winter to kneel beside the man, I grabbed his arms and pulled. He was too heavy.

"Hey." I shook him. He didn't move. "Hey!" I slapped him, and he wheezed, his eyes snapping open. I gestured to the horse. "I can't lift you. If you want to live, you must help me."

I thought it pointless to explain, but I saw a glimmer of recognition at my words. I pulled his arms, and he pushed with his legs, until he was draped over Winter's back. The effort exhausted him. Within moments, he was unconscious again. Winter stood slowly beneath her burden. I led her up the sloping path from the shore to the top of the cliffs, making it into the forest just as I heard the shout of a sentry.

The bodies had been discovered, but by fate or the will of the gods, we had not.

Winter reached the old hovel—a shed once used for storage, now abandoned—and knelt beside it. An inch at a time, I managed to drag the man off my horse and inside the shed. The floor was dirt, the wooden walls and roof filled with holes that did little to keep out rain or cold, and the hovel crawled with vermin, but there was nowhere else to hide him. I laid out the supplies I'd taken from the stables: woolen blankets, candles, flint, a waterskin, liniment that healed men's wounds as well as horses'. I stared down at his shivering form. He wouldn't last long if I didn't get him dry.

I unlaced his leather jerkin and his tunic, pulling off the soaked garments. Though his face was boyish, his powerful build was that of a grown man, and his flesh was etched with blade-shaped battle scars that marked him as a warrior. But all my attention was drawn to the arc of blooming bruises that curved along his collarbones, over his ribs, across his waist. The bruises flared around small, spear-shaped gouges in his skin. Teeth marks.

He'd been *inside* the Brine Beast's mouth. It should have ripped him to shreds like the others. Instead, it spared him. The same way it had once spared me.

There wasn't time to ponder this. I pulled off his boots, his trousers, and finally his breeches. I'd seen men naked—the men of clan Stone weren't shy about shedding clothes after a long day's work or to bathe in the sea—but this was different. He was not of my clan, and he was unconscious. Stupidly, I felt myself blushing.

"Pity I can't build a fire," I said. I couldn't risk the smoke being seen in the village.

I eased one blanket beneath the man, wrapped another around him. I wrung out his wet clothes and hung them to dry, scattering spiders hiding in the eaves. I shook him awake and held the waterskin to his lips, forcing him to sip, but he retched the water back up.

"Determined to die, are you?" I asked, scowling through my worry.

Why should I care if he dies? He's a stranger. He's nothing to me.

Except no man was a stranger after I'd touched his soul, and my experience touching this warrior's soul was unmatched. We'd shared something beyond physical touch, deeper than heartfelt conversation. With him, for the first time, the soul I touched had felt what I felt. It left me shaken.

His trembling worsened. His breathing was sluggish.

Concern made me bold.

"I went through the trouble of saving you." I pulled off my damp dress and slid beneath the blankets in my smallclothes, cringing at the coldness of his skin. I couldn't build a fire, but I could lend him my body's heat. "You owe me answers, and you can't give them if you're dead."

He shifted onto his side and huddled against me, pressing his face to my breast.

"*Mordir*," he murmured.

CHAPTER 3

My body was on fire.

Flames crept along my skin. Soft thread tickled my cheek, smelling of salt and earth. I heard labored breathing next to my ear, and my eyes opened to a flash of gold.

I didn't know where I was. Someone lay next to me, an arm slung across my waist—a heavy, muscled arm. I gasped, sitting straight up. The person next to me jolted up too, startling me. Instinctively, I swung my fist out, and my knuckles met bone.

With a grunt of pain, the gold-haired stranger scrambled away.

I drew my knife; Garreth had given it to me years ago, trained me how to use it. Slowly, my mind extracted itself from the mist of sleep. I was in the hovel. Across from me, crouching defensively, was the young man I'd pulled from the harbor.

He snarled, glaring at my knife.

"I am Lira of Stone, granddaughter to the chieftain. You'll treat me with proper respect or I'll turn you over to my father and his warriors to punish as they see fit."

His brows rose. Crouching seemed too much effort for him, and he slumped to the floor, holding his head. He coughed, the force of it racking his body.

"Do you know where you are? Do you remember what happened?"

He glanced up sharply, rubbing his jaw where I'd punched him.

I bit back an apology. "Don't give me that look. My fist feels worse than your face." I gestured to my swelling knuckles.

As we eyed each other, I noticed the flush in his skin, the glassiness of his gaze. Another coughing fit overtook him.

I slid my knife back in its sheath. I was no healer, but I knew what lung-fever looked like—Rhys had nearly died from it as a boy. A nasty illness, reducing even the strongest man to a shivering waste. I held my hand out. "Come here. You need to lie down."

He didn't move. He glared at my hand like it offended him.

"Stubborn, aren't you?"

I shoved him onto the blanket. Between coughs, he unleashed what I assumed were vile insults. I wet strips of cloth, arranging them over his chest, neck, and forehead. "Calm yourself. I'm trying to help."

It wasn't my body that had been on fire when I woke, but his, pressed against me like smoldering coals. The fever struck quickly. Hours ago he'd been freezing, and now he burned. Pale and drained, he stopped fighting and settled into the blankets, closing his eyes. I coaxed some water into him, relieved when his stomach didn't reject it.

It seemed cruel to leave him, but I had to return to the village. Rhys would assume I went riding and cover for me as long as he could, but I needed to get back before Father noticed my absence.

I brushed my fingers over the black flames of the man's warrior-mark, feeling the slight ridges of the inked skin above his eye. The near-matching scar on my wrist tingled. There were secrets behind these markings. This man, with his prismatic soul, was full of secrets, and I wanted to unravel them.

"Try not to die while I'm gone."

—◆—

The village was abuzz over the corpses.

Rather than go home, I went straight to the harbor and stood on the cliffs beside other villagers, studying the commotion. Father and Madoc paced the shore, shouting at each other. Sons of Stone—my brothers among them—dragged the half-eaten bodies into a pile, tossing them atop the ship's wreckage.

"Westlanders," someone near me mumbled. "Giants with hair like straw, eyes like water. The beasts of the Frozen Sun."

I remembered sitting cross-legged between my brothers, listening raptly as Mother told this tale: Long ago, pieces of the sun broke free, landing in half-frozen seas. The sulfurous rocks spat fire and belched smoke. The leviathans dwelling there—the only creatures that could survive in realms of fire and ice—birthed monsters deceptively covered in human skin.

Beasts.

"Bollocks," I said. The warrior I'd saved was strange, but he was a mortal, not a monster.

An old man pointed at the corpses. "Their warrior-marks prove it, flaunting the serpent scales beneath their skin."

A tattoo proved nothing. Besides, my warrior's mark was fire, not scales.

I wanted to hear what the Sons of Stone were saying about the dead men, so I grabbed a jug of whiskey from the great hall's kitchens and lugged it down to the harbor, winding my way through the tired warriors, refilling their flasks. "A drink to usher the dead," I called.

"To the otherworlds with you," each man replied, raising his flask and taking a swig. An old superstition, meant to remind any lingering spirits that they must move on.

Our village priest had come to examine the bodies. I caught him scowling at me, and I wondered if he saw through my guise of tradition. My brothers certainly did. Garreth pursed his lips, and Rhys tilted his head—silently asking where I'd been last night—but neither of them tried to stop me. Meanwhile, the Sons of Stone circulated the same rumors as the villagers: these men were frost giants from the Frozen Sun.

My skirts billowed in the breeze as I shuffled toward my father and uncle. The wind carried their voices across the sand. "Another clan of mercenaries looking to settle on our island," Madoc was saying. "As if we don't have enough barbarians already. The Kelpies wedding their horses, the Ravenous eating their own dead. The bloody Bog Men, those mud-wearing, serpent-loving savages."

I thought back to books I'd read in Father's library about the history of Glasnith. It was said that the mercenary clans weren't descended from Lord Llewlin and the first men of Glasnith, as clans like ours were. Their ancestors had been dispossessed barbarians from the Auk Isles who had settled in southern Glasnith, taken Glasnithian wives and lands. They had their own clans, their own cultures. Most mercenaries believed in the Immortal Scriptures and the True Gods, as we did, but it was their own barbarian gods that they worshiped and prayed to.

Madoc never missed a chance to complain about the mercenaries.

Father sighed, weary of this argument. "The mercenaries keep us free. No one wants to cross them. Without their backing, the clans of Glasnith could be influenced to disband and appoint a High King. Do you want to bow to some rich, foppish nobleman? We're meant to rule ourselves, as Lord Llewlin before us, as the True Gods intended. Look what happened the last time some fool got it into his head to declare himself king."

The Great Betrayer—a god who came down to Glasnith wearing a mortal's skin and tried to take our country from us before he was defeated. We'd burned his name from the pages of our history, but we all knew what he'd done, how he'd nearly destroyed our island.

"I bow to no one," Madoc said.

"Then we'd best hope all the frost giants want is women and land." Father nudged one of the bodies, an ox of a man, with his boot. "Especially if they're as fierce as stories portray."

When all the bodies had been gathered, the priest took a torch and set the heap of corpses and timber aflame. I watched the dead men burn, thick smoke curling into the bright sky. There were no songs, no prayers—a lack of respect that meant these men were regarded more like animals than enemies.

My sickly warrior would join his dead brethren if I couldn't heal him.

I abandoned the pyre and hurried back up the path through the village.

Stony Harbor crouched on the edge of the Shattered Sea. Shaped like a crescent moon, it was bordered to the north and west by the sea's gray waters and to the south and east by the towering trees of the Tangled Forest. The rolling hills were dappled with modest cottages. I stopped at one, letting myself in without knocking.

Tables dominated the parlor, cluttered by vials, bowls, and herbs. Ishleen stood chopping roots at one of the tables, light-brown curls falling into her face. Though she wasn't god-gifted as I was, her mother, Olwen, the village midwife, had taught her well. Ishleen had a talent for potions—she knew precisely what concoctions could cure any variety of ailments.

"Lira," she called. "Have you come to gossip? I hear my uncle Fergus soiled himself when he saw all those dead frost giants washed up on the shore."

As soon as I saw her mother was out, and we were alone, I wasted no time. "Ishleen, I need a potion and your discretion. No one can know of this."

"Hmm. Rescuing helpless wild animals again?" she asked, teasing me over my childhood fascination for aiding wounded creatures. "Let me guess. Fox? Hawk?"

"A young wolf," I said quickly. I thought of the warrior, snarling at me, his eyes blue as a wolf pup's. "Sick with lung-fever."

Ishleen stopped chopping and gave me a worried look. "You must be cautious. Even young wolves can kill."

"He won't hurt me." Did I actually believe this? So he'd cut my bindings and shoved me off a boat five years ago—could such a thing be called an act of kindness? I'd felt the man's soul. There was darkness in it as well as light, guilt as well as innocence. "But I've my knife, if he tries," I added.

"And your fist, it seems." She gestured at my swelling hand.

"Will you help me or not?"

I knew she would, otherwise I wouldn't have come. Ishleen stared at me, deliberating, and then she nodded. "I hope you know what you're doing, Lira."

"I do," I insisted, even though I didn't.

Ishleen loaded a sack with vials of lung-fever potion and handed it to me. "Put a poultice on those knuckles. Your harmless wolf must have an awfully hard head."

―――――――

I couldn't return to the hovel until well after dark, so I went about my day like it was any other.

Our village was home to some two hundred men, their wives, and their children. They were tough, hardworking men, laboring as sentries, fishermen, trappers, farmers. The women supported them, running the households. I'd proved hopeless at cooking and sewing, little better at healing and potions, so I helped in the stables—a boy's job, but one I loved well enough that Father allowed it.

I threw myself into my work, feeding, brushing, picking hooves clean. Our clan wasn't rich, but we had many mounts and treated them well.

When I finished, my heavy heart led me down the path to the gallows.

A group of boys, young warriors-in-training, gathered at the foot of the scaffolding. A nervous-looking boy stood on the raised wooden platform, beneath the beam Dyfed had hung from yesterday. Beside him stood Madoc, waving a birch rod. "To fall asleep on your watch," he said, "risks the lives of every villager. Such negligence will not be tolerated."

This boy had been on watchtower duty when the bodies washed ashore. My warrior lived because the boy had fallen asleep.

"Strip," Madoc ordered.

Trembling, the boy removed his tunic.

"Kneel."

The boy obeyed, curling into a supplicant pose. Madoc brought the rod down on his bare back in rapid strokes. I cringed as the branches lashed him, leaving pink welts from his neck to his waist. He endured his punishment with barely a whimper.

"Rise," Madoc said when he was done. The boy did, stiffly. "Now go, all of you, and don't let this lesson be forgotten." The boy held his head high, descending the stairs. The other young warriors followed, nodding respectfully as they passed me.

All except one, whose eyes bored into me.

Ennis. Dyfed's son.

Madoc remained on the platform. My father's older brother looked much like him, only shorter, his hair and eyes a darker shade of brown. There was starkness in the lines and hollows of his features, as if his bones were trying to break free of his skin.

"Did Torin give you leave to birch that boy?" I asked.

He folded his arms behind his back. "How I discipline my warriors is my choice. I don't answer to him. Or to you."

"They're Torin's warriors as much as yours. You could've made that boy empty chamber pots to teach him a lesson. Your discipline was cruel." I shouldn't have said it, but I was as adept at holding my tongue as I was at sewing.

"If I were cruel, I'd have made the boy drop his trousers like a child and birched him until he couldn't sit. I left him his pride and beat him like a man." Madoc leaned against the gallows. "Why are you here? To pay homage to the thief you killed?"

"His name was Dyfed, and it was you and Torin who executed him." My eyes flickered to the beam above Madoc's head.

"Yet you're as guilty as the souls of those you condemn." My uncle's smile was laced with poison. "Your mother damned you from the start, naming you after a traitor."

Aillira, the first god-gifted daughter of Glasnith, who was so loved by the gods they blessed her with the gift of mind-reaping and vowed to bless her female descendants with gifts of their own. Aillira, who fell under the spell of the Great Betrayer and turned against the gods who loved her, bringing about decades of plague, war, and strife.

Her name was a curse. She was mother and villain, loved and hated. Many questioned my mother's sense when she bestowed me with the short form of a traitor's name. I supposed it a mark of her boldness that she didn't listen.

I took a slow breath. "If there's nothing you want of me, I'll be going."

"You've so little to offer, Lira. But I'm sure I'll find use for you, when the time comes."

The anticipation in Madoc's voice sent prickles along my spine.

That night I entered the hovel cautiously, as if walking into a wolf's den.

Over the years, I'd taken in all sorts of injured creatures. I'd bandaged wings and paws, fed and soothed each animal until it was healthy and strong enough to set free. For my efforts, I'd been growled at, scratched, bitten. I knew the risks of aiding dangerous predators.

As soon as I stepped inside, I was knocked to the ground.

The warrior pinned my wrists, bending over me. Naked, glistening with sweat, eyes bright with madness. Even now, I didn't see a monster. I saw a wounded wolf, alone, afraid.

I pulled one wrist free, smacking him on the nose, showing I was neither adversary nor prey. "You won't hurt me. I'm the only one who can help you."

Eyes wide, he slouched back.

I sat up slowly, lifting a hand to his brow. "You're burning up."

He regarded me suspiciously, until something captured his attention. My skirts had bunched at my thighs. In a blink, the warrior snatched my knife from its sheath.

"You won't hurt me," I said again, less certain. I plotted a path around him to the door, the dodges and strikes I could use to evade him.

He pressed the blade to his own throat. Crimson leaked down his skin.

"No!" I wrestled the knife from him and tossed it away. The warrior's shoulders sank, as if I'd stolen his last shred of hope.

Gripping his jaw, I examined the wound—the cut was small but deep. I tore cloth from the blanket, pressing it to his neck to staunch the blood. "What were you thinking?" I asked, even though I knew. Pulling him from the harbor wasn't saving him, but capturing him. Too sick to leave, he was a prisoner in this hovel, waiting to be tortured, executed. That's what men did to their enemies. That's what the Sons of Stone would do if they discovered him.

"I'm no warrior. I mean you no harm."

He stared at the fallen knife.

"No." I leaned to block his view. "That is not the way."

If he'd had the strength, he would've shoved me aside and grabbed the blade. I saw him calculating his odds as it was, but then the fever took hold. He coughed, fighting for breath, the sound wet and sharp, sawing through his lungs. Of course he'd not hesitate to slit his own throat, when he faced death from every direction.

I thought of Rhys as a boy, ravaged by lung-fever, moaning in his bed. This warrior wasn't Rhys, but he was someone's brother, someone's son. "You'll be all right. I'll look after you."

"*Draepa*," he wheezed, pointing at the knife, then me, making a stabbing motion into the side of his neck. "*Draepa mir.*"

"You want me to kill you?" I shook my head. "I won't."

"*Draepa mir!*" His shout made him cough again. Between coughs, other sounds rose. Laughter. Sobs. He laid his forehead in the dirt, hacking and gasping, crying and laughing, fingers clawing at the earth. Had the fever cracked his mind?

"Shh." I eased his head onto my knee. At my touch, he tensed. He coughed, growled, and wept, face buried in my skirts. One hand curled around my ankle, as if searching for an anchor to hold fast to in a storm. His fingertips traced the ring of scars there.

To distract him from his misery, I moved my leg closer and told him my story.

"I was nine years old, playing with my brother and his friends in rowboats just beyond the harbor. I'd begged Garreth to take me along, and he took pity on me. The weather turned foul, and a wave as high as a horse capsized our boats. Something circled us in the water."

The sensations came back fresh: the churning sea, Garreth's arm around me, slick scales brushing my leg. "It was the Brine Beast. A giant sea creature that sinks ships and devours fishermen. It took three other children first."

I couldn't bear to speak their names. Their bodies had washed ashore in pieces, just like the Westlanders' corpses. My cousin, Madoc's only son, had been one of them.

"Then it came for me."

I slid my fingers under his, feeling the indentations of needle-sharp teeth. "I remember fangs closing around my foot. My brother screaming as I was snatched from his grasp. The cold, dark heart of the sea as the Beast dragged me down. Staring at the slithering shape of my own death. I didn't realize the Beast had let me go until Father pulled me to the surface. The men had run for boats when they heard our cries. Mother ..."

I swallowed hard and tried again.

"My mother was on the shore. After the Beast pulled me under, she walked into the sea. No one stopped her. No one knew what she'd done until she didn't resurface. They searched, but never found her body. Many in Stony Harbor believe the Brine Beast came that day to steal one child from each of the wealthiest families in the village as payment to the sea goddess Faerran, who provides for our people. My mother offered herself to Faerran in my stead, and the goddess accepted."

I looked at the warrior lying quietly in my lap, listening. I didn't wipe away the tears flowing down my cheeks. "Now we've both bared our pain."

He'd shifted onto his side, hair falling across his face. One of his hands still held my ankle, rubbing the scars. The other touched the matching bites on his torso. "*Sjaeskjir?* Beast?"

"Beast," I confirmed, watching him. Did he understand my language? "*Mordir?*"

"Yes. The Beast took my mother." Easing my legs from beneath his head, I fetched my satchel. "Medicine. To cure you." I held up a vial of bright-green liquid. He eyed it dubiously. "If I meant to harm you, I'd have done it already. And so would you, when you had the chance. We must learn to trust each other."

His stare was unrelenting. Seconds passed.

Finally, he gave a slight nod.

Before he changed his mind, I opened the vial and held it to his lips. When he gagged, I clapped a hand over his mouth until he swallowed.

With his last bit of strength, he crawled onto the blanket and submitted to sleep.

The teeth marks the Brine Beast left on him were inflamed. I bathed his fevered flesh with what was left in the waterskin, rubbed liniment into the wounds along his stomach and chest to stave off infection. "Not an ice-hearted beast under there, are you?"

He grabbed my wrist, startling me.

"Lira." My name sounded beautiful and strange on his tongue, swelling from a drop to an ocean between the cradle of his mouth and the space separating us. He folded my hand into his, rapping my knuckles against his chest. "Reyker."

Ray—like a sunbeam. *Ker*—like a kerchief.

"Reyker," I repeated.

His lips twitched. Not a smile; more like a tiny flame in a dark cavern. It was the smallest of gestures. But it was a beginning.

CHAPTER 4

REYKER

Once, when Reyker was a boy, he let his brother, Aldrik, stuff him in an empty ale cask and roll him down a steep hill. His body bounced inside it, and as he stared past his feet, the world spun—grass and sky, mountain and stream. Reyker passed out. He woke inside the cask, covered in his own vomit, too dizzy to walk. Aldrik nearly had to carry him home.

That was nothing compared to this.

Everything was spinning. Scattered. Time twisted, forward was backward was sideways. Thoughts and memories and nightmares intertwined. Reyker couldn't make it stop.

Was it the world or his head that was broken?

A boy in a rowboat, screaming that I'm a monster. Or am I the boy in the rowboat?

A boy covered in blood, kneeling in the snow, in the shadow of a monster. I am the boy. And I am the monster.

A girl in a boat, screaming at me, words I almost understand. I know what the warlord wants her for. I cut her free, push her into the water. She glides like a fish.

Sometimes when the warlord punishes me, I think of her swimming away and smile.

Pain. Skin and muscle and bone. Splintering. Throbbing. My head is trapped in a vise. My lungs are filled with knives. How is it possible to swelter and freeze all at once?

A veil-dweller sits beside me, a spirit guarding the cusp between the living and the dead. She can free me. Help me, *I beg her.* Release me.

Kill me.

I rip my sword from the chest of the young warrior at my feet. My first kill. I am nine years old. My brother puts a hand on my shoulder. "Now you are a man," Aldrik says proudly.

Now I am damned.

I scrub the tears from my face before he sees.

Lira. The veil-dweller's name is Lira. Her hair is violet; her eyes are green— bright as the unearthly fires that flare across the skies of my homeland. Her whispers are balm; her fingers are gentle. I cannot trust her.

She won't let me die. I hate her for this. She makes me feel broken and whole.

The warlord slaps me hard enough that I spit blood. I disobeyed his order to slaughter an entire village that dared to speak out against their sovereign.

I only killed half of them.

"You're worthless." Draki sighs, circling me. "If you had a woman, I would throw her to my dogs. If you had a child, I would toss it into the sea. They would be better off."

I will never have a woman. I will never have a child. I won't give Draki the satisfaction of destroying something I love.

Never again.

———⊹———

Dragonmen will come here. They'll burn Lira's village, murder her people. I thought I was dead inside, beyond caring.

I'm not.

CHAPTER 5

Days passed. Slowly, my warrior healed.

A fragile trust formed between us. I forced doses of Ishleen's potion into him, fed him cold broth, tended his wounds. When coughing fits racked him, I rubbed his back until they passed. He no longer flinched at my touch. I sat beside him by candlelight, reciting stories from the Immortal Scriptures—of my forefather Lord Llewlin and his daughter, Aillira, and the terrible rift she caused among the gods.

"The Great Betrayer didn't understand why his immortal brethren loved Aillira. So he went to her, first as a lammergeier, then a deer, then a hound." I moved my hands as I spoke, using gestures and shadow shapes to animate the story. "He experienced her kindness and purity firsthand, and he became covetous of the beautiful maiden. Finally, he went to Aillira inside the flesh of a man, seducing her with sweet words and promises. In her innocence, she didn't see him for what he was. He wed her, and she bore him sons and daughters. When her love ran so deeply she would not dare question him, he asked her to use the gift of mind-reaping the gods had blessed her with to enter their thoughts and steal the secrets of their power."

How much of the stories Reyker understood, I wasn't sure. Misery fractured his thoughts; sometimes he shivered, staring at nothing, barely aware of my presence. Other times he watched me, face wrinkled in concentration, listening to my voice if not my words.

"Aillira told her husband everything she'd heard inside the gods' heads. The Great Betrayer used it against them, and his own power grew. He declared himself king of Glasnith and built a grand kingdom in the center of the island. When the gods discovered what Aillira had done, they came for her, but the Great Betrayer would not give up his prize. Some of the gods joined him, and others fought him. Thus began the Gods' War. Their battles caused seas to rise and lands to shake. The skies broke open. Fire swathed the earth. The gods had no time for mortals, so they were abandoned. People froze, starved, endured terrible plagues. They fought their own wars, and much blood was shed.

"It was Gwylor, the god of death, who finally defeated the Great Betrayer and his followers. They were cornered and bound, stripped of their names and powers—they are known simply as the Fallen Ones now. Gwylor imprisoned them for eternity in the deepest, darkest realm of the otherworlds."

Usually Reyker lay quietly, but sometimes he repeated a word, asking questions with his eyes. Now, he looked up and whispered, "Aillira?"

"Yes," I answered, "Gwylor captured Aillira. She repented, begging forgiveness, pleading for the lives of her children. Mercifully, the gods spared them, but Aillira couldn't live with what she'd done. She went mad and died from the bite of a bog adder she found in her garden. She kissed it, mistaking the serpent for her husband returning to her in animal form."

At some point in my stories, I always glanced down to find Reyker sleeping. When the tension in his jaw loosened and the shadows haunting his expression softened, he looked vulnerable. It was difficult to see him as an enemy.

Before stealing back to the village each night, I tucked the blankets around Reyker, brushing my fingertips along the black flames of his warrior-mark, praying I wasn't wrong about him. Praying I wouldn't someday regret saving his life.

—◆—

"Have you decided yet?" Ishleen asked.

"Hmm?" I glanced up from the tome of ancient poetry. Ishleen and I sat by the hearth in my father's library, reading and conversing and drinking tea, a thing we did most evenings when Father and my brothers were away, occupied with clan business.

"About whether or not to pledge yourself to Aillira's Temple?"

"Not yet." It was a question I'd mulled over constantly since finding Reyker in the harbor, wondering if there was more I could do for him, some way to ease his discomfort with my abilities. But my only way of finding answers was to give up my freedom and be confined to dusty class-rooms, abandon my life in Stony Harbor and devote myself to the gods.

"I wish I could study at the temple," Ishleen said. She couldn't, because only the god-gifted were allowed, and for each clan descended from Aillira, the gods only blessed one girl per generation. "There are potion masters there. And I heard they teach the Forbidden Scriptures."

"What? Where did you hear that?" I knew little of the Forbidden Scriptures—the contested accounts of our island's history—but I'd heard whispers. They were contrary to the Immortal Scriptures. Two versions of the same story, different as night and day.

"When we visited the temple as children. Everyone was distracted while the priestesses tested your abilities."

I remembered it well. I'd been exhausted and annoyed by all the questioning and examining I'd been put through. Ishleen was jealous, but I'd have gladly traded places with her. I often wished I could trade places with her now. What a relief it would have been to be skilled without being god-gifted, to have an ability that belonged to me and not to my entire clan.

Ishleen continued. "I slipped away to explore. One of the priestesses followed me. She took me aside and told me ..."

"What?" I sat up straighter. "What did she tell you?"

There were no copies of the Forbidden Scriptures left; they'd all been burned after the Gods' War. But in certain circles, the stories had been conveyed from one person's lips to another's ear, passed down through generations. In clan Stone, even speaking of the banned verses was considered blasphemous.

Ishleen craned her neck, peering into the hall to ensure we were alone. "The Forbidden Scriptures said that it was not Aillira and the Great Betrayer who brought about the Gods' War, but Gwylor himself."

I inhaled sharply.

"The Immortal Scriptures erased the Great Betrayer's name from its pages, but some still remember—Veronis, he was called."

"Veronis," I repeated. The sound was like a chord struck on a harp.

"According to the Forbidden Scriptures, when Gwylor saw the love between Aillira and Veronis, he grew envious. He tried to seduce Aillira, but she spurned him. Gwylor did not want anyone, especially a lesser god, to have what he could not. So he began the Gods' War to destroy Veronis and steal Aillira for himself." She paused for dramatic effect.

"Go on," I said. "Finish the story."

"After he defeated Veronis and his followers, banishing them to the prison-realm, Gwylor forced Aillira to be his mistress. He took her children away, turned them against her. When he tired of her, Gwylor cast her aside. She took her own life out of grief."

The tome fell from my lap, thumping noisily to the floor. "So Gwylor is either a hero or a villain. How are we to know which version is true?"

"I asked the priestess that same question. She said, 'You must ask the gods, both the victors and the defeated. Listen with your heart. The truth will open within you like a blossom to the sun.'"

"Bloody fates." For several moments, the only sound was the crackle of the fire. "Ishleen, we visited the temple ten years ago. Why didn't you tell me of all this sooner?"

She leaned forward and took a sip of her tea, her hands trembling. "I forgot. As soon as it ended, it was as if my conversation with the priestess was wiped from my mind. But I had a dream the night the frost giants washed up in the harbor. In the dream, you and I stood together on a cliff as a flock of lammergeiers circled us. When I woke, I remembered what the temple's priestess told me. I've had the same dream every night since." She placed her shaking hands in her lap, studying them. "It's an omen. Something dreadful is coming."

This was a side to Ishleen I wasn't used to. Of the two of us, she was usually the sensible, dependable one. She wasn't the kind of girl to let a nightmare trouble her.

I clasped Ishleen's fidgeting hands. "Only a Daughter of Aillira can dream of omens. Your dreams mean nothing."

"Maybe." She shrugged. "The priestess said something else. That if I truly wanted to know more about Veronis, I had to seek the blind mystic."

"The seeress?" She was the Great Betrayer's most devoted vassal. She not only worshipped the Fallen Ones, she guarded the portal to their prison-realm. "If you want answers, we'll track her down together." Ishleen had been at my side through many of my reckless escapades. I owed her this much. And unlike many of the villagers, I was more curious about the mystic than I was frightened.

"Lira, we can't! The mystic is mad. She'll try to ensnare us with her visions." Ishleen pursed her lips. "You don't actually think we should go see her, do you?"

It hurt to see Ishleen unsettled, so I cocked my head and said, "Aye, let's ride like the wind into the Tangled Forest seeking the mad mystic who guards the Grove of the Fallen Ones. While we're there, maybe I'll chop off my toes as an offering and beg the Fallen Ones to make me a charmed dancer." I poked her in the ribs. "How daft do you think me?" I stretched down to retrieve my book of poetry from where it had fallen on the floor.

Ishleen swatted at me, a grin easing the tension in her face. "You truly want me to answer?"

I lifted the tome as if to throw it, and she squealed and ducked.

The door to the antechamber opened, followed by the sounds of my brothers clomping through the cottage, calling my name.

"What are you two chattering about?" Garreth asked, leaning in the doorway. He was convinced Ishleen and I were always up to no good. He was often right.

"How brave and clever my brothers are." I smiled sweetly.

Rhys snorted, pushing past Garreth to scan the library's shelves. "Let's have a story, eh?"

Garreth folded his arms. "Lira, what's that frayed rope around your neck?"

My hand went to the cord Reyker had been wearing my medallion on when I took it from him. I'd meant to replace the rope with a proper silver chain; I'd even walked to the silversmith's cottage earlier today, but then stopped. I wasn't quite sure why. "I found Mother's medallion," I said, lifting it from inside my bodice.

My brothers stared at the medallion, this small piece of our mother we'd thought was lost.

Before they could ask, I said, "It was in a corner at the back of my wardrobe. I must've dropped it."

Garreth raised a brow. He had a knack for sensing my lies, but he said nothing more.

Rhys grabbed a book. "Move over, Lir." He settled himself in front of the hearth between me and Ishleen, flipping through pages. "I'm bloody tired of hearing about frost giants. Ah, here's an old Bog Men legend."

"Bog Men," Garreth muttered. "Mercenary half-breeds, tainted with foreign blood. They have no loyalty to our country. I don't understand why Father insists on treating with them, doling out shares of our profits to those barbarians."

It chilled me how much Garreth sounded like Madoc sometimes.

"Barbarians or not, they spin a good tale," Rhys said.

I listened vaguely as Rhys read about foolhardy travelers lured deep into the bogs by glowing green lights, only to sink into the lair of the venom-spitter—a monster who was half-woman, half-serpent, and delighted in swallowing men whole.

But my mind kept wandering to other stories—those from the Forbidden Scriptures, with their starkly different interpretations of Gwylor, Aillira, and the Great Betrayer. *Veronis*.

How much of what I'd been taught to believe was built upon lies?

CHAPTER 6

The next afternoon, I was working in the stables, so absorbed in picking pebbles from a horse's hoof that I didn't hear someone enter the stall. The sudden tug on my braid would've startled me, had the teasing gesture not been so familiar.

"That's how you greet a lady?" I asked, wiping my hands on my smock. "I should command the horse to trample you. Or gut you with my pick." I turned and brandished the tool.

Quinlan stooped to one knee, holding a butter-colored daylily. "A thousand pardons, Lady Lira. Forgive your humble servant." He peered around me at the sable-coated mare. "I meant no offense. Please, gentle creature, have mercy."

"Get up, you jackanapes." I put the pick away and snatched the flower from his fingers.

"Tell me how much you've missed me."

I stroked the lily's sun-warmed petals. "Not a whit."

The young man who stood before me now was a handsome highborn warrior of Fion, the clan that ruled the neighboring village of Houndsford. But once, many years ago, Quinlan had been a rude lad who taunted me, ripping the ribbons from my hair, until I tired of it and punched him hard enough to blacken his eye and earn his undying respect.

"What's wrong?" he asked. "You look weary."

Tending to my warrior and worrying after Dyfed's family made for restless nights. Only one was safe to speak of. "There was an execution."

"Garreth told me. I can help."

I waved a hand at him. "There's nothing you can do."

"I could marry you."

I leaned against the horse to steady myself. "Quinlan. I refused your first proposal. Did you think the second would be different?"

"No. I'm betting on the third." He regarded me with soft eyes, so dark they were nearly black. "If you married me, I'd never let anyone use you for your gift. You'd never have to be anyone's judge. That's what you want, isn't it?"

The offer was tempting—to never condemn another person. For my gift to be my own.

"I care for you, Quinlan. You're as dear to me as a brother."

"I'm not your brother."

His tone surprised me. "I'm aware."

"Are you?"

Quinlan was comely. He made me laugh. I felt safe with him. Most marriages were based on far less—landholdings, lineages, alliances.

"I have to think of my brothers, my father," I said.

"They know I'm trustworthy, that I'd protect and cherish you as few men could. Houndsford is close enough for you to visit them often. I'll bring you back to Stony Harbor whenever you wish. Please don't reject me and place the blame on your family. If you feel nothing for me, you must say it. I'd rather lose my pride than hold to false hopes."

Lira, wife of Quinlan—I didn't hate the idea. I feared it. I didn't want to leave my home. I didn't want to be any man's property. And there was still the possibility of joining Aillira's Temple. When it came to pledging myself to Quinlan or the temple, I wasn't ready to choose one and lose the other forever.

"I can't say I feel nothing, only that I've no wish to marry yet."

"Well. Until you can better dissuade me, I suppose I must keep asking." Quinlan smoothed a hand along my braid, drawing it over my shoulder. "I need to go."

"You aren't staying?"

"Much as I'd like to, there are pressing matters. A ship en route to Stalwart Bay found a boy drifting in a rowboat. He told a mad tale about frost giants attacking the Skerrian islands, massacring people. Before we could question him, he ran off. I'm leading the search for him."

"Westlanders." My mind went to my warrior—could he have done such a thing? "Do the clans think they'll attack Glasnith?"

"Word is spreading about those corpses that washed ashore here. Between that and the Skerrian boy, the clans are worried. The men of the Frozen Sun have been quiet far too long," he said. "But Glasnith isn't Skerrey. If they think to conquer us, they're fools. I'll be the first to tell them so, if they dare make landfall."

"So if frost giants storm the shore, you'll saunter out and cock a snook at them?"

"Precisely." He stuck his tongue out, pressed his thumb to his nose, and waggled his fingers at me. "What? This doesn't strike fear into your heart?"

I laughed. "Not quite."

"Quinlan!" Garreth called from the doorway at the far end of the stables. "Not making an arse of yourself to my sister, are you?"

Beside him, Rhys chimed in. "Stop pulling her braids or she'll blacken your eye again!"

I looked at Quinlan, already missing him. He raised my hand to his lips. "Gwylor keep you, Lira."

"And you, Quinlan."

He ran to join Rhys and Garreth. They carried on up the path, pushing, teasing one another as they had since they were children. I watched until they were out of sight.

An inexplicable sadness lapped at the shores of my heart.

When I entered the hovel that night, the candle was already lit. Reyker sat, clothed in his trousers and tunic, resting his back against the wall. His hair hung to his shoulders, bronze-gold like barley. His gray pallor was fading. His eyes were clear.

We looked at each other with uncertainty.

A coughing fit battered him, and I put a hand to his brow. It was tepid; the fever still stalked him, but it had loosened its deathly grip.

"Despite your best efforts, it seems you'll live." I smiled.

He returned it, and my breath caught in my throat. I was suddenly very aware that I was alone with him, too far from my village to be heard if I screamed.

Reyker hooked a tentative finger beneath the rope around my neck, brushing my collarbone, and a shiver ran through me. He lifted his finger and the medallion emerged from my bodice, dangling between us.

"You stole it," I said. "The night you let me go."

He pantomimed a series of gestures—finding something, picking it up, placing it around his neck. The medallion's chain must have broken when I was struggling in the boat.

"Where did you come from? Why are you here?"

No reaction.

I held up my wrist, pushing the scar of flame toward his face. "You did this. You cut me." Every time I was near him, the scar warmed, as if responding to his presence. "Why? What does this mark mean?"

Reyker looked at me blankly.

"First, you eat. Then you give me answers." I wasn't sure how to get information from someone who couldn't speak my language, but I'd figure something out. I unpacked fruit and bread from my satchel. "You need more than broth or you'll waste away."

"Lira." When I glanced up, his features were grave. "Go, Lira."

"Go?"

He pointed to his warrior-mark, spreading his arms and drawing them in to form a circle. Stabbing violently at the air. Pointing toward the village, then at me.

"Westlanders—your people—will come here. To raid."

He stabbed at his neck. "*Draepa.*"

To kill.

"My clan is strong. The harbor is well guarded." I used my own flurry of gesticulations to buttress my words. "What do you want me to do? Tell my people to lay down their arms and bow to the Westlanders when they come ashore?"

"Go," he said again, pointing inland, away from the village.

"You mean run? Abandon Stony Harbor, where my clan has lived for centuries?" My voice rose in disgust. "My ancestors were carved from these stones by the gods, our blood formed from the seawater, our hearts from the earth. This is our land, and we'll fight for it. The Sons of Stone are mighty warriors. Let your people come."

Reyker laughed—a dark, dour sound. He took one of my hands and slid it beneath the loose laces of his tunic, my palm flat against his chest. "*Leifa.*"

"No." I tried to pull free, but even in his weakened state he was strong.

It wasn't my choice. I kept my mind closed, and still he pulled me in. I fell, past sharp black canyons and bright sloping valleys, through molten red rivers and skies that shattered around me like glass. My vision flickered. For a moment, I was blind, and then …

I stand on solid ground, men spinning and shifting around me in waves through blood-choked air. The world tilts dizzily. Right in front of me, a blade crashes into a man, half severing his head from his neck. The axe … the axe is in my hand.

Not mine. Reyker's.

I'm inside his memories, inside him, and he's there as well—not just past Reyker, but present Reyker, his consciousness sitting alongside my own, forcing me to watch as he—as we—run a sword through a man's belly. Beside us are other warriors, fair-haired, their right eyes adorned with black-inked scales. They scream with raw exhilaration, silver flashing as their weapons slice their opponents' flesh.

"Let me out!" I push against him from within, like banging on the bars of a cage. He shouldn't be able to do this—drag me inside him,

lock me up, show me what he wants me to see rather than what I seek.

I'm in his soul. There's no need for spoken language. His every thought comes through, clear as water. "You must see, Lira. You must understand."

Now it's a spear we thrust into a man's guts. The venue changes, from mountain to field to beach, every landscape cluttered with dead and dying warriors.

"This is what awaits your people. This is what the armies of Iseneld do."

The scene changes again, and I see women weeping and struggling as Westlanders surround them, grab at them, drag them away. I don't want to think about the awful things the Westlanders will likely do to them.

"If you don't run, your village will fall. This will happen to you."

"Stop!" I cry. "No more!"

With a desperate heave, I ripped myself free, slamming back into my own body.

I commanded my shaking limbs to move, scrambling to the other side of the hovel, unsheathing my knife. Any trust we'd built was destroyed in an instant. How had I been so foolish, thinking him no different than my brothers?

"It's true. You're beasts." I had to warn Father that the Westlanders didn't mean to settle but to destroy. The Sons of Stone needed to know about the foe they faced.

I had to turn Reyker over to them.

He looked at me, as if reading my mind, and held up his hands. "Lira, *stonva*—"

I rushed for the door, throwing it open. Reyker was right behind me, and I slammed the door into him, knocking him off balance. As I ran, I heard him cough and wheeze. I raced ahead, gaining ground.

My eyes were slow adjusting to the darkness, my thoughts muddled from being inside Reyker's soul. It took me a moment to notice the hunched shapes creeping ahead of me.

Two dozen shadowy figures, out in the forest in the heart of night's hour.

One of the shapes drifted in front of me. I bumped into it and bounced off. It spun impossibly fast, bright hair whipping around a pale face, with eyes as blue and cold as ice. A hand closed around my neck, lifting me so my feet dangled.

Had Reyker not just shown me his people's depravity, burning it into my mind, I might have gaped in awe at the huge warrior until I suffocated. Instead, I used Garreth's training, burying my knife to the hilt in the frost giant's throat.

His fingers released me, and we both fell to the ground. I sucked in air as he gurgled and sputtered, a fountain of blood soaking the blond braids of his beard.

I shouldn't have done what I did next.

As if in a trance, I slipped my hand beneath the warrior's tunic, opening my mind.

His soul was cool, smooth, and dim, like a sea cave. I saw images of his lovers, his enemies. His sins washed over me in a flood. Dying, he revealed all—every childhood lie, every theft, every slain foe.

Then, it changed. A darkening. An emptying. The cloth of his soul tore free, one fiber at a time, alighting on unseen winds and crumbling like dead leaves in winter. They slipped away, piece by piece, into the ether. As his body died, his soul was sundered. When the last fiber evanesced, it left only a shell. The desolation penetrated deep into my being.

A voice echoed through the carapace. "*Come out, Lira. We must go.*"

I hesitated, afraid to stay, afraid to leave.

The voice persisted. "*Please. Trust me. Come out.*"

I relinquished my hold. When I opened my eyes, one of my palms still rested on the dead man. The other was pressed to Reyker's chest. He knelt beside me, eyes closed, hands folded over my own. Blood clung to my fingers, sticky and warm.

I wrenched my hands closer, holding them in front of my face. I had done this. Deserving or not, I had killed this man and destroyed his soul.

Reyker gripped my arms. When I met his eyes, I saw more in them than

I'd expected. Empathy. Regret. Reassurance that I'd chosen the best path among the damnable options set before me. I could imagine Father giving Garreth a similar look after his first kill. It was strangely intimate, and despite everything, I was grateful for his rough grasp and piercing gaze, holding me together. He took my hands, wiping the blood off on his trousers.

Why was he helping me? I'd killed one of his kind. And how had he reached me when I was lost inside the soulless vessel of a dead man?

I started to ask as a sound whispered across the earth. Reyker's head snapped up. He clapped a hand over my mouth, scanning the space around us.

My dazed mind snapped back to awareness. All those shapes I'd seen—they were Westlanders. They weren't attacking from the harbor, where the sentries kept close watch. They must have moored their ships farther north and scaled the cliffs. Now they crept through the forest to surround Stony Harbor. The villagers would be caught unaware, cut off from escape.

Reyker hauled me to my feet, swaying unsteadily, his face pallid and damp with sweat. His hand locked around my wrist, but I jerked out of his grip.

I had to look away as I ripped my knife from the dead Westlander's neck. His axe lay where he'd dropped it, and I picked it up. It was too heavy for me to wield, but I couldn't leave my only battle-worthy weapon behind. I took a step toward the village, dragging the axe. Reyker grabbed me again.

"Let go." I held my knife to his throat.

"*Nai*." Reyker leaned into the blade. "*Thu vil doyja*." He pointed at the dead man.

"These are my people. My family. I won't abandon them. If I die beside them, so be it."

"*Nai*, Lira." He wrapped both hands around my arm, daring me to sink the knife deeper.

I couldn't.

I couldn't end the life I'd fought to save. I hated the thought of his blood spilling across my hands, his soul dissolving.

Lowering the knife, I summoned my strength and clenched the axe handle. With a swift thrust, I jammed the flat of the axe into Reyker's stomach. The blow knocked the breath from him in a violent rush and he fell to his knees.

I turned, running after the Westlanders.

CHAPTER 7

"Ambush!" I shouted.

It didn't matter. I was too late.

As I reached the edge of the forest, the warning bell came to life—a clear, frantic sound.

Screams of terror and fury accompanied it—the cries of my people. Fire devoured several cottages, illuminating the night. Women raced past with their children, desperate to escape the blaze and the warrior-beasts. Clusters of men battled, in pairs and groups. Bodies fell beneath deft blades. Blood pooled like lengthening shadows.

Westlanders fanned out, howling, weapons raised. They were easy to spot—taller than our warriors, fair-haired, dressed in fur-lined clothing. Their swords were huge spires of steel, worn across their backs instead of at their hips. They fought with brazen disregard for their safety, as if unafraid of death. A few avoided the battle, dashing from one cottage to the next, kicking doors down, like they were searching for something.

I hid behind a tree, knife in one hand, an axe I could hardly lift in the other.

A Westlander near me crouched down, using flint to set fire to a cloth-wrapped arrow before loosing it. It lodged in the rooftop of a cottage, and the thatching began to burn. He removed another arrow from his quiver.

Securing the knife between my teeth, I hefted the axe, sneaking up behind the man. I pivoted, gathering strength from my feet to my shoulders, swinging the axe into his legs. He stumbled to his knees, and as he tried to rise, to aim his next arrow at me, I swung again, striking his skull. The Westlander toppled sideways, unconscious, but alive.

With a few quick, bludgeoning strikes, I wielded the axe like a hammer and broke several fingers on each of his hands so he couldn't grip his weapons. I didn't lie to myself. This man would die; left defenseless, someone would slay him. But it wouldn't be me.

I took the warrior's dagger, a blade better fit for my skills. Gathering my bearings, I devised a plan. Father and Garreth would be in the thick of the melee; I couldn't get to them. But Rhys would be guarding villagers seeking shelter in the great hall. If I could reach him, I could help.

I crept between buildings, staying low to the ground. I'd made it halfway to the hall when I heard screams coming from Ishleen's cottage.

The main room was in disarray, tables and chairs overturned. A Westlander had Ishleen trapped in a corner, his back to me. I lunged forward, dagger raised, but he heard me coming and dodged my blade. His elbow slammed into my chin, tumbling me to the floor. The dagger fell from my hand.

As I picked myself up, he backhanded Ishleen, knocking her into the wall. Then he came for me. The warrior was stocky, his yellow hair streaked with gray. He snarled at me in his language, the words harsh and garbled.

I scrambled for the dagger, but his axe slammed down between it and my reaching hand. Scooting backward, I ducked behind an upended table. The axe sheared it in half, spraying me with splinters, and the Westlander kicked the table out of the way and raised his axe again, daring me to move.

"Gwylor keep me," I prayed.

A thrumming sliced the air. The Westlander staggered, an arrow jutting from his armpit.

Rhys stood in the cottage's doorway, bow in hand.

I grabbed a broken table leg and slammed it into the Westlander's knees as Rhys shot a second arrow into him. The Westlander sprawled to the floor, and Rhys unsheathed his sword to finish him off.

Ishleen limped over to us, her face bruised and swollen. "Give me your sword." She held her hand out to Rhys.

"Give it to her," I said when he hesitated.

Rhys relinquished the sword.

Ishleen looked at the Westlander. "I pray you find no peace in the hereafter." She drove the sword into the Westlander's chest.

His mouth dropped open in surprise. He cried out once, then fell still.

Cold numbness wound through my veins.

Ishleen's face was shuttered, her eyes distant. She fainted, and Rhys caught her, gently hoisting her over his shoulder. "Lir? Are you all right?"

My bones moved on their own: feet shuffling forward, fingers retrieving the dagger. "I killed a man. I felt his soul die."

My brother gave me the same look Reyker had when he'd wiped the blood from my hands. "They're beasts, not men. Death is all they deserve."

If only I believed that.

"How fare the Sons of Stone?" I asked.

"Our men are driving the beasts toward the cliffs, led by Father. Garreth is with him. Father ordered me to evacuate the villagers to the great hall." There was a question in his voice. "You were missing when the invasion began. I searched for you. I feared the worst."

Guilt twisted in my gut. I'd been offering undeserved kindness to our enemy. "I'm sorry."

"You're alive. Nothing else matters." Rhys peeked around the doorway, ensuring the path was clear. "Let's go."

We crossed the village, darting between cottages. Ishleen awoke and Rhys set her down, supporting her with an arm around her waist. Our progress was slow, the sounds of battle growing louder.

I saw a river of crashing warriors not far from us. The air hung heavy with the clangs of striking metal. Men danced around each other, axes and swords bashing against shields, slicing through skin, lodging into bone.

Shouts and commands resonated as the Sons of Stone faced the beasts of the Frozen Sun.

Bodies littered the ground. It was hard to make out the faces of the dead. I tried not to think of Garreth and Father lying among them.

The great hall was within sight when we heard the pounding hooves. Horses galloped from the stables, Westlanders swinging their weapons from atop their mounts. These were our horses, stolen and used against us.

The three of us stood between the riders and the battle.

"Run, Lir!" Rhys broke into an encumbered sprint, dragging Ishleen with him toward the safety of the great hall and the warriors defending it. I was right behind him.

Something made me stop.

There, sitting atop my father's black warhorse, was a Westlander unlike any other. Long ashen hair trailed behind him. He was bare chested, as if he didn't fear the threat of blades on his skin, and he radiated a sleek, savage sort of beauty.

His gaze locked on me.

Beautiful. Savage.

The Savage prodded his mount. Leaning to one side, he brought his axe crashing down into the Sons of Stone who ran at him, wielding his weapon like an extension of himself. My clan's warriors fell. Blood splashed in waves across his skin.

His eyes never left mine. My limbs were heavy as boulders, stiff as plaster.

A voice called my name. Rhys rushed toward me, sword in hand. His eyes darted from me to the Savage, trying to reach me first.

The horse was coming. My legs wouldn't move.

The Savage veered at the last second, passing between Rhys and me, so close his calf brushed my arm, and I shivered. He circled his horse back in our direction, and Rhys grabbed me, yanking me forward. The warhorse's hooves pounded, nearly on top of us. We only made it a few steps before Rhys stumbled and choked, eyes widening. His hand slipped from my arm. His sword fell into the grass.

A battle-axe was buried between his shoulders.

My scream was the raw, wrenching keen of an animal. I caught Rhys as he collapsed, lowering him to the ground. I looked around wildly, calling for Father and Garreth.

The Savage leaped off his horse.

"Stay away!" I let go of Rhys and picked up his sword.

With a swift kick, the Savage knocked the weapon from my grip. I drew the dagger, and he slapped it away too. He pulled me to him, smelling my hair, running his fingers through it. I hammered my fists against him, but it did nothing. This close, I saw every detail of his face, his body. I absorbed them through a haze of shock.

Older than Garreth, younger than Father. Tall, muscled, with thick hair hanging down his back in braided ropes of silvery white. Eyes a shade of greenish-gold, like a cat's. Black ink crawling across one entire side of his body: up his stomach, chest, and neck, then back down the length of his arm to his fingertips, coiling along one jaw and cheek, to his forehead, disappearing into his scalp. Knotted patterns, with intricately etched claws and tails and reptilian heads interwoven between the twisted links.

If the other Westlanders were frost giants, he was a leviathan; if they were beasts, he was their king.

I struggled feebly, my palms smacking his chest. Anguish had torn my mind wide open, left my abilities untethered; my consciousness plunged into the depths of his soul. Except what I dove into was nothing. Colorless, shapeless, void of sensation. The space was starkly, infinitely empty. A barren abyss.

The Savage had no soul.

I pulled my hands free, snapping back into my body as the Savage grasped my chin. "What you see, soul-reader?" The words sounded cumbersome to his mouth. He took hold of my wrist, bending it to expose the scar of flame Reyker had marked me with, laughing like my scar was a joke meant to offend him. "He is here."

The Savage thrust one of his hands into my hair, holding my head still, and the other tightened around my waist, crushing me against him. He pulled a delicate knife from his belt, pushing my hair back and sliding the stiletto behind my ear. The blade bit into my flesh in short, deep cuts. He was carving me. Marking me, just as Reyker had, only this felt far more violent. I whimpered as blood dripped down my neck. "*Mine*," he said.

A threat and a promise.

His lips pressed against the wound he'd made behind my ear, and his mouth was freezing, burning like ice against the cuts he'd made.

I felt him enter my mind then, slipping inside like a skilled thief. Tendrils curled around my thoughts, coaxing away my fear and outrage. His voice slithered through my head, an uninvited caress. *When I call, you will let me in. You will obey me. You will worship me. I am your savior. I am your god.*

"Yes," I said, dimly aware that the Savage had stolen my will, yet unable to resist.

Just as I was drifting away, losing myself to him, the scar on my wrist grew warm, tingling like a feather fluttering beneath my flesh.

It was enough to loosen the Savage's grip. Enough for a thought to creep through. "Rhys," I gasped, latching on to this vicious truth: my brother lay dead at my feet, by *his* hand. I fought, straining to reclaim my mind. I scratched at the Savage's face, stomped his foot, pulled his hair. Snarling. Screaming. Until suddenly, my thoughts were my own again.

All around us the night screeched, alive with battle.

The Savage drew back. "Little warrior." When he smiled, my blood coated his lips. He eyed me shrewdly. "I come back for you both."

He let go, and my legs gave out. I kneeled in the dirt as the Savage propped a foot on Rhys's ribs, grasped the handle of his axe, and tore it from my brother's back.

I dove for Rhys's sword, but the Savage was already on Father's horse, riding away.

I didn't see the battle ebb or hear the victorious shouts from the Sons of Stone. I didn't know when our men forced the Westlanders against the cliffs and they retreated—some swimming into the harbor where their ships awaited, others fleeing into the forest.

I was conscious of nothing beyond my brother's broken body.

I crawled to Rhys, shaking him, screaming at him. He was still, his eyes open, staring at nothing. I wrapped him in my arms, rocking back and forth, babbling—apologies that came too late, promises I couldn't keep. How much time passed, I couldn't say. I barely registered the sound of my name, shouted, then whispered. I fought against the hands that touched me, the arms that tried to pull me from Rhys.

The darkness was lit with torches, Father's and Garreth's faces swimming within the bright wash of light: pale and exhausted, covered in small injuries, spattered with blood.

"Where were you?" I said. "You should've been here. You let this happen."

It was unfair, but I couldn't stop. There was too much pain inside me.

Garreth loosened my grip, and Father lifted Rhys from my lap, laying him on the ground. Father stared down at his youngest child with such despair that it shattered my heart anew. Then it disappeared, replaced by his stoic commander's mask.

"Go to the healers," Father said. "You both need tending."

I didn't want to leave Rhys; I wanted to live in this moment a little longer, because it was the only thing that kept his death from feeling real. But Father needed to be alone to grieve, and Garreth's arm was already around me, leading me toward Olwen's cottage.

Several men rushed by us on the path, carrying a litter. My grandfather was sprawled across it, his skull cracked wide open, leaking gray sludge. Garreth and I stopped and stared in silence. The men carrying the litter hurried, even though it was pointless; Aengus, our clan's chieftain, was dead.

I should've cried, but my tears were all dried up. I wrapped my arms around myself, around the dark pit forming inside me, and pulled away from Garreth, heading toward the harbor. Garreth protested weakly, but in the end, he simply followed.

When I got to the cliffs, I scanned the horizon. There—the silhouettes of ships moving across the water, back to the forsaken lands they'd come from. And the Savage was on one of them.

"One day I'll find him." My voice cracked. The wound behind my ear throbbed. "I'll cut out his black heart."

"You take his heart," Garreth said. "I want his head." We looked at each other, sorrow unfurling between us at what was missing. What had been taken from us.

Our brother was gone.

CHAPTER 8

Eight years ago, the small bodies of three children had lain on tables in the great hall, draped in linen to hide the horrid bite marks and missing limbs. Victims of the Brine Beast. One table had no body to display, its surface covered instead with my mother's favorite dress. The table that had been meant for me.

I'd wept rivers at that vigil. This one was different.

I sat with Rhys's body, replacing candles as they guttered out, singing the requiems of our ancestors. Every time pain threatened to overcome me—*my brother is dead, he's gone, I've lost him*—I folded it tight, shoved it far from my mind. Later, I would cry. Later, I would ache. I wasn't ready to feel the loss yet.

The funeral ceremony commenced the next day beside the harbor. Rhys was dressed in his best armor, sword on his chest, arms folded over the hilt, warrior-mark facing the sky. Other dead warriors lay on litters beside him. One by one, our clan's priest set fire to each warrior's body, all except Lord Aengus, who would be entombed in a barrow alongside all the chieftains of Stony Harbor who had died before him. Ishleen stood with me, holding my hand as I watched my brother's body burn.

That night the villagers got drunk on wine and ale, stuffed themselves with meat and bread. They laughed and sang, told stories of the dead and made toasts in their honor. They opened the doors of every cottage and let the wind sweep through, ferrying spirits past us in their final farewells.

Our allies sent envoys to offer sympathy on behalf of their clans. Quinlan was there representing clan Fion. He kept a respectful distance, but he was never far, his dark eyes always following me. Whenever our gazes met, the knots inside me loosened slightly.

Well into the reigning hours of witches and wolves, curls of smoke from the funeral pyres rose above the treetops, phantoms traipsing somberly around the cold white moon. I snuck away to where the village ended and the forest began. Dangling overhead from a thick rope, like charms from a necklace, were the heads of the Westlanders killed during the invasion, including the one I'd stabbed in the throat. They were slack-skinned, hollow-eyed. I searched each face.

Reyker wasn't there; he must have escaped with his beast brethren.

I leaned against a tree, trembling with relief, sickened with myself for it.

—◆—

The watchtower was built on a curving lip at the center of the cliffs over-looking the harbor. I mounted the stairs spiraling along its circular stone walls. At the top was a wooden belfry where a sentry always stood watch, ready to ring the bell and alert the village of danger. Usually manned by younger warriors, on this night it was Garreth who paced the belfry.

"You haven't been on watchtower duty in years." I stood to one side of the bell and regarded my brother, his figure framed by the dark sea.

Garreth grunted. "Father says he needs someone he trusts watching the harbor, though I suspect he enjoys how it rankles me. An amusing punishment for my dissent."

How much time had passed since the invasion? I tried to count the days but couldn't keep them separate. The minutes had crawled by, yet the hours had been a blur.

"The men voted today on who they want to be chieftain," Garreth said. "They were evenly split between Torin and Madoc."

I put a hand against the wall, feeling as if the ground shook beneath me.

"But the Sons of Stone are Father's men." Since his twentieth year, Father had trained and led them into battle. They respected him. Madoc was a fearsome warrior, but he preferred scheming to fighting. And his immoral ways were no secret—he was a liar, a manipulator. Even Aengus knew it, publicly favoring his second-born son. "How could anyone vote for Madoc?"

"These men believe in tradition. They fear the precedent set if Torin is chosen, the potential uprisings if younger sons can take what rightfully belongs to the eldest. They fear for the futures of their own sons. With strong divisions over how to deal with the Westlanders, much is at stake. There's to be a Culling."

A chill rose in my blood.

"Summoning a god to choose our leader. Are they mad?" I knew of Culling rituals only through legend, and none of the stories ended well. When mortals made demands of them, the gods didn't play nicely. "No one's attempted a Culling in ages. It's dangerous."

"It was Madoc's idea. The others agreed. Nothing less than a god's decision will satisfy them." Garreth turned. "We have to leave. We'll go tomorrow, before the Culling commences."

"Go? Where?"

"I want to take you to Taloorah. To Aillira's Temple, where you belong. You can train with the priestesses, put your abilities to better use than what Father has made you do with them. I'll join the temple guard."

"You're serious." I gaped at him. "I don't even know if I want to pledge myself to the temple."

He resumed his pacing. "The day the Brine Beast took you … Lira, you were in my arms, and then you were gone. It tore you from me. I thought you died." He squeezed his sword's hilt, as if he could return to that moment and slay the Beast. "I couldn't protect you."

"Garreth, you were twelve."

"I'm the oldest. It was my responsibility to keep you and Rhys safe. I failed you both. Now Rhys is gone, just like Mother. But Mother wouldn't have died if Father spent as much time looking after his family as he does his warriors. Rhys wouldn't have died if Father had listened to me and kept him out of danger."

Garreth had spoken heatedly of Father before but never like this.

"You're wrong," I said. "Father is a good commander. The Sons of Stone defeated the Westlanders."

He whirled and took hold of my shoulders. "The Westlanders underestimated us, bringing only fifty men. We had two hundred, and still our victory was narrow. They'll return with greater numbers. Father is blinded by arrogance. He thinks he can protect Stony Harbor, but he can't. I've seen it. If Madoc or Torin take control of the village, it will be destroyed."

"What do you mean? How could you have seen such a thing?"

"The blind mystic."

"*You* spoke with the mystic?" My steadfast, rational brother had subjected himself to a heretic's cryptic divinations. I could scarcely imagine it.

"Years ago. She showed me things." His eyes clouded over. "Awful things that made me question everything I knew. I told myself they were lies, but half of it's come true."

Abilities like mine, gifted by the True Gods, were natural. The Fallen Ones could bestow gifts as well—for a price—but they were a corruption of the natural order. Those who wanted to speak to the dead might cut out their tongues, those who wanted to see beyond the limits of mortal vision might pluck out their eyes. The blind mystic's power to peer into the past and the yet-to-come was blasphemy, and her prophesies weren't enough to make me abandon my home.

"No, Garreth. I'm not leaving."

"Then you give me no choice." His face became a blank mask, so like the one Father often wore. "Go back to the cottage. I need to think."

As I made my way down the watchtower's stairs, he called out, a disembodied voice floating across space. "Whatever happens, Lira, know that I'll fight to my dying breath to keep you safe."

The sentiment was no comfort. It was a promise that he would die as Mother and Rhys had, for the same unworthy cause.

Me.

Instead of going home, I crossed the rim of the cliffs to the village sanctuary, removing my sandals and rinsing cool water across my hands and face from the basin outside to cleanse myself before paying tribute to the gods.

The sanctuary was tall, cylindrical, its walls decorated with protective symbols painted in our priest's own holy blood. Wooden benches faced the altar in the center of the room. Beside the altar was a stone pillar that held a fire pit—a torch the priest kept lit at all times. There was no floor but the loamy ground, so worshippers could be close to the earth that provided for them, and no roof, nothing above but sky, so prayers drifted straight up to the gods. Incense burned in clay censers, the cleansing fragrance of sage tinting the air.

At this late hour, the sanctuary was empty.

The worn soil was smooth under my bare feet as I approached the altar. I'd brought no offering, no gold or food to bestow, no crops to burn or animals to sacrifice. Only myself.

Unsheathing my knife, I looked up at the dark sky. "I kneel before you, Silarch, goddess-mother of warriors, to confess. I killed a man and aided the battle-deaths of several others, including my brother. For the deaths of these men, I seek your absolution." I drew the blade across my palm, dripping blood upon the altar.

In one of the four windows cut into the top of the tower, something moved. Starlight revealed a lammergeier, perched on the window's ledge. Like the one from the harbor that called me to where Reyker lay dying.

The huge bird regarded me piously with its red eyes. A single feather drifted down, mottled silvery black, landing in the droplets of my blood.

The door in the back of the sanctuary leading to the priest's quarters opened. The old priest emerged dressed in gray robes, his entire body shaved in the traditional style of holy men, symbolizing that nothing but skin separated him from the gods. In that same tradition, he was a nameless eunuch, simply called Doyen, having given up his identity to better serve the gods' will.

"You're the reason for this," he said. "Your blood profanes this holy pantheon." Doyen shuffled toward me. His eyes were like chips of flint, hard and dull, set deep in his wrinkled skin.

"I told Torin all those years ago. What your mother did was blasphemy. You were chosen to die. That you still live is an affront to the gods."

I shook my head. "My mother offered herself in my place to appease the sea-goddess. Faerran accepted. The debt was paid."

"There's a balance to things. The gods don't choose idly. Your mother performed some trickery so the Brine Beast took her instead of you. She insulted Faerran and her kin. The gods chastise us for it, sending those Frozen Sun devils to punish us!"

High above, the lammergeier screeched. I didn't realize I'd backed away from the priest until my spine touched the wall. I wanted to tell Doyen he was wrong, but he was our spiritual leader, closer to the gods than the rest of us. If his words were true …

The possibility sank into me like a dagger.

"You want absolution for the deaths you're responsible for?" Doyen asked. "To save the village and those you love?"

"Yes." I clenched my fists. Blood oozed between my fingers.

"Go down to the harbor. Walk into the sea. Let Faerran take you, as she always intended. As long as you live, we must endure our own destruction. End this cycle of death now, before the gods punish us further." With a swirl of robes, he retreated to his quarters and slammed the door.

Walk into the sea.

The priest wanted me to drown myself.

I'd give my life to have Rhys back. I'd give my life to ensure Garreth and Father didn't meet Rhys's fate. But I didn't want to die. To kill myself would cause them untold anguish and render my mother's sacrifice meaningless.

"Why did you do it, Mother?" I murmured into the still air, the question drifting up, past the burbling lammergeier, into the sky where only the gods could hear. It was a pointless question. I knew she'd done it out of love.

Sometimes I hated her for it.

CHAPTER 9

REYKER

Lira was dead.

Reyker thought of her small hands, cool on his skin. Those hands, lifting water and broth to his lips. Those hands, trembling, coated in the blood of her first kill.

Hands slight and fine-boned, like the rest of her. Bones that would easily break.

He thought of her voice, calming, constant—the thread he'd clung to as his mind faltered into madness. He'd followed its soft sounds when he was lost, letting it lead him out of the darkness.

Her voice, falling silent. Her slender throat, crushed.

If she had stayed with him, he'd have kept her safe, but she'd run after the Dragonmen, lugging an axe as large as she was, determined to die with her people. Stupid girl.

He couldn't help but admire her.

He would not go back. Reyker was a Dragonman no more.

He'd crawled to the hut and collapsed, drifting in and out of conscious-ness for what must have been days. Then he'd woken with a start, realizing what he'd done. Stranded in enemy lands, with no way home. The only one who could help him was dead. She must be.

But Lira wore his mark. Wouldn't he have felt it if she'd died?

He had to be sure.

It was easy enough to avoid the patrolling guards. Reyker was a hunter. He knew how to move quiet as wind, how to hide from prey in plain sight. He prowled the forest's edge, eyeing the layout of the village—cottages, guard tower, meeting hall. Another stone tower, lit up, smelling of spices. A place of worship.

Reyker caught his breath as Lira stepped through the tower's archway, violet tendrils of hair floating in the sea gusts sweeping up the cliffs. Her face was stark white, her eyes pained. Alive, but lifeless. The bright spark in her had dulled.

His stomach twisted. He did not want to know what the Dragonmen had done to her.

"I'm sorry, Lira," he whispered.

She couldn't hear him. It changed nothing. Yet it needed to be said.

CHAPTER 10

I'm on Winter's back as she gallops through the forest. Rhys trails after me on his horse, Victory, trying to catch up. I turn to tease him.

When I look back, my brother and his horse are gone. In his stead is a man with long, silver hair. His face is shadowed, but I see the gleam of golden eyes. His mount is no ordinary steed—its coat is a flourish of black scales, and plumes of steam waft from its nostrils. No matter how fast I ride, he doesn't fall behind.

He draws closer, near enough to grasp my elbow. His touch is ice.

I woke shivering, rubbing my arm where the dream fingers had gripped me; my elbow seemed colder than the rest of me. So did the scar behind my ear, as if the Savage had reached through the dream and frozen it with his touch.

When I rose, I found our cottage empty. Another shiver danced along my spine as I remembered what today was: the Culling.

Father had stationed a guard outside our cottage for my protection, but I snuck out a window and circled around through the forest. It was quiet, as if all of Stony Harbor held its breath. The Sons of Stone were at the sanctuary, consecrating themselves—they were the only ones allowed to attend the ceremony. The women and children of the village sat inside their homes, watchful through slatted shutters. On every doorstep, incense burned beside offerings: ripe fruit, sweet wines, beautifully crafted weapons, precious gemstones. Left in the hopes that whatever god came to our village would bless the villagers and spare them from harm.

When I reached Ishleen's cottage, I found her slipping silently from her bedroom window. "I knew you'd be out here," she said, grabbing my wrist and pulling me up the path. "You simply couldn't resist."

"Nor could you. Your mother will blame me for this."

"Well, you were the one who taught me to sneak out." She glanced around the empty village. "What happens now?"

What little I knew of Cullings came from the Immortal Scriptures. "Doyen will call upon the covenant between the True Gods and the sons of Glasnith. He'll summon a god to judge who's worthy of being chieftain. But which god comes and how the god is called, I don't know." This was dangerous knowledge only priests and priestesses were privy to. "I have to be there. If there's any way I can help Father become chieftain, I need to try."

Ishleen's cheeks blanched. "I thought we were only going to watch."

We passed Madoc's home, where he lived with his wife, Brigid, and his daughter, Slaney. There were no offerings on the doorstep of their cottage, only a strange symbol drawn with ash across the door.

"If Father is chosen, I won't have to do anything. But if it seems like Madoc will be chosen …" I shook my head, unable to stomach the possibility. "I'm a Daughter of Aillira. Perhaps whichever god comes will listen to me."

I led the way, creeping along through the village, not sure what I was searching for until I found it. Tucked between the cells and the forest, on the eastern side of the village, was the barrow—the grassy hill that concealed an inner chamber where every chieftain of Stony Harbor had been entombed. The entrance to the barrow, normally sealed with stones, was open. The stones had been piled into a dais beside the barrow, and a body lay upon it.

Lord Aengus, my dead grandfather.

Ishleen and I ducked behind a tree, watching as Doyen bowed over Aengus's corpse, chanting loudly. "Almighty Gwylor, we offer this flesh as your vessel."

Gwylor.

My fingers dug into the bark of the tree. The priest was summoning the god of death—the most powerful, volatile god of them all.

We both jumped as a voice spoke beside us.

"Men are such fools."

The dark-haired woman standing next to me was radiant, but in a way that set my nerves on edge. She was dressed in a flowing, bloodred gown. Multicolored jewels seemed to be embedded in her exposed flesh—on her arms, her hands, her neck. As I looked closer, I realized they weren't jewels at all, but *eyes*, blinking, watching me. Beneath her long lashes, where her real eyes should've been, there were empty sockets.

"You're the blind mystic," I whispered.

"And you are the mistress of souls." Her sightless gaze fell upon Ishleen. "And the mistress of potions."

Ishleen squeezed my arm.

"No one has summoned Gwylor since Lord Llewlin." The mystic gestured disapprovingly at the scene before us. "Do you know the story?"

Lord Llewlin. Warrior, explorer, leader. Father of doomed Aillira. My ancestor, the chieftain who founded our island-nation thousands of years ago. There were many stories of him, but I knew which one she meant.

"When the Great Betrayer declared himself king of Glasnith," I said, "Llewlin and his sons called upon the god of death to help them overthrow their enemy. Gwylor came to earth in a mortal body and fought together with the warriors of Glasnith. Gods and men battled side by side to defeat the Great Betrayer and his army. Gwylor restored peace to our world."

The mystic's scowl deepened. "'Tis what your dubious scriptures and priests claim. Do you want to hear what the Forbidden Scriptures say?"

I nodded slowly, not daring to speak.

"It was Llewlin and his sons who fought over these lands. They summoned Gwylor to declare which of them deserved to be king.

Whatever the death god did drove them all to madness. They murdered one another."

That couldn't be right. "Lord Llewlin and his sons died with honor during the storming of the Great Betrayer's palace."

Her laughter was high and tinkling, like shattering glass. "Gwylor used them as pawns in his war of jealousy and spite. Now your clan has awakened Gwylor from his long slumber and invited him back into our world, risking his violent whims over sibling rivalry. Piteous fools."

Something was happening. It was midday, but the sun dimmed to a feeble glow. Clouds rolled in from all directions, squatting on top of our village, bathing it in indigo light.

Billows of steam drifted from the stone dais. The suit of armor Aengus had been buried in bulged. Lumps squirmed beneath his skin as if insects crawled inside his flesh. A low thrum reverberated deep in his throat. He sat up slowly, swung his legs off the dais, and stood.

It was Aengus's body, but the god of death had made it his own, stretching the skin and muscles so he seemed four hands taller and two stone heavier. My grandfather had eyes like murky pond water, but these eyes were solid drops of ink. The crack in his skull gaped open, the gray mass inside shrunken and ripe with rot.

"Gwylor." His name dropped off my tongue, crackling in the air. Too late, I realized I'd moved out into the open. The ink-hued holes in his face regarded me with mild interest, like watching an ant crawl across the floor before stomping on it.

"Almighty Gwylor." Doyen bowed. "Thank you for answering our summons. Our humble village is honored to receive you."

"Is the girl a gift?" Gwylor's voice was a sibilant rasp. "One of your own must return with me to my palace tonight. That is my price for answering your call."

"All we have is yours." Doyen swept his arm to include the harbor, the homes, and me.

I couldn't peel my eyes from the god's terrible gaze. Gwylor's tongue flicked out to wet his lips. "I see you, Daughter of Aillira. I know what you are. The sacrifice that lived."

I remembered what Doyen said to me last night in the sanctuary. "Does my life offend you?" I asked.

When Gwylor answered, there was no sound. His lips didn't move. I heard the god's voice inside my head, clanging like a bell: TO BE OFFENDED, I WOULD HAVE TO CARE. YOUR LIFE MEANS NOTHING TO ME.

The god and the priest shifted their attention to the otherworldly woman who came to stand beside me. "Mystic," Doyen snarled. "Worshippers of the Great Betrayer aren't welcome here. Your presence befouls this holy ceremony."

The mystic peered down her nose at Doyen. "I am the eyes of the Fallen Ones. According to the covenant, they too have a right to attend this Culling."

Gwylor waved a hand dismissively. "What do I care if my disgraced kin know the outcome of the ceremony? Let them see."

There was a sudden clamor in the distance: the Sons of Stone, heading for the great hall.

The mystic looked at me. Her long fingers went to my rope necklace, sliding the medallion from my bodice. "No mere trinket, this. A powerful talisman. 'Twas your mother's. This is what saved you from the Brine Beast. And this is how you saved another, without even meaning to." She smiled knowingly. "It was always meant to be yours. Do not take it off."

She dropped the medallion and headed toward the hall, beckoning me to follow.

CHAPTER 11

Ishleen and I snuck through the back entrance of the great hall, hiding in the balcony. When we were settled where no one could see us, I pulled out my medallion, examining it closely. Etched into the silver was a tree, its many limbs curling downward, long thorns sprouting from its branches instead of leaves—a southern thorntree. It was just like the one I had seen growing in the center of Aillira's Temple when I'd journeyed there as a child. The back of the medallion was engraved with Aillira's dying words: *Burn brightly. Love fiercely. For all else is dust.*

Mother had believed it to be a protective talisman, just as the mystic said; she'd given it to me on my ninth birthday, not long before she'd died. I'd been wearing it that day the Brine Beast nearly took me. And Reyker was wearing it when I found him in the harbor. But why would the Beast spare us because of a necklace?

Ishleen nudged me. We peered through the balusters as the god of death entered the hall wearing Lord Aengus's skin. Gwylor didn't walk like a man; his movements looked like someone shaking a sack full of bones. His presence saturated the room. We'd called the god here, but it was clear we weren't in control—Gwylor, scouring the rows of anxious faces, held the reins.

Doyen's voice rang through the hall. "All believers in the righteousness of our people and the honor of our clan must offer part of themselves." He drew his ceremonial dagger, with its double-edged blade and jeweled hilt.

The men took turns slashing their palms with the dagger, dripping their blood into a small cauldron. When all the blood was collected, Doyen stirred the cauldron and said, "Who dares think himself worthy of replacing Aengus, chieftain of Stony Harbor? Who submits himself to the god of death's judgment? Those who have the strength to lead us, the wisdom to guide us, and the virtue to keep us faithful to the laws of gods and clan, step forward."

My father was the first to go to Doyen. Madoc was only a second behind him.

That should've been the end of it, but another candidate stood and followed them. Murmurs rose from the men.

"You've lost your bloody mind," I whispered in disbelief. This could not be my brother, openly defying Torin and Madoc. Garreth was too young, too inexperienced—he had no chance of becoming our leader. He'd set himself up for humiliation and punishment.

This was what he meant when he said I'd left him no choice, what he'd resorted to because I refused to leave Stony Harbor. In his own stupid, misguided way, Garreth was trying to protect me.

Ishleen pulled me back down as I tried to rise. "You can't go down there, Lira. That's not just any god, it's the god of death."

"I have to." My brother stood before Gwylor, about to be judged. I was afraid what might happen to him if he was found wanting. I couldn't let him face the god alone.

Below us, the god of death came forward. He sliced his palm—Aengus's palm—and drained a thick stream of black blood into the cauldron. Smoke rose in curling gray clouds. He dug his hand in, pulling something out: a grayish-pink hunk, like a rotting melon. "The heart of Llewlin, first chieftain of Glasnith," Gwylor said.

He squeezed the heart in his fist, forcing it to beat.

The entire hall quaked. The vibrations roared through me. Gwylor pressed the heart again, and my bones seemed to rattle beneath my skin.

I pulled away from Ishleen and descended the balcony stairs, my steps accompanied by the throb of the screaming heart.

"There is another." Gwylor's words were razors dancing in my ears.

Every head in the hall turned toward me. My every impulse commanded me to stop, hide, run. But I wouldn't abandon Garreth.

The screech of the organ in Gwylor's hand beckoned me closer. Was it Gwylor who'd done this, or was it my ancestry as a Daughter of Aillira that made Llewlin's heart call me forth? Whatever the cause, my feet marched me to the front of the hall. Doyen, Father, Madoc, and Garreth were all fixated on the beating heart in the god's hand, as if they couldn't look away.

From a corner of the room, the blind mystic's gemstone eyes watched me. Her lips curled into a smile.

"Four Stones stand before me," Gwylor said, "but only one can lead." He blew on the heart and flames erupted from it, white and shimmering like liquid silver—it should have blackened and turned to ash, but the organ remained whole, unburnt. "Whoever withstands the flames of the otherworlds long enough to declare himself chieftain shall reign."

The god handed the heart to Madoc. The moment my uncle touched it, he screamed. His clothes caught fire. He tried to toss the heart away, but it seemed glued to his hands.

"Confess or burn," Gwylor said.

Madoc chewed his tongue, but the pain won out, ripping the truth from him. "I am chaos. I am destruction. I ... am ... no ... chieftain!" The heart dropped from Madoc's fingers. He beat at the flames on his tunic, shuttering his features.

Gwylor presented the heart to Father. Jaw clenched, my father took the heart and held it to his chest. Flames skipped across his knuckles, up his arms. His face reddened. Sweat dripped down his brow, but he didn't flinch or cry out.

His eyes pooled with the same blackness that rippled in Gwylor's. His lips parted, and he roared, "I am Torin, son of Aengus, and I am chieftain of Stony Harbor!"

The hall filled with shouts and whistles.

It was over. Father had passed the trial.

Even so, Father offered the heart to Garreth, taunting him. Garreth accepted the challenge, reaching for the heart. He held it, embracing the fire. It tested him, and Garreth bit down, grinding his teeth as the inferno threatened to tear him apart. "I am Garreth, son of Torin, grandson of Aengus. *I* am ch—"

His neck snapped back, an agonized groan rising from his throat. The fire was too much for him. I wanted to run to my brother, to pry the heart from his fingers and end his misery, but I was restrained by unseen forces. "Confess or burn," Gwylor repeated.

"Torin will die by my hand! If I'm not chosen, this village will fall to ruin and you'll all meet the edge of a sword!"

The hall went deathly silent.

The heart fell. Gwylor caught it, smiling.

The shock on Garreth's face was mirrored by the Sons of Stone. He'd just threatened the life of their newly appointed chieftain and our entire village. This was high treason.

Gwylor moved toward me. I tried to explain that I didn't belong here, that I'd only come for my brother, but my mouth was nailed shut.

"Wait!" Garreth said. "She's not a Son of Stone. Don't make her do this."

The god of death ignored him.

"There's no point in her going through the trial. Torin's been culled." Garreth appealed to our new leader. "Stop this. She's your daughter."

"Yes," Father said. "She's my daughter. And you are my son. Yet you both stood against me. *Betrayed* me. You've felt the consequences of your disloyalty, Garreth. It's your sister's turn." His eyes shifted to me. "Lira, pick up the heart."

My hands were already open, waiting, though I didn't remember lifting them. Garreth yelled at me not to touch it, his shouts fading as Gwylor set the heart on my palms.

The world exploded.

The pain was instant, all-consuming. Suffering swallowed me. Flames stampeded down my arms and legs, blossomed up my shoulders and neck, whipped my hair into a blinding halo. Engulfed me. The fire was no longer silvery white, but deep violet.

My bones ignited. My nerves were kindling. My skin was fuel.

There was something beneath the flames, brushing against me, pressing into me. Hundreds of *things*—shuddering, tangible pools of darkness. Pounding at my mind, shrieking to be let in. Livid that I refused.

The floor dropped out beneath me. I raised the heart above my head, begging Gwylor to take it, except I couldn't speak. I was in the air, floating, my skirt fluttering like incandescent wings. I glowed. Boiled. Screamed.

Gwylor's voice drifted up to me. "Confess or burn."

The admission spilled out of me, an unstoppable flood. "These are not my lands! This is not my clan! You are all my enemies!"

The heart disappeared from my hands. My toes touched ground. The fire dissipated, relief and horror washing over me. The words I'd spoken—they weren't true, so why had I said them? What did it mean?

The Sons of Stone gaped at me.

I wrapped my arms around myself, hissing at the pain of my own touch. My skin was scalded and blistered.

Garreth stared at me for a beat before lunging at Father.

"You did this!" he said, the two of them crashing to the floor. "You let your wife drown. You sent Rhys to his death. You forced Lira to burn. What kind of man are you?" He threw punches, bloodying Father's face. "I'll never serve you. I'm taking Lira away from here. We're leaving you."

For a moment, Father didn't fight back. He stared at his son, accepting the blows. Then his eyes seemed to pulsate, and wispy black vines coiled around his pupils.

Something was inside him. A piece of Gwylor's essence? A splinter of the otherworlds?

Father punched Garreth's temple, knocking him sideways. While Garreth was dazed, Father pinned him, ripping off his sword belt, tossing the weapon aside. Madoc sidled up to my father, mumbling things I couldn't hear.

Father nodded, pulling out his dirk with a ferocity that proved he meant to use it.

I didn't stop to think. I rushed at them, jumping on Father's back, reaching for the dirk, but he slung me off. As I clamored to my feet to attack Father again, other warriors came forward, grabbing me, holding me in place.

Madoc restrained Garreth—my uncle's first act as the new chieftain's sycophant. Father spread Garreth's right hand, exposing the tattooed swords marking him as a Son of Stone. He edged the blade into Garreth's skin, below his knuckles, and sliced all the way to his wrist.

My brother's cries filled the hall. When Father peeled the flesh back, the white of Garreth's bones peeked through under layers of tendons and blood.

My stomach churned, but I couldn't look away.

Father bound Garreth's wrists, jerking him to his feet and addressing the warriors. "My first order is to clear this clan of traitors. Let it be known: This man committed treason against his chieftain. He's forsaken his people, his inheritance, and his name. He's no Son of Stone, and no son of mine." Father called for a sentry. "Take him to the other end of the forest and leave him," he ordered. "If anyone sees this traitor again, kill him on sight."

Exile. The harshest of all penalties, short of execution.

"Please, Father," I said. "Don't do this."

Madoc and the sentry dragged Garreth out the door. I drew my knife, slicing into the arms of the men who held me until they let go. By the time I was outside, Madoc had thrown Garreth over the back of a waiting horse. I ran after them, shouting my brother's name.

I was only a few paces from the horse when another set of hands gripped me—my father's. "Let him go. You have no brother. He's nothing but a ghost to you now."

"It's all right, Lira," Garreth called weakly, blood dripping from his hand, staining the ground beneath him. "Remember what I told you in the watchtower."

I couldn't think. He'd said many things, and I couldn't remember a single one.

The sentry mounted the horse and spurred it. I didn't dare stab Father, our culled, god-chosen chieftain. All I could do was give Garreth a parting message, the last words he might ever hear from me. "You are my brother! You are my family!"

The horse kicked up a cloud of dust, carrying Garreth away. I watched helplessly as he vanished over the slope of a hill.

Both my brothers were gone.

"How could you?" I shrugged off Father's hands and turned, seeing the ambivalence he tried to hide. The realization was like salt in my wounds— Father hadn't *wanted* to exile Garreth. "Did you do this to prove your power? Did you renounce your own son to set an example?"

He said nothing.

I couldn't assault my father, but I could still hurt him. "If Garreth isn't your son, then I am not your daughter. I'll never forgive you for this."

Father's expression crumpled for a moment before flattening into indifference. "You're a fool to think I care." His eyes turned black once more. I looked to see if anyone else was watching, if they saw what I saw, but the Sons of Stone paid us no heed as Gwylor stepped from the great hall into the sallow sunlight. Men milled about in the god of death's wake, afraid and uncertain, all of them waiting to see what Gwylor would do next.

The god's eyes scraped over me. This was the god I'd spent my life worshipping. I didn't wonder why Gwylor was so revered—he was powerful, immense, worthy of every ardent prayer I'd ever whispered in his name. But I did wonder why he enjoyed our fear. Why did it please him, or any god, to play with mortals—to sow discord among us, spawn storms to test us, send monsters to kill us?

"You're nothing more than a sacrifice, soul-reader," Gwylor said. "The question is whose hand will hold the weapon that finally sends you to me."

He strutted toward the cliffs, and the crowd of warriors followed. Near the bluff's edge, two familiar figures walked hand in hand. Brigid and Slaney, Madoc's pretty wife and daughter. They should've been locked inside their cottage. When I was close enough, I saw that their eyes were vacant, as if under a spell. Gwylor licked his lips.

Madoc came up the path slowly—Madoc, who'd already lost a son to the Brine Beast.

He looked up. Too late. Gwylor discarded Aengus's body in a pile of bones and skin. The deity was reduced to a spectral glimmer, slithering straight for mother and child.

Madoc cried out. His boots pummeled the earth. But a man is no match for a god.

The women waited. They weren't pushed, they were carried—up, backward, over the cliff. Landing with a sound that froze my heart in my chest.

Madoc got to the cliff first, his cry falling silent, fighting the men who pulled him back from the edge. I reached the cliff and looked down at Madoc's wife and daughter—my kind aunt, my sweet cousin—splayed upon the boulders below, their bodies broken. Lovely, even in death.

Lammergeiers circled overhead. A few had already landed and begun to pick at the mess of bones and blood. Soon the raptors would swarm. They would feast.

I clapped a hand over my mouth to keep from screaming.

CHAPTER 12

The grass blurred beneath my feet. My burned flesh pulled taut, but I ignored the pain. My lungs sucked in air, spit it back out. I ran across the village, leaving the Sons of Stone behind. In the frenzy of the Culling and the death of Madoc's family, I slipped away unnoticed.

I mounted Winter, galloping through the Tangled Forest, avoiding the path so I wouldn't pass the sentry on his way back. I burst from the trees a few hours later, thinking I'd find Garreth waiting for me.

My hopes sank. He wasn't here.

I searched until dusk, riding along the forest's southern edge, over heather-strewn meadows and hills, all the way to the foot of the Silverspires, the lofty mountain range that cut across the northern head of Glasnith like a jagged noose. I rode in circles, making wide loops, scouring the land. Calling for Garreth until I had no voice left.

There was no sign of him.

I rode back toward the village in a daze. All this death and loss. Doyen was wrong—it wasn't punishment from the gods because my mother traded her life for mine. The Westlanders had come of their own accord, to kill and conquer. They brought this scourge upon my people. And I'd stupidly saved one's life—an act I would remedy, if given the chance.

I was scarcely aware that I'd steered Winter toward the hovel.

Dismounting, I drew my knife, not sure why I'd come here, but compelled to see it through. I shoved the hovel's door open.

My eyes adjusted to reveal an empty room. No man. No beast. I bit my lip, swallowing bitter disappointment. Of course he was gone. Surely he'd joined his fellow monsters during their invasion, or at least run off with them when they retreated.

Behind me, the door creaked shut. A figure unfolded from the corner, clamping a hand across my mouth. A body pressed firmly against my back and a blade pricked my side. He was taller than I'd realized—the top of my head rested on his collarbones. I felt the strength in his muscles, the heat of his skin. "Lira?" he whispered, lowering his blade.

I spun and kneed him in the groin.

He grunted. I saw his weapon, a crude spear he'd fashioned from a heavy stick and rusted nails from the hovel's walls. He was a clever brute, I'd give him that.

I kicked him in the ribs where the Brine Beast had bitten him, and he groaned. "It's your fault. You come to my village, kill my brother, murder our chieftain. You tore my clan apart!"

I aimed my knife at his stomach and lunged.

He dodged and twisted behind me, locking his arm across my throat. My fingers squeezed the knife's hilt, but I didn't use it. I let my knees slacken, let my body sag, so my neck pressed harder into the crook of his elbow.

Was this what I'd truly come here for—hoping I'd find Reyker, not to kill him but to goad him into killing me?

Bright mosaics burst along the edge of my vision, washed away by a swamp of darkness.

———◆———

The hot ache in my skin fizzled beneath a mantle of frost. I smelled the balm of sunflower, aloe, and mint. My eyes slid open. I was on my back, a blanket beneath me. A candle glimmered, tossing shadows along the hovel's walls.

"*Duma soolka*," Reyker muttered when he saw I was awake. Whatever it meant, it wasn't a compliment. He knelt over me, tending my burns with liniment, his hands gliding in slow trails across my blistered flesh. I wore only my breeches and shift.

"Get away from me." I jerked upright, a wave of dizziness clubbing me over the head as I stumbled toward the door.

Reyker blocked my escape. In a panic, I screamed and shoved him.

"*Jai vil nai skad thu*, Lira." His words were soothing nonsense. He held up his hands as if to show he meant no harm.

"Move." I found my knife lying on the floor and pointed it at him. He shook his head.

I attacked again. He caught my wrists and spun me, so my back was against his torso, my arms crossed over my chest. My knife was still in my hand, the blade pressed against my own throat. Under different circumstances, I'd have been impressed.

"Do it," I said.

Reyker bent his mouth close to my ear, his breath rustling my hair. "*Nai*." He disarmed me and turned me loose. With the warmth of him gone, cool air slapped my bare skin. Reyker pointed to the blanket. "*Sittja*."

I spat at his feet. "I don't take orders from beasts."

"*Sittja!*"

I glared at him. He had my weapon. I couldn't get past him to the door. If he wanted to kill me, I couldn't stop him. So I sat.

My dress was draped across the rafters. He'd taken the time to hang it up—a considerate, unexpected gesture that was undermined when he yanked the dress down and threw it at me.

"You had no right to undress me." I pulled the charred dress over my head, though the ruined garment barely covered me. "No right to touch me at all."

He crouched on his heels, cocking an accusatory brow. Beside me sat the tin of liniment he'd rubbed on my burns. The same liniment I'd rubbed into his wounds. After I'd stripped him. And bathed him. While he was unconscious.

Well. I was trying to save his life. And if my hands had strayed a bit farther than necessary, it was innocent curiosity, nothing more.

"You choked me." My fingers grazed my tender neck.

His brow rose higher. "*Thu stukketh a mir.*" He lifted my knife and mock-jabbed himself. "*Tvisger,*" he added, holding up two fingers.

"Not like you didn't have it coming," I shot back.

He responded with a nasty string of noises I could only assume were words.

"How do you understand so much of what I say? Do you know Glas-nithian?"

Reyker held his thumb and forefinger close together, confirming my suspicions. He gestured at me and twisted his features into a series of dramatic expressions. Mocking me. What he missed in my words, he interpreted from my face and body language. It angered me how easily he could read my emotions.

"Why did you come to my village all those years ago? Why did you let me go? What do you want from me, Reyker?" I'd not meant to say his name—I'd meant to call him beast, monster, invader—but it slipped out.

He scowled. "Reyker."

"That's what I said. Reyker." I couldn't do it justice. From his mouth, the name was a purr and a hiss, a kiss and a strike. But it dropped leadenly off my tongue.

"*Rrrey-kerrr,*" he repeated, drawing out each syllable so it curled and danced.

"*Rey-ker,*" I echoed in a whispery growl, scrunching my face into a snarl because it was the only way I could get my lips to cooperate.

Reyker laughed, and the sound startled me. For an instant, I saw the boy beneath his warrior's guise. For an instant, I laughed with him. Until I remembered the Savage's axe slamming into Rhys.

I fell silent, pulling my knees to my chest. Reyker was a beast, not a boy.

When he reached for my hand, I jerked away. "*Treyst mir,* Lira," he said, cupping my right hand like an injured bird, rubbing liniment over the blisters. For some reason, I let him. He tore strips off the blanket, winding them over my palm. When he finished, he did the same with my left hand.

"*Hvurdig?*" He gestured at my burned skin, my singed dress.

"I tried to hold a god's fire."

Reyker glanced up from his work, taking my measure. "*Thu aer trubbel.*"

"What does this mark mean?" I pointed at the scar of flame on my wrist, but I was thinking of the one behind my ear. "Is it a mark of ownership? Because I don't belong to you, Westlander, so if that's what this symbolizes, I'll cut my bloody arm off right now."

"*Nai. Skoldar,*" he said, tracing the scar lightly with his finger. It pulsed with heat in response, like a molten heartbeat. He spoke in gestures— pretending to hold a shield, then circling his hand around my head.

"Protection? From what?"

He shrugged, as if he didn't know how to explain.

"What do you want from me?" I asked again.

Using my knife, he dug a square into the dirt floor, filling it with shapes. As he added details, I realized the waving lines were rivers, the triangles mountains. "A map?"

He nodded. "Reyker go. Lira *hjalp?*"

"Why should I help you?"

Reyker sawed the knife across the air in front of his throat, pointing toward the village. He'd seen the string of Westlanders' heads hanging there. I ignored the twist in my gut that came at the thought of his head joining theirs. "It's what you deserve. You're one of them."

"*Nai meer.*" He waved a hand like he was erasing his past, erasing anything that connected him to the men who invaded my village.

"I wish I could believe you. But a deer cannot trust a wolf." He gazed at me blankly. I acted it out, spreading my fingers into antler-like branches, then growling, my hands astride my head like pointed ears.

He smirked at my impressions before doing his own, touching his heart after snarling like a wolf, standing tall and proud after lowering his finger-antlers. His meaning was clear enough: *The wolf must be kind-hearted, and the deer must be brave.*

"No." I rose and faced him. "I shouldn't have saved you, but you let me go when your people captured me. Consider my debt repaid. This is the last time you'll see me." He tilted his head, struggling to understand. "Goodbye, Reyker."

His eyes widened. "Lira—"

"Your kin killed my brother! He died in my arms!" My fingers balled into fists.

Reyker paled. "*Jai kleggur*," he said softly.

"I don't speak your stupid beast language." The Culling had drained me past the point of fear. I stepped closer, only an arm's length away. "Kill me or let me go."

He smiled. It wasn't the boyish smile he'd worn earlier; it was a cold twitch of lips, a tightening of his jaw. Reyker held my knife out. I took it, the blade hovering between us. I could kill him. He could kill me. That's how it was meant to be—as a Glasnithian and a Westlander, there could be nothing else between us now.

"Thank you," I mumbled, holding up my bandaged hands.

He inclined his head, his expression unreadable as I brushed past him. I stepped out into the quiet night, shutting the door behind me.

Mounting my horse, I took a last look at the hovel, ignoring the conflicting urges inside me—to go back and bury my blade in his chest, to go back and sit with him and tell him stories until he fell asleep. I clucked my tongue, and Winter headed toward home.

"May your gods have mercy on you, Westlander."

CHAPTER 13

The next morning, the air was thick with the stench of death. Torin declared a Day of Sacrifice to honor the gods for helping our clan defeat the beasts of the Frozen Sun. A massive bonfire was erected near the sanctuary. Doyen handpicked the best of our animals: lambs, goats, pigs. He slit each animal's throat, throwing their corpses into the flames.

I was sitting with Ishleen near the edge of the forest when a chestnut mare was led to the fire.

Rhys's horse.

Ishleen and I shared a look. "They can't hurt Victory," she said. "We can't let them." I was already pushing my way through the crowd, Ishleen right behind me.

We stepped between Doyen and the horse. "What are you doing with Victory?" I asked.

Sunlight glinted off the priest's bald pate. "Your brother longs to be reunited with his beloved mare. We honor him by granting his wish."

"Rhys would never wish for this. He wants Victory to live."

"Do you speak for the dead?" Doyen challenged. "Your brother calls out, asking for a blood sacrifice to send his horse to the otherworlds."

I knew my brother's heart. Rhys would despise this. And that meant

Doyen, whom we relied upon to tell us the will of the gods, was a fraud. "Liar!"

Gasps and protests surged from the crowd.

"Blasphemer!" Doyen hissed back.

From the other side of the fire, Torin moved toward us to put an end to our squabble. The man he'd been before the Culling might have listened to me, but the man who'd exiled Garreth was someone I no longer trusted. He'd side with Doyen. Victory would be sacrificed.

I wouldn't let that happen.

Neither would Ishleen. With dramatic flourish, she put a hand to her forehead and moaned before flopping to the ground in a mock faint. Heads turned toward her, several people moving to see if she was all right.

While most of the crowd's attention was on Ishleen, I leaped onto Victory's back. Kicking the horse's haunches, I braced my thighs around her flanks and braided my fingers into her mane. Victory bounded forward, scattering villagers, and we flew past the fire, past the sanctuary, into the Tangled Forest.

I could ride southwest to Ballygriff, or southeast to Houndsford, where Quinlan lived—they were the closest villages to Stony Harbor, on the southern border of the forest. I could find a kind family in need of a horse. But even as I thought of it, I knew it would never work. Victory bore the brand of three swords, marking her as property of our clan. No one would accept Rhys's horse without proof of my chieftain's permission.

The trees grew thicker, enough that we had to slow down. "What am I to do with you, Victory?"

A shape appeared in front of us.

Victory reared, and I clutched her mane to keep from being thrown. A dark-haired woman stood beneath the trees. She tipped her chin up, revealing her empty eye sockets. "Mistress of souls," the mystic said in greeting.

Victory danced sideways nervously. "Are you trying to kill me?"

"I am not the death god." She reached out and rubbed Victory's muzzle. "Pretty horse. You will give her to me."

"Pardon?"

"A gift. The horse becomes mine, and in exchange, I will give you the answers you seek. 'Tis why I was sent."

"Sent?" I asked uneasily, reaching for my medallion. "By whom?"

She only smiled.

"What answers will you give me?" *Garreth,* I thought desperately. "I need to find my brother. Can you tell me where he is?" Sliding from Victory's back, I came face-to-face with the mystic. I forced myself not to stare.

"I cannot tell you of your brother's fate, only your own. If you want to know what the gods have shown me, you must come with me to the water."

The mystic walked deeper into the trees. Though I was afraid of what she might tell me, curiosity compelled me to follow her. She stopped at a narrow brook burbling over moss-slicked stones. The eyes studding her flesh were green and blue, brown and gray, and all of them regarded me critically. "The gods' fingerprints are all over you," she said. "Can you feel them?"

"No." I looked down at myself, thinking to see whatever she saw, but there was nothing.

She knelt beside the brook. "You were chosen to die. Yet you live."

"You said my medallion saved me from the Brine Beast. How?"

"The Beast is a feral monster, but it loves its master."

"Faerran, the sea-goddess."

"Faerran is a feeble substitute. Veronis is the Beast's true master. Before he was a prisoner, Veronis was the god of all creatures, great and small. Your clans turned against him, but the animals of this island did not. They remember. At Faerran's insistence, the Brine Beast came to take four souls that day. When it sensed the symbol around your neck, the symbol of a worshipper of its true master, it hesitated. And when your mother offered herself instead, the Beast took her and let you live."

I struggled to absorb what the mystic was saying: I'd been spared not just because Mother had taken my place, but also because I'd worn her medallion. A talisman tied to Veronis. Which meant … "My mother worshipped Veronis. She believed the Forbidden Scriptures."

The mystic cocked her head. "Of course. Why else would she name you after a holy traitor, a woman both beloved and abhorred?"

Why indeed. "How did she hide it from my father? Why didn't she tell me?"

The mystic held up a hand. "I know much, but I do not know all. Those are your mother's secrets. The answers died with her."

Sorrow bloomed in my chest. Maybe I'd never really known her, and never would. "Doyen said what my mother did was blasphemy. That my life insults the gods." Although Gwylor claimed to care not one bit whether I lived or died.

"All men think they know the gods' minds. But to know a god, to see his true face ... 'Tis a cost few are willing to pay." She tapped the hollow sockets where her eyes should've been. "If the gods are angered, you will not need to be told. You will feel their wrath, and you will have no doubts. Tell me, what do you think of your death god now that you've been burned by him?"

I felt the ghost of violet flames and shuddered. "Gwylor frightens me. I don't trust him." I sat down beside her on the grassy shore. "You follow the Forbidden Scriptures. You worship the Fallen Ones. How do you know their version of the stories is true?" Were Aillira and Veronis heroes and Gwylor the villain, or was it the other way around?

Her many eyes seemed to laugh at me. "Truth is not what matters, only perception. Whom do you side with? Love or power? Strength or innocence? Which qualities are most admirable? Which qualities do you desire most in your warriors, your chieftains, your gods? You must decide for yourself. The Culling was meant to show you this."

"Show me what? Why was I drawn into Gwylor's trial?" My body had been pulled toward the beating heart in the god of death's hand like iron to a lodestone.

"It was your gift that answered Gwylor's call. To read a soul is to see the true nature of another being, to observe the beauty and cruelty that exist alongside each other within every one of us. This was what you wished to know. That there is another side to your death god. Another side to your father. Another side to your own heart, and where its loyalties lie." She gestured at the medallion dangling against my chest. "That is why you entered the trial. It is why I came to find you. To show you another side to a story you only think you know."

The mystic waved a hand over the brook. An image materialized across the water's surface: a man rubbing a stone against a shard of wood, whittling a crude weapon. Reyker. He blinked heavily, gold hair falling as his head drooped, blue-gray eyes disappearing beneath fluttering lids. His chin sank against his chest, weapon abandoned in his lap, as he drifted to sleep.

"What has he to do with anything?" I said. "He's no one. I wish I'd let him die."

"Lies," she hissed.

"He's a monster."

"Yes." She traced Reyker's face along the water. "He is everything you fear, and worse. He is also everything you hope, and more. His soul is a battleground. You've seen it yourself."

I had—the play of light and darkness within him, hidden layers of gentleness among harsh crags and slickened gloom.

"His gods—the Ice Gods—marked him as well. He's a weapon, forged and forgotten, fallen into the wrong hands. His gods cannot help him in Glasnith, where the Green Gods reign. But you can." The mystic took hold of my scarred ankle. "You did, accidentally, when he took your talisman and was spared by the Brine Beast because of it. And when you dragged him from the harbor, entwining your fate with his. You wield the lost sword of the Frozen Sun. A weapon of the Ice Gods in the hands of the Green Gods' soul-reader. 'Tis a story poets will pen, a tale fit for the scriptures."

"Are you mad? I want nothing to do with any beast of the Frozen Sun."

In the water, the rippling mirage showed Reyker gritting his teeth, murmuring in his sleep. The mystic smiled. "The choice is yours. Even those touched by gods chart their own paths. But before you decide, you must bear witness to the other side of his story. To the nightmares of your beast."

Her fingers dug hard into my arm. She flung me headfirst into the brook.

I crashed through the surface, colliding with Reyker's watery image.

———◆———

The world spun around me. There was no brook, no forest. I lay in an awkward heap on a snowbank in the center of a village dotted with cottages. In the distance, mountains rose up from the white tundra. The sun was a pale orb, little brighter than the moon. If this was Reyker's nightmare, these were the lands of the Frozen Sun.

In front of me, a man sprawled across the ground, his blood staining the snow red. His sword lay beside him. A gold-haired child huddled over the dead man. "I'm sorry, Father," the boy whispered. "I failed you."

I called to the boy, but he couldn't hear me. No one could. This was past, it was memory, and I wasn't really here.

There were other corpses scattered across the white field. Warriors swarmed through the village, boots crunching over snowdrifts, ignoring the boy and his dead father. The skin around the warriors' right eyes was inked with black scales. They herded crowds of women and children into a nearby pen, tied up rows of injured men and made them kneel. This was the aftermath of a battle.

I saw him then, and my knees shook.

Somewhat younger, but no less terrifying, the Savage eclipsed the other warriors; it was the intensity of his features, the assurance in his gait. He circled the captured men. "Your betrayal wounds me deeply, my friends."

He spoke in his mother language, but within the vision I understood every word.

"You are the traitor, rising against your jarl!" one of the captives called.

"Jarl Gudmund lets his settlements and his people waste away. I fight to make Iseneld the powerful nation it's meant to be. It grieves me to do this, but you've left me no choice. Since you will not pledge loyalty to me, all of you must be fed to Ildja. Summon the executioner," he ordered one of his scale-marked followers.

From the guarded pen, women screamed and children cried.

The boy hugging his dead father stood. He couldn't have been more than twelve. There was no mark of black flames beneath his brow yet, but there was no mistaking who the boy was.

In a flash, he claimed his father's sword. Bruises lined one cheek, and tears cut trails through the dirt smudged across his face. His clothes were stiff with his father's blood. "If you want to kill them, you must go through me." It was the voice of a boy but held hints of the man he would grow into.

The scaled warriors laughed. The Savage grinned. "You think yourself man enough to fight me, little lordling?"

The warrior I saved. Not peasant-born, as I'd assumed. Stubborn, proud, chin held high, glaring daggers at the Savage—who was twice his size and a thousand times more menacing.

"Reyker, no!" the captives shouted. "This isn't what your father would want!"

"My father is dead." He pointed his blade at the Savage. "Because of you."

"And you're anxious to join him." The Savage slid his sword from its sheath. "Show me what you've learned of swordsmanship among these cowards."

Reyker let loose a furious roar and swung his father's sword. He was strong for his age and size, handling the blade skillfully. If his opponent had been smaller, less experienced, perhaps he'd have stood a chance, but the Savage met each enraged strike with effortless parries.

The snow fell hard, glazing their hair and clothing. Over the clash of their blades, the Savage offered advice. "Elbows higher. Widen your stance. Don't grip the hilt so tight, son."

"Don't call me that!" Reyker spat, thrusting the sword. "Don't you *ever* call me that!"

The Savage stepped aside, avoiding the blade. Reyker shot past him, and the Savage delivered a sharp kick between the boy's shoulder blades that knocked him flat. He braced himself with his left arm and it turned beneath him. The bone snapped.

I swallowed the bile in my throat.

Reyker grunted, struggling to his knees. The scaled warriors heckled him. "Get up," the Savage said. "Finish your battle like a man."

"May the Destroyers drag you into the Mist if you harm that boy!" a captive shouted, wrestling against his bindings. "May Ildja devour your soul for all eternity!"

"I am the serpent-goddess's greatest Destroyer," the Savage said, his eyes gleaming. "Ildja, eater of souls, blesses and exalts me."

Reyker climbed unsteadily to his feet, lifting the heavy sword one-handed, broken arm dangling at his side. Something oddly close to pride touched the Savage's features as Reyker jabbed the sword at his heart. He yanked the blade from Reyker's hands and gripped his broken arm, bending it behind his back. "You are defeated. Say it, lordling."

Still the boy fought. Struggling, biting his lip against the pain, he refused to speak the words the Savage demanded. Then the Savage twisted his broken arm, and it was too much. Reyker gasped, color draining from his face.

I thought of Garreth, injured and exiled. I thought of Rhys, staggering into my arms as his life slipped away on the edge of the Savage's axe. Such cruelties men enacted upon one another.

"He's only a boy, you bastard!" This scream came from me. No one else heard. I clawed at the discarded sword, but my fingers went right through its hilt. This wasn't my world. There was nothing I could do.

"Cede, Reyker." The Savage spoke softly. "Say it, and I'll let go."

A spark of defiance burned in Reyker's eyes. He spoke in whispered gulps, through gritted teeth. "You'll ... never ... find her."

The Savage laughed, the rich rumbling joy of a man tasting victory. "I already have."

An indescribable sound of horror leaked from Reyker's throat. The spark inside him guttered. The Savage pushed on his arm, and Reyker finally submitted to the pain. His eyes closed and his limbs went limp.

The circle of warriors chuckled and clapped as the Savage lowered Reyker's body to the ground, and he turned a murderous glare upon them. "Back to your posts!" he ordered half of them, and they scattered. To the rest, he said, "Bring forth the traitors."

The first captive was led forward. The doomed man trembled as a hugely muscled warrior appeared with a massive broad-bladed axe. The executioner. He smiled, cracking his knuckles and hefting the axe higher. Something was wrong with his teeth. Instead of being square, they were sharpened into fangs, like a shark's.

The Savage pulled Reyker to his feet as the boy awoke.

"Kneel," the executioner said.

The axe rose. The kneeling man prayed. A woman and child screamed in the distance. "One day you'll thank me for this," the Savage told Reyker.

The axe fell.

Watching a man's head being severed from his body was chilling. It was an insult to sunder what was born whole, to cleave mind from heart, leaving them forever divided, eternally broken. Only then did it strike me how vicious it had been for my clan to dismember the slain Westlanders.

The next captive was brought out to a chorus of more screams.

The axe fell again. Again.

The icy ground turned crimson. Families wept. Snow spiraled from gravid clouds, settling like dust upon the growing pile of corpses. The executioner wiggled his stiff fingers, shook his tired arms.

The Savage held Reyker, but the boy no longer fought. What I saw in his expression, when I tore my eyes from the endless stream of executions, was nearly as hard to bear as the beheadings. It was the smothering of innocence, the death of hope.

His nightmare.

I wanted to wash his tear-streaked face, splint his arm, tell him everything would be all right—such was the vulnerability in those damp eyes, the crushing burden weighing upon his shoulders. But it was a lie. Nothing would save him from becoming the half-drowned warrior I found in the harbor. This boy would mature into a beast of war who would swing axe and sword and split men open like animals.

Here was where it began.

The sky above me darkened. The ground bled from white to green; there was no snow here, only emerald hills. The executioner and the headless corpses were gone.

I stood at the gallows in Stony Harbor. Dyfed dangled from a noose, his face a swollen purple mess, his tongue protruding from his mouth.

"I'm sorry," I said, as if it did any good.

And then, in a flickering blur, the figure changed. It was no longer Dyfed who hung from the noose, but Reyker.

"Not so pretty like this, is he?"

I spun to see the mystic behind me. "Is this what's going to happen to him?" I asked.

"Or perhaps this." She snapped her fingers, and Reyker lay in the grass, a gaping sword wound in his chest. "Or this." Another snap, and Reyker's chest was whole, but his head was some distance away, eyes still open, aimed blindly at the stars. "There are a thousand ways he could die. He is a trespasser in these lands. Many forces seek to destroy him."

"Please," I said. "I've seen enough."

The mystic snapped her fingers, and the gallows vanished.

I blinked up at the tangled trees of the forest, wavering high above me. I was underwater. Spluttering to the surface, I wiped my face, pushing my hair back. The mystic sat on the brook's shore, waiting, as I climbed out of the water.

"Darkness claimed your beast and sharpened him into a weapon for wickedness," the mystic said. "He was lost long before you found him. The only way for him to find redemption is to reach whatever light remains within his soul. Who better to lead him to it than a soul-reader?"

"Me?" I shook water out of my ear. "I'm not … I can't …"

"'Twill be no easy task. You must reignite the spark of hope within him and send him back to his own gods before the darkness finds him once more. There are dangers. Consequences. Tolls you may deem far too steep."

I twined my fingers in the rope my medallion hung from. "Why should the Green Gods or a daughter of Glasnith care about the redemption of this Westlander?"

The mystic skimmed her fingers across the water; it boiled and frothed at her touch. "Because the wars of the west have spilled onto our soil, and the Ice Gods' lost sword is the only weapon that can end the reign of the Dragon."

Two greenish-gold spheres took shape on the water—calculating eyes, alluring and terrifying. I stared at the eyes of the Westlander who killed my brother.

The Savage. The Dragon. They were one and the same. Inside the mirage of his eyes, other images emerged. Fires burning. Armies colliding. Blood spilling.

If I couldn't bring Reyker into the light, the Dragon would crush us all.

CHAPTER 14

The mystic mounted Victory, promising the mare would come to no harm. At least I'd managed to keep Rhys's horse safe.

"Heed me, soul-reader," she said. "When the time comes that you've need of us, enter the forest. Seek the grove and you shall find it. The Fallen Ones await your offering."

Travel to the Grove of the Fallen Ones, where the portal to their prison-realm was located, and make an offering of flesh to the fallen gods? Never. To do so meant gifting them a piece of my soul. Nothing was worth such sacrifice.

I'd not spoken aloud, but the mystic shook her head. "*Never* is not so long as you think, and *nothing* is worth far more than you'll admit." She nudged Victory's haunches.

Choking back sadness, I watched my brother's horse disappear.

I walked home as dusk unfurled. Around me, the night came alive. Animals howled in unearthly intonations, prowling among the trees: boars, coywolves, catamounts, and other, stranger beings. They let me pass, sensing kinship. I was the forest's child as much as they were. Or perhaps it was my medallion, bearing Veronis's symbol, that kept them at bay.

When I reached the village, the Day of Sacrifice had ended, but Torin, Madoc, and Doyen still hovered around the dying fire. They moved aside as I approached.

Coils of smoke drifted from the carcass lying in the embers. A dead horse, its shape as familiar to me as my own—even though the body was charred, I knew it had been a mare with a coat the color of sea pearls, slaughtered and sacrificed in Victory's place.

Sorrow threatened to stifle me, but my anger took over first. I ran to where our chieftain stood. "You killed Winter!"

"We had to give the gods their due," the priest said. "It's unwise to leave Gwylor and his kin unfulfilled."

I ignored Doyen, focusing my fury on the man who used to be my father. "She was my horse. I loved her. How could you do this?"

"You disobeyed." Something dark and dangerous twitched inside Torin's eyes. "Your actions have consequences, Lira."

Doyen and Madoc smiled. Madoc's period of mourning his dead wife and daughter had been shockingly brief. He seemed as callow and cruel as ever.

"Liars and butchers, all of you," I said.

"Careful," Madoc replied, "or you'll lose your tongue as your insolent brother lost his hand."

I raised my fist to strike my uncle, consequences be damned.

Torin caught my wrist. "Peace, daughter." He looked worn, bereft. This was the toll death had taken—the loss of my mother and Rhys, the pain that transformed him long before the Culling sundered him from himself. "Peace," he said again, watching me like there was something more he wanted to say but the words had abandoned him.

He called for a sentry to escort me home. I turned my back on him, and on the waning fire and drifting ashes that were once my horse.

———◆———

I lay in bed and wept, mourning for Winter and my brothers. When my mind finally released me, I slept, enough to curb my exhaustion and give the village time to retire.

I rose late, donning Rhys's clothing. The trousers and tunic were too long, but they would serve. I tied my hair back with a leather thong, strapped on the small sword Garreth had taught me to wield years ago. If spotted, I'd be mistaken for another sentry.

For a moment, I wrapped my arms around myself, inhaling Rhys's scent, still clinging to his clothes, and blinking back tears at the fresh wave of loneliness overwhelming me. Once it passed, I slipped through a window and into the forest.

The hovel was dark.

"Reyker?"

There was no answer. Reyker must have left Stony Harbor already. A violent mix of emotions coursed through me—relief, fear, disappointment. Hope that the mystic was wrong.

I opened the door to leave and ran right into him.

A second later, I was pinned flat to the ground, with a knee in my spine and a spear at my neck. I mumbled his name through a mouthful of dirt, and he flipped me onto my back. "Lira?"

Sitting up, I spat out clods of earth. "A fine welcome that was. Stupid bloody Westlander." He wouldn't stop gawking. "What?"

Gesturing at my odd outfit, my dirt-smeared face, he chuckled.

"Funny, is it?" I grabbed a handful of soil and shoved it into his face. "How do you like it?"

Reyker's skin was smudged from forehead to chin. He blinked and smacked his lips, bits of dirt trickling off. Then he threw his head back and laughed.

I tried to hold it in, but I couldn't. I lost myself in the moment and laughed with him. Looking at Reyker, I saw the cold-blooded warrior who'd slaughtered men like cattle, and I saw the boy who'd fought to avenge his father and defend his village. He was both: a boy and a beast, a hero and a villain. But only one of them was worth saving.

Reyker picked up the waterskin he'd dropped and pulled off his tunic, holding them out to me. I rinsed off, scrubbing away grit with Reyker's tunic. It smelled like him, like salt and sweat, blood and earth. When I was done, he rinsed his own face, missing a smear beside his nose, another below his eye. It made him look even more like that boy he'd once been.

"Who are you, Reyker?" I asked.

He wrung out his stained tunic and put it back on, shrugging. "*Jai veth enki.*" There was pain in his voice. It must have been hard to live as he did, caught between light and darkness, his soul at war with itself.

I'd only ever used my gift to condemn men. If I could heal Reyker, perhaps I could redeem us both.

He stood, offering me his hand.

I hesitated.

Part of me would always hate him for what he was. But I'd been beside him in his nightmare and watched the man who slew my brother destroy Reyker's childhood. I could blame him for the evils of his past and the evils of his people, or I could try to forgive him and allow him the chance to prove he was more than just a beast.

I clasped his hand, letting him pull me to my feet.

We stood close enough for me to feel his warmth, inhale his scent. I wanted to be sickened by it, but I wasn't. I wanted to step away, but I didn't.

"If you still want my help, it's yours." I glanced up at him, bolstered by the flicker in his eyes—the first glimmer of dawn upon the night-black sea. "Lira will *hjelp* Reyker."

His mouth twitched in amusement. "*Hjalp,*" he corrected. "Lira *vil hjalp* Reyker."

"Help," I said. "Lira will help Reyker. Now, you say it."

We eyed each other stubbornly. I put my hands on my hips. With a groan, he repeated the words; his accent was thick, but his pronunciation was clear.

Humoring him, I did the same. "Lira *vil hjalp* Reyker," I said, "because the gods have willed it. They showed me what happened to your father. Your village. The man who did it is the same one who led the raid on Stony Harbor. The man who killed my brother. Who is he?"

Reyker's jaw locked. He shook his head. Again, he said, "*Jai veth enki,*" as if he didn't know, or couldn't understand me, but he was lying. Something in his expression told me I'd get no answers if I pushed him. This truce between us was a delicate thing. Patience was far from my greatest strength, but I would have to bide my time.

Reyker's eyes widened suddenly, and he pointed at something behind me. I turned and saw blue lights flitting among the trees. "Sparkflies. You don't have them on your islands?"

"*Nai.*"

"Well then. Come with me."

Reyker followed as I led him through the forest, stopping at a copse of trees so thick and gnarled we had to turn sideways to slip through them. Inside it was dark, but above us, the canopy was filled with thousands of twinkling insects, like a net full of stars. Reyker stared in wonder, bathed in their soft luminescence.

"In my village, we call this a glow grove. Sparkflies gather where the trees are packed tight. It's sheltered, so they feel safe. My brothers showed me how to find the groves."

I saw them in my mind: Garreth's brooding observations, Rhys's patient explanations. They were bookends, balancing each other, holding me up between them. "Safe," I said wistfully, wondering if I'd ever feel safe again without them.

"Safe, Lira." Reyker put his hand over his heart, like it was a pledge.

I didn't trust him yet. But I'd have to try.

Beneath the dancing flares of sparkflies, beneath the steady gaze of his eyes, I placed a hand over my own heart. "Safe, Reyker."

CHAPTER 15

The shifting of power from Aengus to Torin was near-seamless, a flip of an hourglass. It was the same sand, only it seeped in a new direction, marking a new hour.

No one else noticed the change in him, that his words and gestures were laced with hostility, as if another man wore my father's face, performing insincere imitations. Torin moved into his father's manor, the largest house in the village. He held council in the great hall. He appointed Madoc as head magistrate to settle disputes over land and labor. Whether Torin trusted his brother or was simply keeping his enemies close, I couldn't say.

The village settled back to its old ways, the ordinary routines from before the Westlanders' invasion and the Culling. Except for those who'd lost too much, tragedy carving holes too deep to ignore. Those like myself.

Torin said nothing about me moving into the manor with him, so I remained in our family cottage. Every step I took in the village, suspicious eyes followed. The people of my clan had always been wary of me because I was a soul-reader, but things were worse since my confession at the Culling, and Doyen's spreading theory that my very existence had brought the gods' rage upon Stony Harbor, in the form of the Westlanders. There were whispers that I was cursed—the fact that I still drew breath would bring calamity to their doorsteps until the mistake was rectified.

No one would dare hurt me so long as Torin forbade it, but I couldn't trust that he cared about my well-being anymore. I was little more than a shiny token to him, a coin kept in his pocket until he found something worth trading it for.

Every few days I oiled and sharpened my sword with a whetstone until the steel drew blood with a featherlight touch. I imagined the Savage standing behind me. Spinning, I swung the blade and watched his eyes dim, his head toppling from his body.

It was one of the few things that made me smile.

⸺✦⸺

For my first attempt at redeeming Reyker, we sat in the grass beside the brook where I'd spoken with the mystic. I reached my hand out, fingertips resting lightly over his heart. "I want to help you, but you have to let me in. Understand?"

His eyes narrowed. I'd explained to him, as best I could, what I wanted to do—to enter his soul so I could heal it. In exchange, I promised him supplies, a horse, and a map for his journey home. He'd agreed, and I could tell it wasn't just about the map. He wanted to be healed. Even so, he remained skeptical.

"Please, Reyker. Let me see who you are."

He lowered his head. I worried he might refuse, but he took my hand and slid it beneath his tunic, pressing my palm to his chest.

He didn't pull me into his soul. He allowed me to enter on my own.

With a deep breath, I opened my mind, letting myself fall.

His soul was deep. I imagined this was how it felt to leap from a mountain. When I finally touched down, I floated along the surface of an ebony river, surrounded by sheer canyon walls. The river churned, frothed, and ... steamed. Black water. Black fire. Two incompatible elements—they merged and became one, cutting through the core of Reyker's being. I dipped my hands in, lifting curls of liquid and flame that danced together within my cupped fingers.

Lights twinkled around me like diamonds, studding the rock walls. Some glinted below the fiery river. I reached for one, but the river rejected me, spitting my arm out. When I tried again, I found the surface impenetrable.

"You're hiding things." My words rippled through the canyon. "You don't trust me."

No more than you trust me. His answer came from everywhere: the rocks, the waves, the expanse of red sky high above. *But we must begin somewhere.*

A shiny bauble glinted in the rocks at the river's edge. "Aye. We must begin somewhere." I plucked the gem. It glowed warm in my hands. Light spilled out, enveloping me.

When I could see again, it was from behind Reyker's eyes.

A cottage-strewn hamlet. Bodies everywhere. The sun is low on the horizon, disappearing behind the steely waters of the sea. My axe is stained with gore.

I go to the barn to get away from the other warriors, their cheering and celebrating. Horses whicker in the stables; chickens babble and goats bray, but underneath is another sound, muffled. Near. There's a trapdoor, hidden under the straw. It opens with a groan when I jerk the handle. From the bowels of the barn come soft cries of terror—a cellar, crowded with women, young and old. Children cling to the skirts of their mothers and sisters.

The blood on my axe belongs to their men.

A young woman passes the doe-eyed babe she holds to someone else, climbing out to face me, her fear tempered with courage. She pleads, unlacing her bodice as she comes closer. I struggle to make sense of her language, distracted as she bears her milk-swollen bosom. Offering herself.

I grit my teeth, ashamed. "That's not necessary. Stay here. Be quiet. I'll make sure no one finds you."

The woman doesn't understand my tongue. I lift a finger to my lips and usher her back into the cellar, shutting the trapdoor, kicking straw to conceal it.

I stay close to the barn, watching. As the other warriors sleep,

*I sneak food and blankets to the women. The trapdoor is still open
when the floor behind me creaks. A fellow warrior, a friend, stands in
the doorway. He starts to shout for the others.*

I bury my axe in his chest.

*Pressing a hand to his mouth as his life slips away, I whisper,
"I'm sorry. I'm sorry."*

I let go and opened my eyes, returning to the brook.

"You kept them hidden." This was the last thing I'd expected to find in
his soul. He'd defied orders for the sake of people he owed no allegiance,
people the Westlanders viewed as enemies. "You saved them."

Reyker pulled away. "*Jai draepa* … I kill …" He searched for a label,
coming up empty.

"Your comrade," I said. "But if you hadn't, what terrible things would
the Westlanders have done to them?" Reyker had traded his friend's life for
the lives of those villagers. "You did the right thing."

His laughter was dark and ugly.

"Reyker—"

"*Nai.*" He rested his forehead on his knees. My fingers reached out to
touch him before I realized what I was doing; my hand froze, hovering just
above his head. "Go," he said without looking up.

I snatched my hand back.

Walking home, I cursed myself, the mystic, and Reyker. This shouldn't
be my responsibility. I was no savior—I was just a girl who could peer into
souls, a paltry trick in the face of the task set before me.

How could I help Reyker when even the lights in his soul were fraught
with shadows?

———※———

Two weeks after the Culling, an assembly of warriors rode into the village.
Representatives from allied clans had been coming and going from Stony
Harbor for days, deliberating with our chieftain over how to best defend
Glasnith against further Westlander invasions. This time, Quinlan was
one of them.

I went down to the harbor to wait. It didn't take him long to find me.

At the funeral, we'd been limited to formalities, but when Quinlan walked across the rocky beach and joined me, all decorum was abandoned. There was no one else here but the chattering gulls. He put his arms around me, and I huddled in the shelter he offered, my cheek pressed to his shoulder. "I'm sorry, Lira," he said. "About Rhys. And Garreth."

"Has there been any word of my brother?"

He shook his head. "Not yet. We'll find Garreth, I promise. I still can't believe Torin exiled him."

"The Culling changed him. When you met with Torin, did you notice anything different since you saw him last?"

"Different?" He paused. "Not really, no. Why? What have you noticed?"

"He's become vicious. He carries on conversations with himself. His eyes fill with this swirling blackness." Quinlan gave me a blank look that solidified my fears. The villagers, the Sons of Stone, warriors from outside our clan—none of them saw it. Was I the only one who did? Was it because of my gifts, or because I'd also gone through Gwylor's trial?

I brushed at imaginary flames climbing up my arms.

"You're unwell, Lira," Quinlan said.

It was on the tip of my tongue to tell him about what happened to me at the Culling, what I'd learned of the Forbidden Scriptures, even the blind mystic's prophecy. He was my oldest, dearest friend—I should've been able to tell him anything—but I couldn't get the words out. There was a kernel of doubt that made me wonder if I could trust him with such dire secrets.

Quinlan's arms tightened around me. "You need someone to look after you. Let me take you away from here. Come with me to Houndsford."

"I can look after myself," I said, but I was too weak-willed to pull away from him. It felt good being in Quinlan's arms. Familiar. "Besides, I can't live with your clan unless …"

He gazed down at me, his eyes full of something that must have been love. "Let me take care of you, as your brothers would want me to. Let me heal your wounded heart. I'm asking you for the third time. The last time. Say yes. Marry me."

My throat tightened.

I looked at the handsome face of the wild boy I'd watched grow into a stately young man. I'd imagined this moment, when I finally said yes to Quinlan—which some part of me always assumed I would. I'd imagined how he'd sweep me into his arms and press his lips to mine.

It should've been easy to say yes. I was lonely. I missed my brothers, and Quinlan was the only one who understood, the only one who'd been as close to them as I was.

"Quinlan …"

Part of me still dreamed of a simple life, the one I'd expected to have back before the Westlanders destroyed everything. Before a beast of the Frozen Sun washed up in the harbor and blew my entire existence off course.

"Quinlan …"

Why was this so hard? Why couldn't I say yes and let Quinlan take me away from Stony Harbor, saving me from the wreckage that had become my life?

"Torin will never give his consent," I blurted out.

"Let me worry about Torin. Do you love me, Lira?"

"I've always loved you."

"That's not the kind of love I mean. Am I the first person you think of when you wake, and the last you think of before you fall asleep? Does your pulse quicken when you see me? When I touch you, does it feel like sparks set to kindling? Because that's what I feel for you." He pulled away, studying me. "Do you *love* me?"

I couldn't hold his gaze, and I couldn't admit, not even to myself, who it was that sometimes made me feel such things.

Quinlan bowed his head.

"You make me happy." I reached out, taking hold of his hand. "Isn't that enough?"

"Not for me. Nor for you. We both deserve more." He squeezed my fingers. "You cling to me out of fondness and loyalty, but all the while, you've been waiting for someone whose secrets and dreams you don't know as well as your own."

I groped for something to say, finding nothing.

Quinlan released my hand and stepped closer to the water, letting the frothy tip of a wave splash over his boots. "I hope you find the man you're looking for," he said.

"I'm not looking for anyone."

"That doesn't mean he's not looking for you."

After Quinlan left, I went to the stables. My horse was dead and Rhys's was gods-knew-where with the blind mystic, so I sought Garreth's stallion, Wraith, pressing my face against his neck, running my hands over his smoke-gray coat. He peered at me with the curious dark mirrors of his eyes.

I caught sight of my own reflection in them, loathing what I saw, envying Wraith's ignorance. Though part of him must have sensed Garreth's absence, Wraith didn't know he was gone. He didn't know the world had changed and would never be the same again.

CHAPTER 16

On the nights when I could escape notice, I crept from my cottage and passed the hours with Reyker. We walked through the forest, sat in the glow grove, or lounged beside the brook. I stole food from the great hall's kitchens, and we dined on salted fish and oaten bread. We flailed and fumbled our way through conversations, speaking with our gestures as much as our mouths, collecting crumbs of each other's languages.

Each time I visited, I entered his soul.

I experienced his boyhood: training at combat, playing with other children, hunting with his father. I witnessed the man he'd become: honing his battle skills, laughing and drinking ale with comrades, hunting alone in snow-covered mountains that spewed liquid fire. I learned the terrain of Iseneld, his homeland, as we swam in cold rivers and climbed black-rock cliffs beneath skies streaked with green and violet light. I learned Reyker as well, immersed in his past. For every warm, light-filled experience I drew out of him, I unearthed another made of cold darkness: bloody battles, betrayals, loss.

Never had I spent so much time in someone's soul. Reliving his history drained us both. I might have given up if it hadn't been so important, if the fate of my people didn't rest on healing Reyker's soul. He might have refused, had he not wanted his redemption as much as I did. Over and over, he consented, and I failed. The light in him, the hope I found, wasn't strong enough to defeat his darkness.

I'd learned nothing more of the Savage—who he was, why he'd murdered Reyker's father. Why he'd marked me. There were things Reyker kept hidden, memories he wouldn't let me touch.

"How do you do it?" I asked. "No one's ever been able to control what I find inside their soul or speak to me while I'm there. Why can you?"

He shrugged. "*Nai enki.*"

We were headed to the northern bluffs, one of the only places along the coasts near Stony Harbor where no sentries had been stationed because they were impossibly tall for an enemy to climb. It was a long walk, but I wanted to show Reyker my favorite place. "I'm the only one who's read your soul?"

"Yes," he said.

"Can you sense me inside you? What does it feel like?"

Cupping his hands, he captured a sparkfly floating nearby. "*Oppne.*" He jerked his chin at my hands. I obliged, and he slipped the insect onto my waiting palms. The sparkfly's legs tickled my skin. Blue light seeped between my clasped fingers.

"You." Reyker tapped his chest then spread his fingers around his heart, like rays of a small sun. I smiled shyly. It was odd, the intimacy we shared. I'd stumbled through his soul, inhabited his skin, yet we were still near strangers.

I opened my hands, setting the sparkfly free.

When we arrived at the bluffs, I told him about the time I'd spent here, alone and with my family. I told him how often I'd looked to the west and wondered what was out there. "Iseneld," I said, pointing at the horizon.

His eyes followed my finger, clouded with longing. "Home."

"You miss it." It wasn't a question. In his memories, I'd felt his love for his homeland. As much as I wanted to explore the world, I couldn't imagine being stranded a thousand leagues from Glasnith. "You'll see it again."

Reyker said nothing. He turned away.

That was when I heard the noise: a murmur, barely audible. The scar behind my ear grew cold and my head began to ache. I closed my eyes, listening.

I find you, he said. *You are mine, little warrior. Come to me.*

Dread pooled in my veins, spreading through my limbs. In the darkness behind my eyelids, greenish-gold eyes glowed. Staring into me. My legs moved at the Savage's command, drawing me forward. I struggled to pull free from the waking nightmare, but I was trapped.

The scar of flame on my wrist tingled with warmth.

"No," I told the Savage.

As quickly as his influence had overtaken me, I clawed my way through, cast it off, and my body was my own again. My eyes flew open. Before me, there was nothing but ocean, infinite and gray. I was poised on the rim of the bluffs. A gust of wind set me off balance, and I tipped forward.

Gray. It was everywhere. It was all that was left of the world.

Something jerked me back. Reyker's arms gripped me, pulling me from the edge.

He crushed me against him, just for a moment. Beneath my cheek, his heart pounded. Then he pushed me away, still holding my arms, talking fast in Iseneldish.

My fear was gone, leaving only anger—Reyker knew who the Savage was, and he was hiding it from me. While he struggled to ask me what happened, I slipped my hand into his tunic, pressing my palm to his chest. I barged into his soul, finding it unguarded, and plucked a forbidden memory from beneath the river of black flames.

I sit in a small, dark room. The floor is hard beneath me. Sunk into one wall is a heavily barred door.

"Lay down, Reyker." A woman with ivory skin and golden hair sits beside me. Her eyes are a deep, unyielding blue. "You've not slept in days."

My voice is young, fragile. "I can't. He finds me there."

Outside the walls are sounds of war—clashing steel, men shouting, heavy feet racing about. Tears slide down the woman's cheeks. "I'll never let anyone hurt you."

"I'm no child." I squeeze the sword at my hip. "I'm a warrior. I'll defend you, Mother."

"I forget you're nearly a man." She smiles through her tears, and then she begins to sing, her voice sweet and clear and lulling.

My eyelids flutter. I'm so tired. She leads my head down to rest upon her lap, singing a cradlesong about lambs huddling together for warmth in winter. Before drifting off, I hear her whisper, "You'll be a good man, my son. I know you'll make me proud."

The memory dissolved. I floated on the black river, cupped within the canyon walls, my mind crowded with confusion—this was not what I'd gone looking for. Why was Reyker hiding memories of his mother?

How could you? Reyker's thoughts spooled around me, dripping scorn. *This is my life you trespass in; my scars you rip open so carelessly!*

"I never meant—"

We're done with this, Lira. Your gods were wrong. I cannot be redeemed.

He shoved me from his soul and I returned to myself with a gasp. Reyker still gripped me, panting with fury.

I should've let it go, but I couldn't. "Did she die? Your mother?"

Reyker stiffened. "Yes."

There was a world of pain in that one gruff word.

The mystic had shown me how Reyker lost his father. And Reyker had shown me a memory of his older brother, Aldrik, riding away to join a patrol in the service of their jarl. Reyker had stood on the tallest hill in the village every day for weeks, watching the horizon, waiting for Aldrik's return. But his brother never made it home.

These losses had damaged him, but the loss of his mother went deeper. I'd felt it inside his soul as he watched the memory of her. It had gutted him.

I knew how it hurt to lose a mother.

"I'm sorry." I rested my forehead lightly against his chest. He leaned forward in response.

It started as comfort, but then his breath quickened. So did mine. I could put my arms around him. I could reach up, touch his face. His lips. He'd let me, if I wanted to. Did I want to?

The night grew silent. We teetered on the crest of a wave.

Enemy. Killer. Beast.

We broke apart, pulling away at the same moment, avoiding each other's eyes. The crash of sea against rock, the drone of insects, the shiver of wind returned. The only silence was between us.

"Let's head back," I said hoarsely. He grunted in agreement.

If the night's events had ended there, it would have been plenty, but the gods weren't done with us yet.

We'd not gone far when a scuffling sound made us both go still.

A silhouette emerged beneath a thatch of trees a stone's throw from where we stood. The thing that stood there was as tall as a horse, as wide as an ox, but it was neither. Its sleek blue-black coat blended perfectly with the night. I couldn't see it clearly, I could only make out hooves and talons, messy shards of bone jutting from the sides of its head like antlers. Glowing orange eyes that were almost human.

I stared at the forest demon. It stared back.

There were many tales of what they were, where they'd come from. They had dwelled here long before my village existed, protectors of the forest, killing those who harmed the land or its people.

Reyker snatched my sword from its sheath, moving between me and the monster. Its orange eyes shifted to watch him, black lips stretching into a grimace over carnivore-sharp teeth. All it saw was a Westlander, one of the men who'd used the forest to conceal themselves when they came to unleash their destruction.

"No." I stepped forward.

"Lira!" Reyker put an arm out, barring my path. The demon hissed.

Every child in Stony Harbor was taught the ancient tongue of Lord Llewlin and the first men of Glasnith. I was rusty, but I remembered well enough. "Stop in the name of Veronis," I commanded in the old language. I pulled the medallion from my bodice, holding it up so the demon could see. If Veronis had been the god of all creatures, perhaps the forest demon remembered his master as the Brine Beast had. "I am a scion of Glasnith, a Daughter of Aillira. This man is under my protection."

The demon stamped its hoof.

"I'm a guardian of this land, as you are." I shoved past Reyker. "He's not like the others. He's done no wrong. If you mean him harm, you must go through me."

There was an uncanny sentience in the demon's watchful gaze. Tense moments passed before it widened its jaws and loosed a bloodcurdling bleat. I never saw it move, but between one heartbeat and the next, the demon was gone.

Only then did I realize how badly my legs were shaking.

Reyker stared at the space where the demon had been. "What …?" He looked at me, dumbfounded. "What …?"

"I believe the words you're looking for are *thank you*." I braced myself against a tree until I felt steady enough to walk.

"*Duma soolka*," he grumbled. *Stupid girl*.

But his eyes held a hint of respect.

CHAPTER 17

Ishleen's blade caught mine, and my sword sailed out of my hands. Again.

"Where's your head?" she asked. "I've never beaten you at swords before."

We'd been practicing our swordplay in a sheltered cove off the harbor. Since the invasion, Ishleen had taken a renewed interest in learning to defend herself. Garreth used to instruct us, but today we fumbled through on our own.

I'd lost my sword at least ten times. "I'm tired is all. Didn't sleep well."

There were many things I trusted Ishleen with, but Reyker's life wasn't one of them. She'd been attacked by a Westlander. She'd never understand.

"You're hiding something," Ishleen said. "Traipsing about with that up-to-no-good glint in your eye, like some bonny lad just blew you a kiss. Is it Quinlan? Have you abandoned pledging yourself to Aillira's Temple and decided to marry him at last?"

"No." I didn't want to speak of Quinlan. I missed him, and the ache of our parting was still too fresh.

She pursed her lips, thinking. "Then perhaps you have a secret suitor?"

"Of course not. And I don't have a glint."

"Do so. You may as well tell me. I'll find you out, one way or another."

Ishleen's sword flew at me. I blocked her strike, thrusting it aside. "Think what you like," I said. "There's nothing to tell."

At least, not for much longer. Reyker's patience had already been waning, and when I stole the memory of his mother, it had run dry. He'd decided to leave Stony Harbor, with or without my help. The blind mystic had told me to lead Reyker to the light and send him back to his Ice Gods. I'd done what I could to redeem him. Hopefully it was enough.

The time had come to set my wolf free.

⸻

Before I sent Reyker away, I needed to get him a map of Glasnith, as I'd promised.

It was easy enough to get past Torin's attendants and into his library while the chieftain was off meeting with his councilors, to rummage through his desk until I found a stack of maps, setting aside a suitable one that shouldn't be missed right away. I secured the roll of parchment beneath the folds in my skirts and was about to leave when I heard Torin and Madoc enter the manor and head for the library door.

There wasn't time to sneak out a window, and there was nowhere to hide except under the desk. It would be far worse to be caught hiding than to stand in plain sight, as if I'd done nothing wrong. I steeled myself and waited. As they came closer, I listened to their heated conversation.

"Threaten the mercenaries," Torin was saying. "Tell them we'll withhold their cut of herbs, grain, and lumber. They'll get nothing if they allow an envoy from the Frozen Sun into their village."

"I'm handling the barbarians," Madoc said. "I've already sent missives to the chieftains of the Bog Men and the Ravenous."

"If they're considering this, it means they're considering an alliance. If the mercenary clans ally with the Westlanders, they'll try to take control of Glasnith. It will be civil war. We cannot let such a thing happen."

I stifled a gasp. The library door swung open.

When they saw me, the two men fell silent. "You should be more careful about leaving your doors unlocked, brother," Madoc said. "You never know what sort of vermin might slip inside."

"What's the meaning of this, Lira?" Torin asked.

I scowled at Madoc, clearing my throat. "I was hoping to speak with you, Lord Torin."

Torin paused. "Leave us, Madoc. We'll finish this discussion later." He shut the door behind his brother and waved a hand at me.

"I've made my decision," I said. "I wish to pledge myself to Aillira's Temple."

It was an excuse. It also happened to be the truth.

Trying to help Reyker heal the wounds in his soul had been exhausting and frustrating, but it was also the first time my life had ever felt truly meaningful. I had a gift that could help people. I was weak, untrained, but I could learn. I could get stronger. When I'd visited the temple as a child, I'd been awed by the libraries filled with books both new and ancient, the lecture halls where priestesses taught lessons on history and literature. Now I could feel the knowledge contained in the temple walls almost within my grasp.

"This is what the gods made me for," I said. "It's my chance to have a life that matters."

Torin remained silent. I played the one card I had that might make him listen.

"This is the best way to honor Mother's sacrifice." I toyed with my medallion. At the temple, maybe I could find out more about the followers of the Forbidden Scriptures and the things my mother had believed. "Please, Father. Let me go."

Torin studied me for several tense moments. When he slowly nodded his head, my heart lightened, my spirits lifted. "No," he said.

"No?"

"You were born to serve this clan. The temple doesn't need you. And nothing you do will ever justify your mother's death." He brushed past me and sat at his desk, considering the matter closed.

I stood there awkwardly. I'd hoped, but had I truly believed he'd say yes after everything that had happened since the Culling? With nothing left to lose, I spit out the question that had haunted me for years. "Do you wish it was me who'd died instead of Mother?"

Torin stared out the window. "Sometimes."

The word hit me like a punch. Had he said yes, I could've told myself he was being cruel, but this answer sounded more like a confession.

I stopped in the doorway. With my back to him, I said, "So do I."

CHAPTER 18

I arrived at the hovel earlier than usual that night and found it empty. Making my way to the brook, I saw Reyker through the trees, rinsing off in waist-deep water. Tendrils of hair clung to his face and neck. Water trickled down his shoulders and chest.

I made a small, involuntary sound.

Reyker grabbed his spear, searching the woods. When he spotted me staring, he stared back. Finally, I found my voice. "I didn't mean to startle you."

He put the spear down. I turned my back as he climbed out of the brook and pulled on his trousers. "Hope you're hungry," I said, holding up my satchel.

Knowing this would be his last full meal for some time, I'd raided the great hall's kitchens. I forced as much food on Reyker as he could eat while we pored over the map I'd stolen from Torin's library. Reyker traced the path he would take—through the Tangled Forest, between the Silverspire Mountains, across the Green Desert, down to Stalwart Bay on the eastern coast.

"It's the biggest village in Glasnith. From Stalwart you can seek passage on a ship to the Auk Isles." My finger traveled east over the sea, to the archipelago. "Their language is similar to Glasnithian. You can hide out there until you find a ship heading west. But I'm still not sure what to do about all this." I gestured to Reyker's hair, his face, his body.

"What?" he asked.

"*You.* You stand out. You're too tall. Your hair's too light. Your eyes—" They looked into mine curiously, and I lost the thread of my thoughts. I tore my gaze from his and focused on the maps. "Your eyes are too blue. You're a bloody frost giant."

For some reason, he found that hilarious.

"I'll give you some of Garreth's clothes. They'll be tight on you, but serviceable. If you wear a cloak and keep the hood pulled low, you'll draw less attention. I could cut your hair or try to dye it with powder."

He grabbed possessively at the long strands of gold.

"Vain, aren't you?" I teased. "It doesn't matter. Hair or no, you'll never blend in."

We'd received messages from other clans that Westlander invasions were escalating along the coasts—possessions stolen, men slaughtered, cottages burned. Men and women put in shackles, taken as slaves. When the invaders took their leave, entire villages were left in ruins. The clans wanted vengeance. Reyker wouldn't be safe until he was off Glasnith.

I pulled out the skin of wine I'd brought, drinking deeply to ease my nerves before passing it to him. We ate and drank, discussed and planned.

Once the details were settled, I asked to read his soul one final time. "I know I don't deserve it, after what I did, but I'd like to try. All this time, I've been pushing my way into your memories, choosing which ones you relive. This time, you choose. I'd like to see one of your happiest moments, if you'll let me." I offered a contrite smile, making it hard for him to say no.

He narrowed his eyes, like he could see right through me, but after thinking for a bit, he took my hand and placed it on his chest.

I drifted into his memory.

I gather my spear and bow, strap knives to my belt, readying for the hunt.

Mother's voice carries from down the hall. "I don't want him to go. The ice is melting. It's dangerous."

"The winter stock is depleted," Father says. *"Our people are starving, Katrin. If we don't replenish our stores, Reyker will starve with them. He knows the land. He can hunt and track as well as any of the men."*

"You push him too hard."

"He pushes himself."

"To be like you. To be like his brother, whose thirst for glory earned him an early grave. Can't we let him be a boy for another year?"

Father sighs. "This is what it means to be lord. One day the village will be his to protect and lead. He must prove to himself that he can. No one will follow a man who doesn't believe in his own abilities."

I stomp past them, heading for the door.

"Reyker?" Mother calls.

I ignore her, rushing outside to my mount, joining the other men. There's little snow. The earth is brownish green, budding with life, on the cusp of spring. The women of the village watch from their doorways, clutching their children, faces drawn with worry. They have a shadowed, gaunt look about them. We all do.

Father leads the hunting party, heading for the mountains. "That was disrespectful," he scolds, riding beside me.

"Mother thinks me a child," I say. "She doesn't believe in me."

Father chuckles. "Yes, she does. That's the problem. She sees your fate, Reyker. You'll lead by example. You'll march beside your men into battle. You'll give all of yourself, sacrifice everything to defend your lands and your people. It will make you a great lord, but it's a hard life. Your mother fears the treacherous road you must travel. So do I."

I ponder this as the party arrives at the foot of the mountains. There are fresh hoofprints. We follow them until we spot the giant elk near the high banks of the Fjokull River, chewing on tufts of newly sprouted grass, forked antlers rising above its bowed head. It's thin from the long winter, but huge. Enough meat to feed the entire village for days.

The men surround the creature. Arrows slice the air, hitting home. The elk arches its broad neck and bays. Glassy eyes rolling, it bolts, hooves slipping on the rocks.

"No," the men say, a quiet prayer that becomes a shout as the elk trips and falls over the banks. "No!"

I don't think. I leap from my horse and sprint to the edge, barely hearing the gasps and cries of the men, of my father, as I jump after the elk.

I land feetfirst, arms at my sides. The cold is jarring, but I'm used to swimming in frigid water. What I don't expect is the current. The river is swollen with snowmelt, and it sweeps me into its fierce grip. I slam into rocks, white water sucking me under. There's a moment of panic, of death's shadow looming, and then I fight, breaking the surface.

The elk floats ahead of me, and I swim, grabbing its hind leg. I dig into the water with one arm, kicking, towing the elk.

Before me, the land suddenly ends. The water drops. How tall are these falls? Trapped in the veins of the gushing river, I hear little else. Tall enough, I assume.

Death for me.

Death for the villagers.

I push myself, fighting the water, pulling the elk, aiming for the bank. Rocks are everywhere, and the river beats me against them. The falls are close. The rocks—it's the only way. I let the river shove me. Slammed into two rocks, I thrust a leg into the space between them, sling my free arm around one, clinging desperately, still clutching the elk with my other hand.

Water batters me. I shiver, cold seeping into my bones. My leg is squeezed, sharp needles climbing from ankle to hip. My arms ache, each pulled taut, muscles cramping. I could let the elk go, clamber onto shore.

Death for the villagers.

"No," I growl through chattering teeth. I can do this. Mother believes in me.

How long am I there, freezing, beaten, wrenched by the river? How long until I hear Father's voice calling, feel arms reaching for me, securing my burden, lifting me from the water? Hours, it seems. Their hands dig and pull. With the relief of letting go of the elk comes a flood of pain. Father already sent for healers, and they bend over me, prodding and fussing. I'm stripped, bandaged, wrapped in blankets.

The ride back is hazy, but the reception clears my head—villagers cheering, shouting my name, greeting me as a hero.

Even Mother, furious as she is with me, with Father, smiles and hugs me proudly. There's a celebration: wine and ale and heaping bowls of elk stew. People crowd around, slapping my shoulder, toasting me. I'm sore and limping, but I am so alive.

I opened my eyes and took a steadying breath. Reyker looked back at me with a bright, unfamiliar grin.

"I wish you'd shown me this memory sooner," I said. "Were you hiding it from me?"

"No." He patted his chest. "From me."

"Why?"

"Death." He stared into his lap. "Mother, Father, village. All."

I knew what had happened to his village, to the people in it. Those tragedies couldn't be undone. But if Reyker could move beyond his loss, he could rekindle the purpose he'd lit upon when he dove into the river. "Hold on to this memory. When darkness surrounds you and you fear you'll give in, remember it. Hold it as tightly as you gripped the elk."

He bowed his head. "Thank you."

"You can be a good man, Reyker." I clasped his hand. "I believe in you."

He put his hand over mine and his gaze changed subtly, like a veil had fallen from his eyes. "*Thu aer vakk*," he said.

"*Vakk?*"

"Beautiful."

You are beautiful.

I looked at Reyker, really looked at him, feeling the weight of everything that had been slowly building between us these last weeks. "*Thu aer vakk*, Reyker."

As if he couldn't help himself, he brushed a strand of my hair with his fingertips.

My pulse sped up, spiked by fear and something else I didn't yet understand. This wasn't supposed to happen. I was only meant to redeem him; I was never supposed to care about him. I *couldn't* care about him—it was a betrayal of my country, my clan. Of Rhys.

I stood abruptly, backing away.

"Lira?" Reyker moved cautiously toward me, aware of our roles: he the wolf, and I the deer that might spring away.

If I was smart like a deer, I'd have run before the threat cornered me, but the closer he got, the less willing my limbs were to evade him. He stood in front of me, the heat of his skin caressing me across the gap between our bodies. "We can't."

"No?" His hands were at his sides, waiting for permission. He wouldn't breach the space between us unless I consented.

"You're a Westlander!" I was suddenly furious at him for making me feel so weak. "I hate your kind. I hate …" I couldn't say it. It wasn't true.

"Hate me."

I raised my eyes to his. My reluctance was a speck of snow landing on a fire—trifling, dissolving. Here, now, he wasn't an invader. Just a man.

"I wish I hated you." I leaned my head against him and his arms settled lightly around my waist. His eyes closed as I trailed my fingertips over the faded bite marks on his torso. His face was relaxed, but his hands twitched as if it took boundless effort not to use them.

"Reyker?" My voice was a hoarse purr, asking for things I couldn't put into words.

When his eyes opened, they reflected my own longing. His palm pressed the small of my back, drawing me closer. His fingers glided through my hair, curling behind my ear. Brushing over the scar the Savage had left there.

The change in him was instant.

His body tensed, the blood rushing from his face, hand shaking as he traced the wound. He angled my head to the side, gathering my hair out of the way. Phantoms eddied in the dark pools of his eyes as he stared at my scar.

The sweetness between us shattered, my desire buried by my rage.

"Who is he?" I trembled with fury. "The Westlander who marked me and killed my brother?"

Reyker looked haunted. I should've been kinder. I'd been inside his nightmares; I knew how the Savage had made him suffer. Yet all I could think of was Rhys dying in my arms. "Tell me his name." When Reyker said nothing, I hammered his chest with my fists. "His name!"

He wheezed like he was choking on the name, fighting to cage it. It forced its way up his throat, and he spit it out in a strangled rush. "Draki!"

"Draki." My tongue rolled over the thick tiers of each syllable. The name tasted of blood and bile, the dank must of a bottomless abyss. "He's the one you came here with years ago, isn't he?" I'd sensed it, when the Savage grabbed me, that I had felt his touch before. "He leads the invaders. Has he marked others?"

"*Magiska*," Reyker said through clenched jaws. "Girls with gifts."

My mouth went dry, thinking of how Draki had looked at me. Like I belonged to him: my mind, my soul, my abilities. "He wants to use me."

I worried briefly about Aillira's Temple, and what Draki might do to the pledges if he found them, before remembering how protected it was—by guards and spells and every defense the Daughters of Aillira had been gifted with. It was probably the safest place in all of Glasnith.

"Will Draki come back for me?"

Reyker pressed his lips into a thin line, wrath contorting his face, telling me all I needed to know. "I stay here," he said. "When Draki comes, I kill him."

I'd already lost my brother to Draki's blade. Westlander or not, I couldn't abide Reyker sacrificing himself. "You aren't staying. I won't let you die for me."

"I *will*—"

"No!" I smacked my palms into his chest. "Go home. Defeat Draki in Iseneld, where your gods can help you."

"Gods aflame, Lira! Why you do not listen to me? The Dragonmen will return, and they will do worse—"

"Reyker? How are your words so clear?" He froze. Lowered his head, averting guilty eyes. "You speak as if ... you already know the language." I took a step back. "Where did you learn Glasnithian?"

He raked a hand through his hair. "Prisoners."

Of course. The first time I saw Reyker, there were other prisoners tied up in the boat. I wondered what horrors befell those men after Draki was done using them.

"You lied." All the nights Reyker and I had spent together, speaking in gestures and broken sentences. All an elaborate ruse. I felt like a fool.

"Not a lie." He sighed, chasing after me as I stormed off. "I did not speak Glasnithian for many years. I forgot. I came here and spoke with you. I remembered."

"Yet you let me believe you needed to be taught."

"It was safer if you did not know."

Safer for him if I babbled on and spilled secrets, thinking he didn't understand.

He blocked my path, sidestepping when I tried to go around him. "And I like how you teach. How you listen and understand without words. Forgive me."

I glanced up at him, then quickly away. He was giving me that look again, the one that threatened to undo me. "Fine. You're forgiven." What did it matter? He was leaving tomorrow; we'd never see each other again. I swallowed hard. "You look tired. We should go."

We walked in silence, Draki's shadow hovering between us. By the time we got to the hovel, Reyker was swaying on his feet. I pointed at the blanket. "Sleep."

His eyes narrowed. "You give me orders now?"

"Please," I added with false sweetness.

He sat down, arms crossed, scowling like a stubborn child. Blinking heavily. Slumping over almost instantly. Knowing how little he slept, how much he needed rest before his journey, I'd slipped one of Ishleen's sleeping draughts into the wine when he wasn't looking and let him drain the skin.

I took off his boots, adjusted the blanket beneath him, and told myself to leave.

I didn't. I sat beside Reyker, watching him sleep.

His body twitched, jaw stiff, teeth grinding. Nightmares. No wonder he fought off sleep. How long had Draki haunted Reyker's dreams?

How long would Draki haunt mine?

Reyker gasped, clawing at the blanket. "It's all right," I said, pushing hair back from his forehead. "You're safe, Reyker."

When I touched him, his hand shot out, clenching my arm. I started to wake him, but stopped, remembering how his mother sang to him. In a hushed half whisper, I sang the ballad about the woman whose love was lost at sea, the song I'd been singing just before I found Reyker in the harbor. At the sound of my voice, he quieted, his breath slowing. He curled onto his side and burrowed his head into my lap.

"I don't care that you're leaving," I told him. "I won't miss you at all."

He mumbled softly in his sleep. I traced the ridged skin of his warrior-mark, feeling the pull of time rushing onward, the inevitable flux of darkness fleeing the encroaching day.

This was all we would ever have.

CHAPTER 19

I moved through the day in a fog, chewing my nails and pacing, going over lists and plans in my mind. There was nothing more I could do. It was up to Reyker whether he made it off Glasnith or …

I couldn't finish that thought.

Seeking solace, I made my way toward the sanctuary. I was nearly there before I realized someone was following me. When I turned, Dyfed's son froze, glaring; it wasn't the first time I'd caught Ennis haunting my steps. "If you're going to stalk me, at least let me apologize."

The boy spat in my direction and ran.

I found the sanctuary empty. From the niche within the stone wall, I chose three brass lamps, holding each to the torch that burned at the center of the sanctuary. One for Garreth. One for Quinlan. One for Reyker. I spoke their names into the fire as I lit the lamps, offering prayers for their protection.

"Is it truly your will that I aid a Westlander?" I asked the gods. "That I redeem him and help him escape, as the mystic instructed?"

A squawk answered. Lammergeiers perched in the arched windows of the tower, watching. Veronis—the Great Betrayer—had worn the guise of lammergeiers as he observed the mortal world. Perhaps these were gods looking down upon me now.

I bowed to them, just in case. "I'll take that as a yes."

—◆—

Night came. I donned Rhys's clothes and snuck to the stables, where a sentry was posted to watch for thieves. Stomping on a branch, I cracked it beneath my foot.

The noise brought the sentry running. From the trees beside the stables, Reyker snuck up behind him. One quick punch to the sentry's head, and he was unconscious. Reyker took the sentry's sword and dragged him into the stables, tying him up and pushing him into one of the stalls so it would look like the work of a vagabond horse thief.

I saddled Wraith, Garreth's stallion; I didn't want to lose my brother's horse, but Wraith was fast and would serve Reyker well. As I buckled the straps, my sleeve slipped, exposing the scar on my wrist.

Skoldar, Reyker called it. A shield-scar, meant to protect me. And it had. Draki had been furious when he saw the *skoldar*. Somehow it dampened the effects of the mark the warlord had cut into me. Without it, I'd be Draki's prisoner. His slave. I allowed myself to accept what I'd suspected for some time—when Reyker had marked me, he'd saved my life.

The blind mystic's warning echoed in my mind: *Many forces seek to destroy him.*

It was these thoughts that made me take off my medallion. I tried to slip the rope over Reyker's head, but he took hold of my hands. "No."

"It'll protect you."

He slipped the medallion around my neck, his fingers sliding down the rope, brushing my skin in a way that made my breath catch. "You keep this. For your mother."

"If you won't accept the medallion, there's another way." I pricked my finger on my knife, mixing my blood with a handful of earth, motioning for him to open his collar. On his chest I drew four blades with a moonflower blooming where the steel-tips touched, an ancient protection symbol: Llewlin and his three sons were the blades, and the flower was his daughter, Aillira, uniting them. "This marks you as one of us, so forest creatures won't harm you."

We stood beside the horse, looking at each other for the last time. There was something in Reyker's eyes I didn't want to acknowledge. It was death, certain and unavoidable. Not his, but mine. He was sure Draki would come for me, and I would die.

I was afraid he'd insist on staying. I was afraid if he did, I'd let him.

Forcing a smile, I raised my hands above my head, fingers spread like antlers, chin high. A brave deer. "Trust."

He placed his hands like pointy ears on either side of his head, then touched his heart. A kindhearted wolf. "Trust." He held his hand out. "Come with me?"

"What?"

He tapped the sword. "I will keep you safe."

"I can't. My brother will send for me." If I went with Reyker, Garreth would have no way of finding me.

"Lira—"

"No." I had to look away when I said it. "I won't leave. Not yet."

His hand closed, arm dropping to his side. I felt as if a piece of myself had come loose, rattling inside me. As if I'd lost things I'd not realized were mine.

"Go, Reyker." It hurt me to say it. It hurt him to hear it, judging by the tight lines of his features as he spun and mounted Wraith. "Take care of him." I hid my face against the horse's coat. "When you get to Stalwart Bay, sell him to someone near the docks. Only foreigners would buy a stolen horse from someone who looks like you. Don't accept less than gold specie. He's worth it, and you'll need it in Longshore."

"*Takka thu*, Lira."

With a deep breath, I looked up at him, memorizing each detail—eyes as deep and blue as oceans, hair that gleamed like sunlight through honey.

"Thank you," he said. "I will not forget. *Aldri.*"

"*Aldri,*" I agreed. *Never.* "Go," I whispered, biting my lip to keep it from trembling.

He didn't move.

"Please, Reyker."

He sighed and took the reins, squeezing his heels. Wraith pranced forward, hooves clomping the dirt—slowly, then faster, until they were a streak of gray and gold, barreling out of the stables, the green forest swallowing them.

I watched him disappear, calling after him silently.

Farewell, my wolf.

CHAPTER 20

REYKER

The horse was fast and knew its way through the forest; the blurring trees and pounding hooves led Reyker's mind to wander more than it should have.

You abandoned her.

He had to. What could he do in his weakened state? He needed to fully recover from his illness if he ever hoped to confront Draki. He needed the blessings of his gods, who'd been silent since he had reached the Green Isle. He needed the healing shores of his homeland.

Lira will die.

She was only a girl who'd taken pity on him. She helped Reyker because she believed her gods asked it of her. It had nothing to do with him. He owed her nothing.

You owe her your life.

No. She wasn't his kin. He'd vowed on his parents' ashes to end Draki's reign. That was why he'd carried on, why he'd endured. So one day he could stand in defense of his island, his people, who'd been tyrannized by the warlord and his Dragonmen for years.

The purpose Lira helped you reclaim.

Yes. Reyker could not deny it. The darkness that had been a noose around his neck, tightening with each bloody battle he fought, had loosened.

He'd lost himself, and Lira had found him.

And you'll let her die for it?

"I asked her to come with me!" he said aloud, forgetting the need for stealth. "I tried to stop her from going into the village when the Dragonmen attacked. If she'd listened, Draki never would have seen her."

If you'd not disappeared, Draki would not have come to the Green Isle's north harbor looking for you, finding her instead. Her death will be your fault. Like your father's death.

And your mother's.

Reyker's growl was loud enough to startle the horse. It stumbled, nearly crashing into a tree. He jerked the reins and the horse stopped, panting. Reyker looked back the way he'd come, then urged the horse into a gallop once more.

You've seen what Draki does to girls he marks. What he'll do to Lira.

Long-buried memories rumbled in the crust of his mind, bubbling up from beneath the black river—Reyker saw his mother, thrashing, crying, fighting Draki's compulsion in vain, begging Reyker to save her.

Bile splashed up his throat. Reyker pushed the images away. His fingers sank into the horse's mane as if it was the only thing grounding him. Rubbing a sleeve across his mouth, he glanced up and saw an open field.

He'd made it past the forest. In the distance was a shadowy mountain range. The Silverspires. That was where he was bound.

Reyker's head cleared. He gulped crisp air. It was the forest that had brought forth his nightmares. Like the forest demon he and Lira had encountered, this place saw him as a threat. The forest, the island—they wanted him gone.

"Leave me be. I'll go."

He looked back again. The horse snorted its impatience. Reyker's palm went to his chest, where Lira's blood was smeared across his skin:

This marks you as one of us, she'd said. He stared down at his hand, so used to feeling hers there, resting over his heart.

The choice was already made.

He'd made it the moment he found the scar behind her ear.

"I'll go." He turned the horse around, dug his heels into it, steered it straight for the forest. "But not without Lira." He'd bind and gag her if he must. They would leave together. He would find somewhere to hide her, somewhere safe from Draki's reach. If such a place existed. "I will not leave her to die."

The darkness of the forest, the darkness of his soul, ceased to touch him. This was his purpose—to protect those he cared for, kin or no.

Reyker felt more alive than he had in a long time.

When he heard noises ahead, he thought it was the wind. But as the sounds spread out, flanking him, he recognized the stomping of horses, the calls of men.

And when the rope appeared, held between two riders, too late for him to duck, he laughed darkly. The rope snagged on his shoulders as his horse kept running, flinging him backward, slamming him to the ground.

Four men surrounded him, swords pointed.

Reyker unsheathed his stolen sword. With a howl, he rose to attack, but found he couldn't move his right leg. A knotted rope was looped tight around his boot; a snare, meant to trap game. He laughed harder as his sword was knocked away and boots and fists pummeled him.

You fool. This voice was not his own. It was the deep rasp Reyker hated more than any other. *See what happens when you think to take what belongs to the Dragon?*

PART TWO
DEALS WITH DEVILS

CHAPTER 21

I woke in a tangle of sheets, feeling a snare around my foot, a sword at my throat. It took a moment to realize what had woken me: an ominous, insistent clang. The warning bell.

My stomach lurched. I jumped up and dressed, bursting through the cottage door into the soft blue light of dawn. *A dream*, I told myself. *It was only a dream.*

I met Ishleen on the path, a knife clutched in her hand. "Is it another attack?" she asked. Whatever she saw in my face made her stop. "What's wrong, Lira?"

I raced past her.

It's not Reyker. Reyker is safe beyond the forest, on his way home to Iseneld.

People trickled from their cottages nervously, women and children hovering in doorways, men coming out armed. I ran to where a crowd had formed in the clearing beside the great hall, shoving through them until I was at the front.

My heart plunged into my stomach.

Madoc and several sentries stood in the middle of the circle, all of them cut and bruised, glowering at a hunched figure. A young man, beaten bloody, his arms tied behind his back.

Somehow Reyker managed to lift his head, to growl at his captors and the buzzing crowd. Covered in blood, his clothes torn, teeth bared, he looked every bit the feral beast my clan believed him to be. His wild eyes rolled over me, paused an instant, drifted away.

Ishleen pushed through the crowd until she was next to me. She stared at the Westlander.

Madoc drew his leg back and slammed his boot into Reyker's ribs. I barely flinched, but Ishleen saw. Her gaze darted between Reyker and me.

The crowd parted like trees bending in the wind as Torin strode into the clearing. "Madoc. You've brought us a guest."

"The beast attacked a sentry, stole a horse. We tracked him through the forest." Madoc held up the satchels Reyker and I had tied to Wraith's saddle, tossing out the supplies. When the map fluttered into the dirt, stamped with the three-sword symbol of our clan, the villagers rumbled. The rest could've been taken from the sentry or the stables, but this had come from the manor.

Beside me, Ishleen stiffened.

"We believe these items were stolen from the village, but not by the invader," Madoc said. He gripped Reyker's head and wrenched it back. Reyker's tunic was torn, exposing the protection symbol I'd drawn on his chest. "Someone took good care of our beast." Madoc's pitiless eyes rested on me. Somehow, he knew.

I spotted Ennis, my stalker, in the crowd, confirming my fears. Dyfed's son smiled victoriously. Ennis must have followed me last night and told Madoc what he saw.

"A traitor in our midst. What does our guest have to say of this?" Torin asked. "Show us who helped you and your death will be quick."

Reyker's lips curled with contempt. He cursed Torin in his native language, insults about the chieftain's manhood, insinuations about what he did with barn animals, and many other things I couldn't even guess at.

Torin drew his dirk, the same one he'd used to cut off Garreth's warrior-mark, pressing the blade under Reyker's chin. "We have ways of making guests talk."

He wouldn't tell. They could beat him, stab him, break every bone, and he'd never speak my name. I knew it with an unshakable, unexplainable certainty.

Reyker grinned, blood dripping from his mouth, streaking across his teeth. He spit in Torin's face.

There was a beat of silence, then Torin's fist cracked into Reyker's jaw, his head whipping sideways. Torin's arm formed a bar across Reyker's throat as he dragged the Westlander to his feet, marching him around the circle, forcing his head up so his eyes connected with the mob calling for his blood. For the second time his gaze slid over me, betraying no recognition.

"Silence will only bring you suffering," Torin said. "Name your conspirator, and your torment ends."

"Your mother."

Torin spun Reyker around, grabbing his collar, yanking him close. Too close. Reyker thrust forward, head-butting him with the crack of bone on bone and Torin staggered back, his nose bleeding rivers. But he recovered quickly, raising his fist for another punch.

"Fight," Reyker said, nodding at Torin's sword.

The chieftain stopped, baited. "You're challenging me to a sword fight? You think you can beat me?"

Laughter pealed through the crowd. I wanted to scream at Reyker. He could hardly stand. How could he fight?

Duma strenge, I thought ruefully. *Stupid boy.*

The chieftain wouldn't back down from this public challenge; his pride was too bloated. "Cut his bindings," he told one of the sentries. "Give him your sword."

The sentry gaped at Torin. "Are you sure—"

"Do as I command!"

The sentry cut the ropes pinning Reyker's wrists and tossed his sword down. Reyker glanced around, expecting a trick. "Pick it up," Torin said.

Reyker complied, taking a defensive stance. Torin hadn't touched his weapon yet. His back was to the Westlander, vulnerable. "What are you waiting for?" he taunted.

Reyker charged, quick but limping. In one swift, smooth motion,

Torin whirled and unsheathed his sword, swinging straight at the West-lander's neck. Reyker blocked the strike just in time, the heft of clanging steel driving him backward.

Their blades untangled, arced, clashed again and again. It took several narrow misses, but Reyker watched how Torin attacked, adapting to it, adjusting his form. Teeth grinding, muscles straining, the two men fought.

Sweat trickled along Torin's neck. His arrogance faltered.

Reyker was remarkable with the blade. Agile. Strong. But he'd nearly died from lung-fever only weeks ago. He'd taken a beating that might have killed a lesser man. And Torin was the finest swordsman in our clan, perhaps in all of Glasnith. Reyker's fluid strikes and blocks forced Torin to his toes, but Torin bided his time, waiting for a lapse in his opponent's guard.

It came as Reyker stepped in a fraction too close. With a final flourish of steel, Torin's blade caught Reyker's near the hilt. Torin's arms swept low, then high, and the sword slipped from Reyker's hands. Torin's blade sliced across Reyker's torso.

There wasn't much blood. If he'd wanted, Torin could have eviscerated Reyker, but this strike was meant to shame, not to kill.

Reyker dove to retrieve his sword and met Torin's boot, slamming into him, the force knocking him flat on his back. The boot settled on his stomach, grinding him into the dirt. Torin pressed the tip of the blade over Reyker's heart, both hands wrapped around the hilt, ready to cleave the Westlander's chest and lay him open.

Reyker's face was calm. He waited for death with absolute acceptance.

This was what broke me.

"Wait!" The scream was out of my mouth before I could stop it. I stepped forward.

Every head turned, eyes torn from the climax of the battle to stare at the girl who dared interfere with the chieftain's justice. Torin's glare was its own monster, clawing at me. Reyker's mask slipped briefly: a flash of anguish, begging me to hush and fade back into the crowd.

It was too late. I took a deep breath. "I helped the Westlander."

A chorus of murmurs traveled through the crowd.

"You?" Torin's eyes were nearly black with the god of death's twisting shadows. Beside him, Madoc grinned—this was why he'd kept my secret, to see what I would do.

I had one chance. Whatever I said next would either save or condemn us both. I spit the words out as quickly as they came to me.

"The True Gods commanded it. I found the Westlander hiding in the woods, so I pretended to be his friend. He's one of them. He knows things. That makes him a weapon we can wield against his own people. Through him, we'll defeat the beasts of the Frozen Sun. This is what the gods told me." Not exactly a lie; the mystic claimed to speak on their behalf.

More whispers rose among the villagers. A robed figure emerged from the crowd to join us in the clearing. The old priest. "The gods told *you*? A girl? A child?"

"I am a Daughter of Aillira, god-gifted in her blessed name."

"Cursed Aillira," Doyen said. "Betrayer-whore Aillira."

I appealed to the suspicious crowd, holding the gaze of everyone I locked eyes with. "Kill him, and we gain nothing. These beasts don't respond to force, but this one trusts me. He is like a wild dog, but I can tame him. I've been teaching him our language so we can question him. I'll learn his people's weaknesses so we can use him to overthrow the Westlanders and invade their lands as they have ours."

The look Reyker aimed at me was searing. *Betray Iseneld to save your own skin:* this was the deal I'd struck on his behalf. He hated Draki, but cared deeply for his homeland, his people. I was encouraging my clan to use him to destroy what he held dear.

"You will read the beast's soul and tell us what he knows," Torin said.

"I've tried, my lord. His soul is shielded from my gift. I can see only what he allows. With a bit more time, I can convince him to let me in and give up his secrets."

Torin wiped his bleeding nose, thinking, blade still poised over Reyker's chest. The chieftain was as cunning as he was ruthless. Keeping a Westlander alive to extract information was an effective scheme, one he'd undoubtedly been considering before Reyker's challenge distracted him.

"The invaders are a plague on our island," Doyen said. "This beast is a curse. Keeping him alive will bring us nothing but scorn. He must be sacrificed to appease the gods."

"This Westlander is a *gift* from the gods," I said. "He was on the ship sunk by the Brine Beast. It killed every Westlander except him. Why would the Beast spare him unless the gods desire him to live?"

The darkness in Torin's eyes seemed to dance. "Lira did us a great favor keeping our enemy alive. Why didn't you tell us what you were up to, child?" Torin pressed his boot on Reyker's ribs while Madoc retied his wrists. "If you meant to turn him over to us, why did you give him a map? A map stolen from *my* home?"

"I—It was … a ploy. To gain his trust."

"Of course it was," Torin replied.

I didn't see Madoc move behind me, but I felt him. There was uncertainty in Torin's expression, but it fizzled and died. He nodded at Madoc.

I twisted toward my uncle as his hand flew at me. The world burst with white-hot light. The side of my face went numb. I floated a moment before slamming to the ground, the taste of blood and dirt filling my mouth.

From far away came an enraged growl. Reyker was shouting threats, struggling to stand, but Madoc and another sentry grabbed hold of his legs and dragged him off.

"Take the beast to the cells," Torin ordered. "Lock my daughter in the manor. Councilors, report to the great hall. We must decide what to do with our guest and our traitor."

Someone wrenched me up, forcing me to walk. Reyker and I were pulled in opposite directions. He was alive at least, and so was I.

But for how long?

CHAPTER 22

The room was a sparse cube. There was a bed in the corner, and a tiny window over it, too small for me to fit through, but it was otherwise empty. I was given a pitcher of water and a chamber pot by a sour-faced guard who refused to acknowledge me. After he left, I wasted an hour shouting myself hoarse, pounding on the door.

In the afternoon, the door opened. A woman entered—Ishleen's mother, Olwen. Our clan's midwife. Olwen was accompanied by a sentry, who stood in the corner with arms crossed and eyes averted as she explained that she needed to examine me for signs of violation.

"You mean Torin wants to know if the Westlander's been up my skirts? He hasn't."

"Good. Let me prove it." Olwen motioned patiently for me to lie back. Swallowing tears and curses, I obeyed.

When it was over, Olwen patted my hand and nodded to the sentry in approval. After they left, I resumed my fuming and pacing.

Later, I sat down and promptly drifted off, unaware I'd fallen asleep until I jerked awake, sore from my slumped position. I put my ear to the door, hearing only silence. I went back to beating on the door and hollering for someone to tell me what was happening.

No one responded. I sat again, slept again. The cycle continued all day, all night, into the next morning. My voice was nearly gone when the door finally opened.

Four guards stood on the other side. They marched me down the stairs, across the clearing, into the great hall. The Sons of Stone watched me enter, expressions clouded with contempt. I was no longer just the soul-reader who damned men with a touch, the girl our priest said brought a curse upon our village. I was also a traitor, the girl who'd aided the enemy.

Torin brooded next to the crackling fireplace. Madoc hovered beside him, stoking the blaze with an iron rod. They observed me with casual disgust, as if I was too abhorrent to ignore, but too pathetic to garner more than fleeting attention.

Our chieftain strode forward to address his men.

"In regard to the recent acts of deception, a decision has been made." Torin didn't look at me; I was merely a prop on his stage. "Since the invader seems to trust my daughter, Lira will visit him in his cell under the guise of teaching him our language. She will beguile the beast into letting her search his soul so we can glean all information he has of our enemy. Should Lira fail in her task, we will resort to torture. Either way, we will get as much out of the invader as we can, and when he is of no further use, his life will be forfeit."

Imprisonment. Torture. Execution.

I hadn't saved Reyker; I'd only delayed the inevitable.

Torin spoke so only I could hear. "You have until the conclave to get the invader to let you into his soul and show you all he knows. If he cooperates, I'll allow him to die with honor. If he doesn't, he'll be slaughtered like the beast he is. You can bear witness, as you did with the herdsman."

The conclave—a yearly event where the leaders of the most powerful clans in Glasnith met to discuss the most pressing issues facing our country. It was three moons from now. Three moons until I had to watch Reyker die.

"Bring the beast," Torin called.

Four sentries entered the great hall with Reyker between them, his wrists and ankles chained. Reyker glared at anyone who looked at him, his lips twisted into a snarl. The sentries shoved him to his knees at Torin's feet.

Madoc retrieved the iron rod he'd set in the fireplace, and I saw the design on the end, glowing with heat: a triangle of swords, our clan's warrior-mark. A rod used to brand cattle.

Torin took the rod as Madoc pinned Reyker down. "Never forget," the chieftain said, "that I am your master." He pressed the red-hot metal into the side of Reyker's neck.

Reyker's skin sizzled. He gasped, his pain-filled gaze finding me. In it, I saw confusion, anger, betrayal. As if I was the one burning him. Did he truly think I'd turned against him to save myself?

I clenched my fists.

I couldn't go to him. I could never let Torin know I cared for Reyker. If he found out, things would get much worse for us both.

Torin stood back to admire his handiwork. The triad of swords blackened Reyker's skin, stretching across one side of his neck. I choked on the smell of seared flesh permeating the room.

"If you escape," Torin told Reyker, "you'll find no shelter. Our allies will return you to us. Our enemies will kill you to spite us. Your life belongs to the Sons of Stone."

Reyker growled, but Torin had already turned away, dismissing the Westlander to speak to his men once more. "As a maiden and only daughter of her chieftain, Lira is valuable. I'll pursue a marriage for her that will strengthen our alliances."

Marriage. He would give me to a stranger who would take me far from my village, force me to lie with him and produce heirs—a thing Father had promised never to do. But this man wasn't my father. "I prefer death, my lord," I said coolly.

"Do not tempt me!" Torin's hand slid to his dirk.

The men in the hall glanced at one another. I wondered what they would do if Torin ordered my execution. Would anyone stand against him?

Regaining control of himself, Torin continued. "Lira has proven herself foolish and weak. I believe her treachery was misguided, the result of the fragile state she's been in since the loss of her brothers. To remedy this, I've chosen a fitting punishment."

He nodded to my escorts. They ushered me after Torin as he left the hall and headed across the village. I didn't let myself look back at Reyker as I was led away.

When I saw the plumes of black smoke, I understood.

The cottage came into view. My cottage, containing every last trace of my brothers and our old life. All I had left were the clothes I wore and my mother's medallion around my neck. Everything else I'd ever owned was on fire. Orange waves shivered across the roof and lapped up the walls. My home, the only one I'd ever known, fell beneath the flames.

"You will not leave this spot," Torin said. "You will watch until the fire burns out. Henceforth, you'll reside in the manor and be accompanied by an escort at all times."

"This was your home too. They were your sons. Or have you forgotten?" I searched his face for a sign of regret. I saw it, like peeking beneath a shawl. His expression shifted, revealing the deep sorrow known only to a parent who'd lost a child.

To my surprise, he answered. "Do you know how hard it was to send Rhys into battle, ill-suited as he was? But how can I ask other men to sacrifice their sons if I'm unwilling to sacrifice mine?" These questions weren't for me. Torin spoke as if interrogating himself. "How could I let Garreth defy me in front of my men and do nothing? The clan comes first. The clan must be strong, or we all die."

He turned to me, and the grief etched in the lines of his features seemed heavier than any man could bear. "You think I don't feel the loss of them in every part of my being? That I don't blame myself every moment of every day?"

"Father?" I laid a hand on his arm.

At my touch, he gritted his teeth, muscles twitching up and down his body in a silent struggle. The grief vanished. My father was quickly buried beneath the impenetrable facade of Torin—our powerful, heartless chieftain.

I'd lost him once more.

"You'll not lie or keep secrets from me again," Torin said. "You'll do nothing to bring shame upon me. Because if you do …"

He let the warning hang there, unfinished, filled in by my worst fears.

—✦—

An armed guard unlocked my bedroom door when I knocked the next morning—Sloane, who I used to play with when we were children. He'd grown up to be short and stocky, with a thick beard that made him look far older than his years. Sloane gave a curt nod and followed me to the washroom, standing outside. He stood nearby as I ate. Not only had Torin burned down every shred of my old life, he'd taken my privacy, and with it my dignity. His spies would never allow me a moment of solitude.

Sloane shadowed me as I crossed the village. I saw Ishleen walking on the path, a basket of herbs slung over her arm.

"Ishleen!" I called, chasing after her. Ishleen didn't turn or stop to wait. She walked faster, disappearing into her cottage. When I knocked on the door, her mother opened it. "I need to speak with Ishleen," I told her.

"Ishleen isn't here," Olwen said.

"Bollocks. I just saw her go inside."

Olwen peered down her nose at me. "She isn't feeling well."

"Which lie is it—is she not here, or is she not feeling well?" I'd known Ishleen was angry that I'd helped a Westlander, but I'd hoped she would let me explain. We were as close as sisters. With my brothers gone and my father mad, she was the only family I had left. I needed her to hear me out, even if she had every reason to turn her back on me.

"Both." Olwen shut the door in my face. I slapped my palm against the wood, cursing. When I stepped back, I saw Ishleen peeking out through the shutters over her bedroom window. They snapped shut as soon as she caught me looking.

"Ishleen!"

The shutters stayed closed.

Sloane grunted. "I don't think she wants to talk to you."

"I don't remember asking your opinion." I spun on my heel and headed to the cells as Sloane followed. A single sentry was stationed at the entrance, and he slid the heavy door open at my approach.

"Commander Madoc told us to let you enter alone," Sloane said. "But I'll come with you if you're afraid."

I was afraid of many things, but Reyker wasn't one of them. "The Westlander is locked up. No harm can come to me."

I entered the cells and shut the door behind me.

The smell hit me instantly—musty, rank. There was only one narrow, barred window in the whole structure, letting in slatted shards of light that touched the open space on the right side of the room, where I stood. None of the light made it into the two cells on the left. The cells themselves were made of stone walls and an iron grate. The floor was hard-packed dirt, the thatched ceiling reinforced with wood to prevent escape.

The first cell was empty. In the second cell, Reyker lay on his side, facing the back wall. His hair was clumped with dried blood. One hand pressed on his neck, covering the slave brand. The only sound was his breath, scraping in and out of him—the sound of a man trying to breathe through bruised lungs.

I sat in front of the cell, fingers curling around the cold bars. "Reyker," I called, my voice splintering. His spine stiffened, but otherwise he didn't acknowledge me.

What was left to say? I had no excuses, no promises, no hope to offer. "Are you all right?"

A bark of bitter laughter.

"Reyker. Look at me." I needed to see his face. He felt so far away. "Please."

Sighing, he pushed himself up, moving awkwardly, breathing sharply. He shifted into the corner, head hung low, matted hair hiding his features.

"I brought food. It's fresh, better than that rubbish the sentries give you." I lifted the parcel in my lap, nudging it toward him through the bars.

He ignored it.

"You have to eat."

Another burst of humorless laughter. Reyker pulled the parcel closer with his foot, unfolding the cloth. A hunk of bread sailed between the bars, over my head, bouncing off the wall behind me. He threw the cheese and meat next, and they splattered against the stones.

"Why are you doing this?" I glanced at the smears.

When I turned back, he was in front of me, hand shooting through the bars, gripping my throat. His fingers squeezed tight enough to hold me in place, not quite tight enough to hurt.

Our faces were so close they nearly touched, giving me a clear view of his ruined beauty. Blood crusting in his nostrils, the corners of his mouth. Gashes cracked the skin of his brow and jaw. Bottom lip split open. One eye purple and swollen. Bruises speckled his cheeks and forehead. The conspicuous black burn on his neck, raw and inflamed.

He stared into me, snarling. This was not the Reyker who'd shared his life with me by letting me touch his soul. This was the feral beast my uncle had bound and beaten, that my father had branded like a steer, that my clan had crowded around and shouted and spit at, cheering over his spilled blood.

I met his rage with my own. "Did you really expect me to keep my mouth shut and let Torin kill you? I'm no coward. I didn't think you were one either."

I watched him read my expressions the way he always did. He blinked a few times, as if awakening from a heavy sleep. His violent glare wavered, receded, dissolved into bewilderment. The fingers on my throat loosened. His hand strayed to my cheek, fingertips skimming the ugly patchwork of discolored skin where Madoc had struck me.

I closed my eyes, leaning in to his touch, suddenly overwhelmed by how much I'd missed him these past days, how I'd missed the strange hours we spent together, connecting in ways that went far beyond words. I knew more than just his soul—I knew the cadence of his voice, the pattern of his breath. I knew the curl of his lips when he smiled, the angle of his brow when he was confused. Our bodies absorbed and translated the unspoken messages.

I felt it now, with my face cupped in his hand, his fingertips expressing all the things he couldn't say, sharing all the pain and anger and fear bearing down on him. I put my hand over his, opened my eyes, took a shuddering breath—silently telling him the truth I'd not accepted until I'd been forced to watch as he was beaten, his life hanging precariously beneath the tip of my father's sword. *I need you to live, not just for the gods. For me.*

He pulled away. "Go, Lira." *Don't waste your anguish on a dead man.*

"You didn't make it this far just to give up." My fingers tapped the lock on his cell door. "I'll find a way to get you out." *No matter the cost.*

"No!" he shouted, banging his fist against the grate. "They will hurt you. Maybe kill you." He wasn't wrong. If I set Reyker free, would Torin execute me?

The door to the cells creaked open. "I'm fine, Sloane," I called. "Wait outside."

My uncle's mocking voice responded. "How is our beast faring in his new cage?"

Icicles formed along my spine at Madoc's approach. I didn't want Madoc near Reyker, no more than I wanted him near me, especially in the dark privacy of the cells. But it did present an opportunity. He'd been too calm since the Culling, too quick to accept Torin's leadership. I wanted to know what he was up to.

"Well enough, my lord." I rose and stepped toward him, pretended to trip. Reaching out to steady myself, one palm aiming for his chest.

His hands clamped down on my wrist. "Did you really think that would work?"

"No." My free hand had already slipped past his guard while he focused on the hand he'd grabbed. My other palm hit his chest.

I saw the great hall. The Culling. The trial. Gwylor stood before Madoc, handing him the flaming heart. Madoc held it, and Gwylor whispered into Madoc's mind: I SEE YOU, SON OF STONE. YOU ARE CHAOS. YOU ARE DESTRUCTION. YOU ARE NO CHIEFTAIN. On the outside, Madoc screamed, but on the inside, he smiled—the joyful, evil smile of a man about to be given the things he'd always wanted. Things he would kill for. The heart in his hands changed form, spongy tissue molding into a hardened circle of gold.

I fell from Madoc's soul as he shook me, both my wrists now locked in his grip.

"You'll pay for that," he said.

"Let go of me. My father—"

"Your father no longer cares what happens to you. Do you know why Torin was culled? Because he was the only one foolish enough to let Gwylor get his hooks into him. You, me, your brother—we chose self-preservation over power. Torin wanted so badly to be chieftain that he invited the god of death into his body and gave up his soul."

Was that what I'd felt slithering over me when I'd held the heart—some part of the god, trying to implant itself in my mind? Was that what slithered behind Torin's eyes now?

"That's the price Torin paid," Madoc said. "He's Gwylor's puppet. So if a dreadful fate befell his wayward daughter, I doubt he'd spare a second thought."

I kneed him in the groin and groped for my knife.

Before I could stab him, he wrenched my arms behind my back. "You're an unruly whelp, just like your brothers," he said. "Another mark of Torin's failures. If you were my child, I'd have beaten the willfulness out of you ages ago."

My cheek was pressed to cold stone, facing the grate, my limbs locked in Madoc's grip. Reyker prowled back and forth inside his cell, a stalking predator whipped into a frenzy, growling and punching the bars.

"Look at that, dear niece. Torin might be blind, but I saw right through you. You have feelings for this beast, as he does for you." Madoc twisted my arms, sending jolts of agony from my wrists to my shoulders.

Reyker reached between the bars, straining to grab him. To rip Madoc's head off, judging by the Westlander's expression.

"Stop, or I'll break her wrist."

Reyker stopped. He stood still, his hands resting tensely at his sides. Only his snarling lips and the fire in his eyes revealed his wrath.

"Clever beast," Madoc chuckled.

Without warning, Madoc released his hold on my arms and shoved me toward the cell. I snatched up my knife and whirled to meet his next attack, my spine pressed against the grate. I felt Reyker's hand, resting lightly on the small of my back, lending me strength.

"I should expose your perversion and watch the villagers burn you both at the stake," Madoc said. "However, it may prove more interesting to watch you burn yourselves."

I blinked. "What are you plotting?"

"Do you know my favorite verse from the Immortal Scriptures? 'As the gods warred, the seeds of chaos rained down across mortal lands, and foolish men, both lord and peasant alike, did sow their own destruction.'" His gaze darted between Reyker and me. "You should've taught your beast to use the map you gave him. He was heading the wrong direction when we found him."

With that, Madoc left us.

I turned to face Reyker. He eased himself down into the far corner of the cell. "You were coming back? Why?"

He closed his eyes. "Go, Lira."

"For me?"

He didn't answer. He didn't have to. I'd refused to go with him when he had asked. He'd risked himself to come back for me anyway. Now he was trapped here.

I started to leave, pausing in the open doorway, light spilling around me into the cells' dark spaces. "Whatever it takes, Reyker," I whispered, "I will get you home."

CHAPTER 23

REYKER

There was nothing to do but sleep. Sometimes Reyker wasn't sure if he was awake, lying in the darkness of his cell, or asleep, wandering the dark halls of his mind. Sleep was torment. The nightmares—the memories—were relentless. They'd haunted him for years, but they were worse now, locked up, with no way to escape them.

He would die here, alone with his nightmares.

He didn't want Lira to watch him waste away. "Go," he told her when she came to the cells again, keeping his eyes closed so he wouldn't have to look at her.

"You really love that word, don't you?" Something landed on his face. She'd thrown a wet rag at him. "I'm not going anywhere, so you might as well stop saying it. Come here. I brought you food and water to rinse with."

"Don't bother."

"As you can see, I already did bother. And I'll continue to bother until you bring your stubborn arse over here to eat and wash the bloody mess off your face."

He knew what she was doing. She was from a family of warriors, and she knew sweet coaxing wouldn't work half as well as barked orders when it came to men like him. Reyker sighed, but he eased himself forward until he was across from her.

She passed him a hunk of bread. "Eat."

He bit into the bread, glaring.

"If you think I find that snarl the least bit intimidating, you don't know me very well." She badgered him until he ate every last bit of food, and then she pulled out a tin of liniment. "Wash your face so I can tend to your wounds."

"Gods aflame." He glanced up at the ceiling, as if his gods could hear him, as if they weren't a thousand leagues away. "Don't talk at me as if I am a child."

"Then stop acting like one."

Reyker mumbled a few unpleasant phrases beneath his breath, but he saw the tightness of her jaw, the sheen of her eyes—the regret over what her kinsmen had done to him. Tending his wounds was her way of apologizing for things she couldn't control.

"Fine." He dipped the rag into the pail, mopping his face.

Lira reached through the bars, dabbing salve on his cuts and bruises. He caught her studying the black flames etched above his swollen eyelid. "Why is your warrior-mark different from the other Dragonmen?"

Reyker had never wanted to wear a Dragonman's symbol. As with all things, Draki had given him no choice. "It marks me as an outsider, a warrior who can't be trusted."

"Why would Draki want a Dragonman he couldn't trust?"

"Draki murdered my father when I was only a boy. He thinks himself to be like a father to me. The warlord would not kill me, and he would not let me go. He preferred to keep me with him, to torment me. To shame me."

Lira rubbed a glob of liniment over the inflamed brand on the side of his neck, and he hissed, but it wasn't just from the pain. Her clan had shamed him too, derided and spit on him, held him down instead of letting him stand to face their blows. Branded him like he was a bull instead of a man. They were no better than Dragonmen.

She pulled at his tunic. "Take this off."

"No."

"Yes." She balled a handful of fabric into her fist.

It made him laugh, something he'd not thought possible in this wretched place. "You want to tear off my clothes?"

She blushed. Lira was bold, but her bashfulness emerged with a word, a glance, a touch. Reyker enjoyed watching her bite her lip, color rising in her cheeks. It was like watching a nymph yawn—a vulnerable, human gesture from a fey creature.

"I will." Her shyness ebbed. She wasn't going to give up. Reyker realized he wanted her to see, to know that her kin were as monstrous as his own. He eased out of the tunic, dropped it to the floor. She stared hard, her eyes glistening. "Trousers," she said firmly.

Reyker slid them off. Clothed only in his breeches, he could hide nothing. Bruises stained his torso, arms, and legs. Gashes split his skin. He reached for the rag, wiping off blood and dirt.

She scooped out more liniment, her fingers treading cautiously over his injuries. He shivered beneath her touch. For a long time neither of them spoke, and then Reyker broke the dense silence. "Stop looking at me like that."

"Like what?"

"Like I don't deserve this."

"Reyker. Why would you ever believe you deserve this?"

He laughed again, but this time there was no light in it—the sound was thunder and rain, matching the tempest brewing inside him. "You think you know me because you read my soul? You saw only half my sins. If you knew all, you would hate me. You would fear me."

"No, I wouldn't." She rubbed a nasty bruise on his stomach, pushing down the waistband of his breeches. He inhaled sharply and caught her wrist.

Did she not know what her touch stirred in a man? The vile things he could do to her if he were a man who did such things?

He'd nearly been that man once.

Reyker laced his hand with hers, examining how they fit together, her fingers dwarfed by his. Her body was too small and fragile a shell for the fires it contained. "You will."

It was better if she hated him.

He slapped her palm against his chest.

The memory Reyker sought was buried in the bones of his past. It took effort to dredge it up, like ripping a sprawling root from a poisonous tree. He fell into it—into his own body, staring out through his own eyes as a boy. Lira was there with him, a warm spark in the cold heart of his fear.

Bodies litter the settlement's ruins—crushed skulls and shattered limbs sticking out from blood-drenched armor.

My first raid. I killed six warriors. During the fight there was no pain, no hesitation, nothing but the black river's whispers flowing through me, guiding my sword. Now I shake, I sweat, my stomach threatens to expel its contents.

The Dragonmen notice. "We've deflowered the battle-virgin!" They laugh. "A raging demon on the field and a quivering boy off it."

I hate these dishonorable men. I'm only here because the warlord gave me a choice that was no choice: become one of his warriors or remain a hostage.

Dragonmen don't deserve to call themselves warriors. They are warmongers.

"Leave the lad alone." This from Einar, one of the older Dragonmen, a defector from Jarl Gudmund's army. "You lot were all pissing your breeches after your first battles, as I recall." He winks and tosses me a flask.

Perhaps good men are hidden among these fiends. I drink deeply from the flask, the burn in my throat blotting out the echoes of the river's call.

Two Dragonmen haul a woman from the rubble of a bathhouse, arguing over her.

"Hey, give the battle-maiden his due." The Dragonman nearest to me grins. It's not friendly. "Go on, take first claim of her."

I look at the woman. She's comely, older than me perhaps by ten years. She stands between the two Dragonmen, eyes vacant. Grief and fear have stolen her wits.

I've longed to discover the pleasures of a woman, but not like this. Never like this. "No," *I say quietly, a tremor in my voice.*

"Prefer boys, do you?"

"Lad doesn't know how to use his flesh-sword!"

"A virgin of battles and bedchambers!"

Flushing with anger and shame, I reach for my weapon just as it slides from its sheath. The warlord stands beside me, my sword in his possession. The Dragonmen hush.

"How old are you, Reyker? Fourteen?" Draki places a hand on my shoulder, and I cringe. "Old enough to spill blood, to take life. Old enough to enjoy the spoils of war."

"It's wrong. She is kin, a child of All-God Sjaf and Seffra."

"She stands against us, against Iseneld. She's a traitor to Sjaf and all his children."

"No." I glare at Draki. He knows what I'm thinking—I will never hurt a woman this way. I will never be a monster like him and his minions.

The warlord turns to the others. "Reyker is pretty for a boy, isn't he? Soft hair. Fair skin. In the shadows, it would be easy to pretend he was a girl. And we do seem to be short on girls."

In his words, I hear another choice that is not a choice.

Around me the Dragonmen rise, eager for the hunt.

I run. They chase me gleefully. The warlord has challenged them, making a sport of it. They want to please him. I'm fast, but they call out to their comrades ahead of me. Hands trap me, and I'm set upon by a mob, pushed down, my clothes ripped, my hair torn out in clumps. I cannot move. I cannot breathe. They laugh and shout, fight one another for first claim.

"Draki!" I scream. The men stop, looking to the warlord. "I'll do it."

Dragonmen crowd in to watch the spectacle. The woman is limp as seaweed, silent as a tomb. She's not there, not really. The men shove me toward her, shouting instructions, passing around ale, chuckling. Einar shakes his head and walks away.

The warlord smiles.

Lira jerked her hand back, pressing it to her mouth. She closed her eyes as if she couldn't bear to look at him. Reyker didn't blame her.

"This is who I am," he said. "This is why I deserve to die."

She grabbed a handful of the dirt floor and threw it in his face. "How could you? You're no better than the rest of them. A Dragonman at heart."

She rushed to the door and was gone.

This was what he'd wanted.

Reyker punched the stone wall until his knuckles bled, thinking of what happened to that woman whose name he didn't even know, and to so many others. What might happen to Lira if he could not stop it.

———◆———

Lira didn't come the next day. Reyker held his breath when the door opened, hopeful despite himself. It was only a guard bringing food and water, shoving it at him, spilling most of it. She didn't come the day after either.

On the third day, when he'd given up hope, Lira stormed into the cells.

Reyker stared, dumbfounded. Lira sat in front of the bars, offering her hand. "Show me the rest. Show me what you did to that woman." The challenge in Lira's voice told Reyker she'd figured out he didn't go through with it.

He'd pretended not to know how to lie with a woman, feigned ignorance until the other Dragonmen tired of waiting and pushed him aside.

"It doesn't matter," he said. "That I considered it at all is unforgivable." And the end result was the same. The woman was used. The warlord had made him watch.

"You were only a boy, Reyker. What you nearly did was monstrous, but you refused. You didn't let Draki turn you into a monster." Her next words were tentative. "Did the Dragonmen ever … hurt you?"

"They tried." Over and over. A continuous game. He'd broken men's arms, jaws, and noses as he fought to get away; he'd broken his own knuckles and fingers. Each time, his escape was narrow. Each time, he feared they would succeed. "I trained until I was strong enough that they stopped trying."

Others weren't as lucky. When Reyker could, he protected captives from the Dragonmen's appetites, but usually he was forced to witness, helpless to stop it.

Reyker squeezed the cell bars so hard the scabs on his knuckles split open and oozed bloody tears.

"What happened?" Lira asked.

"I picked a fight with the wall."

"Stupid boy," she chided in Iseneldish. Though she spoke his native tongue awkwardly, it charmed him to hear it.

She tended his knuckles, then made him sit with his back to the bars as she rinsed blood from his hair, her fingers teasing loose the tangles, sending shivers down his scalp.

Why did her mercy hurt more than her hate? Why did it terrify him?

Because you aren't worthy of it, a voice from the scarred crevices of Reyker's soul answered. *Because you'll fail her, as you failed your mother.*

"I've never told anyone about what the Dragonmen tried to do to me," he said. "Do you think me less of a man for it?" It was easier to ask when he couldn't see her.

Her hands stilled. Her voice was soft.

"No. You are a man, Reyker. More so than most."

CHAPTER 24

Days crashed on the shores of time, piling into weeks, each one pushing me closer toward the conclave. I did my best not to think on it. My life settled into ritual and repetition. I awoke behind a locked door every morning, retired behind it every night, and during the span between, I was followed and watched, escorts hounding my every step. The small sprig of this world that had once been mine narrowed to a splinter.

Other things changed as well. It started with the mirrors.

I rose one morning to find them gone, every last one in the manor. When I asked Torin's attendants, they said he'd ordered them removed without explanation.

Another oddity: Through the floor of my room, I often overheard Torin in the parlor, arguing. With Madoc, before my uncle left to treat with our allies and the mercenary clans. With his other councilors. But there were times when no visitors called, yet he bellowed and bickered until dawn, and I couldn't be certain—were there two voices in the parlor, or only one?

One evening, Torin bid me to dine with him.

"Tell me of your language lessons with the beast," he said over a plate of roasted pheasant and a flagon of ale.

"They go well enough, my lord. The Westlander speaks, but his words are jumbled, his accent heavy." A stretch, but not exactly a lie. Reyker's command of Glasnithian was impressive, but not perfect.

"Have you learned anything of value yet?" It was more of an accusation than a question.

I was summoned to the council once every week, to update them on my progress. I fed them details Reyker gave me about Draki and his Dragonmen—enough to keep up the charade, but never enough to satisfy them. Never enough for them to decide Reyker had nothing left to offer.

I cut my meat meticulously, taking my time answering. "Nothing more than what I've reported, but I'm getting closer. There's still time."

"The date of the conclave has been moved up, due to the escalating Westlander threat. We leave for Selkie's Quay in a fortnight. You and the invader will accompany me. If the beast has not spilled his secrets by then, I'll oversee his interrogation alongside the other clan leaders."

"A fortnight?" I'd thought I had more than a moon left.

"At least we're getting some use out of the invader in the meantime," Torin added.

The Sons of Stone had put Reyker to work loading rocks, hauling wood, digging trenches. His hands were shackled and he was surrounded by armed men who wouldn't hesitate to cut him down if he made a wrong move. The workers and sentries harassed him—spitting on him, upending chamber pots over him. I saw what it did to Reyker, the defeat in his eyes. It made me hate Torin and his men all the more.

"Why did you get rid of the mirrors?" I asked.

"Because they lie," Torin muttered into his chalice. "The mirrors are wrong. That man is not me." His fist slammed the tabletop. "Cursed frost giants invading from the west, barbarian mercenaries squabbling to the south, and my own council full of half-wits."

"What do you mean *squabbling*? What's happening with the mercenary clans?"

He ignored me. "I'm surrounded by enemies and simpletons. Madoc is the only one I can depend on."

I couldn't believe what I'd heard. "You can't trust Madoc. He still wants to be chieftain. Given the chance, he'll kill you for control of the village."

"You lie!" Torin hurled the flagon across the room. It crashed to the floor. "All of you, nothing but liars!"

I jumped up, reaching for my knife as he stalked toward me. He stopped, gazing with morbid fascination. "When did you become so beautiful?" He touched a lock of my hair.

Why was he looking at me this way?

"You seem tired. Take yourself to bed." He kissed my forehead. "Good night, Iona."

Iona. My mother.

I wanted to cry, to scream. I wanted this man gone and my father returned. I ran to my room and slammed the door, for once thankful for locks and guards.

———

Offers of marriage arrived daily from clans hoping to strengthen or forge alliances with the Sons of Stone. Some sent messengers. Others came in person to present their proposals to Torin—lords and merchants and warriors, old and young, handsome and repulsive alike.

I wanted nothing to do with it, but Torin commanded a host of attendants to clean and dress me so that I might be paraded in front of these guests, like bait dangling on a fishing line. I wore an empty smile, keeping my tongue silent and my gaze upon the floor as I envisioned the ways I would murder these men if they ever tried to touch me. Torin sent them all away with promises to consider their offers carefully.

I was clever enough to understand his plan. This was an auction, and he was creating a frenzy to raise the stakes. When it was over, the prize would go to the highest bidder. I was no better than a fertile plot of land or a well-bred mare.

Every week the chieftain made me read the souls of his councilors, to ensure none plotted against him. All except Madoc, who was exempted from this indignity for some reason, no matter how much I tried to convince Torin this was a mistake.

"What will you do when I'm gone?" I asked after what felt like the hundredth time I'd delved into the guilt of the councilmen, searching for betrayal. I'd found various misdeeds, but none committed against the chieftain. "How will you trust anyone without a soul-reader to ensure their loyalty, when you've married me off and I no longer belong to you?"

"You'll always belong to me." Torin stood at a window, looking out at the village. He was cagey as usual, like he was waiting for someone to come and burn down everything he'd built. "A husband won't change that. When I call, you will come."

It sounded eerily similar to things Draki had said when he tried to get inside my head. I realized then that there would be no escaping Torin. No matter what I did, no matter where I went, the chieftain would never let me go.

Though Torin's order for me to teach Reyker our language was meant as a ruse, I followed through. Reyker wanted to improve, and I enjoyed teaching him. He knew a great deal of Glasnithian, but there were always grammar rules to practice, new words to learn. For everything we spoke of in Glasnithian, Reyker taught me its equivalent in Iseneldish. We grappled through each other's muddy lexicons, teaching, correcting, learning. We told jokes, sang songs, shared the legends of our people and our gods. I was as fascinated by his language and the stories of his people as he was by mine.

As I sang the ballad about the woman whose love was lost at sea, Reyker tilted his head and smiled. "Do you think her love found her after?"

"After what?"

Reyker rinsed off with the water I'd brought him. His time in the sun had darkened his pale skin. He was one of several laborers clearing the remains of my family's ruined cottage—salvaging stones, building a new home on the site. I wondered if anyone had dared question the chieftain's decision to burn it down in the first place.

"After she died. In the world after death."

"Maybe. It's up to the god of death. If Gwylor judges a person worthy, they enter his Eternal Palace. If not, the person wanders hopelessly in the black depths of the Halls of Suffering. What of your gods?"

He scratched absently at the slave-brand on his neck. "Seffra is mother of us all. She is love. Sjaf is our father, god of tides and sea. He is strong-ness."

"Strength," I corrected.

"Strength, yes. You must have love for your country and kin, and you must fight for them. If you have love and strength, no matter how you die, you go to Skjorlog Felth." Fortune's Field: a lush, infinite meadow, a place without pain, where the dead were united with their ancestors. The Westlanders' Eternal Palace, in the otherworlds. "If a man is weak, if a man has a heart full of hate and he hurts his people, when he dies he will go to the goddess Ildja, queen of the worlds underground. It is a place of demons, a place of ... cloud?"

"Mist." When the mystic showed me Reyker's nightmare, I'd heard one of the captured warriors say this to Draki. *May the Destroyers drag you into the Mist.*

"The Destroyers—the demons—bring souls to Ildja. She is a woman, but also a ..." He searched his mind for the word. "Serpent."

I thought of the Bog Men's legend of the venom-spitter—a snake-woman who lived deep in the earth and ate unsuspecting wanderers. Could Ildja be a venom-spitter? Were the two creatures related?

"Ildja tortures, burns, and eats the souls of enemies and traitors." That familiar expression crossed Reyker's face, where the warrior crumbled to reveal a broken boy—one who feared he wouldn't be allowed into Fortune's Field, but would be condemned to a place of torment, where a snake-goddess would prey on him for eternity.

He'd risked damnation for those he'd saved from the Dragonmen.

He'd risked damnation for me.

"Don't let Draki decide who you are, Reyker. Don't let him drag you into the Mist with him. Your soul doesn't belong to him, or to Ildja." I'd grasped his hand through the bars without realizing. I stared at our twined fingers, thinking I should let go, but not wanting to. "It was Draki who killed your mother, wasn't it? He marked her, as he did me?"

"Yes." Barely a whisper. "She was a *magiska*, like you. Her gift was her voice. Her songs. When she sang, she could soothe a spooked horse, a feral dog, a rabid wolf. She could coax a warrior into dropping his sword in the middle of battle."

"But not Draki?"

"Draki is part god. His father was mortal, but he is the goddess Ildja's son. Years ago, Draki offered the mortal part of his soul to Ildja in exchange for an immortal's power. *Magiskas'* gifts are weak against him at best. They cannot harm him."

A demigod. Reyker had said as much before, that Draki was godlike, unstoppable. But Ildja's child? This was the first he'd spoken of Draki's lineage. It explained why I'd found nothing when I touched Draki's soul— Ildja had already claimed it. As Gwylor had claimed part of my father.

I'd seen firsthand what a god could do wearing a mortal's skin. How could my country stand against someone so powerful? How could anyone?

"My father tried to hide my mother," Reyker said. "Draki still found her. He ensnared her mind and used her gift against his enemies, as he does with all *magiskas* he takes. But *magiskas'* gifts are not meant to be controlled in this way; it drains them, destroys them. I didn't know about the *skoldar* then. I tried to help my mother ..." Reyker stopped and closed his eyes. "In the end, I could only watch her die. It was my fault."

"I don't believe that."

A shadow passed over his face. Reyker traced the *skoldar* on my wrist, and it warmed beneath the caress of his finger.

I touched the other scar, the cursed one behind my ear. "If Draki comes for me, I'll run. But if I must, I'll give myself over to Gwylor's judgment." And pray the god of death was more merciful than he seemed. "I'll die before I let Draki take me."

"I'll stop him. Draki will not have you." Reyker pressed my palm to his chest. It was sweet and it was bitter, knowing he would fight Draki to protect me, knowing it might cost him his life—that the heart flexing under my fingers could be silenced. "I think her love found her," Reyker said, staring into his lap. "In the Eternal Palace, or Skjorlog Felth, or even the Mist. Wherever she was sent, he found her."

"Or perhaps she found him."

He looked up at me. A smile tugged at his lips.

My escort opened the door to the cells. Our time was up. As I stood to leave, Reyker pressed something small and cool into my fingers.

I didn't look until we were nearing the manor. Opening my palm, I stared at the blackened metal. The small buckle from one of Rhys's belts. It wasn't pretty or well-made. It wasn't what I'd choose, if I had my pick of objects to survive the fire. Yet it brought me to tears, this tiny piece of my brother Reyker had found as he dug through the wreckage of my old home, keeping it hidden so he could return it to me.

I held it against my heart.

"*Takka thu*," I said, setting my thanks upon Anad's winds, hoping the god would carry the message to the Westlander, delivering it with the fullness of the gratitude I felt.

CHAPTER 25

REYKER

The door to the cells opened. He rubbed his eyes. "Lira?" It was dark outside; she never came at night.

"Guess again, beast."

Just the sound of Madoc's voice stoked his hatred. As Reyker rose, the commander came closer, standing just out of reach. Smart. Otherwise, he'd have torn Madoc apart.

"You and I share a mutual contempt, Westlander. We also share a mutual enemy. I believe we can help each other. Torin wants to show you off to the other clans soon. This presents a unique opportunity." Madoc slipped a piece of metal from his pocket, setting it on the floor. The key to the shackles Reyker wore every time he was let out of his cell. "Kill the chieftain."

Reyker held his tongue.

"I know who you are," Madoc said. "Reyker of Vaknavangur. Son of Lagor and Katrin. A lordling, before your village was destroyed."

Reyker felt like he'd been punched in the chest. He didn't blink.

"Your family was influential in your homeland, and that makes you valuable. Unlike my brother, I believe our people can coexist. But I need a contact I can trust, and I need Torin dead by an invader's hand, so it cannot be traced back to me. We have much to offer each other. Lira, for instance."

Reyker took a slow, controlled breath.

"Unless you don't want her. In which case, I'll find someone who does." Madoc placed a finger behind his ear. "The Dragon, perhaps."

Briefly, Reyker's composure slipped—a twitch of his jaw, nothing more.

Madoc's eyes lit up, victorious. "Torin's always been soft on the girl, indulging her. Lira won't break cleanly. After enough time at Draki's mercy, her mind will crack, her spirit will dim. A terrible way to die, don't you agree?"

Reyker gripped the bars, thinking of Draki's mark cut into Lira's skin. It had kept Reyker alive through beatings and insults, through hopeless nights lying in the dirt, cold and aching and lonely. He had to live, to kill Draki when he came for her.

"It doesn't have to end that way." With his boot, Madoc pushed the key closer. "Agree to my terms, and the girl is yours. Refuse me, and you'll die in this cell tonight."

There was a trap here. This was a dangerous man to make deals with. But Reyker had no other options. He picked up the key—a symbolic acceptance.

"You're smarter than you look, beast."

Madoc explained what he wanted as Reyker listened. When the commander was done, he drew his dirk. "You should know, if you fail to carry out your end of the bargain, I'll make it my mission to ruin you." He stabbed the blade into the dirt floor to punctuate his words. "And I'll start with her."

There was no turning back.

Lira had tied herself to Reyker when she'd dragged him from the harbor, and again when she'd saved him from her father's sword. Reyker had cinched the knot tighter with this deal.

If he failed, they would both pay for it in blood.

CHAPTER 26

Winter is beneath me. The Savage rides beside me on his demonic black steed, his hand closing around my elbow. Jerking me from my horse. The forest vanishes as I fall, and the world turns white. I land on an icy surface that crackles under my weight. Silver droplets of snow drift from the sky. Before I can move, Draki is on top of me, pinning me down.

"I am your god." His voice is deeper than the frozen loch we lay on. "You will forget him. He cannot save you."

"Forget who?" My own voice is a frightened wisp.

He smiles. The sight makes me shiver. I try to pull away from him, pressing my back harder against the ice. There's a sharp crunch as it shatters.

I plunge into waters darker and colder than anything I've ever known.

My eyes opened to the waxen light of morning spilling through my bedroom window. I touched the icy scar behind my ear, the terror of the dream slowly fading as another took its place.

Today we would leave for the conclave. Reyker had refused to tell me anything vital that Torin could use against Iseneld. By Torin's decree, torture awaited Reyker in Selkie's Quay, and likely death. I could no longer protect him.

I dressed slowly, avoiding leaving my room as long as possible, but from the other side of the door, Sloane called out, "You have a visitor."

Ishleen awaited me in the parlor. She hadn't spoken to me since the day Reyker was caught. I'd been naive to hope she'd not judge me without hearing my side. I didn't blame her, but it still stung.

"Good morrow." I spoke as if she were a stranger.

Ishleen hesitated before returning the stiff greeting. "You're journeying with Lord Torin and the others?"

"I am."

"Well." Ishleen fidgeted. "Safe travels."

"Is that all you came to say?" I couldn't hide the hurt I felt. "Why are you here? I thought you were mad at me."

"Bloody right I'm mad at you!" she shouted, making me jump. "What were you thinking? You protected one of those *things*. You lied to me, and you made me complicit, healing an invader with potions I made for you. Don't you know what could've happened, what that beast could've done to you?"

"I'm sorry I lied, but Reyker wouldn't hurt me. You don't even know him."

"*Reyker?*" Her eyes threatened to pop out of her head. "You gave the beast a name?"

"He had a name before he came here. That's what I'm trying to tell you. He's just a warrior, not so different from us—"

"Don't compare me to an invader." Ishleen's shock turned to revulsion. "You know what the villagers call you? Traitor. Beast-whore. I've stood up for you, told them they're wrong. But here you are, talking about a beast like he's innocent. You're making it hard to defend you."

"Then don't. Think whatever you wish. I've nothing left to say to you." I started back up the stairs.

"Wait," she said. "I came to warn you, to tell you … do you remember the dream I told you about, with the birds? I still have it each night, only now it's changed. The lammergeiers swarm around us, but your hand has slipped from mine. I can't see you. All I see is feathers. But I hear a voice calling to us. 'Arise, daughter,' he says." Her eyes were damp, her voice trembling. "Oh, Lira, I'm so frightened of what it could mean."

"Ishleen. Everything will be all right." I tried to sound convincing, but her dreams frightened me as well. They could be omens, as she suspected. If they were, it meant Ishleen was also a Daughter of Aillira. Two in the same clan. It wasn't supposed to be possible, according to the Immortal Scriptures, but I no longer trusted the scriptures' assertions.

Sloane called my name.

Impulsively, I stepped forward and wrapped my arms around Ishleen. "I have to go. We'll talk more when I return?"

We'll heal the rift between us, I told her silently. *We'll be as sisters once more. Together we'll discover the meaning of your dreams and defend ourselves against whatever may come.*

After a moment, Ishleen hugged me back. "I hope so," she replied.

Warriors milled about the stables, awaiting our departure. Torin was overseeing the organization of mounts and supplies. Madoc came to see us off, attached to Torin's ear as usual. Something in my uncle's gaze unsettled me. He gloated, as if he'd already achieved victory and was awaiting his prize.

Another figure stepped into the bright day's warmth. Sunlight sparked Reyker's hair to spun gold, thawed the frozen pools of his eyes into crystal springs. He glanced up, his eyes snagging mine before we both looked away.

A stable boy brought our mounts, and I was overjoyed when he handed me Wraith's reins. I had Rhys's belt buckle affixed to my knife's sheath, and now I had Garreth's horse. These small remnants of my brothers strengthened me. I stared into the distance, taking in the rolling hills and the cliffs, the cottages and the sanctuary. A small fear nagged at me, the feeling that I might not see my village again, or that if I did, everything would be different.

"Mount up and move out," Torin called.

Thus, our journey began.

Selkie's Quay was roughly thirty leagues from Stony Harbor. We traveled through the Tangled Forest, into the meadows beyond, and along the pass between the Silverspire Mountains. As we rode, I studied the men around me. There were thirteen of us in all—me riding in the center, flanked by guards. Torin was in the lead with Reyker close behind, his wrists manacled and a metal collar around his neck, its long chain fastened to Torin's saddle. A leash, meant to restrain a wild beast. That's all Reyker was to them.

That night, we made a simple camp. The guards took turns keeping watch in pairs, making escape near impossible and dashing any hopes I'd had of helping Reyker get free.

We spent the next day crossing the rim of the sprawling moorlands known as the Green Desert. If the Tangled Forest was the head of Glasnith, the Green Desert was the island's broad shoulders, stretching from one coast to the other. The desert was hilly and wild, unsheltered from storms, too barren to plant crops, too rugged to raise cattle. There were no clans in the desert, only pockets of nomads—exiles, fugitives, and undesirables, forced to abandon their lives and reside in the wasteland, outside of clan rule. They were skittish folk, and many people referred to them as ghosts. True to form, when our procession happened upon a few of their tents, the nomads scattered and vanished.

I searched for Garreth among them, before realizing he'd never resort to hiding under rocks with lepers and thieves. But where was he? My brother wouldn't leave me alone in Stony Harbor, I was certain of it. If he hadn't found help after his exile, he might have succumbed to his wound. Had Gwylor taken him, as the god of death had taken Rhys?

It was a possibility I wasn't ready to face yet.

We reached a rustic inn that night, the only one for many leagues. I slept on a cot in a room I shared with Torin, while the rest of the men camped outside.

Just before nightfall on the third day, we reached Selkie's Quay. We turned our horses over to the stable hands, heading for the pier. The conclave would take place at the village stronghold, built on the black rocks rising out of a notorious patch of the Shattered Sea.

A wooden vessel waited for us and we clamored into it, barely able to fit. The boatmen pushed off, ferrying us into the sloshing tides. A hooded woman stood in the bow, holding up a lantern, and wherever she pointed, the boatmen steered in line with her finger, avoiding the most turbulent currents. She was guiding us. This must have been clan Selkie's Daughter of Aillira—a god-gifted tide-teller.

The water was a swirling mess. The boat rolled and shuddered, knocking us about like marbles in a jar. Spindrift dampened my skin and coated my tongue as I held fast to the thwart, sandwiched between two guards. When the bow slammed down into a deep trough, several warriors started to topple overboard. A wave broke over us, and the men grabbed onto one another, pulling back those about to be swept out.

No one could get across these waters without a boat and a tide-teller. There would be no escaping the fortress. It loomed over us, the end of our journey.

The end of Reyker's life.

Cold, wet, and tired, our party climbed the long, winding stairs cut into the rocks that led to the stronghold. My legs were numb by the time we reached the top. Fort Selkie, its black walls glazed with salt, looked more like a haunted castle than an active stronghold. I followed the men into the damp, meandering passageway.

Torches burned in sconces, lighting the gloom. Voices and laughter seeped from the centrum, and a cheer went up as we trickled in. A hundred men from at least fifteen clans crowded around tables, gorging themselves on food and ale, already drunk. The Sons of Stone were the last to arrive, but they caught up quickly, draining ale-filled tankards as they talked and laughed and slapped one another's shoulders.

There were several mercenary clans here as well. Bog Men with mud smeared across their faces and bodies, venomous spears and bows strapped to their backs. Others who wore armor that looked like fish scales, or shirts woven from horsehair, or vests studded with tiny metal spikes. The two groups—mercenary and nonmercenary—interacted cautiously, keeping their distance, making me wonder about what I'd overheard Torin and Madoc discussing when I'd been caught in Torin's library all those weeks ago: the possibility of the mercenaries allying with the Dragonmen.

I picked at my cold plate of food and watched the clans' raucous behavior from a bench near the back. These were the men who were supposed to save us from the Westlanders? I shook my head. "We're all doomed."

Next to me, Sloane bristled. "Men strategize better with food in their bellies and drinks in their hands. Reminds them what they're fighting for. Lord Aengus taught us that."

"Didn't think to teach you about moderation, did he?"

Everyone's attention was suddenly drawn to the front of the room. I turned to see Torin taking his place like a performer on a stage, pulling the metal leash, forcing Reyker to stand before the rowdy warriors who'd stared at him since he was led in. Reyker kept his head high, his expression defiant.

The centrum fell silent, waiting for the show to begin.

"No doubt you've all heard rumors that the Sons of Stone have gone mad," Torin said, his voice intimidating, commanding. The voice of a fearless chieftain. Or possibly of a demented, vengeful god speaking through him.

"Rumors that we captured an invader, taught it to speak. That we aim to use the beast to help us kill other invaders and drive them from our lands. I'm here to tell you it's true."

Torin's eyes swept the room. "The Westlanders and that yellow-eyed giant who leads them are a menace, and no longer to just the coasts. They've breached inland, burning and stealing, taking our people as hostages and slaves, establishing long-term camps where they can. They aim to destroy us and claim Glasnith for themselves."

This was information I'd garnered from Reyker and reported to the council, but I didn't know it had all come to pass. Glasnith was in more danger than I'd realized.

"Our tactics are antiquated. Predictable." Torin tugged the chain and Reyker stumbled. "His aren't."

There were jeers from the clans.

"If you doubt it," Torin said, "step forward and fight the beast. To the death."

Sloane's arm clamped down on mine as I tried to rise. "Stay in your seat."

"He's not an animal to be gutted for sport. Torin cannot do this."

A colossal warrior swaggered to where Torin stood. There was a harbor seal emblazoned on the man's tunic—the symbol of the Order of Selkie, our hosts. "I'll fight the filthy Westlander," the man said as his clan hooted and clapped. His belly spilled over his belt, but his arms rippled with thick muscles as he drew his sword.

Torin motioned to a sentry, who removed Reyker's manacles and handed him a sword. His collar stayed on, but Torin let go of the chain and turned the floor over to the two men.

I counted the seconds.

The duel was over before I reached thirty.

The seal was rent in half. Reyker had dodged the warrior's heavy blows, ducked under his guard, and slit him up the middle, from navel to breastbone. The man toppled like a tree, landing in a puddle of his own blood.

The room filled with gasps.

Reyker spun, sword dripping, assessing the mob. Calculating how many men he could take out before they cut him down.

"Lira!" Torin called. My name bounced off one wall, slapped against another, filling the air. I nearly fell off the bench. "Come here."

I padded to the front of the centrum, feeling every eye watching me. One set stood out from the others—warm brown, lit with humor and affection. Sitting with the representatives from clan Fion, the warriors known as the Hounds of Vengeance, Quinlan smiled at me, but I didn't have it in me to smile back.

Torin put his hands on my shoulders. "For those who don't know, this enchanting maiden is my daughter." There was a mocking edge to the compliment. "Lira, bring me the invader's sword." He pushed me toward Reyker.

Did he know Reyker wouldn't hurt me, or was he gambling with my life?

I stared at my feet, forcing my legs to move. I lifted my eyes to look at Reyker. I forgot to breathe.

Invader. Ally. Friend. Beast. The traits were all there, rioting in him, like he wasn't sure which one to wear. He wanted to keep the weapon. He wanted to use it.

I held my hands out, palms open. "Sword," I tried to say, but I was mute; I only mouthed it. I tilted my head, let my hair fall across my face to shield it from the spectators so I could drop the mask and let him read my expression. *Please, Reyker. They'll kill you. Please don't.*

Some of the savageness drained from him—clenched muscles loosening, shoulders dropping. He lowered the sword. Slowly, he angled the blade toward himself and placed the sword across my palms. *For you*, his eyes said. *Never for them.*

I took the sword to my father, hating his triumphant smile. I held on to the weapon a second too long—long enough to see Torin realize I'd contemplated stabbing him myself—before surrendering it. Maybe it was punishment, or maybe he'd planned it all along, but the next words out of his mouth made me wish I'd gored him. "Daughter, bring me the invader."

I went rigid.

"I won't ask twice," Torin said under his breath.

Jaw set, I stomped back to Reyker. Swallowed the bile in my throat. Picked up the end of the chain. Led him to Torin, like he was a dog. I slapped the chain into Torin's hand. He put the manacles in mine. "Shackle him."

A thousand curses ran through my head. I bit down on them.

Reyker held his forearms out. I felt his eyes on me, but if I looked into them I might fall apart. I fit the metal cuffs around his wrists, as gently as I could, clicking them shut.

Torin kept me by his side. I was his shield, should Reyker turn violent. He jerked on Reyker's leash. "Tell them what you are," he ordered.

Reyker looked at the clans. At Torin. At me. "An invader from western lands," he said. "My island is Iseneld. What people of Glasnith call the Frozen Sun."

Shock flowed through the centrum. *The beast can speak our language.*

Torin took out his dirk. "Our people tell elaborate legends about the invaders. The beasts of the Frozen Sun. My prisoner here fights with the wisdom of a warrior twice his age, the strength of a warrior twice his size. He's a savage. A brute. But a man regardless. With a man's weaknesses." His eyes flickered to me. "The Westlanders are not gods, nor demons, nor beasts."

Torin kicked the back of Reyker's legs so he fell to his knees. The chieftain grabbed a fistful of Reyker's hair, holding him in place as he sliced the dirk shallowly across Reyker's neck, just above the slave-brand. "Gods do not bleed," Torin said, swiping a finger through Reyker's blood, lifting it for all to see. "They are flesh and blood, mortal men. And all men can be defeated."

Cheers exploded throughout the room.

"Tomorrow we shall talk of methods for crushing our enemies. But tonight, my fellow warriors, my honored friends, let us celebrate our impending victory!"

The men beat the air with their fists. Jumped up from the benches. Howled at the ceiling.

Hungry for war.

CHAPTER 27

I leaned on the windowsill, sipping wine, staring at the waves crashing on the foot of the islet. Behind me, men clinked tankards, chugging more ale. Some passed out at their tables. My guards had downed enough drinks to forget they weren't supposed to let me out of their sight.

Torin was in deep conversation with several other chieftains. He surveyed the room, cold eyes falling upon me. The hard lines of his mouth deepened.

"There's the enchanting maiden, subduer of savages, tamer of beasts." Quinlan appeared at my side, looking handsome and mischievous as ever.

I punched his shoulder. "Not to mention a harpy, slanderer, and sorceress."

"Ow." He rubbed at the rising bruise I was sure I'd given him. "What was that for?"

"I've not heard from you in ages. You couldn't send a letter to let me know how you fared? Or … Or if you'd heard anything. About Garreth."

His expression softened. "There's been no word, Lira. I would have come to you straightaway if there had been, I promise you."

"Oh." There was no hiding my disappointment. I took another swig of wine and said, "I'm sorry for what happened ... for what we spoke of that day in the harbor. I never wanted to damage our friendship."

"You didn't." He inched toward me, leaving little space between us. "And no apologies are necessary, though I'm sorry as well."

"Careful. Torin won't appreciate us standing so close. It might raise questions about my virtue. He plans to marry me off soon." I was trying to sound glib but failing miserably.

"I heard." Quinlan's grin faltered. "I think we're safe. They're too busy plotting or getting pissed to notice us. All but that one." I followed his gaze to find Reyker, chained to a table, watching me. "Did you give him a black eye too?"

"I held a knife to his throat. And I tried to stab him. Twice."

"Well. A black eye can't compete with that. Must be love."

I choked on my wine. "No," I said, swiping at the juice spilling from my mouth. "I'm his—" Keeper? Companion? What was it that lay between us? "It's not like that."

"Don't worry. Only a jealous heart would notice the way you look at the invader. But every man here saw the way he looked at you. If he keeps it up, he won't be long for this world."

"What are you talking about?"

"You have no idea, do you?" He cocked his head. "Most men look at you and see just another pretty girl. Some of us see past that. We see the fire in your soul. It speaks to us."

"You're drunk."

"Perhaps. But I hear it. So does he." Quinlan nodded at Reyker, being led away to the dungeons by guards, glancing over his shoulder to look back at me.

"What I hear is a stronghold full of drunken idiots, screaming for a war they aren't prepared for." I put down the chalice. "If you'll excuse me, I think I'd rather go sleep on a hard cot in a dreary bedchamber than stay here any longer."

"They summoned a Daughter of Aillira to torture him," Quinlan said.

I went cold all over.

"That's what your father is whispering about over there. Tomorrow, the pain-wielder will ply the invader for information. She'll make him tell Torin everything he knows. And if he doesn't, he won't be leaving here whistling and dancing a jig."

It wouldn't be Torin and the other chieftains beating Reyker until he answered their questions. It would be a pain-wielder, a Daughter of Aillira skilled at making an art of agony. I'd met a pain-wielder when I visited Aillira's Temple as a child. She'd shown me the instruments she used—blades and spikes, bone crushers and boiling oil. My stomach had turned just looking at the tools. And now those vile devices were going to be used on Reyker.

My hand shook, knocking into the chalice.

Quinlan caught it before it fell off the sill. "I can sneak you into the dungeons to warn him. Meet me at yonder stairwell." He polished off his ale and disappeared into the throng of carousing warriors.

———◇———

The spiral staircase was narrow and cramped, its turns tight as a corkscrew, ending in a desolate hallway. Quinlan showed me to a heavy iron door, the back entrance to the dungeons. "There's no guard?"

"Only one, stationed at the front. They don't bother guarding this side. Truth be told, I think the Selkies love letting prisoners escape, watching them try to swim for shore." He slid the metal bar out of the way and cracked the door open. "No one's ever made it, so I don't recommend letting your man try."

"Why are you doing this for me, Quinlan? He's a Westlander."

Quinlan was silent a moment. "Because even after what his people did to your village, to Rhys, you still looked at this invader like it killed you to shackle him. Like witnessing his torment was breaking your heart. Some men only dream of being looked at that way by a woman. If you were mine, and I was in this dungeon, I'd be dying right now. And I'd be praying someone would help you find your way to me."

His usual swagger was stripped away. I saw Quinlan for the man I'd always known he was—noble, kind. I took hold of his jaw and turned him toward me. "One day a woman will look at you that way. I've no doubt."

I kissed him lightly—a brief, sweet touch of lips—and was rewarded with a warm blush that lit up his entire face.

The stronghold's cellblock was bigger than Stony Harbor's, built deep enough into the rocks to make captives feel as if they'd been buried alive. There was only one other prisoner and he was passed out, snoring loudly. I crept to the other side of the dungeon.

Reyker sat in the corner of his cell, knees pulled to his chest, head tilted back, eyes closed. I called his name softly, and his eyes shot open. He rushed to the bars. They were vertical rods rather than a grate, heavily rusted by the salt air, but otherwise the same as the ones we were used to. "How?" he asked.

"Quinlan—a friend—snuck me in. I don't have much time. Tomorrow, Torin is going to use a Daughter of Aillira to interrogate you. You have to tell the chieftains what they want to hear, give them something they can use, or the pain-wielder will kill you slowly. She'll make you beg for death."

There was weariness in his face, emptiness in his eyes. "I don't care."

"Don't be stubborn."

"Me? You are stubborn, always giving me orders." He spoke in a falsetto voice, imitating me. *"Do not fight, wear chains, sleep in cages like a dog, tell my people secrets of your people."*

"That sounds nothing like me."

"I live, Lira. I live for you!" He raked a hand through his hair. "When will this end? When will I have peace? If I die in a cage tomorrow, or I die in a cage in ten years—what is the difference? A cage is not a life."

"Don't say that."

"Tomorrow I will tell them nothing. I will die and hope I wake in Skjorlog Felth. Even being damned to the Mist would be better than this."

"No." I gripped his hand through the bars, fastening us together. "I won't let you."

"Why?"

What could I say? How could I explain to him what I didn't under-stand myself? *Because I found you, I saved you, and that makes you mine. Because my soul is tied to yours, for reasons beyond my comprehension. Because*

without you, my life is as icy and dim as this dungeon. "Because I can't!"
A paltry excuse that didn't come close to answering his question.

The threat of his death had hovered over us since the day I dragged
him from the harbor, an invisible blade that could fall any moment. I'd
erected flimsy shields of lies and excuses to slow the descent, but it wasn't
enough. The blade would fall. The times when I let that truth sink in were
crushing. It was happening now. Before it overtook me, before I fell at his
feet, weeping and pleading and making a spectacle of myself, I turned my
anguish into anger.

"Listen to me, you stupid bloody Westlander." I grabbed the collar of
his tunic. "You think letting Torin kill you makes you a hero? He'll tell
stories for the rest of his days about the weak invader who broke so easily.
Is that the tale you want to be spread about you, that Reyker Lagorsson
was a lily-livered milksop?"

I'd gotten up on my knees, my eyes level with his, exhaling in furious
pants, like a bull about to charge. He glared back, but his lips twitched.
"Milksop?"

"Yes, milksop! It means you crumble like soggy bread."

He snorted.

"It's not funny," I insisted, fighting a smile. "It's a damning insult."

He snorted again, and it was too late, we were both laughing—quiet,
reserved, but laughter, nonetheless. Reyker's hand moved to the nape of
my neck. He leaned forward, resting his forehead against mine through
the gap between bars.

"Stupid girl," he said softly.

"Mule-headed idiot." His fingers cautiously stroked the line where my
skin and hair were wed. "I won't let you leave me."

"I know." His eyes were hazy blue in the dungeon's faint torchlight.

I edged the collar of his tunic open, set my palm lightly on his chest.
"Show me the day we met." It was another memory he'd never shared with
me; I needed him to remember it when he faced the conclave, how our
fates had been tangled together from the beginning.

Reyker sighed, putting his hand over mine.

The memory was a hard lump of rock; when I touched it, the rock crumbled to reveal a cloudy jewel. But this time, Reyker put distance between me and his past self. This time, he took me by the hand and led the way.

The woods are dark. The warlord and his men pick their way through the trees, and I follow. I don't want to be here. Draki forced me to come, to see the places he plans to conquer. A scouting expedition to the Green Isle, to gather information on the country's landscape, its resources, its people. Draki wants prisoners. Warriors with knowledge of the island's defenses. And women to inspire the Dragonmen.

Draki and I spot the girl at the same moment.

Why is she here, alone in the forest at night?

Dragonmen move to grab her, but the warlord waves a hand. The way he looks at her squeezes my lungs so tight it's hard to breathe. I know that look. Like he can see something no one else can—a glow within her, shining like a beacon. It means there's something different about her, something he can use to get what he wants.

She's not much more than a child. When he grabs the girl, she tries to scream. He takes his stiletto, about to mark her as his own.

I call out. "I heard something. Surely someone else is with her. We must check."

"You heard nothing," Draki growls.

"Yes, I did! Do you want us to be discovered, for the whole north harbor to find out we're here? Tie the girl up. I'll take her to the boat with the others."

He doesn't truly believe me, but he won't chance it. He gags the girl, blinds her with a sack, ties her wrists together. He throws her at me.

I carry her to the boat. She fights the whole way, strong for such a little thing. When I remove the hood, she spies the other prisoners. She spits out the rag, shouts at me.

I know what the warlord will do to her. I cannot let it happen. It isn't because the girl is beautiful or even because of the way she fights. It's because of the brave defiance in her eyes, showing me how the world has already hurt her, declaring that no matter what is done to her she will not break.

I never want her to find out how wrong she is.

Grabbing her bound hands, I stare at my knife. My knowledge of skoldars *is part rumor, part myth, a cryptic passage in a volva's text, surmising how someone god-gifted can link their life to another. I put the blade against her wrist and cut a mark of flames into her skin, a symbol to match my own, the same way I've watched the warlord do countless times. Then I slice my palm, smearing my blood across her wound. Warmth pulses where our blood mingles.*

I cut the ropes binding her, asking if she can swim. She nods, but I'm not certain she understands. We're out of time. I hear the Dragonmen coming.

I shove her into the sea.

When she doesn't come up, I think I've killed her. I'm about to jump in after her when I see her below the surface, gliding through the water as gracefully as a sea creature.

I spy the silver pendant lying in the hull moments before the Dragonmen arrive. It must be hers. I snatch it up, hiding it before they see.

When Draki steps aboard, I tell him the girl leaped overboard and sank. He knows it's a lie. I'm expecting another beating, but instead of taking it out on me, he grabs one of the prisoners, ripping off the hood. Underneath is a frightened warrior, about my age. "Reyker fancies himself a hero," Draki says to the Dragonmen. "But only life can pay for life."

He slits the boy's throat and drops him into my lap. The boy's eyes beg me for help, but there's nothing I can do. I hold him as his life bleeds out, staining my clothes, coating my skin. When it's over, Draki flings the boy's body over the side of the boat.

"You think you saved that girl?" Draki says. "She will grow up. We will return to this place and destroy it. I will find her once more. You saved no one."

I have no doubt Draki will do as he says.

No matter what I do, the Dragon always wins.

Reyker pulled my palm from his chest but didn't let go. We sat in silence a moment, letting the cobwebs of the memory fall away.

"He was wrong, Reyker. You did save me. But you were wrong too. Draki has lost. I'm here with you, instead of with him. And I will never break."

"No. Because I will be there, to keep you whole."

Footsteps moved toward us. "Lira," Quinlan said. "The festivities upstairs are ending. Time to go."

Reyker and Quinlan were locked in a staring match, studying each other. Quinlan extended his hand to me. I let him help me to my feet and stood at his side, looking from one man to the other, wondering what they were thinking.

Quinlan thrust an open hand between the bars. "Quinlan of Fion, warrior of the Hounds of Vengeance."

Reyker gaped at Quinlan's hand, like he'd forgotten how it felt to be greeted as a human. Finally he accepted it, and they shook hands—Glas-nithian and Westlander. "Reyker Lagorsson. Beast of the Frozen Sun," he said with no shortage of bitterness.

Even so, Quinlan grinned. "Good to meet you, Reyker. Unfortunately, we must be going before we're missed. I'll make sure Lira gets safely to her room."

"Thank you." There was grief in Reyker's eyes as Quinlan took my arm to lead me away.

Quinlan paused. "Reyker. We aren't all bastards, you know?"

Reyker leaned against the wall of his cell. "We are not all beasts."

CHAPTER 28

REYKER

Reyker was on his knees, shackled, in a room full of men begging for the chance to skin him alive and paint the floor with his blood. All but the dark-haired one in back, watching with furrowed brows—Quinlan, a man he might have befriended in a different world.

The warriors' questions were endless: fighting techniques, ship design and navigation capabilities, the process of selecting which villages to raid. They wanted to know the extent of the Dragon's power. Reyker responded in Iseneldish. "If I tell you, you'll fall apart. You'll weep like frightened children."

This was a game. He'd survived the warlord's games for years. Reyker knew how to play.

Show them you fear neither pain nor death.

Torin called the torturer, a dour young woman with eyes like stone— flat and gray. She turned pain into an art form, using a chest full of tools that cut and bruised and burned, plucking his body like an instrument, playing a song of agony to inflict extreme pain that caused no lasting damage. Had he not suffered for years under Draki's tutelage, he could never have withstood the torturer's skills. As it was, he held his tongue, glaring insolently.

Frustrated, the torturer grew careless. She threw his chain over a beam and choked him with the metal collar he wore, releasing him just before he blacked out. Thinking him too weak to be a threat, she let go of the chain. He forced his empty lungs to breathe slowly, shook off the dark spots clouding his vision.

Give them their beast.

He leaped at the nearest warrior, throwing his shackles over the man's head. Jerking the manacles' chain, strangling the man.

The warrior struggled futilely. The crowd descended, raising their weapons, closing in.

Dangle their prize.

Reyker released the man, stealing his sword before shoving him away. He stared the clans down, sword held high. "I am Reyker Lagorsson, heir to the lands of Vaknavangur, a warrior and lord of Iseneld. Kill me, and you lose your only chance of stopping the invasion of your island."

Torin held up a hand and moved forward. "I'm listening, beast."

"You have no idea what you're facing." Reyker told them a fraction of what he knew, explaining the Dragonmen's training, their defenses, their goals. It was different to be standing, gripping a sword. He wasn't a victim revealing information under duress. He was a conspirator.

The men paled, looking at one another fearfully.

"While all of this is … interesting," Torin admitted, "it's not reason enough to spare your life. Unless you have more to offer?" The chieftain smiled. *Your move, beast.*

Reyker thought of his deal with Madoc, the threats Madoc had made, the key hidden in the lining of his boot. He hadn't used it yet. There had been no clear path of escape for both himself and Lira, and he wouldn't leave without her. And deserving or not, Torin was Lira's father—Reyker wouldn't kill the chieftain without her blessing.

Side with Madoc or with Torin? A devil or a demon. It was a gamble either way.

"You want to kill the Dragon?" Reyker hurled his sword at Torin's feet. "Let me fight for you. Many of my countrymen bear no love for the warlord. I can raise an army of Westlanders to destroy him and his followers. I'll bring you his head myself."

A game.

More dangerous than ever, now that he was playing both sides.

CHAPTER 29

I paced the stronghold's porticoes, listening to the barking seals sun-bathing on the rocks at the islet's base. In the centrum, Reyker was being questioned. I wasn't permitted to attend. I'd lost count of how many loops I'd marched around the fort. Turning the corner once more, I stumbled upon Quinlan.

He answered before I could ask. "Reyker's all right. Injured, but alive."

"How injured? What did they do to him? What did he say?"

"You should go to him. Ask him yourself." Someone called Quinlan's name. He turned and shouted, "Aye, I'm coming!" To me, he said, "I have to go."

"You're leaving?"

He grinned. "Going to miss me, my lady?"

"Not a whit." I hugged him hard. He was always leaving. How many times had we said goodbye?

"Take care, Lira. If the gods are good, we shall meet again soon." He kissed my cheek and ran to catch up with his clan.

A moment later, a young woman stepped into the empty passageway. She was twenty years or so, tall and lean, with long brown hair tied into a series of knots falling down her back. The woman carried a thick case that jingled as she walked, as if it was full of metal. She wore leather gloves that came up to her elbows. They were stained with blood.

I didn't have to wonder whose blood it was.

The woman didn't notice me. Drawing my knife, I followed her as she strode deeper into the stronghold, toward the wing where my own guest chambers were housed. She slipped into one of the rooms, and I snuck in behind her.

Before I could blink, I was pushed against the wall, a dagger at my throat. "Drop your weapon," she said.

My own blade was pointed beneath her chin. "Not until you drop yours."

"You might want to reconsider, poppet. I can do far more damage with my blade than you can." She tilted her head, eyeing me curiously. "I don't believe we've had the pleasure."

"I'm Lira of Stone. A Daughter of Aillira, like you. What's your name? Or shall I just call you pain-wielder?"

"Ah, the soul-reader. I've heard of you." Slowly she lowered her dagger, and I followed suit with my knife. "I am Sursha. And no, you are *not* like me. I've chosen to use my gift for the glory of the gods. You let yours waste away, hiding within your clan in that isolated harbor."

"It brings glory to the gods to torture innocent men?"

Sursha pulled her gloves off and washed her hands in the water basin. "Innocent? That savage? Hardly. But he was quite sturdy, withstanding more than most men I've questioned."

The knife trembled in my hand. "What did you do to him?"

"Do you actually care about that invader? Silly little soul-reader. Don't you know what the Westlanders mean to do to Glasnith? They'll try to kill or enslave us all, steal the island for themselves. He says he's not one of them anymore, but I say once a beast, always a beast."

"If you hate them so much, why aren't you doing anything to stop it? Why have none of the Daughters of Aillira come to help the clans defeat the Westlanders?"

She tossed her hair over her shoulder. "You know as well as I do that Aillira's Temple and its pledges honor the True Gods, not mortals. We take no part in mortal wars unless the gods bid us otherwise, and they've said nothing about the beasts of the Frozen Sun."

"Maybe you're not listening. Or maybe you're listening to the wrong gods."

"Get out." Sursha shoved me toward the door. "I don't want to hear about Veronis and his Fallen Ones. The priestesses teach us the Forbidden Scriptures, but that doesn't mean we all believe in them. The True Gods are the only ones that count. Find your own way to stop the beasts."

So there was dissent among the Daughters of Aillira when it came to the Forbidden Scriptures. How many sided with Aillira and Veronis, and how many with Gwylor? Could I use their division to my advantage?

I shoved Sursha back. "Tell your priestesses the soul-reader is coming to them at last. Someone must convince them to do something besides watch as Glasnith burns."

"And you think you're the one to do it?"

"Aye, since it seems no one else is brave enough to save this island."

Our party left the following morning.

I saw Reyker as we all piled into the same vessel that had brought us to the stronghold. Rage gripped me when I noticed the bright bruises beneath his metal collar. Reyker and I shared a glance, a silent exchange of concern and reassurance, before turning away as the boat splashed toward the mainland.

Mounting our horses, we left Selkie's Quay, entering the Green Desert, following the same path in reverse, reaching the inn shortly before nightfall.

Still emboldened by what transpired at the conclave, the Sons of Stone drank and dined, sharing bawdy limericks and songs. One warrior held a slab of meat to his crotch, hips thrusting, making crude jokes about what the mercenary clans did with their livestock. The men's laughter rang through the hall, making my head ache.

I went upstairs to my room, where Torin was slouched on his cot.

When he spoke, his voice was hollow. "I've found you a husband. He'll collect you after we return to Stony Harbor."

For a moment, it felt as if the floor had dropped out beneath me. "Which one?"

"The chieftain with the most soldiers. I can't remember his name."

"Do you jest?" I asked, though it was clear he was serious. "How little you must care for me, your own flesh and blood."

The black vines in Torin's eyes twitched. "You play the martyr well for a child who has never known suffering. I've provided for you your entire life, and you balk at being asked to make a sacrifice that benefits our clan. After all I've given you, all your mother gave up."

"Perhaps I've known little suffering," I said, "but I've known much loss. If you need a sacrifice, give me a sword. I'll ride with you into battle against the Westlanders. I'll give my life fighting. But don't ask me to sacrifice my heart. It's too much."

"That ought to fill our enemies with fear. A little girl swinging a sword." Torin scoffed. "Sacrificing your heart, you say? You know nothing of hearts, child."

"Give me the chance to find out. If Garreth were here—"

"Garreth." My brother's name was a wound that awakened something inside Torin, like ripping off the scab so it bled anew. He looked at me as he had beside our burning cottage, sadness swelling inside him, drumming a lament on his bones.

"Father?"

His eyes were warm and brown, with no trace of parasitic darkness. "Lira?"

I put my arms around him. I felt like a child and sounded like one when I said, "I don't want to marry. Please don't make me."

Torin's eyes fixed on my bodice. I glanced down and saw that Mother's medallion had slipped free from my gown. He reached out, tracing the thorntree. "I miss you so much, my love." A sob caught in his throat. "Why did you die? How could you leave me?"

He bowed his head, pulling me closer. I didn't understand what was happening until he tried to press his lips to mine.

"Stop!" I jerked away, slapped him hard. "I'm your daughter, not your wife!"

Torin looked at me, dazed. Tentatively, I placed my palm to his chest. His soul—flickering deep beneath skin and bone—was fractured, like a dried-up riverbed baking beneath a noonday sun. He was coming apart. Whatever Gwylor had left in him was devouring Torin from the inside out.

"My daughter?" He sank back onto the cot, staring into his lap. "My daughter."

I bolted from the room, past the rowdy men downstairs, past the guards outside the inn. The half-drunk sentries stationed at the stables were so deep into their card game, they didn't notice me. I crept by, tiptoeing across the straw.

Reyker was in the last stall. "Lira?" he called as I entered. "What's wrong?"

A dam broke within me at the sight of him, shackled and wounded. He wore manacles, and the chain attached to the collar on his neck had been secured with bolts into the stable's wall. I dropped to my knees. "Show me what those bastards did to you." Not just the clans, I reminded myself; this time it was a Daughter of Aillira who had carried out his torture. I reached to touch his chest, but he took my hand and held it.

"No."

"I need to see." There was so much anger in me, so much fear. I deserved to witness the awful things they'd done to Reyker, as punishment for ever trusting that the men of my clan and my island were noble.

"*No.*" Reyker shook his head. "I do not want you to see me that way. I am a beast to them. You are the only one who lets me be a man."

Tears pressed at my eyes, but I held them back. "I wish I'd run with you that night when you asked me. I wish you hadn't come back for me."

"I would do it again. I would spend a thousand lifetimes in those damned cells before I would leave you alone with *them*." He spit out the last word like it was toxic. I didn't need to ask who he meant. Torin, Madoc, Draki—the monstrous men who tormented us both.

He was watching me closely, a question in his eyes. "Did something happen?"

I told him of my conversation with Torin, how he was marrying me off to some man I'd never met, how he'd mistaken me for my mother. Reyker listened silently until I finished. He pulled something from his boot: a key. The same sort Torin wore around his neck that unlocked Reyker's chains. "Run with me," he said.

"Where did you—no, it doesn't matter. Tell me later." I grabbed the key and unlocked his collar and shackles, letting the cursed chains fall to the ground.

Reyker stretched his muscles with a groan. "Quinlan offered aid, should I escape. We can head to Houndsford, unless you have somewhere else in mind."

"When did you speak with Quinlan?" I headed for Wraith's stall, grabbing his saddle.

Reyker gathered up anything he could use as a weapon—rope, a horse pick, the shackles he'd just shed. When he was done, he found the tack for Torin's stallion. "Quinlan came back to the dungeon after escorting you to your room. We talked for a while."

"About what?"

"Our countries. Our people. You." He smiled at me over the top of the stall, and I raised a brow. That was a conversation I'd have liked to listen in on.

Briefly, I debated. We could go to Stalwart Bay and catch a ship to the Auk Isles, as Reyker had planned to do before he was caught. Part of me wanted to go to Aillira's Temple and confront the Daughters of Aillira, as I'd told Sursha I would. But Torin might suspect either of those paths; he wouldn't expect us to head back in the direction of Stony Harbor, and having Quinlan on our side would be advantageous. "Houndsford it is."

Before I could mount, Reyker came and took my hand. "Lira, your father. He will come after us. I could stop him now, but I won't do so without your permission."

Stop. As in *kill*.

Emotions clouded my thoughts, making it hard to answer. My father. My tormentor. My captor—and Reyker's as well. Did I want Torin dead? Did I want what little was left of my father to die? "No. His fate is his own. I want nothing to do with his life or his death."

Reyker nodded. "Are you ready?"

A seed of fear sprouted within me. If we failed, what would happen to us? If we succeeded, where would we go? Who was I if I was no longer Lira of Stone?

Did it matter?

I looked up at Reyker. Moonlight skipped along his eyes like stones across water. I knew they held secrets, things he wasn't telling me. I didn't care. I pushed the hair off his brow, running my fingers through it.

It was strange to be this close without bars between us. Here there were no guards, no devious uncles or mad fathers. There was no one but us. Whatever feelings lay between us stirred. Swelled. Reyker tilted his head toward mine, pausing. I trembled, expectant.

This was the threshold of something. A beginning. An ending. A choice. Once made, there would be no unmaking it.

I pushed through it, stepping into the unknown.

My lips parted, awaiting his, unable to form the words surging through me. *Yes. Please. Finally.* Our mouths met, sweet and gentle, a whisper of a kiss. Carefully, we learned the shape and fit of our merged lips. His tongue brushed mine, and I sighed.

I'd battled my growing affection for Reyker for so long, building walls around my heart. It was a relief to let them crumble.

It happened without warning, like an undertow dragging us from the shallows into the open sea. Our mouths forged deeper, growing hungry, insistent. I pressed my body against his. His hands gripped my waist.

The drunken voices outside seemed to come from the other side of the world.

We froze in each other's arms, reality slowly seeping back, and with it, a shy embarrassment. I flushed, glancing at Reyker from beneath my lashes. "I'm ready."

It didn't take long for one of the stable guards to fall asleep. As soon as the other one walked around the side of the building to relieve himself, we snuck the horses out, and then there was nothing between us and the desert.

We rode through the night, into the morning. The Silverspires were sharp, shadowy vertebrae on the horizon, growing closer with each hoof-fall. Houndsford was on the other side, to the northeast, beyond the pass that cut through the mountains. Above us, the sky was a bright blue, but ahead, it darkened.

Behind us, other riders appeared in the distance.

Reyker and I didn't speak. We pushed our horses onward, until the Silverspires loomed before us. The mountains were barely visible beneath a blanket of mist that spilled down the foothills to where gray rock met the green stretch of desert.

The team of horses was gaining on us, carrying the Sons of Stone. They were close enough now for me to see Torin among them.

How had they found us so quickly?

"Stop, Lira!" the chieftain commanded, taking the lead.

Reyker and I spurred our horses, wading into the thick fog blanketing the pass's narrow opening. "Stay close," he said just before we were swallowed by the white veil.

Wraith snorted nervously as the mist circled us on all sides, vanishing the landscape. This was wrong. Wicked things hid in the mist—like Destroyers, demons who dragged evil men to the serpent-goddess Ildja to be tortured and devoured. It was a Westlander tale, but it still made me shudder.

I couldn't see Reyker; I wanted to call out for him, but I didn't dare.

The sound of hooves grew louder, and then there were horses on either side of me, hemming Wraith in, as a hand shot out from the fog and gripped my arm.

"Where do you think you're going, beast-lover?" Sloane asked.

Unwilling to go without a fight, I drew my knife. A sentry on my other side reached to take it, and I prepared to stab him, but something heavy slammed into the sentry from behind. He hunched forward, face wrinkled with confusion.

His body shifted sideways, tumbling off his horse. An axe was lodged in his spine.

CHAPTER 30

I stared at the sentry's lifeless form, bloodying the dirt where he'd fallen. A sick fear overcame me. I'd seen this before. "Ambush!" I screamed.

Once more, my warning came too late.

Sloane released me and unsheathed his sword. I ducked as a man flew over my head, leaping from a ridge above us to tackle Sloane. The men collided, toppling to the ground.

Through the haze, I could make out flashes of movement—Dragonmen landing on the Sons of Stone, throwing some from their horses. I heard the wild howls of invaders, the answering war cry of Torin and his warriors, the kiss of metal on metal.

How many Westlanders were there? Ten? Fifty? The mist made it impossible to tell.

Was Draki one of them?

A Westlander materialized in front of me, trying to pull me off Wraith, and I sank my knife into his hand. He let go with a shriek, but recovered quickly and was back, seizing me, raising his axe. I pulled hard on Wraith's reins, urging him backward.

From out of the mist, Reyker's horse appeared. The manacles were in his hands, a dead Dragonman dangling from the length of chain by the neck. The invader grabbing at me halted when he saw Reyker, recognition passing between them. He screamed in fury, running at Reyker, swinging his axe. Reyker barely had time to pull his chain loose from the dead man's neck and stop the blade with it.

While the two of them wrestled for the axe, I edged Wraith forward and slit the invader's throat from behind.

I had to bend down over the saddle, to hold his hair to keep his head steady, to push hard and pretend I was sawing through a thick slice of pork or mutton so I wouldn't lose my nerve. My hands shook as blood spilled over them in a warm flood—my second kill only slightly easier than my first.

Reyker claimed the dead invader's axe. Around us was a rising tide of sound, an onslaught of shapes. I stared, trying to make sense of it. I didn't see Torin anywhere, but I could still hear him shouting orders.

"Draki," I said. "Is he here?"

"I don't know." Reyker glanced at me, my question reflected in his features. More invaders pushed toward us through the mist, blockading the way forward. "You have to go, Lira." When I didn't react, he jerked Wraith's reins to the side, so the horse would turn, and then he slapped Wraith's haunches. "Go!"

Already panicked, my horse bolted, with no regard for his rider. Wraith backtracked through the pass, dodging around the bands of fighting warriors too fast for me to make out any faces, emerging from where we'd entered only minutes before.

Half the world lurched by in a heartbeat.

Wraith ignored my attempts to control him. I pressed myself into his neck, clutching the reins. There was nothing but the pounding of hooves, the shrieking wind, smears of white and gray and green unfolding on every side. He ran until the mountains and mist were long gone and we were flying across the hills of the Green Desert, his hooves propelling us forward. Eventually, I remembered my medallion and pressed it to his coat. "In Veronis's name, slow down, you stubborn stallion."

On the verge of collapsing, Wraith finally slowed.

Around us, moorlands stretched endlessly in every direction. I had no idea if there were villages nearby. My sense of distance had been thrown off-kilter. I rode on, not sure where I was going, but certain if I stopped moving I would fall apart.

Reyker is alive. Reyker will find me.

I repeated this, over and over, as I searched for a safe place to rest. I'd been riding for several hours when I spotted tents in the distance. A deserted nomad camp.

I dismounted and searched the camp for supplies, but someone had pillaged it, tearing the tents, scattering belongings. Among them I found a broken spear, its shaft snapped in half. I tucked it into Wraith's saddle.

The sounds of horses made me go still. I motioned for Wraith to kneel behind a tent, and I peered around it as the horses came into view over the top of a rocky knoll. Two Westlanders, riding mounts branded with a triad of swords. Over the haunches of each horse was a body, tied up. Sons of Stone. One man was limp, but the other struggled—even from this distance, I recognized the gruff sound of Sloane's voice as he cursed at the Westlanders. The invaders leaped off the horses, hobbled them with rope, and dragged their captives into a hole in the side of the knoll. The yawning mouth of a cave.

I could leave them. I owed them nothing. But they were my kinfolk, and it didn't matter that they hated me. I wouldn't abandon them to be slaughtered.

Leaving Wraith at the camp, I made my way to the cave. "Help me, Silarch," I beseeched the goddess-mother. "Grant me the courage and strength of a true warrior."

Gripping the broken spear in one hand and my knife in the other, I took a deep breath and stepped through the crevice. The throat of the cave was narrow, but it expanded the deeper I went, until I stood inside a nook the size of my bedroom. A single candle burned, illuminating the earthen vault. Food and furs were piled along the walls. There was more light ahead, and muffled voices.

The passage tapered once more before swelling into a wide, lofty cavity, as spacious as a cottage. A small fire blazed in a pit. Glossy fingers of rock protruded from the floor and hung like amberous icicles from the ceiling high above.

Sloane and the other sentry were tied up at the rear of the cave, with two Westlanders looming over them. I inched closer, raising the spear.

Sloane noticed me, his eyes widening in surprise. Giving me away.

The Westlanders whirled, already swinging their axes. I dropped to my knees as a blade whisked above my head, stabbing my spear into the larger of the two men.

The invader grunted. Grabbing the shaft of the spear, he wrenched it from his belly with a wet slurp and tossed it aside like it was no more than a splinter. He lumbered toward me, firelight splashing across his features.

"Run!" Sloane said.

The invader's long hair was matted, his face heavily scarred. He was tall and thick, with limbs like tree trunks. The widening gap of his mouth revealed rows of teeth filed down to fangs. When he reached for me, I sliced at him with the knife. He sidestepped my strike and grabbed my wrists, tearing the weapon from my fingers as he slung me to the floor.

Sloane kept shouting at me to run, even though it was too late.

The invader leered at me with sharp-edged eyes that promised pain. The Dragonman who had beheaded the men of Reyker's village.

The executioner.

CHAPTER 31

"When you were a wee babe, did someone drop you on your head?" Sloane asked. We leaned against the cave wall, wrists tied behind our backs. "Because there's no other explanation for how you could be so stupid."

"Shut your ungrateful mouth. I came here to rescue you."

"Oh, good! Well, get on with it then."

"*Tystille!*" shouted the older invader stationed at the opening to the passageway. This man's face was familiar to me as well, from Reyker's memories. Einar—one of the few honorable Dragonmen.

Sloane dropped his voice to a whisper. "What's he saying?"

"He wants you to shut your ungrateful mouth too," I whispered back.

"Can you really understand them?"

"Mostly."

After I was caught, the Dragonmen stood over me, arguing. The executioner—Ulver, his name was—had growled and laughed when he found the *skoldar* on my wrist as he bound my hands together. Some of the men's words were gibberish to me, but I'd understood enough to know Sloane and I were hostages. The invaders planned to ransom us to our clan.

The other sentry, captured alongside Sloane, had succumbed to his wounds. The Dragonmen left his body lying near us to serve as a warning.

Sloane didn't know what happened to the rest of the party. The Sons of Stone had scattered, some pushing through the mountain pass, others backtracking into the desert, some still on horseback, others dragged off and fighting on foot. The invaders had split up to pursue them. "That ugly beast ran me down," Sloane said, pointing his chin in Einar's direction. "One minute we were fighting, the next I woke up tied to the back of a horse."

There was a noise at the cave entrance. Ulver tromped up the passage, returning with more goods he'd stolen from a nomad camp, tossing weapons and food and clothing in a pile. The wound I'd given him seemed to bother him no more than an insect bite, but it had angered him that a Glasnithian girl managed to injure him. He glared at me, argued more with Einar. "She's more valuable unharmed," Einar was saying.

"I just want to play with her," Ulver said. "I want to hear her scream."

I squeezed my eyes shut.

Sloane pressed his arm against mine. "I'm sorry I called you beast-lover." He seemed to be apologizing for much more.

"It's all right."

When I opened my eyes, Ulver was sneering at me, licking his lips. Einar tried to hold him back, but Ulver shoved the older invader away, ordering him to go guard the cave's entrance. Sloane fought for me too, throwing himself into the Dragonman. It was short-lived, ending with the Son of Stone on the ground, an axe buried in his gut.

"Sloane!" I screamed as Ulver grabbed me.

The Westlander bit through my bindings with his fangs and grinned, scraps of rope stuck between his sharp teeth. He wanted me free to fight. It was no fun if the deer didn't run. I finally understood how Reyker felt, being treated like an animal.

I ran, but I only made it a few steps before Ulver's hands closed around my arms. I fought, knowing it was what he wanted, unable to deny him the satisfaction. I punched and kicked, scratched and bit, until he let go, only to chase me again. Laughing, he toyed with me—letting me attack him, releasing me, recapturing me.

"*Skriga*," he said. *Scream.*

I bit my tongue.

He pinned me against the rock wall. His jaw widened, and those inhuman teeth darted toward my neck.

Grappling for strength, I let go of the present, shutting myself off from Ulver, sliding into a place where he couldn't touch me: memories from childhood, of Mother holding me after I'd woken from a nightmare. This was just another nightmare. It would end.

It was already ending.

The invader stilled. He clamped a hand over my mouth, listening to something. Voices echoed from the front of the cave—Einar, speaking to someone in Iseneldish.

My *skoldar* prickled with warmth.

Not everything they said made sense, but the context was clear and their inflections spoke as loud as their words, making it easy to fill in the gaps.

"I've come for your hostage," Reyker said to Einar. "Where is the girl?"

"What's become of you, Reyker?" The Dragonman sounded sad. Disappointed. "We thought you dead. We mourned. And here you are, alive, killing your own to protect these dogs, wearing their mark." I imagined him pointing at Reyker's slave-brand. "You sicken me."

"Don't be so quick to judge, Einar. Let me explain."

"I saw you kill men you once fought beside. What more do I need to know?" I heard him stand, heard the slide of steel pulled from leather.

"I don't want to fight you. Give me the girl and I'll leave without bloodshed," Reyker beseeched him.

"You'd best kill me, boy. If you don't, I'll tell Draki where you are, who you're with, and what you've done."

They spoke no more. There was grunting, the clash of weapons. A body hit the floor. Ulver dragged me to the passage to look. Reyker was bent over Einar, whose chest bore a gaping wound. He stared at his dead friend, his face pale.

Ulver chuckled.

Reyker hurtled toward us, and Ulver wrenched my head back, his fangs hovering just above my skin. "Don't come any closer, lordling bastard. I can tear out her throat faster than you can swing that axe."

"Not if you want to live." Every muscle in Reyker's body tensed, ready to spring.

"You think you can kill me, little lordling?" Ulver grinned. "I know what you are. A rebel. A deserter. Draki should have let me take your head that day, but he had such hopes for you. I told him you'd turn out worthless and spineless like your father."

The axe trembled in Reyker's hands. "Tell me what you want, Ulver."

"I have everything I want. I have the Sword of the Dragon at my mercy over a pretty little bitch on this island of mongrels." Ulver's breath crawled across my cheek. "I'll drain her slowly, one slice at a time, and I'll make sure you live long enough to watch the light in her eyes fade. Her last thought before she dies will be how you failed to save her. Just like your mother."

Reyker's eyes darkened with a mindless fury that was as frightening as Ulver's threat. An eerie calm settled over him. "The girl is not mine. She belongs to Draki."

A tremor ran through Ulver. "You're lying."

"See for yourself. She is marked."

Ulver shifted me, peering behind my ear. When he saw the scar, he went rigid. "*Stjorna af Drakin.*"

Star of the Dragon. I was just one shiny dot in the constellation of girls Draki collected.

"Do you know what the warlord does to men who try to steal his property?" Reyker asked. "Have you seen their bodies? Or what's left of them, by the time he's finished?"

"I barely touched her," Ulver protested, shoving me aside. I landed on my hands and knees on the cave floor.

The axe tore the air as Reyker leaped.

Ulver dodged a half-second before the blade reached him, and it slammed into rock in a drizzle of sparks. As Reyker spun, Ulver drew his axe, and they crashed against each other, weapons and bodies colliding, stumbling from one side of the cave to the other.

I scrambled out of their way.

The two of them sliced and ducked and chased, knocking into the walls, a hair's breadth from maiming one another. Ulver was brawny, with monstrous, clumsy strength. Reyker was agile and swift, possessed by unearthly ferocity. They seemed a near-even match.

Between swings, they threw punches and kicks. They weren't just fighting to kill—this grudge ran deep, forged years ago in the blood of Reyker's kinsmen. They wanted to tear each other to pieces.

They didn't notice me pick up the broken spear.

Ulver thrust a kick into Reyker's knee. He staggered. Another kick sent him to the floor. With Ulver bearing down on him, he rolled onto his back, bracing the axe handle across his chest to protect his body from the Dragonman's falling blade. The handle cracked, absorbing the blow.

With another strike, it would snap.

Before Ulver swung again, I stabbed the spear into his ribs. He roared, turning to aim his weapon at me.

Reyker's axe lodged into Ulver's thigh. The Dragonman screamed.

Grabbing his arm, Reyker planted his foot on Ulver's chest and rocked backward. Ulver flew over Reyker's head and hit the ground, his weapon skidding away. In an instant, Reyker was up and the axe was in his hands. He raised it high, brought it down fast.

Bone crunched. Blood flowed.

Reyker stared at the blade protruding from Ulver's skull, fingers clenching the axe handle. His chest heaved, his breath came in rapid bursts. I counted to fifty. To a hundred. Nothing changed. Reyker didn't blink, loosen his grip, or catch his breath.

I called his name.

Savage Reyker answered, baring his teeth. His eyes looked but didn't see. He was lost.

"Reyker." I stroked his cheek, and he flinched. "It's over. Let go." I ran my hands down his arms, coaxing his locked fingers to release the axe. The second he did, he grabbed me, shoving my back against the rock. His eyes were dark pools, unfocused.

"I'm not afraid of you. You aren't going to hurt me." I took hold of his face. "Remember the elk, Reyker. Your parents, Lagor and Katrin. Vaknavangur. Remember who you are."

Moments passed. I felt his body start to relax. His breath came more naturally. Life slowly seeped back into his eyes. I kept whispering his name.

Finally, he looked at me. *Saw* me. He slumped to his knees, arms slipping around my waist, burying his face against my stomach. I combed my fingers through his hair. We stayed that way for a time, silent, holding each other.

When he drew back, I sat beside him. "Did he hurt you?" Reyker asked.

"He didn't get the chance." I looked over at Sloane and the other sentry. My corpse would have lain next to theirs if Reyker hadn't come. I wanted to throw my arms around him, show him how grateful I was, but something the executioner had said was bothering me. "Ulver called you Sword of the Dragon. What did he mean?"

Reyker lowered his head until his hair swept across his face, hiding it. "What happens to me when I fight, my people call battle-madness. When I was a Dragonman, Draki used me. He filled me with hatred for him, and then pointed me at his enemies. I lost control. I killed everyone in my way. Over and over Draki did this. He called me his sword."

A weapon, fallen into the wrong hands, the mystic had said of Reyker.

"You aren't his sword anymore." I saw the invader in Reyker when he fought, but the man sitting next to me now was different. Kind, pensive— the man whose soul I knew inside and out, in all its ugliness and beauty.

"No. You gave me new life." He lifted his eyes to mine. There was naked fear in them, like he was curled in my palm and I could crush him if I chose. "I am your sword now, Lira."

You wield the lost sword of the Frozen Sun. A weapon of the Ice Gods in the hands of the Green Gods' soul-reader.

I ran my fingertips over the black flames of his warrior-mark. "I don't care who you were. I know who you are, Reyker. My friend. My wolf." And so much more, so many things I had no words for.

I touched my mouth to his. Reyker pulled me closer and I sank against him, my arms slipping behind his neck. His hands stroked the length of my spine, settled in the small of my back. I felt the rise and fall of his chest with every breath, the pounding of his heart vibrating between my breasts.

He pulled away too soon, shaking his head. "Not here." He glanced at the pools of blood, the dead bodies. "When I kiss you more it will be in a beautiful place."

I thought of gallows and dungeons, of homes burnt to ash and blood soaking into snow. "There's nothing beautiful left."

"There is," he promised. "We will find it. You will see."

CHAPTER 32

Reyker kneeled beside Einar's body, chanting a quiet prayer. I did the same for Sloane; he'd died a warrior's death, given his life to protect mine, and I hoped he dined tonight in the Eternal Palace.

Though it was nearly nightfall, we thought it better to take our chances in the open desert rather than staying in the cave and risking more invaders returning to it. I found my knife, lying where Ulver had dropped it, and strapped the sheath to my thigh. We gathered supplies from the invaders' stock, bundling food and weapons—I took a short sword, light enough for me to wield, and belted it around my waist—then the two of us stepped out of the cave into the cool evening air. I reached for Reyker's hand.

Together we climbed the knoll. At the top, we scanned the empty moor. No horses. Wraith, Reyker's mount, the Dragonmen's—all of them had vanished.

"Where do we go?" Reyker asked. "Do we try for Houndsford again?"

My answer was swift. "No. To Aillira's Temple." I'd been thinking on it since meeting Sursha at the stronghold, and being attacked by Westlanders in the Silverspires and the Green Desert had shored up my resolve. "They've hidden behind their walls long enough. There are women at the temple who have powers to rival the greatest warriors. If Glasnith is to defeat the Dragonmen, the Daughters of Aillira must come forward to help." I could only hope they'd listen to my plea, since I was one of their own.

The Green Desert was massive, and I wasn't sure which direction the temple was from here, so I headed toward the horizon. Deeper into the wasteland.

"How did you find me?" I asked as we walked. "Did you track Wraith here?"

"I followed this." Reyker ran his finger along my *skoldar*, and my skin seemed to sigh. "After I cut my mark into you, I sealed your wound with my blood. Your *skoldar* links you to me through blood magic. The night my ship was attacked by the Brine Beast, I felt your presence the closer we sailed to Glasnith. When you found me in the harbor, it was like there was a cord stretching between us. If I focus hard enough, it pulls me toward you."

That's why the scar responded to his touch. Maybe it was why my experiences reading his soul were so different. "Why didn't you tell me?"

"Because I didn't want you to think I was like Draki. I didn't mark you to claim you. I just wanted to keep you safe from the warlord, and it was all I had to give you."

"Is that … is that why you have feelings for me? Because we're linked—"

"No," he said before I could finish. "I care for you because of who you are to me."

"And who is that?"

His eyes burned into mine. "Someone willing to listen with her heart, to find the man inside the beast. The girl who pulled me from the water, who saved me from her father's sword. The woman who walks in my soul and drew me out of its darkness."

His words struck the cold block of guilt that had been lodged inside me since the day my mother died—cracking it, thawing it. For the first time, I let myself believe her sacrifice hadn't been in vain. Because if I truly meant this much to Reyker, then my life mattered.

The desert was silent, save the occasional baying of coywolves, the whistling screech of catamounts. The moon rose high and full, a fulgent white lily blooming in a dead black garden. Hours crawled by as we searched for a settlement, someone to give us directions or aid us in acquiring a horse. A few times we came across abandoned tents, the remnants of a campfire, horses' hoofprints. It was as if every nomad in the desert was hiding.

I couldn't stop thinking of the attack in the Silverspires, wondering if Draki was here, in the desert somewhere. My head began to ache. The scar behind my ear itched.

We stopped to rest at a rocky outcrop. I drank deeply from the waterskin and passed it to Reyker. "We'll split up when we reach Taloorah," I said. "You can camp in the woods while I enter the temple."

"No. We stay together."

I scratched at my scar. "The temple guards will kill you on sight."

"We'll find a way. I won't be parted from you again. It's not safe."

"Reyker, the Dragonmen are everywhere. On the coasts, in the mountains, hiding in caves in the desert. Nowhere is safe for either of us."

He touched the axe at his hip. "When I kill Draki, we will be safe."

"And if he kills you?" I put my head in my hands. "You bloody men are all the same, caring more about your battles than your own lives or the people who'll be hurt by your deaths."

Reyker pulled my hands away, peering at my face. "Are you sick?"

My vision blurred, and I closed my eyes against the drums beating between my temples. It felt like someone's fingers were inside my skull, trying to rip it open.

When I opened my eyes, I saw silver hair. Greenish-gold irises.

I lurched to my feet and backed away, until a wall trapped me. I turned, expecting to see the rocky hillside, but it was a solid sheet of blue ice. It stretched out on all sides, rising above my head. An ice cave.

"Little warrior."

I drew my sword, but Draki knocked it away. He grabbed my hair with one hand. With the other, he slid his fingertip along the scar he'd made behind my ear, and it pulsed with cold.

I heard Reyker call my name from far away. The *skoldar* on my wrist tingled. I blinked, and it was Reyker in front of me, gripping my arms. "Lira?"

"He's here!" I glanced around in confusion, seeing only rocks and hills. "Draki."

Another spike slammed into my skull.

Reyker vanished.

Draki pressed me flat against the ice. "I wait for you."

"Get off me!"

"You called me here." He leaned in close. "You want me to release you from your noble choices, so you can taste the freedom of abandoning everything that holds you back."

"I hate you. I want nothing from you."

"I can break your chains," he said, his breath hot against my face. "I can unleash your darkest desires. And all I ask of you is to let me in. Admit that you are mine."

I looked to the scar on my wrist, hoping it would protect me.

Draki grabbed my wrist and squeezed, his thumb pressing painfully into my *skoldar*. "This cannot save you from me. *He* cannot save you."

My knife. I groped for it, aiming the blade at Draki's heart. He caught my hand, but I sliced at his biceps before he disarmed me. I struck his throat with my fist and shoved him off me, running for the mouth of the cave. It opened onto a frozen loch, and my feet slipped across its surface.

I screamed for Reyker. Where was he? Where was I?

Draki's mark burned like icicles piercing my skin. I pressed my fingers to the scar. The ice sheet covering the loch trembled.

"Lira!"

"Reyker?" He sounded so close. There were rocks breaking through the ice, grass dotting its white expanse. Something rippled on the fringe of my vision—two halves of the same world separated by a thin, lacy veil.

Waves of pain. Like my brain was smashing itself against my skull, trying to break loose.

"You cannot run from me, little warrior," Draki shouted merrily from the cave's maw. "I will find you, no matter where you go."

The ice weakened beneath me, my feet sinking up to my ankles.

I pulled myself out, only to sink again, every step harder than the last. Footsteps and shouts echoed behind me. A sudden gap appeared in the air before me, revealing the steep hills of the Green Desert. I hurried toward it, my only means of escape.

A sharp crack, and the ice broke, submerging me to my waist. My limbs were dead weight, my skirts floating around me. I couldn't move.

Draki was coming. He would catch me.

I sank deeper.

My hand was captured in a strong grip, my palm pressed flat to warm skin.

"You're safe, Lira." Reyker's thoughts caress me, calming me. *"Draki isn't here. He's only in your head."*

"No, he found me, Reyker. He came after me."

"Draki's not here, I swear to you. Whatever you saw wasn't real. If you get confused, listen to me. Look at me. Trust me. Now, come out."

My hand slipped from Reyker's chest. I was in his lap, his arms around me. "Lira?"

Rocks rattled inside my head, making me dizzy.

I was in Draki's lap. Silver hair falling across his shoulders, teeth flashing in his glorious face. "You lie to yourself. I know you wait for me, as I wait for you. It won't be long now."

I squeezed my eyes shut.

Reyker's whispers brushed my ear, soothing me. He held my hands firmly in his. I took a shaky breath and tried again.

The world came back into focus.

Draki was gone. Two mounted riders circled us, their spears and arrows aimed at Reyker, threatening to kill him if he didn't let me go. One was a Bog Man, his clothes caked with mud. The other was a young woman with bronze skin and oval-shaped eyes, like the Sanddune natives sold as thralls in the Auk Isles.

"Stop!" I sat up, spreading my arms wide, putting myself between Reyker and the riders. "He's not hurting me. He's my friend. Please, lower your weapons."

"This *yeetozurri* is your friend?" the woman asked in a lilting accent.

"Your screams say otherwise. Who are you? What are you doing in my desert?"

"Lira of—" No. Not of Stone, not anymore. "I'm Lira, and this is Reyker. We were attacked by Dragonmen. We're lost, and our horses—" I noticed the mount she rode, his smoke-gray coat, his brand matching the one on Reyker's neck. "That's my horse."

"And mine," Reyker said, pointing.

They had three other horses with them, tied to the ones they rode—Reyker's, and the horses Ulver and Einar had stolen from the Sons of Stone.

"They were no one's horses when we claimed them." The woman's brows rose. "Your name is Lira? Like the first god-gifted daughter of Glasnith?"

"Yes."

She shared a look with the Bog Man, and they lowered their weapons. "It seems you are a long way from home. I am Zabelle, and my companion here is Mago. This desert belongs to us—to all the nomads. If you seek aid, there is a safe place I can take you. But him …" Her eyes slanted toward Reyker. "His kind does not deserve shelter. They invade our desert, seize our camps, rape and slaughter and steal."

Reyker shook his head. "I'm not your enemy. If you help us, I'll prove it."

"It's true," I said. "He's not one of them. I swear it on my life." The two of us stood, our hands clasped together.

Mago patted his spear. "Try anything, Westlander, and I'll kill you where you stand."

"You are lucky," Zabelle said. "The nomad code allows everyone a chance to prove their worth. Ride with your *yeetozurri*, Lira of Stone. Ensure your friend behaves." She cut one of the extra horses free. Then Zabelle whistled and Wraith took off, Mago following with the other horses.

"Wait. Did she call me …" I glanced at Reyker, but he only shrugged. Maybe Zabelle recognized the symbol of the Sons of Stone branded on the horses, though the way she'd glanced at Mago when I gave her my name made me suspect there was something she wasn't telling us.

We climbed onto the horse's back and I leaned against Reyker, passing him the reins. One of his arms circled my waist. He nudged the horse's flanks, and it raced after the nomads.

"Where are we going?" I asked Zabelle when we caught up.

She grinned. "To my palace in the sky."

CHAPTER 33

As the first hints of dawn burnished the sky, Zabelle stopped by a gorge cutting through the center of the moorlands—narrow enough to hurl a stone from one side to the other, but deep, with a fast-flowing river at its core far below. "We are here," she said.

The nomads dismounted, so Reyker and I did too. "What do you mean?" I asked. "There's no palace here, no settlement of any kind."

"You cannot see?" There was a challenge in her tone. She gestured at the gorge. "It is there."

"This is a joke?" Reyker asked.

"No, it's a test," Mago said, taking hold of the horses' reins and stepping off the edge of the gorge. The nomad and all five horses disappeared.

"A spell." I saw it now, a glimmer in the air—something suspended above the gorge. I'd seen something like it before; the same sort of veil hid the entrance to Aillira's Temple. "What dark power did this?"

"Not dark," Zabelle said. "Gifted."

"You mean god-gifted? Are there Daughters of Aillira here?"

Rather than answer, Zabelle leaped into the gorge and was gone.

Standing at the gorge's rim, I held my arm out as far as it would go.

My fingers met resistance, and as I pushed against it, my whole hand vanished. I yanked it back with a gasp.

Reyker and I looked at each other. There was such trust in his gaze—if I believed, he would follow. I took his hand, and we stood together on the edge. "Ready?"

He squeezed my hand.

My heart pounded as I stretched my foot out, leaning forward. Reyker stepped with me. The air was thick, like walking through a heavy curtain, but we forced our way through it.

Our feet touched ground.

There was no gorge. We stood at the gated entrance of a tent-filled village, bustling with a strange array of people. Men and women of all ages, dark and light skin, hair of varying colors and lengths, familiar and unfamiliar accents, warrior-marks and odd clothing. All of them, here, together. Pausing to gape at us.

We gaped back.

Even through my shock, I was enamored with this place. It was so *alive*. There were people here from all over the world, all those different far-off lands I'd always wished to visit. I wanted them to teach me their native languages, tell me their countries' legends.

One of the nomads drew a sword. "Invader!" he shouted. Other nomads reached for their weapons. I raised my short sword, and Reyker grabbed his axe.

"All is well, my friends. They are guests," Zabelle said, appearing at the village gates. She waved for us to enter.

The nomads stared a moment longer before lowering their blades and going about their business. That was all it took.

I turned to Zabelle. "Are you their chieftain?"

"There are no chieftains in Ghost Village. I am their ally. Their sister. Their queen, and their equal. Now, I must insist you hand over your weapons."

"No," Reyker and I answered at the same time.

"They'll be returned when you leave, or if we deem it appropriate. Until then, you are quite safe."

"Is he?" I nodded at Reyker.

"The penalty for killing a guest in Ghost Village is death. But if it pleases you, I will have Mago guard him. We have much to offer—food and drink, baths and beds. Healers."

I glanced down at myself, then at Reyker. We were dirty, injured, exhausted.

I handed over my sword. My knife, I kept strapped to my thigh. Reyker had knives hidden in his boots as well. Zabelle wasn't stupid; she eyed our ankles but didn't ask. "May your gods curse you, should you prove false," I added.

She slung our weapons over her shoulder. "You are quite spirited. You will fit in well here."

Zabelle led us through the village. There must have been fifty tents made of animal hides, large enough to house families. Children squealed, chasing each other. Dogs, goats, and sheep wandered freely, and horses roamed the hills beyond. People tended fires, cooking and conversing. Some smiled at us, while others glared. All of them seemed curious.

There was a long tent near the center of the village, and Zabelle ushered us inside, where Mago sat with several other men and women on the rug-covered floor. They looked up as we entered. "These are some of the elders of our village," Zabelle said. "Sit, both of you. Let us share our tales."

One by one, we did.

Mago was a mercenary exile from the Boglands. Zabelle was an escaped slave from Sanddune. The others' names I forgot, but they were all refugees who'd fled or been forced to leave their homes. They were not lepers and thieves, as I'd mistakenly believed. They were victims of circumstance. Outcasts.

So were Reyker and I. That much was clear as we took turns telling our own stories.

"For many years," Zabelle said, "nomads were scattered across the desert. The clans of Glasnith bring iron fists down on those they think weak and unworthy. The exiled come to us, and we embrace them. Now the *yeetozurris*—the pretty giants—invade, bringing death and ruin." She looked at Reyker, who returned her gaze evenly. "It was the prince who finally brought the nomads together, showing us how to use our gifts to protect each other. We have cooks and hunters, blacksmiths and warriors, seers and magi. Our settlements grow large and strong. Let the other clans and *yeetozurris* war and die. Nomads will thrive. The prince will lead us."

I leaned forward. "The prince?"

"The Prince of Ghosts," Mago said. "His coming was foretold in the Forbidden Scriptures. A scion of the blood of Aillira and Veronis. An outcast, traveling into the desert when he was needed most, defying death to rise from the ashes. He came to us three moons ago, a warrior half dead from a festering wound. But he lived. He united us."

"Three moons?" I murmured, thinking. "You're telling me the Forbidden Scriptures contain prophesies about nomads?"

"The Forbidden Scriptures contain prophesies about many things," Zabelle said.

So she believed in them too, despite being a foreigner to Glasnith.

"You've come to us on the final night of the Birth of Summer festival. Stay and rejoice with us. We will show you what it means to be nomad. For now, you are in need of baths. Mago will show your pretty giant where to go. Lira, you will come with me."

My fingers were still clasped in Reyker's. I was reluctant to let go.

"You are both safe here," Zabelle said. "My people will not harm you. None would dare break the prince's law."

Reyker kissed my hand and released it.

Zabelle led me across the village, to the women's baths, which consisted of three large tubs inside a medium-sized tent. At a word from Zabelle, several nomad women brought in pails of fire-warmed water, filling one of the tubs. I stripped and sank into it with a sigh.

"You called me Lira of Stone, but I never told you what clan I was from. You trusted me enough to bring us to your hidden village though you don't even know me."

Zabelle's eyes were brown with hints of orange, like topaz, and they displayed shrewd intelligence. She sat on a bench in the corner, arms crossed, regarding me silently.

"You know, I lost something I treasured three moons ago. Perhaps it found its way into the desert." I lathered my skin with tallow. "Tell me, is your prince all Mago claims him to be?"

"More." Her guarded expression slipped. Adoration flickered across her face. "Stay and you may meet him. He is south of here, guiding the dispossessed seeking sanctuary, but I will send word of your arrival. If he's intrigued, he will come."

I ducked under the water, afraid to hope, afraid not to. "Why would he care?"

"Perhaps you are someone's lost treasure as well."

Let it be him, I prayed. An enigmatic prince, cobbling together his own clan of outcasts in the desert. *Please tell me, at long last, I've found my brother.*

Once I was clean, Zabelle showed me to a spare tent, empty but for a fur-covered pallet. Tossing my dress aside, I crawled onto the pallet in only my shift.

I fell asleep and dreamed.

I stand in a green, rock-strewn field. I can't see him, but I feel him: He is near and far, both at once. Waiting. He won't come unless I call him. I shouldn't call him. But I have to know.

"Draki."

His laughter is soft, sensual. I follow it until I find him. He stands on the frozen loch, in a realm of blue ice. "Where have you gone, little warrior?"

"Beyond your reach." Between us, the earth is cracked, separating his world from mine. Mist billows up from the fissure, swirling around us.

"Nowhere is beyond my reach."

"I'm one girl. My gift won't help you defeat armies. So what do you want from me? Why can't you leave us alone?"

"Us." He cocks his head. "Who is with you? Someone who thinks to keep you from me? Someone who believes he can take what is mine? Maybe if you give yourself up, I will spare him. Maybe I will spare those who are hiding you. But only if you tell me where you are."

"How bloody stupid do you think I am?"

"Stupid enough to believe this is only about you."

No. Not me. Reyker helped me escape Draki the first time he came after me. Reyker gave me his skoldar. *For Draki, stealing me is about hurting Reyker—the traitorous Dragonman he thinks of as a son.*

"I will find you," Draki says. "And him. I always do."

Distance makes me feel safe. Without Draki's hands on me, my thoughts are clear, seething with rage. "Not this time, Savage."

Draki smiles. "We shall see."

CHAPTER 34

Sometime later, I woke. I rolled over and found Reyker sitting beside the pallet, hand on his dagger. "Did something happen?"

"No." His hair was damp, his face clean. "I worry."

"About the nomads?"

He shook his head. "The Dragon."

"Draki invaded my mind, Reyker. I felt him inside my thoughts." And not for the first time.

Reyker opened his arms and I crawled into them. He rested his chin on top of my head. "It is the power Ildja gave him." He circled his thumb over the scar of flame on my wrist. "You wear my *skoldar*. He sees it as a challenge. A game, to figure out what it takes to overcome it."

I touched my fingers to the scar behind my ear. The Star of the Dragon. "This is how he finds me. How he tries to control me. His mark." I moved my hair aside, pulling out my knife and putting it in Reyker's hand. "Cut it off me."

Reyker stared at the blade, all the color draining from his cheeks.

"Without the mark, he can't find me. If Draki takes control of my mind again ..." Would I be able to resist him next time? "Please, Reyker."

"I can't." His hand shook. He dropped the knife. "Draki's mark goes deeper than skin. It's in your blood. It's part of you." He ran his fingertip along the veins in my neck, just beneath the scar. "If I remove the mark, you will die."

"But—"

"Stop, Lira. I know what I speak of. I've seen it happen. Do not ask me for this." He picked up my knife, slipping it back into the sheath on my thigh.

"What of my *skoldar*? Is it part of me too?"

He nodded. "Draki's power is vast, so he can mark anyone. My power is limited, so I can only mark another *magiska*, and only once. You're the only one who'll ever bear my *skoldar*."

If Draki was in my blood, then so was Reyker. And I was in his—the only one who ever would be. "Good," I said, surprised at the sharpness in my voice.

Reyker's mouth twitched, like he wanted to smile. He blinked heavily. There were bruise-colored shadows beneath his eyes, weariness weighing him down like an anchor. I remembered something from Reyker's memories: how he'd refused to sleep, telling his mother, *He finds me there*. "Draki's done this to you too. Gotten inside your head. Inside your dreams. That's why you don't like to sleep."

"Sleep leaves the mind weak." He touched my temple. "Draki can sneak inside, like a rat."

"Whatever magic conceals Ghost Village shields us from Draki. He can't find us. We're safe here. Our dreams are safe too."

Reyker eyed me doubtfully.

"Come here. Lie down."

When he didn't move, I tugged his boots off, then his tunic, drawing him onto the pallet. A healer had stitched up the wound on his biceps where I'd stabbed him, when I mistook him for Draki. I ran my finger along the sutures. "I'm sorry. I didn't mean to hurt you."

"I know. You fought well. Like a fierce deer."

I had to smile. "We're not leaving this bed until you do something for me." I pushed him onto his back. His brow arched suggestively, his gaze wandering over my thin shift. "Sleep. At least a few hours."

I closed his eyelids with my fingertips. "Let me guard your dreams."

"Or fierce deer will stab me more?"

"Never." I laid down beside him, propped on my elbow. "I'll just drug you again."

"What?"

"Hush. Sleep, my wolf."

It didn't take long. As I stroked his hair, the tension seeped from his muscles. His face transformed from fearsome warrior to vulnerable young man. I rested my head next to his, watching him for signs of nightmares, but he slept peacefully. "You see?" I whispered, my own eyes drifting shut. "We're safe."

Blessedly. Finally. Safe.

———◆———

I woke to the warmth of Reyker's arms. When I stirred, his lips touched my ear. My neck. My shoulder. I yawned and smiled, turning to face him. "You seem well rested."

"Good dreams." His eyes shone like crystals of sea ice, roaming over me. His fingers slipped along my jaw, brushing my hair back. They stroked the skin of my collarbones, then lower, following the sweeping neckline of my shift.

Dazed with desire, I let my worries slip free. "Is this real, Reyker? You and me?"

He drew back. "You are afraid?"

"Not of you." I brushed my thumb across his warrior-mark. "Of this. Us, together. Is this a passing affection, or something more?"

"It's real for me." He pressed my hand to his chest. "Look in my soul. You will see."

His heart, beating beneath my palm. Solid. True.

Ours was not a patient world—there wasn't time to learn each other gradually, to give part of ourselves until we were sure of things. I could trust Reyker, or not trust him. I could give all of myself, or none. There could be no half measures for us. Not when we risked so much just by caring for each other.

"I don't need to look. I trust you. But everything in our world wants to tear us apart."

"We must fight our world. We let nothing come between us."

"Nothing," I agreed, my hands gliding beneath his tunic. "Is this place beautiful?"

He laughed, a rich rumble filling my ears. "Beautiful enough." His lips brushed the skin left bare by my shift, and I dug my fingers into his hair.

Zabelle chose that moment to barge in unannounced, carrying a stack of clothes, which she threw at us unceremoniously. "There is plenty of time for love later, *yeetozurri*." She waved a dismissive hand at Reyker. "Go to your tent. Mago and the others will ready you for the festival. Soon we dance, drink, and feast to honor the season."

Reyker growled in frustration.

"Later, *yeetozurri*," I promised as he pulled away.

When he was gone, Zabelle helped me with the gown she'd brought. "An odd match, you and that one," she said. "Like fire and water. Yet somehow you fit."

"We do." Being with Reyker felt natural—like rain feeding rivers, sunlight reeling life from the earth. "Speaking of fitting, why am I wearing this?" It was a simple gown of bright green, the same color as my eyes, with tiny flowers embroidered along the hem. The gown was snug, the bodice cut low. Zabelle was dressed in boyish garb, a gray tunic and brown trousers, and I envied her.

"I will let Eathalin explain. Ah, here she is."

A slender girl of thirteen or so with stick-straight apricot hair entered the tent with a pouch slung over her arm and offered me a shy smile. "The gown is perfect on you. It's meant to look like a summer garden. But your hair ... Well, may I?" She gestured at my unruly locks.

I nodded and sat on the pallet as Eathalin combed my hair, winding it with silver ribbons and taming it into braids. She gushed about the Birth of Summer festival. "It's an old tradition, welcoming the season when the world is warm and every creature seeks a mate. It honors the first summer, when Aillira met Veronis. It's custom to reenact their first kiss, and I thought because you're here, and she's your namesake, you should play blessed Aillira."

"I've never celebrated the Birth of Summer. My clan outlaws the rituals of the Forbidden Scriptures. Our priests declared any veneration of the Great Betrayer blasphemous."

The girl gestured to my medallion, bared by my low-cut gown. "Those who follow the Forbidden Scriptures honor the abiding love between Aillira and Veronis. The symbol you wear is the thorntree Aillira planted in the ruins of her palace and watered with her tears after Veronis was imprisoned. It still stands, a living tribute to their love, the oldest tree in all of Glasnith."

Though I'd not known the story behind it, I'd seen this tree with my own eyes. The great thorntree at Aillira's Temple.

I stared down at my mother's medallion. Would I ever know how she came to worship Veronis and the Fallen Ones?

"It seems many nomads believe in the Forbidden Scriptures," I said. "Those from Glasnith, and those from other lands as well."

Zabelle smiled. "From near or far, we all came to be here after ill fortune found us. Nomads have been labeled heathens and criminals. How could we not sympathize with the Fallen Ones, when we too are fallen? We foreigners still honor the gods of our homelands, but we find room in our hearts and prayers for Aillira and Veronis, brought to ruin by their own families, trampled on by those seeking greater power. Not so different from us."

No, not so different. I shared far more with my ancestor than a gift and a name.

Eathalin opened a small tin of crushed petals and glazed my lips rose and my eyelids lilac. "There. A near goddess, wrought in flesh. Worthy of a god's ardor."

I snorted.

"Perhaps in looks, but not manners," Zabelle added. "Come, boorish goddess."

"Wait." Eathalin took a slip of parchment from her pouch and handed it to me.

The parchment was old, worn. I unfolded it and stared at the words, handwritten in the ancient tongue, the ink faded. Several seconds passed before I could speak. "Is this what I think it is?"

Eathalin nodded. "A copied passage from the Forbidden Scriptures. Every book may have burned, but not every page did. Some stories refuse to remain untold."

I read the verse again:

> *From the guise of the great raptor, Veronis gazed*
> *   upon her:*
> *Sweet like honey, fresh like dew, a mortal heart*
> *   thumping within her breast.*
> *Aillira, child of the earth, daughter of the dust.*
> *A moment. A breath. The fire of a thousand suns.*
> *   The rise and fall of empires.*
> *Silence. His choice. The death of a god.*
> *Then, a vibration. A harmony.*
> *His newly mortal heart beating in time with hers.*

Veronis had given up everything—his immortality, his status, his powers—to be with Aillira. There was a time when I would have wondered why, but I was beginning to understand. Some things, some people, were worth risking everything for.

I started to hand the parchment back to Eathalin, but she shook her head. "Keep it. I have my own copy. Read it when you have doubts. It will give you strength."

"Thank you." I folded the page and, as Eathalin and Zabelle ducked out of the tent ahead of me, tucked it discreetly into the sheath with my knife.

We emerged into twilight. This corner of the camp was deserted, but I heard noises on the other side. I was suddenly nervous. "If I'm to play the role of Aillira, what must I do?"

"It's the role you were chosen to play." Eathalin's hand squeezed mine. "When you see Veronis, Aillira's spirit will fill you, and you will know."

The festival had begun. Shouts of celebration rang through the camp. We came upon the crowd, and I saw it clearly, nomads of all cultures and ages gathered together, talking, laughing. Atop a raised wooden platform, a woman and two men played a jaunty tune on fiddles and flutes while people clapped and danced in spirited disorder. The mood was joyous.

In the middle of the gala, one man stood out even among the distinctive nomads. He wore a crisp white tunic, matching deerskin jerkin and trousers—the way Veronis once wore the form of a deer to spy upon Aillira. His hair hung loose around his shoulders, with a few small braids slinking through it. His eyes were a calm, bright ocean.

Eathalin urged me forward. "Not yet," I said, watching Reyker.

Despite their wary reception when we'd arrived, the nomads seemed drawn to him. Men spoke with him eagerly, throwing an arm around his shoulders as they leaned in to hear his response. Women stared with rapt desire, batting their lashes. He talked and laughed, completely at ease. It made my heart swell.

My presence sent ripples through the crowd, nomads elbowing and whispering. The musicians' song ended abruptly.

Reyker was one of the last to turn. His eyes met mine, widening. The nomads between us parted. The men kneeled and the women curtsied, like we were royalty.

Mago lifted Eathalin onto the platform. She stood beside the musicians and cleared her throat, until everyone fell silent. When she spoke, her voice was clear, resonating through the camp. "Once the world had only three seasons: autumn, winter, and spring. On a night like this, many moons ago, Aillira, the first god-gifted daughter of Glasnith, met Veronis, god of all creatures." Translations wended through the crowd, ensuring all the nomads understood. "The heat of their love created summer. It is that love we honor tonight."

Reyker and I stared as if seeing each other for the first time. This was mere pageantry, yet Eathalin had spoken truly. I was filled with the wonder of it, like the gods themselves were in attendance, like Aillira whispered in my ear: *Go to your Veronis.*

We moved toward each other slowly. Aillira and Veronis. Lira and Reyker.

When he was an arm's-length away, Reyker kneeled and bowed his head, hands crossed over his heart. "Aillira, light of my soul."

I took hold of his chin, lifting it to gaze upon his face.

In his eyes, I saw our past. The first time we met, when I was nothing but a captive girl from a foreign land, and he'd cut his mark in my skin to shield me. When I killed a Westlander and he wiped the blood from my hands. Asking me to run with him, killing his brethren to save me, wrenching my mind from Draki's grip.

I saw Aillira and Veronis too, gazing into each other's eyes through us, their love burning hot enough to heat the world and incite wars between mortals and immortals alike.

I didn't know if it was my voice or Aillira's that said, "Rise, Veronis, blood of my heart."

He shot to his feet, arms circling my waist. His lips touched mine, and we burned. Lira and Aillira. We held them hard, kissed them deeply. Reyker and Veronis.

The crowd cheered, showering us with the milk-white petals of moon-flowers, falling over us like summer rain. I heard Eathalin, sounding far away. "My friends, tonight and all nights, I bid you to burn brightly and love fiercely. For all else is dust!"

"All else is dust!" the nomads chanted in response.

Our kiss was enduring. A single moment unfolded into many, with the two of us suspended inside each one. We lived lifetimes in the span of heartbeats, ours and the characters we'd embodied, brought to life by each other's lips.

It went on so long the nomads coughed into their hands. They joked and heckled. When that didn't stop us, they lost interest. The musicians started to play again. The dancing began anew. "Cut the beast!" someone shouted. Others echoed the sentiment.

Reyker tensed, pulling back to reach for his hidden dagger.

No, I seethed. *No one will hurt you. No one will take you from me.* I spun toward the voices, grappling for my own knife, ready to fight with him. Ready to kill for him.

I saw Mago carving up a roasted boar, passing around portions of meat.

"Cut the beast," Reyker said with a laugh.

He pulled me against him, and I relaxed at the soft sound of his laughter. It loosened the spell. The spirits of the first god-gifted daughter and her divine lover left us. I was simply Lira. He was only Reyker.

It was more than enough.

CHAPTER 35

The festival was a chaotic, jubilant affair.

We dined on roasted boar. We drank ale and cider and foul things brewed in casks for months that the nomads swore would help us live a hundred years or conceive ten strong warrior sons. Reyker raised his tankard at me, and I blushed.

Mago beckoned to us from the bonfire, eager to talk of weaponry with a Westlander. He showed us his Bog Man spear, pointing at the white splinters jutting from its tip. "Adder fangs. We use them in spears and arrows. Each fang holds drops of venom. A single drop from a glancing blow sickens a man, weakens him instantly. A direct hit lodges them deep in the flesh, enough to kill within hours. Shower arrows on an army from a distance and you can defeat them without engagement. Even if your enemy escapes, he won't survive. There's no antidote."

I edged back a bit. "Seems unduly risky. What if you nick yourself?"

He pressed his thumb against a fang, drawing blood.

I gasped, but Mago laughed. "I'm immune," he explained. "All Bog Men are. It's only deadly to the rest of you."

Reyker leaned in to inspect the fangs. A knot clenched my stomach suddenly, a finger of unease sliding down my spine. I grabbed his shoulder. "Don't."

He looked at me, reading something in my face, and stopped.

"I've recruited the best archers and spear-throwers among the nomads. I'm training them to use Bog Men weapons," Mago said. "The hardest part is gathering the adders, though we've done a fair job. Zabelle hates the idea, but the prince believes we should make use of all our defensive skills."

"Unlike me," Zabelle said from behind us, "the prince has more faith in his warriors' skills than concern for their blunders. Put that spear away, Mago, before you kill our guests."

Mago gave her a chastised grin and slid the weapon into its thick sheath.

I wondered if Garreth could truly be a leader to these people, some of them from the mercenary clans he'd once hated. Then again, I was consorting with a Westlander. Perhaps Garreth had also learned to see past what his eyes told him and listen with his heart.

Zabelle took my empty tankard and her own, passing them to Reyker and Mago. "Bring your womenfolk more ale, my hearty warriors."

As they left, she sat down beside me. "Even before Ghost Village, nomads came together to celebrate one another's festivals. With so many people from so much of the world, there is one every moon. Though Eathalin proclaims this to be the most romantic Birth of Summer since Aillira and Veronis, thanks to you and your *yeetozurri*."

"What happened to Eathalin?" I spied the girl, dancing with the other nomads. "She's so young to be an outcast already. How did she end up here?"

"She's a spell-caster, blessed by your gods. She created the veil that hides our village. But Eathalin's people tried to force her to use her gift for wickedness. She ran away. We took her in gladly."

Eathalin's story wasn't so different from my own. "Why didn't she seek refuge at Aillira's Temple?"

"She did. They turned her away. Your temple does not accept exiles. Those who run from their clans are considered apostates."

I'd not known this, and it infuriated me. How dare the priestesses deny shelter to a Daughter of Aillira, especially one who needed their protection? It was a heavy blow to my hopes that anyone in Aillira's Temple would listen to my pleas for help against the Dragonmen, because I was an apostate now too.

"We want you to stay," Zabelle said. "To become nomads. Both of you."

"So you can use us."

"No more than your own clan. Your gift, and your *yeetozurri's* knowledge and skills, can help us protect ourselves. But we ask for it freely. No chains, no torture. Where else on Glasnith is he safe? Where else can he court you openly?"

I glanced at Reyker, laughing at something Mago was saying. I'd abandon Stony Harbor to keep him safe from Torin and anyone else who wanted to hurt him, but could I really stay here and hide while Draki slowly conquered Glasnith and enslaved my people? Was that Garreth's plan—to let the clans and the Dragonmen kill each other off?

"Tell me your prince's name, Zabelle."

"We tell no one our prince's identity. It is dangerous for him. If you wish to know, you must wait here until he comes and ask him yourself." Zabelle stood, casting a furtive look at me. "You should stay, Lira. Not only for us, but for you and your mate. Fate is not kind to those who tempt it, and I fear you are not safe beyond this village." She left me to ponder her warning.

The night continued.

Reyker and I were coaxed into joining in the dances. Nearly every nomad wanted a dance with Aillira or Veronis, and it seemed like hours before we finally made it back to each other, too tired to do more than move in slow circles.

I leaned against him. "This morning you were an invader, and now the nomads respect you as an equal. I can't believe you charmed them so quickly."

"I charmed you."

"You grew on me. Like moss. And it took weeks." I ran one of his braids through my fingers. "Tell me. What changed?"

"Before you came as Aillira, the nomads asked me questions. About

Iseneld. My family. You." He smiled. "When I spoke, they no longer saw a Dragonman. They saw a good man. The man you made me."

"Reyker. There was always goodness in you. Others tried to bury it. You lost yourself. I helped find you, that's all."

"You found me." He kissed the top of my head. "It is everything."

I settled deeper into his arms. "The nomads want us to stay in Ghost Village. What do you think? I know you must go back to Iseneld soon." To free his people. By facing Draki. It was his destiny, one I was meant to help him achieve according to the mystic, even though I hated the thought. "But could you be happy here until then?"

I felt him nod. "If we are together, I can be happy."

Reyker started to say something else, but a cry of anguish near the village entrance brought the gala to a standstill. The music and voices died. A cluster of men and horses were at the gates, shouting for help.

Nomads rushed forward, and Reyker and I followed. The men who'd arrived were bloody, some badly injured; healers took charge, barking orders, cleaning and binding what wounds they could. We circled around to where Zabelle questioned one of the men.

"Invaders attacked us," the man was telling her. "We were camped near Moon Hill, about four leagues from here. There were only ten of them, but their leader was there, the giant yellow-eyed beast."

Reyker's arm slid around me.

"They were looking for a girl. When they didn't find her, they killed half our men and took our women."

I put a hand over my mouth.

"Was your party followed?" Mago asked. We all glanced at the gates. If the Dragonmen found their way through the spell, they would invade Ghost Village. They would destroy it.

"No. We made certain of it. But we've a few men still out there." The nomad's voice faltered. "They're bringing along the corpses."

"I did this," I murmured. The dream. *Not this time, Savage.* "I taunted him."

Reyker shook his head, shushing me.

Five men lay injured on the ground, shouting or weeping from pain.

Two others were eerily silent. Healers crouched by each man. "We need you, Lira," Zabelle said.

I let go of Reyker, moving to Zabelle's side. "What can I do? I'm not a healer."

"Not of bodies. But you can calm them."

"I've never—"

"Please." Her expression was grim. These were her friends, her people. They suffered, and there was nothing she could do.

"I'll try."

I went to the man crying loudest. He was spattered with dirt and blood, and a healer was sewing up a gaping wound over his rib cage. Two nomads held him down as he thrashed. I knelt beside him, taking his hand.

"You're all right," I lied. I could see muscle and bone. His chances weren't good.

I laid my palm on his chest, entering his soul.

It was clouded, disarrayed. I waded through images and landscapes, not knowing what to do. I was used to looking for guilt. With Reyker, I'd plucked his memories randomly.

No, not randomly. I'd learned how to read each memory's mood by the way it was presented. Dark pasts were buried, dull-hued. Pleasant ones were easily reached. They gleamed.

Concentrating on the shifting realms of the nomad's soul, I found a meadow full of horses. Some were monstrous and regal, others shaggy and gentle. I wandered among them. Many shied and fled, but a few came close, sniffing me. I chose a white mare that reminded me of Winter, pressing my face to her coat. "Show me," I said.

The mare reared. The memory sprang forth.

He runs through the tall grass, chasing her. She runs, laughing, her long hair trailing behind. He catches her, arms around her waist, swinging her off her feet. She holds his face, kissing him. They whisper sweet words to each other. This, the moment he realizes he loves her.

"Stay here," I tell him. "Stay with her until the pain ends."

I released his soul, pulling myself free.

When I opened my eyes, the man was quiet, lids drooping, face calm. Being inside Reyker's memories was like wearing his skin, breathing his breath, sharing his every emotion. This had been different. I'd experienced, but not embodied. Even so, I'd connected with this man. I bent to kiss his brow and whispered in his ear, "Fight. Live. Return to her."

The healer finished the man's sutures. She nodded her thanks to me, and I stood, looking to aid the next man who needed it.

One of the nomads who'd been attacked was standing nearby, staring at me.

"The Dragon sought a god-gifted girl," the nomad said, his gaze dark and wild. "With hair like ripe plums and eyes as green as leaves. He said she belongs to him and bears his mark as proof." The man darted forward, grabbing me, fingers digging for the scar behind my ear. "It's her! The Dragon said we could trade her for our women! We can get them back!"

The words had scarcely left his mouth before Reyker was there, tearing the man off me, shoving him away.

"They took nine of our women!" the man screamed.

My stomach twisted. Nine women. Taken, because Draki couldn't find me. What would happen to them? Was one my injured nomad's woman, whom I'd told him to fight to return to?

"We just give him the girl and he'll give our women back unharmed! He swore it."

"He won't," Reyker said, blocking the man, keeping him at bay. "He lies."

"They took my wife, my sisters!" The man addressed the gathered crowd, pointing at me. "She's one girl, not even one of us. Why protect her?"

Other nomads mumbled, divided. Some nodded agreement, others shook their heads. "She's a guest. The code says we owe her sanctuary," one said.

"We owe her nothing. The Dragon followed her here. I say give her to him!" shouted another. The crowd became a mob, nomads jostling, arguing, pushing at each other, eyeing me.

I searched for Zabelle and Mago, but they'd rushed off to meet with the other nomad leaders. There were few friendly faces here. Those who had danced with us and cheered for Aillira and Veronis's first kiss had turned against us when forced to choose between us and their own people.

Reyker drew his hidden dagger.

At the sight of his weapon, the mob drew swords and spears. "See how they deceive us! They violated the code themselves!"

The man who'd started all this was losing his wits, sobbing and shouting. "My wife! My sisters! Give him the girl and he'll give them back." He tried to dodge around Reyker to get to me.

Reyker was too quick, locking his arm around the man's neck. "I'm sorry. He lies. He will never give your family back."

"The girl! Take the girl!" The man pleaded with the crowd.

A few of them stepped forward. Reyker unsheathed the sword of the man trapped in his grip, lowering it at them.

"You're one of them." The crazed man squinted up at Reyker in sudden realization. "He's one of them! A beast!"

"Stop!" I leaned around Reyker, who stood like a shield between me and the mob. I sought words they couldn't ignore. I sought Garreth's fortitude. "You nomads call yourselves a clan? You want respect from the rest of Glasnith? Then stop acting like barbarians! What would your prince say if he was here?"

There was more mumbling. "Who does she think she is? She doesn't know us."

"She's right, though."

I pointed at the man who said this. "Go find Zabelle and the other leaders. No killing or trading will happen without consulting them first."

He ran. The mob stared at me.

Reyker kept his sword raised in warning. The wild-eyed nomad struggled in Reyker's grasp. "Let go of me! He'll kill us all! Vile, soulless beast!"

I hadn't noticed the lagging group of nomads riding through the gates toward us, bloody and weary from the attack, ferrying their dead. I caught a flicker of movement and turned to see a boy on a horse, his familiar face bright with rage.

His bow was drawn. Arrow nocked. String taut. I remembered where I'd seen him, in Reyker's memories, just as his finger slipped from the string.

My vision blurred, washed in red.

My scream was slower than his arrow.

CHAPTER 36

REYKER

Reyker's eyes were on the circle of nomads, his ears full of shrieks from the man he'd pinned. He barely heard it, the snapping *whisk* of an arrow. But he felt it, slamming into his shoulder blade, throwing him off balance.

He heard Lira scream.

His grip loosened on the nomad. As the raving man tried to slip away, Reyker punched him at the base of his skull and the man fell to the ground, unconscious.

Where the arrow hit, Reyker's skin tingled, a slow pulse throbbing deep in his flesh.

He saw the boy, sitting atop a horse, already nocking another arrow. The witness from the Rocky Isles. The one Reyker saved. The boy carried death in his eyes.

Retribution.

"No!" Lira screamed.

Mago had appeared and had both arms around her, holding her back. If she got free, she would throw herself in front of Reyker, thinking the boy wouldn't risk shooting her. Reyker knew better. The boy's hate blinded him. He would go through Lira to reach his target.

"Do not let her go!" Reyker shouted at Mago.

The boy aimed the arrow at Reyker's chest. "To your knees, beast." He looked at Lira. "Your woman? I'll hear you beg for your life before her. Let everyone see how weak you are without an army at your back."

Reyker closed his eyes briefly. The black river roiled.

A boy, he is only a boy. "I'm sorry for what I did to your people. You deserve vengeance. But I can't let you take it. Not like this."

"Silence, frost devil. You will cower before me. Listen to your woman wail. It's the last sound you'll hear in this world."

Reyker's fingers tightened on the sword hilt.

"Brayen, put down your weapon." Zabelle crept forward, hands steady on her bow. She had an arrow aimed at the boy. "This man is our guest. We do not allow bloodshed within Ghost Village."

"Guest?" Brayen spit. "He killed my kin! I won't suffer him to live!"

"You forget yourself, Skerrian. This is the prince's village, and in his absence, *I* am prince. Do as I say or I'll shoot between your legs and let Eathalin dress you in skirts."

"The prince will understand. This, I do for Skerrey." Brayen released the string.

Reyker lunged sideways, sweeping the sword in an arc, slicing Brayen's arrow in half. The sword was heavy in his hand. Too heavy.

Zabelle fired a half second after, her arrow catching the boy's arm. She dropped her bow and leaped, grabbing Brayen's leg, pulling him off the horse. "It doesn't matter," Brayen said. "He's already dead. I already killed you, beast!"

Reyker concentrated on the pain, the dull ache spreading from his shoulder, down his arm, up his neck. Liquid fire, seeping through his veins.

Brayen's quiver had fallen, arrows scattering across the ground. Zabelle picked one up, frowning at the arrowhead. The white splinters sticking from its tip.

Fangs.

Reyker's arm twitched. The sword slipped from his fingers. He stared at it, lying at his feet. He'd expected death to catch him, but not like this. Killed by a mere boy. A boy he'd saved.

A spate of wild laughter burst from Reyker's lungs.

Lira broke out of Mago's grasp, running to him. His knees shook from the effort of bearing his weight. He let them quit, kneeling in the dirt, laughing like a madman. Lira reached him, cupping his face, whispering his name.

His veins were on fire. He scratched at them, clawed at them, until he was tearing bloody gouges into his skin, trying to rip his veins out. Lira trapped his wrists, calling for a healer.

Reyker bowed his head, laughing at the pain, at the gods, at the inevitable justice of it all.

He stood outside himself, watching from a distance, as Lira fed him liquor from Zabelle's flask, cut his jerkin and tunic off, slipped a belt between his teeth. He bit down on it as Zabelle worked the arrowhead backward through the muscles in his shoulder, blood spilling down his back. When the arrow was out, a healer dug into the wound with pincers, extracting two curved slivers—venom-filled adder fangs—before bandaging his wound.

Reyker was dazed from blood loss and the venom coursing through him, half-drunk on liquor. The veins in his shoulder had turned deep violet; the color was spreading, already traveling down his arm.

"How do we get the venom out?" Lira asked.

The healer put a hand on Lira's arm. "You don't."

"There must be something! Aillira's Temple—couldn't a god-gifted healer help him?" Lira rushed at Mago, shoving the Bog Man backward. "You're the one who made the damned weapon! Don't tell me there's nothing. Don't tell me to stand here and watch him waste away from the venom of a bloody bog adder like—"

Like her ancestor Aillira. This was how she'd died.

"Inevitable," Reyker said, not sure who he was talking to, or whether he'd spoken in his native language or another. He shivered, and Eathalin came forward to wrap a cloak around him, tears slipping down her cheeks.

"No one at Aillira's Temple would agree to help a Westlander," the girl told Lira, "but there is another way." Some unspoken knowledge passed between the two Daughters of Aillira.

Reyker shook his head. "Whatever you're planning, stop it now. Draki is out there. No one is safe outside the village."

Lira's eyes met his. She gave him a fiery look, one that meant she might have slapped him if he wasn't already injured. Dying. "You sound like a coward, little lordling."

She was provoking him, as she always did when he was on the verge of giving up. She wanted him angry, so he would fight.

It worked.

Lira looked at Mago and Zabelle. "Tie him to a horse."

They rode hard.

Zabelle and Eathalin were in front, then Reyker, then Lira. Mago brought up the rear. They had tied Reyker as Lira instructed, his hands to the reins, his feet to the stirrups, his waist to the saddle. He'd cursed them for it, but he swayed in the saddle, wilted by pain and fatigue. His horse was swift and sure-footed, needing no guidance. Reyker pitied the creature. All their horses would be pushed to breaking. That was the plan.

As his body failed, Reyker's mind cleared, and the conversation he'd overheard at the camp pieced itself together slowly. The venom was wending its way through his bloodstream—he had hours left, half a day at best. There was a place in the Tangled Forest, some sort of grove with mystics and gods, where Lira insisted he could be healed. At a reasonable pace, it was more than a full day's ride. Lira meant to cover the distance much quicker. Zabelle would lead them to hidden nomad camps along the way to exchange the worn horses for fresh ones.

But leaving Ghost Village meant exposure. Eathalin was there to conceal them with one of her spells. Reyker didn't trust it; Draki was near, and he wasn't easily fooled. The warlord could still find his way inside Lira's head.

Reyker knew how it felt. Draki had done it to him for years, until he learned to build walls around his mind. They weren't impenetrable, but it kept the warlord out when he was awake or sleeping fitfully. Lira had no such shields. Draki would toy with her.

Reyker saw it when they stopped at the first camp—Lira rubbed her temples, scratched at the scar behind her ear.

Mago cut his ropes, helping him onto a new horse like he was an invalid. "How could you let Lira do this?" Reyker asked the nomads.

It was Zabelle who answered, tying Reyker's hands to the fresh horse's reins. "Look in her eyes, *yeetozurri*. No force on earth could stop her. She would battle the gods themselves before she let you die quietly. Such loyalty is rare. You'd best live to repay it."

When Lira was mounted, she rode to Reyker's side, holding a water-skin. "Drink," she ordered, lifting it to his lips.

"How's your head? Full of dragons?"

She waved her *skoldar* in his face. "I can keep Draki out, thanks to you."

"Not forever."

"As long as it takes." She peeled back the bandages to check his wound and flinched at the sight. Reyker couldn't see the wound, but he felt it swelling. His arm was numb, and all the veins from his shoulder to his wrist were bright violet.

"You tie me to a horse with no care for my pride, drag me into the desert so I can see Draki take you before I die." Anger fueled him, sharpening his tongue. "You didn't ask me what I want. It's *my* life. Do I get no choice in this?"

"No." She used the edge of the cloak to wipe the cold sweat from his forehead and neck. "Remember what you told me in the cave? Your life belongs to me. You are my sword. And I will not be disarmed."

Before Reyker could respond, she slapped his horse's haunches. They were off again.

The desert flew by in a green haze. Curled into himself, Reyker hardly noticed. The horse's steady gait jarred him, the ache piercing deep into his bones.

They reached the second camp. This time when the nomads aided him onto another horse, he cried out. It felt like their fingers had ripped off his flesh. The cloak scoured him. His skin was white as bone, all his veins glowing violet. Lira came with the waterskin once more, but he could barely sip past the tightness in his throat.

Mago lingered nearby on his mount. "We must slow down. He cannot take it. You may kill him before the venom does."

"We aren't slowing down." Lira's fingertips brushed Reyker's knuckles, as much of a caress as he could stand. "Do you trust me?" she asked.

"Can a wolf trust a deer?" He tried to smile. "I trust you. With my life. My soul. With all that I am." He coughed and droplets of blood sprayed his lips. "Lira," Reyker whispered hoarsely. There were too many things he wanted to say. There was no time.

"Ready?" Zabelle called.

No, Reyker tried to say, but Zabelle raced ahead, and all their horses followed.

He drifted in and out of awareness.

The third camp was close to the mountains. When the ropes holding Reyker in place were cut, he fell. His limbs were limp, useless. Mago caught him, struggling to settle him onto the next horse.

"Your giant cannot ride," Zabelle said. "Not like this."

"He doesn't have to." Lira climbed into the saddle with Reyker, sitting backward. She put the waterskin to his lips, but he couldn't swallow. His throat constricted, his tongue swelled. It took effort to breathe. When he spoke, his words slurred.

He'd missed his chance to tell her. One final regret added to a lifetime's worth.

Lira's face swam in his dimming vision. "We're almost there, Reyker. You can hold on." She turned, folding his arms around her. "Tie him to the saddle, and to me."

"You cannot hold him up," Mago warned.

"Don't tell me what I can do."

They entered the mountain pass.

Reyker tried to sit up, tried to stay conscious; it was like wading through snowdrifts. Lira was warm and soft, tucked inside his arms, bearing too much of his drooping weight. He held on to her. This girl, this woman. She wanted him to live. She needed him to fight.

Wait, he told the soul-eating serpent-goddess pulling him to her poisoned bosom. *Not yet.*

CHAPTER 37

As the Tangled Forest came into view, I kicked my mount hard. My horse dove into the trees, and my companions fell back. This last leg of the journey I had to do on my own.

I knew the lore. The Grove of the Fallen Ones was temperamental. It *moved*. It never left the forest, but sometimes it lay near the northern bluffs, other times it could be found at the southern edge. Occasionally it popped up right beside Stony Harbor. But it always appeared to those who sought its powers. The blind mystic had confirmed it.

Come to the forest. Seek the grove and you shall find it.
The Fallen Ones await your offering.

The mystic had seen it—she'd known something would happen to Reyker. And she'd known what I'd be willing to do to stop it.

"Hurry! Show yourself," I beseeched the grove. I led the horse around tight-knit trees, sharp roots, thornbushes, fast-moving streams. Pushing it mercilessly.

My senses were saturated by Reyker's ragged breaths, the waning heat of his body. He leaned on me heavily, but I managed. I had to.

The sounds of the forest suddenly tapered. The knotted trees we passed were covered in pestilent sores, their leaves brittle husks, their fruits rotted upon the vine. Grass and flowers withered, bleached of color. Raw pink animal carcasses hung from branches or slouched out of holes. The acrid stench stung my nostrils and turned my stomach. The grove was in a state of perpetual death. What sort of horrid place was this?

In the distance was a loch. That's where the portal was, where I had to give an offering to gain a favor from the Fallen Ones.

The stallion staggered, its legs giving out. It went down onto its knees, taking us with it. I dug for my knife, sawing through the knots binding Reyker to me and the saddle, easing him onto his back beside the horse. His skin was marbled with veins, every one of them glowing in violent shades of purple.

"Reyker." I shook him. He didn't wake. I pressed my palm to his chest, over the fraying thread of his pulse; his heart limped sluggishly. Any moment it could stop.

I opened my mind and entered his soul.

It was too quiet, too still. A yawning emptiness. The black river inside him ebbed, returning to sea. The shiny baubles of his memories flowed with it, draining, disappearing.

"Reyker, don't go." My words echo off the canyon walls. There is no answer. "You said you would stay with me. I need you."

There is movement. A gust of wind, a ripple on water.

I let his soul go and looked down. His lashes fluttered. The flaring violet veins were stark against the whites of his eyes.

"Help me," I said, taking his hands, dragging him away from the horse. He scrabbled with his feet. We made it to the bank of the loch, where I knelt beside him, but he was gone again, eyes rolling back in his head. I brushed the sweat-drenched hair off his face. His lips moved, mumbling feverishly in Iseneldish. He called for his mother. He called for me.

"I'm here, Reyker." I kissed the cold skin of his brow, pressed his icy palm to my cheek.

His spine went rigid. His body convulsed.

"Mystic!" Cradling Reyker's head, I screamed for her until she stood before me.

"Mistress of souls."

When I looked up, I nearly fainted. A hunchbacked crone stared down at me, draped in robes as gray as her thinning hair. Her eye sockets were still empty, but the eyes covering her body were buried in folds of decaying flesh. "You've brought the pretty beast," the mystic said, voice muffled by her rotting windpipe.

"Please. He's infected with a bog adder's venom. I have to save him."

Her colorless lips split into a smile, revealing corroded shards of teeth. "You must make an offering in exchange for his life. What will you give the Fallen Ones?"

I stared at Reyker, dying in my lap. I didn't care if he was a weapon, a savior. I cared only that he was my friend. My wolf.

"Whatever the gods want, I will give." Fingers. Eyes. I'd cut out my heart if they asked.

The mystic cocked her head toward the loch, as if listening to the whisper of the waters, the wishes of the fallen gods swimming underneath. "Blood. They desire to drink of your veins."

Grabbing my knife, I hurried to the loch's edge. Bones and various organs bobbed atop the coppery waters. Noxious gas bubbled up, stinking of carrion. The loch expanded, contracted—a shifting, horrifying entity.

I pressed the blade into my wrist, just below the *skoldar*. The blood flowed over the water's rust-colored surface. I knew what this meant: The Fallen Ones owned a piece of me. They could ask for more. I could run to the ends of the earth, and they would still find me.

It was a small price to pay.

A dark slick of my blood pooled atop the water. A mouthless tongue drifted by, lapping at it. Disembodied eyes—one brown, one green—floated to the murky surface, staring at me.

"Enough," the mystic said. "The gods are sated for now." She peered at Reyker with her numerous eyes. "Put the boy in the water. The gods must touch him to heal him."

"What?" I'd paid the gods' price so Reyker wouldn't have to, and they wanted to take from him anyway, to touch him with their decay.

"Be quick. He's fading."

There was no time to pause, no time to think. I removed Reyker's cloak, his boots. I lifted the silver medallion from around my neck and slipped it over his. "To keep you safe," I whispered. "To bring you back to me."

With my arms locked around his chest, I pushed him off the bank into the water, feetfirst. I lowered him up to his waist, hesitating. "Let go," the mystic said.

This was wrong. Everything about it was wrong.

There was no other choice.

I unclasped my hands. Reyker sank beneath the water, vanishing into its opaque depths. I held my breath, waiting. Waiting.

Waiting ... Sucking in air.

"Where is he? How long does it take?" I watched the surface for a sign, a ripple or wake to prove something was happening.

"The gods cannot be rushed. They will take care of him."

I glared at the mystic. "Will the gods give him gills?" My heart was an animal, howling, clawing at my ribs. He'd been under too long. He would drown. How could I have placed my faith in a mystical madwoman and her disgraced gods?

I looked back at the water.

"Don't be a fool, girl! If you dare disturb their work, the gods won't look kindly on it."

What if she was wrong? What if Reyker was drowning at the bottom of the loch? He'd trusted me, and I'd dumped him unconscious into a slime-filled sinkhole.

What have I done?

A cold certainty gripped me. I didn't trust the fallen gods, or any others. All they did was smash and burn and destroy. We mortals were nothing more than toys to them. I wouldn't leave Reyker's life in their hands.

Ignoring the mystic's cries, I leaped from the embankment and dove into the loch.

CHAPTER 38

The water was darker than pitch, thicker than stew, so dense I couldn't swim—my arms flailed, my legs kicked, but I sank straight down. Things touched me: spongy, cold, sticky, sharp. Eyes and bones, mucus and blood, tongues and teeth. They skimmed over me, lapped at me, tangled themselves in my hair.

Hands grabbed me—drifting, skeletal hands, lopped off at elbow or shoulder. Bony fingers latched on to me, too many to count. Pulling. Dragging me deeper.

My toes touched the bottom, only to feel it split open. Swallowing me. There was no bottom. The loch was the wide mouth of a monster, disguising itself. Its throat was an endless trench cut through the heart of the earth.

I'd damned Reyker by bringing him here. I'd damned myself by jumping in after him.

An unearthly chorus erupted, speaking in long-forgotten tongues. The words sewed themselves together into skeins of meaning: "WHY IS SHE HERE?" "LOOK WHAT SHE'S DONE!" "WHAT SHALL WE DO WITH HER?"

The black depths collapsed my lungs, crushed my skull to dust. Everything inside me shattered and dissolved. The gods dug their claws into me, tearing off my skin.

I was a broken doll, a rotting skeleton. Empty.

The water receded. The throat-chasm was empty too, and the void closed around me, folding me into itself, until I didn't exist. I was nowhere, and nothing, and there was no one left to care that I'd ever lived. I suffocated on oblivion. I *was* oblivion.

A voice cut the infinite silence: "LIRA."

Other voices joined it, calling my name. Some I recognized. My parents. My brothers. Madoc. Quinlan. Reyker.

Draki.

I fell through space. My body was gone. I was a glowing spark, a violet sphere of flame, brushing along the threads of my own life. The past and the may-come-to-pass. The possibilities sang as I touched them, but they were cobwebs and mist, shapeless, barely tangible. I might have fallen forever, but something reached out, plucked me from the chasm, held me close.

"AT LAST." His voice was stars blazing across the sky, silver drops of death raining down. "LONG HAVE WE WAITED FOR ONE SUCH AS YOU TO COME."

Veronis. The Great Betrayer.

During the Birth of Summer ritual, I'd seen him in a mortal body, through Aillira's eyes. There was little left of that man. Here he was a dark, twisted form—molded by eons of isolation, filled with an infinite well of rage. I was a speck of dust in his hands.

"YOU BELONG TO US NOW." The drumming of a thousand heartbeats. "YOU WILL BREAK OUR CAGE." The thunder of a thousand beating wings. "YOU WILL BRING HER BACK TO ME." The crack of the earth splitting in two.

Far away, someone was singing—a melody I vaguely recognized, though I couldn't hear the words. I strained, listening, feeling as if it was important, but then Veronis let me go, the song faded, and I was falling again.

"WE WILL COME FOR YOU SOON."

———◆———

I opened my eyes with his voice still vibrating painfully through me. I was the same violet spark, once more encased by bones and flesh, as I was meant to be.

When I tried to breathe, I vomited up the loch. Water and pulp, bile and viscera. The taste tainted my tongue. I coughed and spit until my mouth was clear.

I lay on my side. Underneath me was damp soil. It was too dark to see, the air muggy and stifling. When I put my hands out, they touched cool stone above me, beside me. I pushed on it, but it didn't budge. I was in a prison of rock.

No. I was in a grave. I felt the bones beneath me, digging into my skin.

"Let me out!" I pounded my fists on the stone lid. "I'm not dead!"

A sliver of light peeked through. I braced my hands near it, pushed with all my strength, and the gap widened. I slid my fingers into the small space, grunting and shoving at the slab until it scraped open enough for me to fit through.

Slipping out of the heavy darkness, I sprawled onto the ground under the bright rays of midday. It had been dusk when I dove into the loch. Had an entire day passed?

I sat up, expecting to see putrefied trees, to hear the blind mystic scolding, but I wasn't in the grove. I turned slowly, taking in the landscape. It was a valley, enclosed by green mountains dusted with snow. Around me was an old burial yard perched on the slope of a hill, pocked with tombs like the one I'd climbed out of, the names on them too faded to read. Beyond the burial yard were the somber ruins of an ancient kingdom—the remains of several manors, great halls, a once-magnificent palace. Walls, arches, pillars, towers. Some still stood, but most had crumbled. The glass and wood of windows and doors had long since broken and rotted. Ivy and moss clung to the outer shells. Trees burst from inside the ruins, their thick roots snaking over the stones.

I'd never been here before, yet it stirred a torrent of emotions in me. Comfort. Passion. Grief. Terror. The ruins were almost-but-not-quite familiar, like the ghost of a memory.

I descended the slope, drifting deeper into the valley. "Is anyone here?"

The only answer was the chirrup of songbirds perched on a sunken archway. What was this place? How had I gotten here? And where was Reyker?

I came upon a small waterfall spilling down over a bank of jutting rocks, splashing into a glassy pond. Clovers and moonflowers sprouted across the land like a dense carpet. In the center of the valley stood an enormous tree, its bark a deep blushing red, its myriad limbs curved downward, adorned with long white thorn-needles that looked sharp enough to pierce straight through flesh. The same thorntree that was carved into my mother's medallion.

I *had* been here before. I knew this place—it was Aillira's Temple, except the ruins at the temple were nearly dust, and there were classrooms, libraries, dormitories, and monuments surrounding the grounds. But those things weren't here. I was in a realm where Aillira's Temple hadn't yet been built.

I was in the ruins of Aillira and Veronis's kingdom, as it must have looked centuries ago.

This was Veronis's doing.

I wanted to explore the ruins and search for Reyker, but the need to wash away every filthy trace of the loch took precedence. Peeling off my soiled gown, I waded into the pond's cool, clear water, swimming to the waterfall, letting it drench me, opening my mouth to rinse the rancid taste from my tongue.

A shape blurred on the edge of my vision, and I rubbed my eyes. He stood at the rim of the pond, coated from the crown of his head to the soles of his feet in the loch's dredges. Staring at me like I might be an illusion.

I stared back, feeling the same.

Reyker stepped into the water. I was already moving toward him. We met in the middle of the pond, standing silently in front of each other. I pressed my palm to his chest; his heart pulsed steadily, its rhythm strong and familiar. His soul, when I opened myself to it, held darkness and brightness, like sunlight on the ocean.

I threw my arms around his neck. He tipped my head back and kissed me hard—the kiss of a man who'd beaten death.

CHAPTER 39

Reyker and I lay curled together beside the pond, dozing beneath the warmth of the sun in our undergarments. My gown and his trousers dried on the rocks. Our hands wandered over each other's skin. "Do you remember being in the loch?" I asked.

"I remember being cold and wet. Darkness everywhere. Things tearing at me, screaming inside my head." He started to say something, stopped himself.

"What is it?"

"Nothing. Then I woke in the ruins."

"I thought I'd lost you, Reyker. I thought I'd killed you, putting you into the loch."

I traced the thin white scar where the venomous arrow had pierced him. He kissed the raised line of flesh where I'd cut my wrist and offered my blood to the Fallen Ones. Our injuries were nearly healed, as if we'd sustained them weeks ago instead of hours.

"You saved me, Lira. With your blood. And with this." He took off the medallion and put it around my neck. "The things in the loch. I felt them touch the necklace. They were careful with me because I wore it."

I glanced between the carving of the thorntree on my medallion and the real thing, sprouting up from the valley floor. "I wish I knew what it all meant. This place. The thorntree. The differing stories of Aillira and Veronis."

"Maybe we can find answers." Reyker stood up, offering me his hand.

Together we wandered the ruins, from one fallen structure to the next. Up close, I saw the scorch marks on the stones. Once, this had been a beautiful fortress. Gwylor and his army had razed it to the ground. I ran my finger through soot and ashes, shuddering.

Reyker circled the ruin, caught up in his own thoughts. He motioned to the piles of broken stone. "For love."

"Where do you see love in all this destruction?"

"I've seen this before. Men fighting over a woman. One to protect her. One to take her."

His words stirred something within me. I removed my knife from its sheath and pulled out the slip of parchment hidden there; it had survived the loch unharmed, likely Veronis's doing, as all of our current circumstances seemed to be. "Eathalin gave me this. It's a page from the Forbidden Scriptures."

I read it aloud.

"Look," he said. "There's more."

I turned the page over and saw another verse, though I'd have sworn it was blank before.

> *The flaming gates fell aside, the screaming masses streamed through.*
> *Men. Gods. A host of destruction, riding upon the wings of Death.*
> *The last kiss. Two bodies separating, two hearts torn asunder. Love became a wound.*
> *Veronis raised his mortal sword. Gwylor raised his immortal fist. The earth shook. The sky fell.*
> *Alone, Aillira watched and wept as the world burned.*

"For love," I repeated. Reyker was right.

A sudden whim wormed its way through my thoughts. Curious, I pressed my palm to a stone, opening my mind as if the ruins were a soul. The change was instant—I was pulled forward, and then my vision faded briefly before brightening again.

Two shapes entwined—a man and woman, smiling and singing to each other, whispering of their undying love, in this very room. I feel their affection, clear and true.

The image shifts and the woman is on her knees, sobbing at the feet of an imposing figure who wears the skin of a man awkwardly, as if it's a coat that doesn't quite fit. "You will never see him again," the man says. "Not in life, nor in death. I will make sure of it."

Through her tears, she glares defiantly. "He will come for me. He will find a way."

My hand dropped from the stone.

"Gwylor defeated Veronis, locked him away, and took Aillira," I said. "When she died, she couldn't join him in the otherworlds. Not while he's imprisoned. They've been separated thousands of years. Veronis wanted me to see this. He thinks I can free him so they can be together again." I touched the medallion. "The thorntree. Eathalin said Aillira planted it herself, that it's the symbol of their love."

I spun on my heel and ran from the ruins, bounding across the valley. I didn't stop until I reached the thorntree. Ivory blossoms circled its roots, the moonflowers' petals just beginning to open now that the sun embraced the horizon.

I put my palm against the trunk.

Aillira digs her hands into the soil, planting the seed of a thorntree, watering it with her tears. She hums a haunting melody, the same song she and Veronis used to sing to each other.

She spies the creature slithering toward her. A bog adder, scaled in rippling blue-black patterns. She snatches it by the head, pinning its jaws shut, and gazes at the ruins of the home she once shared with Veronis. "I will wait for you in the otherworlds, my love. I will never stop waiting." She loosens her grip on the adder, holding it to her breast.

Aillira and the adder lock eyes, and there's a strange sentience in the creature's black-slit pupils. "I see you, goddess," Aillira says. "I know what you did. Open wide. Devour my soul if you dare."

The serpent's jaws snap, its fangs sinking deep into the flesh over Aillira's heart.

I let go, stumbling backward. Reyker was there to catch me.

The verse from the scriptures, etched on the back of my medallion—*Burn brightly. Love fiercely. For all else is dust.* They were not Aillira's final words. They were a pretty lie, poured over an ugly truth.

What had Aillira's words to the adder meant? Who was the goddess she saw in the serpent's eyes?

"I felt her pain, Aillira's pain, being separated from Veronis. It was the same way I felt when you were dying, Reyker." Behind us, I saw the graves crowding the hillside. Everyone who stood with Veronis to protect Aillira had suffered—the mortals were dead, the immortals imprisoned in a dark netherworld. The same thing had happened to Reyker's village—Draki took Reyker's mother, killed his father and all the men who'd fought with him.

"Don't fight Draki," I said. "If you do, you'll die. I'll lose you, like Aillira lost Veronis."

"You will not lose me. Look at me, Lira." I raised my eyes to his. "*Jai elskar thu.*" He placed my palm on his chest. "I love you."

For a moment, I couldn't breathe or speak or think.

Reyker waited, anxious. As if he didn't know what I would say.

"*Jai elskar thu.*" I'd sensed it growing between us all along, no matter how much I tried to deny it; I'd known it when I gave my blood to the fallen gods beneath the loch. "Of course I love you, stupid boy."

His mouth crashed into mine, shattering my thoughts, scattering them to the wind.

We lay down in a patch of moonflowers, my hands traveling up his ribs, his fingers tracing patterns across my flesh. He nudged my shift up, kissing his way down my stomach.

My body clenched with anticipation. "I'm not yours until you've had all of me," I said.

Reyker stilled. "All?"

I tugged my shift over my head, tossing it aside. I fumbled with my breeches, and Reyker nearly ripped them off. Then his were gone, and we were nothing but skin on skin, scent and heat mingling. Fingers twined, feeding each other's hunger, breathing each other's names—we unraveled even as we held each other together, burning fierce and bright. Like sparks to kindling.

The moonflowers tickled, soft as a blanket. Aillira's thorntree swayed above us, the only witness to our awakening.

—◆—

Dazed and sated, we lay on our backs, scanning the night sky for falling stars—sometimes the sky god's children begged to visit our world. Sometimes Nesper let them, and they raced from the heavens to the earth before he changed his mind.

In the morning, Reyker and I would try to find our way out of this realm and back to our own. I wanted to return to Ghost Village, to be there when the prince arrived.

Reyker touched my temple. "No dragons in here?"

"No." I'd not felt Draki scraping at my mind since I'd woken in the ruins. I brushed my fingers across Reyker's face. "You look weary."

"I believe that's your fault. You were quite demanding."

It was true—we'd drunk deeply of the blessings of ardor bestowed on us this night. I felt my cheeks flush, and Reyker grinned. "I mean it," I said. "You need rest."

"I passed out from the venom."

"That doesn't count." I poked him in the ribs.

Reyker caught my hand and kissed it. His voice was wistful as he said, "I wish I could take you with me to Iseneld."

"Would you? I want to see all the places you've shown me in your memories. The mountains and rivers, the ghost lights dancing in the sky."

"Those lights mark the gateway to the sacred sky-well of creation, where my people fell from the realm of gods into the realm of men. It is said that if you stare into them long enough, you will glimpse your fate." He tucked a strand of hair behind my ear. "One day, I will take you to see them."

"Good." I kissed him softly. "But for now, you must sleep."

He slipped an arm beneath me as I settled against him. The night was mild, the air pleasant enough that we were comfortable wearing only our smallclothes. "You sleep, Lira. I'll keep watch."

"Stupid boy," I mumbled. "You'll be sorry one of these days, when you fall asleep on your feet in the middle of a battle."

He stroked a hand along my cheek. "You assume I've not fought while sleeping. Plenty of warriors aren't worth waking up to kill."

"Oh, you're so clever." I smiled drowsily at him in the starlit dark. "That's why I love you, *min vulf.*"

My wolf.

He pressed his forehead to mine. "As I love you, *min dyre.*"

My deer.

I closed my eyes, feeling the breeze around us, the bed of flowers under us, the rise and fall of Reyker's chest beneath my head with each breath he took, the steady thump of his heart next to my ear. The sound lulled me. This was a blissful moment, one I wanted to savor. One I hoped would be the first of many.

I walk through the ruins, circling the fallen remnants of castles and manors and towers that surround the giant thorntree.

"This is a lie," a cold voice beside me says. "Remove it."

A girl with apricot hair waves her hands, and the image of ruins lifts like a drawn curtain, revealing Aillira's Temple. Not a broken kingdom, but a sanctuary. The girl turns, and I recognize Eathalin, but she isn't herself. Her face is blank, her eyes unfocused. A young

gray-eyed woman beside her wears the same vacant expression—
Sursha, the pain-wielder.

An army of Dragonmen is with them. A sharp whistle from their
leader, and as one, they march on the temple.

The temple guards meet them, their swords colliding with the
Dragonmen's axes. The Daughters of Aillira do not sit idly by; old
priestesses and young pledges greet the warriors with arrows and
swords. Between the guards and the women, dozens of Dragonmen
fall. But the man in front, leading the charge, walks right through
them all, untouched.

The Daughters with the deadliest gifts fight with what the gods
gave them. Wind-wafters send gales at the army, knocking Dragonmen
into one another, slamming them to the ground. Yet the wind seems to
bow before the leader, not even ruffling his silver hair. Fire-sweepers
pull the flames from lanterns into their hands, tossing blue fire over
the heads of the warriors, burning them alive. When sparks rain
down on the leader, he reaches up to catch them. The light curling in
his hand reflects off his gold-green eyes.

Draki hurls the fire at the temple library, and the building bursts
into flame. It spreads to the lecture halls, the dormitories. As the
women scramble to put out the flames, Draki's forces cut through the
guards, pressing closer to the ancient thorntree at the temple's center.

I move like Draki's shadow, drifting after him, not certain if I'm
inside his head or if he's inside mine. This cannot be real. The temple
cannot be taken. It's a dream, only a dream.

The Dragon places his palms against the thorntree. "Ildja sends
her regards," he says. Something flows out of him, into the tree—
energy, power. The bark blackens, the branches wither and slump. The
roots break off and the giant tree topples, coming down with a crash.

The enduring symbol of Aillira and Veronis dies without fanfare.

While the battle rages, Draki enters a tower and finds what he
seeks—an elderly woman, furiously writing in a ledger, recording
details of the attack on the temple for posterity, as if it is the most
important thing she can do. The head priestess looks the same as she

did when I visited the temple a decade ago; she squints at Draki without fear, speaking Iseneldish. "So you have finally come, son of the Ice Gods. Did you know the earth shook beneath our temple the day you were born?"

"Your temple is full of superstitious crones." He clucks his tongue. "Dragons are not born; they are made."

He ushers the priestess out, and she goes with the composure of a woman who has awaited this moment for quite some time. Draki puts a knife to the old woman's neck. "Surrender," he calls out in Glasnithian to the Daughters of Aillira, "or she dies."

The women glance at one another. "Don't," I whisper as they lower their weapons and the Dragonmen close in.

Draki's blade opens the head priestess's throat as his guttural laugh pierces my soul.

I cry out, shoving at him, but I'm no more than a ghost here.

The Dragon drops the priestess's body and turns, staring at me, even though I'm nothing but shadow and air. It is a dream, I tell myself desperately. Only a dream.

"The temple has fallen, little warrior," he says. "Now I'm coming for Stony Harbor. I'm coming for you."

CHAPTER 40

REYKER

YOU WILL CHASE WHAT YOU CANNOT CATCH.

YOU WILL LOVE WHAT YOU CANNOT KEEP.

Reyker couldn't expel it from his mind—those hideous phantom-gods beneath the water, tearing at him; their shrieking voices, solid and painful as a pounding hammer, divining his fate. Each word had slammed into him, so loud he feared he would dissolve beneath their blows.

He didn't trust this prophecy, foretold by dethroned deities. Lira lay beside him, head pillowed on his shoulder, breathing the deep soft breaths of sleep. "I will keep you," he whispered to her, his eyes drifting shut. "Nothing will take you from me."

———————

"Well, what have we here?"

Reyker sprang from deep sleep into full consciousness, jumping to his feet, reaching for weapons that weren't there. In an instant, he absorbed his surroundings: the snorts of horses, the rustle of boots treading over leaves. Five armed warriors—Sons of Stone. Familiar faces, men who'd beaten and tormented him. Including Madoc.

"Torin's had me out searching for his missing beast and his prized daughter for days," Madoc said. "Now here you are, right under our noses."

They were no longer in the ruins. This was the Tangled Forest.

Reyker didn't bother to wonder how such a thing had happened— these were the ways of gods and magic. He kept his eyes on the men while he spoke to Lira in Iseneldish. "I'll distract them. You take one of their horses and go. I'll find you."

Madoc had a sword, but the others held poleaxes. One of the men stepped toward Reyker, swinging his weapon, and Reyker ducked beneath it, lunging at the man, punching him hard enough to break the man's nose and send him sprawling. Just like that, the poleaxe was in Reyker's hands.

"I'd warn you not to be stupid, beast, but it's too late for that. Quite a deal you offered Torin at the conclave. An army of invaders at his disposal? Wherever did you come up with such a plan?" Madoc's shrewd gaze said what his words had not: *You offered Torin what you promised me. You'll pay dearly for your betrayal.*

The black river surged. Reyker swung the poleaxe at Madoc's torso.

Madoc narrowly dodged it. "At least you had a little fun before the war starts. Gave the girl something to remember you by, did you?" He shot Reyker an icy smile. "Don't worry. I'll look after her while you're gone."

"Go now, Lira," Reyker said, launching himself at Madoc. The poleaxe's spike sliced through the flesh over Madoc's ribs, spilling the commander's blood.

Lira rushed for the horses.

Madoc brought his sword up, blocking Reyker's next swing. "Stop her!" Madoc said as his blade met Reyker's poleaxe again.

Reyker kept one eye on Madoc and the other on Lira as she leaped onto a horse. She kicked it so it reared, its hooves smashing into one warrior when he tried to grab her, but another warrior slammed the flat end of his poleaxe into her hip and knocked her from the saddle. Reyker was edging toward her when he saw the shapes out of a corner of his vision, heard the movement of more warriors coming from the woods behind him.

A heavy net was thrown over his head. Before he could slice his way out of it, the bottom of the net pulled taut around his ankles, jerking his feet out from under him, and ten warriors fell on top of him, holding him down, prying the poleaxe from his fingers. They tightened the net, pinning his limbs, and tossed him on the back of a horse.

"Stupid beast," he heard Madoc sneer, slapping the horse, and then it was running, carrying Reyker away from the commander. Away from Lira.

CHAPTER 41

I didn't understand how I'd gotten here. Reyker and I had fallen asleep in one world and woken in another, as if the ruins had spit us out during the night, back to our bitter fates. Back on a path that led straight to Stony Harbor.

Avoiding my gaze, one of the warriors handed me his tunic, and I slid it over my thin shift, the hem coming down to my knees. I wondered if he'd done it to spare my shame or Torin's.

Madoc wrapped a piece of cloth around his bleeding torso. He kicked my knife, where it had landed when I fell from the horse, and picked up the square of parchment beneath it. When he unfolded it, his eyes widened. "It seems I underestimated you, niece. You have far less regard for your own life than I imagined."

He tucked the parchment under his clothing and mounted his horse. The warrior whose tunic I wore lifted me into the saddle behind my uncle. Madoc whistled a grating tune that set my nerves on edge as we rode.

"You could let us go," I said. "Tell Torin you never found us."

"And miss an opportunity to degrade my brother and his whelp? No, I'm going to ensure you and your beast get exactly what you deserve."

"Why are you so cruel?"

"Maybe because the Brine Beast spared you, but ate my only son and heir," Madoc said. "Or because the god of death robbed me of my wife and daughter. Maybe because my younger brother stole all that is rightfully mine." Turning his head, he regarded me coolly. "Maybe it is simply how the gods made me. Does it matter?"

"I'm sorry about your family. I wish—"

"Does it matter?" he asked again, silencing me.

Our arrival in the village caused an uproar. Villagers halted their chores, hurried from their cottages. I spotted Ishleen among them. Her lips moved, and though I couldn't hear, I knew what she'd said: "What the devils have you done, Lira?"

Madoc hauled me off the horse, presenting me to our scowling chieftain. My uncle leaned over, whispering to his brother. His words made Torin's eyes blaze. Reyker and I had run off together in the night; we were found wearing barely a stitch of clothing, locked in an embrace. No lies could absolve us.

"Lira," Torin said. "Have you been defiled?"

I held my chin high. "No."

"If I had you examined, we would find your virtue still intact?" he asked doubtfully.

"No." If I tried to deceive him, he'd make Olwen examine me as he'd done before. I would spare myself that indignity.

"No?" He cocked his head, furrows creasing his forehead. "Which is it?"

"No, I am no longer a maiden. No, I was not defiled. I gave myself willingly."

Torin's gaze flickered to Reyker; a group of warriors were dragging him off the horse, still trapped in the net. "To this *invader*?"

"To Reyker. The man I love."

Black spirals shuddered in Torin's irises, sending chills through me. Who was he now? He was my father, yet not my father. Puzzling over it hurt my head. It hurt my heart.

Madoc muttered something that made Torin's mouth twitch. A grimace, or a grin?

"No," Torin said. "I will not—"

"You're her chieftain." Madoc gripped Torin's arm. "She defied you in front of your clan. She chose a beast, one of the men who murdered your son, over her own people."

"Reyker had no part in Rhys's death," I said.

Neither of them listened. "She had this on her when I found her." Madoc pulled out the page from the Forbidden Scriptures. "The girl is a whore and a heretic."

Torin took the parchment and read it. The muscles in his jaw tightened; the demons in his eyes danced. He crumpled the page in his fist. "You're right. Fetch it."

My uncle headed for the armory.

I couldn't hear the orders Torin gave his men, but some paled, looking stricken, while others sneered, eagerly awaiting whatever was about to befall me. Torin escorted me up the path, past the cells. To the gallows.

My knees shook. Surely, he didn't mean to hang me?

"String her up," Torin said. I was led up the stairs onto the scaffold, forced to kneel between the vertical beams. Right beneath where Dyfed's body had hung from a noose.

A public whipping? They were reserved for serious crimes, mostly theft or destruction of another man's property. Women were never whipped in public, but punished privately by a husband, father, or brother—though Torin and my brothers had never raised a hand to my mother or me.

"Open her tunic."

I jerked my head toward Torin. He really meant to do this. If I begged, he might change his mind, but I wouldn't demean myself. I would take my beating as bravely as I could. I would show no weakness.

One of the men ripped the sentry's tunic that covered me, and my shift beneath it, leaving my back exposed. Each of my wrists was tied to one of the beams so my arms were spread wide.

Villagers crowded around the scaffold to witness my punishment.

At Torin's command, Reyker was bound to the thick trunk of a nearby tree. They tied enough rope around him to pin a wild bull. Torin tested the knots himself, then grabbed Reyker's chin, lifting his head up. "Keep your eyes open, beast. You're the one who did this to her."

Reyker looked from Torin to me, his eyes darkening with dread. With wrath. "Please," Reyker said. "You cannot do this."

"Tame your tongue, beast, or I'll have you muzzled."

Madoc returned from the armory, and Torin went to meet him. My uncle held the whip out to Torin, and the chieftain hesitated; he must have assumed Madoc would wield it. He glanced at me, then at the villagers who watched him expectantly.

He accepted the whip.

"Lira of Stone, you are charged with fornicating with an invader, an enemy of this clan." Torin addressed me but faced the crowd. "Do you deny this charge?"

"No." I spoke loudly, without shame. Gasps and chattering arose.

"Your marriage could've secured crucial alliances for the Sons of Stone. With your virtue spoiled, by a savage no less, no respectable man will accept you as a wife. You've betrayed your clan, your country, and yourself. Are you ready to pay for your crimes?"

Again, I let my voice ring clear. "I'm prepared to be beaten by my own father for bedding a man I chose instead of one forced upon me."

More jabbering from the audience.

"Five lashes is your punishment. Let it be known that no one is exempt from this clan's judgment. Not even the chieftain's daughter." Torin lowered his voice, so only I heard. "I hope he was worth it," he said, revealing the tool Madoc selected for my castigation: not a regular whip, but a rawhide knout, its thongs made of branches tipped with long, slender white needles. Branches from a southern thorntree.

A nasty, deadly tool.

The moment hung there. It was so brief, yet it stretched on forever. *Help me*, I thought, not sure who I called upon. The gods? The crowd? My father?

Help me.

Torin swung the knout. The thorns tore at my flesh before I could blink.

The ache. The shock. It was like jumping into freezing water, knocking the breath from my lungs. My back was on fire.

"One!" the crowd counted.

There were gasps. There were cheers too.

Torin jerked his arm, ripping the branches free before lashing me with them again. My breath came in tight spasms as pain washed over me. I strained against my bindings.

"Two!"

There was an animal nearby, howling and rabid. The sound burned holes in my ears. It spoke in Reyker's voice. "I forced her! I raped her!" he kept shouting.

Finally absorbing the words, Torin stopped. "Is this true, Lira?"

I twisted my head.

When I looked at Torin, I saw a broken man who didn't have the stomach for this and wanted me to accept the lifeline Reyker had thrown me. Say yes, and I would be released, tended to, forgiven, my earlier confession ignored. Say yes, to save myself and damn Reyker. Paint him as the savage they all wanted him to be. Let him take my place, strung up and tortured for ravishing the chieftain's daughter. Beaten. Castrated. Hanged. His death would be slow. They would do much worse to him than they would to me.

When I looked at Reyker, I saw my lover. My wolf. Begging me to say yes and condemn him. Reyker was willing to die to spare me this pain. I wanted to tell him I loved him, but I only had the strength to utter one word through my clenched teeth: "No."

Torin drew back his arm.

Was this how you felt, Mother, when you walked into the sea?

The knout fell again.

"Three!"

Screams and cries swirled around me, a maelstrom of noise. Some of it spilled from my own mouth. Some was that ceaseless, inhuman roar coming from Reyker.

"You chose an invader over your own clan! Over your own father!" Torin said, and there was more than rage in him. There was disbelief. Jealousy. Sorrow.

Father—my father was there, beneath the surface. I cried out to him.

"I have no daughter, remember—that's what you told me after the Culling. Just as I have no sons. No wife. I loved you, and you left me. You all left me!"

He let the knout fly.

"Four!"

My vision flickered. The pain was in me and apart from me, all around me and happening to someone else.

"Leave her be!" Torin grunted, struggling with someone. "Get away from my daughter, you demon!" And then, "She did this. She must be taught a lesson, like her brother."

Himself. Torin was fighting himself.

The knout's thongs licked me, the thorn-needles pierced me.

"Five!"

All the voices surged and shrank. I could no longer tell if it was my body that trembled, or the earth itself. There were more screams now, replacing mine, which had faded.

"Mother," I whispered.

Screams. Roars.

Then, nothing.

PART THREE
COMETH THE DRAGON

CHAPTER 42

REYKER

Warriors circled with swords and spears when they finally cut Reyker down from the tree. He planned to fight them anyway, but one of the men caught his gaze—Quinlan, his expression carrying a coded message: *Calm yourself. You're no good to her dead.*

Why was Quinlan here?

They marched him to the great hall, filled to capacity with warriors. Not just the Sons of Stone, but others, some of whom he remembered from the conclave. The guards shoved him to his knees before Torin and Madoc.

The black river pulsed. Reyker wanted to wrap his hands around the chieftain's neck. He wanted to bash in the commander's skull.

"Behold," Torin said, silencing the men. "Our secret weapon. The invader who will win us an entire beast army."

Reyker's laughter was a harsh, hateful thing.

"Don't balk yet, beast. You will sail to the Frozen Sun with a band of emissaries. You will raise me the army you promised. You will bring them to Stony Harbor to fight for us."

Grumbles and groans from the men.

"I won't fight with invaders," someone said.

Torin stalked forward. "Stalwart Bay has been taken over by the Dragon and his legion of fiends. We must take back what's ours. Would you rather fight with some of the savages or bow to all of them?"

"But we can't trust this beast, nor any he brings back with him," another warrior shouted.

"Yes, we can. We'll offer lands, titles, women. And our beast commander here will keep them in line." Torin smiled. "Because we have a hostage he doesn't wish to see harmed."

Reyker's breath lodged in his throat.

The black river turned to ice in his veins.

CHAPTER 43

Urgent, muffled voices. Cool hands on my back, my face. Liquid poured down my throat. I coughed and swallowed. I was on my stomach, something soft beneath me.

Someone was petting me. My mother.

No. Not Mother. Mother was dead. Was *I* dead?

Mother smoothed my hair, cooing. Crying. Her tears spilled onto my cheek.

Then nothing.

——◆——

I dreamed of flying arrows and falling thorns. Of bones beneath me and stars above. Of white petals showering down on me like rain.

Every time I woke, Ishleen made me drink her bitter potions. She spoke to me of her own shifting dreams. "The lammergeiers are circling, Lira. But something worse hides behind them, with claws and fangs and yellow eyes. It speaks of terrible secrets, but I can't understand its tongue."

My head was too heavy to lift. My back throbbed. The world tilted and bucked, trying to throw me off.

I dug my fingers in and held on.

Reyker's hand clasped mine.

I was dreaming again.

He kneeled beside the bed, head down. I stirred and he looked up. His eyes bore a wet shimmer, and they were clouded like a tempest. He spoke my name, quiet and crackling. The sadness in his voice frightened me. "I'm sorry," he said.

"Don't leave me."

"*Never.*" His fingers moved gently across my face, through my hair. He would never leave me, he swore, but he had to go away for a little while. He promised to come back for me soon, to take me far from here, where no one could hurt me.

I tried to sit up. Gasped at the pain. He made me lie still.

I fumbled with the medallion. "Take it. Please." He helped me slip the rope off. "It brought you back to me before. It will keep you safe again."

He fastened the medallion around his neck. Told me he would never take it off, not until he returned. Brushed his lips over my knuckles, my forehead. Pressed my palm to his chest, so I felt the strength of his heart. Whispered that he was mine and I was his.

And then he was gone, the light was gone, the dream was gone.

Light and dark played across my eyelids. Night and day blended like paint on a canvas. Time bent and swayed around me.

I dreamed of the ruins, before they were ruins. The grand, lavish castle it once had been. I stood at a high window inside one of the towers. Outside, the kingdom burned.

Below me, Reyker was tied to the thorntree, staring up at me, roaring.

There was a soft swish of boots behind me. A black-inked arm snaking around me. A firm body pressing into my back. A voice like poison poured into my ear: *Mine.*

A threat and a promise.

"Pray for death."

I opened my eyes. Doyen lingered beside my sickbed. He held something out toward me, a crumpled piece of parchment—the verses from the Forbidden Scriptures Madoc took from me.

"To possess this page of filth and lies is blasphemy." Doyen ripped it in half.

My head swam; my vision wavered. Was this another dream?

He leaned closer, but my eyelids drifted shut. "Pray for Gwylor's mercy, for you'll receive none from me," the priest said. "Pray the knout's kiss kills you, for if you live, I'll end you myself."

When I forced my eyes open a moment later, no one was there.

The world came into focus, bit by bit.

I was in a spare bed in the cottage Ishleen shared with her mother. This was where I'd been hauled, bleeding and unconscious, after Torin allowed me to be cut free and cared for. Days had passed since then, I wasn't sure how many. My wounds had become infected. I'd burned with fever for so long that Doyen had been called to perform the final prayers to send my soul to the otherworlds.

Ishleen cleaned and bandaged my wounds, coaxed food and water into my fragile stomach. Quinlan had come to Stony Harbor on clan business and stayed to help Ishleen look after me. As soon as I could make my mouth align with my thoughts, I asked about Reyker. Over and over. "He's in the cells," they told me. It was all they would say.

"Take me to him. I need to know he's all right."

"Soon," they assured me.

Always *soon*. Never *now*.

My medallion was missing. No one could tell me where it went.

When I could walk on my own, they left me alone for longer spans of time. The first chance I got, I eased a cloak around my shoulders and snuck to the cells.

My legs were unsteady. My back shrieked in protest. But I had to see him.

There was no guard out front. I pushed the door open and went to his cell. I wrapped my hands around the bars, pressed my forehead against the cool metal.

There was no prisoner inside.

Reyker was gone.

CHAPTER 44

Quinlan found me in the cells. This was where I'd spent so many hours with Reyker, where we began to fall in love in spite of the grate between us, in spite of the horrors our people inflicted upon both of us. I could still feel him here.

"You lied to me," I said.

"You weren't strong enough to accept the truth yet." Quinlan sat down beside me. "Otherwise you'd remember him coming to see you. You'd remember his goodbye."

"I didn't think it was real. I thought Torin would kill him, or at least never let him near me again." I replayed the sparse moments of Reyker's visit—the strain on his face, the reluctance. He hadn't wanted to leave me. He'd had no choice.

"You don't know what's happened," Quinlan said.

"Tell me."

He did. While Reyker and I had been missing—time had indeed passed differently for us on the other side of the loch's portal, our single day in the ruins equaling more than a week outside—scores of Drag-onmen had sacked Stalwart Bay. They'd killed or expelled every villager, confiscated or burned every ship, and taken up residence. Stalwart was the largest port in Glasnith, the only ideal port for ships coming and going to the rest of the world. Our island couldn't survive without it.

"The invaders sent a message to Torin and the other chieftains. They plan to stay. They're demanding allegiance and tariffs from any clans that want to use the port. They're attacking incoming ships as well, plundering their goods, taking foreign hostages."

"It's beginning," I said. "Draki seeks to conquer us."

"The clans are desperate. They voted to form alliances outside of Glasnith to help defeat the Dragonmen. Emissaries have been sent to the Auk Isles and Sanddune. And to Iseneld, because Torin thinks it'll take one army of beasts to destroy another. Reyker swore at the conclave that he could deliver an army of Westlanders to fight with us."

I wrapped my arms around myself, feeling Reyker slip farther away from me, the distance an unbearable pressure. "What makes Torin believe Reyker will return? Why would he help those who enslaved him?"

"He'll come. For you." Quinlan shifted uncomfortably. "Torin's using you as a hostage. He gave Reyker two months to raise an army and sail back to Glasnith. At the second month's end, he plans to lock you in the cells and starve you. He told Reyker once the cell door closes, you won't be fed so much as a crumb until his army is delivered."

"Oh." Nothing should've surprised me, not after Torin took the knout to me, yet it did. He'd put me in the cells like a common prisoner, let me suffer a slow death.

Before Reyker departed, Torin had allowed him a brief visit to my bedside. A last look, to remind him what he was leaving behind, and to remind him—by the bloody bandages on my back—that Torin didn't bluff. The chieftain would make good on his threats.

"What happened to him, Lira? Your father was one of the most honorable men I've ever known. Why would he do this?"

I told Quinlan everything. Not just of Torin and Madoc and the Culling, but of the nomads. Of Reyker. And Draki.

Quinlan sighed. "Sweet Silarch, this is a right fine mess you're in. When Reyker came to see you before he left, I promised him I'd get you out of Stony Harbor. I aim to keep that promise."

My hands went to my chest, found a hollow space instead of my medallion. "I'm going to Ghost Village."

"To stay with the same nomads who nearly gave you to the invaders?"

"Zabelle would never have let that happen. I trust her. And their Ghost Prince will come." *Garreth*, my heart whispered. "I have to see him. I have to know. If it is Garreth, he can take me to Aillira's Temple so I can speak with the priestesses." Perhaps Eathalin would accompany me. Together we might be able to convince the priestesses to join the fight against the Westlanders, now that things had become so dire.

"Aillira's Temple." Quinlan filled those two words with so much regret. "Lira, the temple fell. The Dragon and his men found their way inside. They destroyed the temple and took the Daughters of Aillira."

The dream came back to me: Draki storming the temple with his army, setting fire to the buildings, slitting the head priestess's throat. It wasn't a dream after all, but a vision. I never saw how it ended, but I knew—I could almost hear the Daughters of Aillira screaming as Draki cut his dragon star into their flesh.

Quinlan touched my shoulder, but I pushed his hand away. "Took them where?"

"The Westlanders are using them. It's part of how the invaders were able to take Stalwart Bay. The Daughters of Aillira are being forced to help them."

No, not simply forced. Compelled. Controlled.

"We have to leave *now*." I tried to get to my feet, but the pain in my back brought me down again. "I need to find Garreth, and then we can form search parties to track down the Daughters of Aillira."

"You'll need a month to heal before riding across the desert."

"I can't leave them, Quinlan. Draki will mark them, if he hasn't already. You don't know what it feels like to be preyed upon by the warlord's power." Though I'd never met most of them, the Daughters of Aillira were my sisters, and they might be Glasnith's only hope to reclaim our country.

"I've seen your back, Lira. Your wounds—" He caught my stricken look and halted. "I'm sorry. They aren't … I'm just concerned. If you push yourself too hard, you'll never heal."

I didn't know how my back looked. No one would help me with the mirrors, and I couldn't do it myself. I imagined an ugly mass of wounds that would leave hideous scars. My body was covered with the remnants of injuries inflicted by the monsters in my life.

I cleared my throat. "We must leave as soon as possible."

"Three weeks," Quinlan said firmly.

"One week."

"A fortnight, and not one day less."

I glared at him, but he crossed his arms stubbornly. "A fortnight, and not one day more," I agreed with reluctance. "What will you do after we arrive in Ghost Village?"

"I'll stay until I know you're safe, but then I must leave. There's a war on the horizon. I want to fight. I have to help defend our lands."

"I wish you wouldn't."

He offered me a halfhearted grin. "Still worrying about me?"

"Not a whit," I said, trying to smile. So much had changed between us. I wanted to tease him, to laugh with him, but I felt so awkward.

A scuffling sound outside startled us. Quinlan and I looked at each other. *Stay here*, he mouthed, rising to his feet, creeping out the door. Through the window, I heard a shout. A moment later, Quinlan dragged a cursing, scowling boy into the cells.

Dyfed the herdsman's son.

"Vile, murderous witch!" Ennis hissed. "Stay away, beast-whore!"

Quinlan tightened his grip on Ennis's shoulders, keeping him in place. "Watch your tongue or I'll box your ears, boy."

"You're spying for Madoc," I said. "And not for the first time."

Ennis writhed under Quinlan's fingers. "You helped that beast attack a sentry and steal a horse. I saw it. Traitorous beast-lover! I wish they'd killed you both. You murdered my father!" Ennis jerked forward and spit in my face.

Quinlan shook the boy hard, until I held up a hand for him to stop.

"My father was a good man. He didn't steal weapons. He had permission. But you didn't know that, did you? You condemned him for something he was ordered to do."

I wiped off his spit, chills flickering up my spine. "Ordered by whom?"

"I don't know." Ennis pressed his lips together, on the verge of tears. Despite his bravado he was still just a boy, overwhelmed with grief. "Father only said he was doing clan business."

"Do you know what he did with the weapons?"

"Hid them on carts. Sent them south."

The chill became a blizzard. I looked at Quinlan, reading his thoughts, knowing they were the same as mine. *Madoc.* "Tell anyone what you heard today, or what you told us," I warned Ennis, "and I'll curse you. I'll turn you into a traitorous beast-lover like me."

Quinlan turned the boy loose, and Ennis ran from the cells.

"Sowing the seeds of chaos," I mumbled, remembering the verse Madoc had quoted from the Immortal Scriptures. "None of the Glasnithian clans would dare cross Torin like this. If Madoc was sending weapons south, he must be securing alliances with the mercenaries. Even before Aengus's death, he was planning a way to overthrow Torin." And spouting insults about the mercenaries at every turn, to ensure no one ever suspected he was making deals with them.

"This is bad. It's *treason.*" Quinlan leaned against the grate. "Madoc will kill to keep this from getting out."

"He already has." An image of Dyfed swinging from the gallows flashed through my mind. The herdsman had tried to tell me, asking me to look in his soul again, before Madoc knocked him unconscious. My guilt over his execution stung me anew. "We've no proof. A story forced out of a grieving boy by a traitorous, beast-loving hostage. Torin will never believe us. If we don't stop Madoc ourselves, no one will."

It was too much—expose Madoc, get to Ghost Village, find Garreth, free the Daughters of Aillira, save my island from the Dragon. I was one girl, and not even a warrior. How could I accomplish such feats? But how could I live with myself if I didn't try?

Quinlan tipped his head back. "Gwylor help us," he prayed.

I thought of the ruins, of Aillira dying from an adder bite and Veronis rotting in his prison-realm.

Help us? No. Gwylor wouldn't.

CHAPTER 45

REYKER

The ship rocked beneath him. Reyker closed his eyes, breathing in the briny air, tasting salt on his tongue. His mind returned him to a place he did not want to go: *Lira, strung up like a carcass, blood flowing down her back. I feel every blow as if it is my own flesh being torn. I cannot move. I cannot get to her. All I can do is add my scream to hers.*

Reyker's eyes snapped open. Waves rolled across the dark ocean plains, smacking into the hull. He stretched his sea legs, moving as nimbly on the pitching ship as he could on land. The cog was taller and wider than the knarrs and longships he was accustomed to. He circled the upper decks again, checking the riggings, squinting at the stars to ensure their course was true. Trying to keep his head clear, but the image was always there, lurking—Lira, bound and bleeding.

He pressed his hand to the silver medallion hanging over his heart.

I'll come back for you, Lira, army or no.

They were headed northwest, to Iseneld. It would take a few more days to reach, even with the wind in their favor, but he felt his homeland calling. As he drifted farther from Lira, his only solace was being closer to home.

The other men on deck watched Reyker warily. They'd left him unchained but allowed him no weapons. Wherever he went, an armed man followed. His constant pacing unnerved them. When he spoke in their language, they stared like he was some sort of demon trying to steal their souls.

This alliance wouldn't work. Not if the clans of Glasnith and Iseneld couldn't trust each other. How could such enemies ever become allies?

———

It was the next day when they spotted the other ship, just a speck on the horizon behind them. They watched the ship creep closer as the sun slid lower, the blue veil of night casting a pall across the wide expanse of sea. The ship's silhouette faded to a shadowy smudge, but by this time they knew it was following them.

"One of yours?" the other men asked suspiciously.

Reyker shook his head. He knew the look of his people's vessels, the patterns they made cutting through water. Even with darkness and distance, he could tell this one was different.

"No innocent fishing boat, that," said the Selkie warrior, who had spent the voyage looking far too green for a man who lived beside a maelstrom. "Rovers?"

"Not this far out," Reyker told them. "There are no close shores yet, nothing but islets with hermit priests. Marauders wouldn't venture such a great distance from settled lands."

"It's a caravel," said the warrior from the Hounds of Vengeance later, when the ship drew close enough to make out its three towering masts and triangular sails. The others murmured in nervous admiration. "No wonder they caught us."

A long spur was rigged at the waterline on the enemy ship's prow. The caravel pulled abreast of the cog, two dozen men scrambling across its deck, fumbling with the sails so it turned into the cog's broadside. The ship headed straight for them, gaining speed.

"Assassins."

They'd all been thinking it, but when Reyker spoke the word aloud the other warriors stood up straighter, fingers on their swords. Readying for a battle that would likely send them to their graves. They were fifteen men in a smaller, slower ship.

"Well, invader." This warrior was from the Cast of Hawks or Kettle of Vultures or something of that nature—these men took such pride in their silly mascots. "Suppose we'll have need of your skills." He handed Reyker a sword.

Reyker looked into the man's face, bowing slightly before accepting the weapon. This was how you made allies out of enemies. Unite them against a common adversary.

The caravel was bearing down on them. "Hold on!" Reyker called.

They braced for collision. The caravel's spur rammed the cog with the grating sound of shivering wood. The force of the impact was like smashing into rocks, knocking both ships off course. Reyker and the other men were thrown hard against the bulwark. When he picked himself up, Reyker saw the two ships were stuck together. Men from the caravel scaled the gunwale, shields and weapons drawn.

"Mercenaries," the Selkie snarled when he saw them. "The Ravenous. Filthy cannibals."

Reyker had overheard tales of the mercenary clans from the Sons of Stone. He'd seen some of them at the conclave, but none who looked like these men. The warriors boarding their cog had long beards and were dressed in leather vests and woolen kilts. Their heads were shaved and painted with bright red stripes that looked like blood. They carried scythes instead of swords.

Reyker and the rest of his crew raised their weapons, rushing forward to meet the Ravenous head-on. They fought side by side, crossing blades with the enemy.

The black river rippled through Reyker, keeping him focused. He sliced a man's throat. Pierced another's heart. Kicked one over the gunwale, the man's body slamming into the small gap between ships before sinking beneath the water. But for each mercenary who fell, another rose. There were too many. Reyker's companions died around him.

He was defending a strike from above by one mercenary as a second man sliced a blade across his leg. A third snuck behind him, smashing the handle of a scythe against his skull.

His grip loosened. His sword was knocked away. He was shoved, pinned down.

The Ravenous traversed the decks, pouring containers of foul-smelling liquid across the planks. One man stood out among them, his posture rigid, his mouth a grim line in his weathered face. The other men saluted as they walked past, calling him captain.

"Toss the bodies on our ship," the captain said. "We'll have a feast on our sail home."

The mercenaries laughed. Two of them yanked Reyker to his feet. "What about this one, Captain?"

"It's no good eating frost giants. They taste like a frozen pig's arse." The captain spit, drawing his scythe. "I've a message for you, beast. From Lord Madoc."

The scythe stabbed into Reyker's chest.

He drew a hissing breath. Blood flowed from the wound, splashing across Lira's medallion. The captain ripped out the blade and tore the rope from Reyker's neck, holding up the bloodstained circle of silver. "We'll make sure this is returned to its rightful owner. Torin's sweet little daughter can wear it as she warms the Dragon's bed."

A growl burst from Reyker's throat as he barreled forward, breaking free from the men holding him, slamming into the captain. They landed in a sprawl and Reyker rose, pressing his knee over the captain's throat.

Mercenaries dragged him back. The captain sat up, touching his tender throat. "Tie him up," he said. "Let the frost giant burn."

Sulfur and oil, some devilish incendiary—that was what he'd smelled before, what the mercenaries had doused the decks with. The last mercenary off the cog set it alight, and the flames spread quickly, crawling from bow to stern, engulfing sail and mast. The smoke was suffocating. Reyker used his teeth to work his hands free from the hastily tied knots that bound him to the railing. With no other options, he vaulted over the gunwale into the water.

The cold cut deep, like diving into broken glass. He unlaced his boots, relinquishing them to the sea. The caravel had detached itself from the disabled ship and was gone. The cog was now a sinking mass of blackened timbers and shuddering flames, lighting the dark with an eerie orange glow, like a colossal funerary candle.

Reyker treaded water, sputtering, each breath causing spasms of pain. For the first time since he'd left Iseneld with the Dragonmen, he called upon his gods. All-God Sjaf, guardian of the sea. Velkk, champion of warriors. Efra, goddess and protector of young lovers. *Help me*, he prayed.

He waited, but no answer came.

The steaming vessel disappeared below the waves. Lost in this vast darkness, with nothing but the winking stars for company, Reyker was as alone as any man had ever been. He had faced death before, and in those moments he had longed for it, or accepted it, or, at most, held it at arm's length. But now, he raged.

"You will not leave me here to die!" he told the gods. "When Draki is dead and the world is safe, you can have me, but you will not take me this night."

He forced his arms to slide through the water, forced his legs to kick, even though there was nowhere to swim to. Above, the green and violet lights of the sky-well flickered to life, mocking him; he'd been so close to standing on his home shores.

Reyker pressed a hand to his chest wound, where the medallion had been.

Lira.

He stared into the lights of creation, the realms from whence his ancestors came, and an image flared across the sky—Reyker, standing in a storm, crossing swords with Draki. His unfinished destiny.

His muscles cramped, so numb he no longer felt the cold.

As if the veil between life and death had lifted, specters drifted along the water in a slim longship, drawing closer, their bone-white fingers reaching for him. He prepared to fight them with his last dregs of strength. "You cannot take me. I will not die here," he told them.

"No," a specter replied. "You will not."

CHAPTER 46

*My chest throbs. I'm freezing, shivering, my blood flowing into the sea
in dark red clouds.*

I woke up gasping.

Something was wrong. Something had happened. The dream was
too real—it had felt the same as being inside Reyker's soul. Was he lost,
hurt? Or worse?

I opened my mind, reaching for him across the distance …

Finding nothing.

———

One week slipped by, and then another.

Bit by bit, I healed and grew stronger.

I tried to convince myself that the unsettling dream of Reyker was the
product of worry, nothing more. Quinlan had left, promising to return
soon to help me escape from Stony Harbor, into the Green Desert. In the
meantime, I'd spent my days watching Madoc's comings and goings as
discreetly as I could, but he'd done nothing suspicious yet.

Eventually, the chieftain deigned to visit me.

"I heard your health had improved," he said. For some reason Torin wore a suit of chain mail over his tunic. I thought of how he'd argued with himself while he'd whipped me and wondered how much his madness had worsened.

I sat tall in my chair. "What do you want?" I couldn't look at him without seeing the knout in his hand. It sent fresh pinpricks through the flesh of my back.

"I …" He stopped, glancing around the room as if surprised at where he was. His face twitched and he bent over, gripping his knees. "I've done terrible things. I hurt you, Lira. I know that. I didn't want to, but I couldn't stop."

His voice changed. The cold confidence was gone. His eyes were wide, the deep brown of molasses, with no hint of black vines.

"Father?"

"I only wanted to protect our clan, to protect you and Garreth. At the Culling, Gwylor showed me who I must be, what I must do."

"Father, listen to me." There was no telling how long he would be free of the darkness. I had to get through to him. "Madoc sent weapons south to the mercenary clans to bribe them. He's plotting to overthrow you. You must lock him up before it's too late."

"I can't." He stared at his hands. "Every man has an instinct for wickedness—a desire to take whatever he wants, to crush all who defy him. Good men can suppress it, but once it's free, there's no shoving it back in its cage. That's what the Culling did to me."

"You can fight it." He was Torin of Stone, our greatest commander, the strongest man among us. I put my hands over his. "I'll help you."

"Oh, Lira. You've no idea. The power. The control. I …" Father's face reddened with shame, but when he spoke, there was joy. "I like it."

"You like it?" My fingers clenched into fists. "Attacking your children. Burning our home. Making me your hostage. All because you like feeling powerful?" My voice rose from a whisper to a shout. "A good man would fight it. A good man would never *stop* fighting."

His chin dipped. "You're right. And now you know." When he lifted his head, black thorns crowned his pupils. "Deep down, your father was never a good man."

I sifted through memories of Father, sitting with my brothers and me beside the hearth, teaching us legends of our gods and ancestors, riding through the forest with us. He wasn't perfect, but he'd loved us. He was a good man.

Or had he pretended all along?

"If you give in to the god of death, then you are not my father! You're nothing but a weak, broken coward who failed your clan and your family."

His face, his eyes—they were as expressionless as a corpse. What would it look like, if I dared to touch his soul? Would there be any trace left of the man I'd known, or would I find only Gwylor's strings, wrapped too tightly around Torin to ever release him?

"Your disdain should mean something to me," he said, "but it doesn't."

He left without another word.

Too angry to cry, too restless to stay here, I strapped my knife on beneath my skirt and walked to the cells, where I'd sought solace each day since discovering Reyker was gone. The cell seemed to hold his scent, just as the dirt floor held the imprint of his body where he'd slept so many nights. I lay next to it, stroking my fingers through the dirt. I whispered my hopes and fears, as if he could hear me.

Where are you, my wolf?

When I woke, it was dark. Hours must have passed. I sat up, blinking, startled to find Madoc standing on the other side of the grate, holding an oil lantern.

"Dear, sweet Lira. You couldn't have played your part more perfectly if I'd written it for you myself." Madoc's eyes were black pits amidst the shadowed lines of his face.

Outside, I heard the rumblings of a coming storm.

"What are you talking about?" I tightened my cloak around me.

"When I convinced Torin to let you teach the beast our language and instructed your escorts to leave you alone in the cells with him, I never imagined how quickly your sickness for each other would grow. Or how thoroughly it would distract your father. The look on Torin's face when I presented his precious deflowered daughter was priceless. For that, I'd have let you live. You are my blood, distasteful as that fact may be. But you had to tell Torin that I conspired against him."

I had left the grate open, but now it was shut. I pushed it.

Locked.

"Where's my father?"

"I convinced Torin to march the Sons of Stone to Stalwart Bay, to help the bay clans launch an attack on the invaders. Unfortunately, they'll never arrive. A legion of Dragonmen awaits them in the Green Desert with orders to leave no survivors."

"What?" Panic fluttered its wings beneath my breast. "You sent them to a slaughter! How could you betray your own people?"

"I only want what's best for my island." Madoc opened the collar of his tunic. "Would you like to see what else I've done?"

He grabbed my hand and jerked it through the bars, placing it against his chest. I didn't want to look, but I had to.

I sank into Madoc's soul.

The inside of his soul was a massive castle, its walls lined with spikes—heads were impaled on each spike, wearing the faces of the Sons of Stone. The iron portcullis protecting the castle shuddered and rose. Out of the depths of Madoc's soul slithered deeds and whispers, swarming around me like wasps, so fast I could hardly absorb them.

His sins spread out before me: bribes, theft, blackmail. Using Dyfed to smuggle weapons. Feeding Torin's fragile, ravaged mind with disastrous lies. There were so many misdeeds it was hard to focus, though I saw the threads knotting together, how so many of them led back to manipulating his way into an alliance with the mercenary clans.

One crime stood out from the others like a flare at night, like Madoc wanted me to pay close attention to it. A command he'd dispatched: *Sink the ship.*

I snatched my hand away and the castle disappeared. "What ship?"

Madoc held something aloft. A medallion. "I told the mercenaries to bring me proof the deed was done."

The world tilted. I braced a hand against the grate to keep from falling. "No."

He tossed the medallion in front of the bars, and I scooped it up. The rope was broken. Blood had drained into the carving and dried there, staining it the color of the real thorntree. Another flash came to me, from the medallion itself. The image ripped through me: *A blade slides into a man's chest. Pain. His heart's blood, spilling forth.*

Just like in my dream.

Reyker. My wolf. My love.

"No!" A crack of thunder punctuated my cry. My heart twitched like a dying animal.

"I couldn't have your beast complicating things. I already forged a deal with the Dragon." Another sound rose beneath the growling storm: distant, muffled screams. "The beasts will do what they do best. Burn. Kill. Destroy. Stony Harbor will blaze so brightly the Sons of Stone will see the flames as they're massacred. They'll die knowing everything they love is gone."

The screams grew louder.

"Bastard!" I swiped futilely at him through the bars. "How? Gwylor chose Torin at the Culling. No one usurps the god of death's will."

Madoc was drawing something in the dirt floor with the toe of his boot. He stopped, staring at me like I was a fool. "My brother was chosen, given the blessings of Gwylor. Just as Llewlin and his sons were."

Lord Llewlin, father of Glasnith. According to the Immortal Scriptures, he and his three sons had called upon the god of death to help them save our island from the Great Betrayer's uprising, after Veronis declared himself king. Llewlin and his sons perished nobly during the battle at the Great Betrayer's palace.

But according to the mystic, the Forbidden Scriptures said it was Llewlin and his sons who wanted to be kings, and they called upon Gwylor to crown the worthiest among them. The god of death toyed with and tricked them, driving them to kill one another out of madness. Just as my father had descended into madness since the Culling.

Gwylor was a trickster. A manipulator. He didn't play by anyone's rules, save his own.

Neither did Madoc. I'd glimpsed the answer months ago in the cells, when I read his soul and saw the trial from Madoc's point of view—the way he'd pretended to scream as Gwylor whispered to him, the way he'd smiled as he held the burning heart that turned into a circle of gold. A crown, I realized with sudden horror.

The trial had been a farce.

"Gwylor didn't choose Torin," I said. "He exploited Torin's weakness, used him to destroy our clan from within. Gwylor chose *you*." Madoc finished drawing the symbol on the floor. I recognized it—I'd seen it drawn in ash on the door of his cottage before the Culling. I remembered dresses stained with blood, the sound of cracking bones, as another realization, more sickening than all the others, came to me. "The god of death didn't steal your wife and daughter. You *offered* them."

"Yes." His hollow gaze regarded me, and I saw that Madoc wasn't completely heartless. His mourning had been genuine. It pained him to lose his family.

Somehow, that made it worse.

"It's true, what I said at the trial. I am no chieftain." Madoc raised the lantern. "Because I was meant to be king."

King of Glasnith. That's what he'd wanted all along.

"The Dragon will take Glasnith and appoint me high king. Then he'll take the Auk Isles, and Sanddune, and Savanna. He'll create an empire. He'll conquer the world."

Gods be damned. Madoc, Torin, Draki, Gwylor. They had doomed us all. "You said you bowed to no one. But you would bow to Draki?"

"If that's what it takes to get a crown upon my head. Mark my words, girl. Before this is over, all of Glasnith will bow to the Dragon."

Even Madoc—blustering, bloodthirsty Madoc—had been cowed by Draki.

"I'll never bow." I gripped the bars so hard my knuckles were white. "Not to him, nor to you."

"Perhaps not." He smiled. "I promised you to that crafty, yellow-eyed beast, but unfortunately, you know too much for me to let you live. So instead, I've offered you to Gwylor." He nodded at the symbol he'd drawn on the floor. "Think of this as a parting gift—death by my hands, rather than the Dragon's."

Madoc swung his arm, hurling the lantern at the ceiling. It caught fire instantly.

CHAPTER 47

The only man with a key to the grate I was locked behind strolled off into the night, leaving me to burn. Clutching the medallion to my chest, I tried to think of a way out, but shock and grief clogged my thoughts, slowing my mind.

The fire gorged itself on the wood and thatching of the roof, a shrieking orange sky swelling above me. Death had touched me in the loch, through the hands of the fallen gods. It had touched me in the sharp thorns of a knout, through the hands of my father. Gwylor was the god of death, but Death was its own entity, its own animal—a god could command it, but it was the teeth of Death itself that sank into your soul and wrenched you from this world. I felt it near me, slavering with anticipation.

Wet drops dampened my cloak.

I squinted up through the smoke at the water splatting down into the cells, molding the dirt floor into mud. Above me, past the harsh haze of flame, was a wide black scrim. Night. Rain. The fire had torn a hole in the roof.

I tied the medallion around my neck and pushed my grief down, away, into a dark corner. Later, I'd let it out and hope it wouldn't destroy me. Now, I focused on surviving.

Wrapping my sodden cloak around me, I stood and put a foot on the grate. I gripped the bars and pulled myself higher, scaling them carefully, until the fire was directly overhead, a wall of orange-yellow spikes, shimmering beneath the pouring rain.

I pushed into the flames, the heat like a battering ram trying to shove me back into the hole I'd climbed out of. Crawling through it, and past it, I clambered onto the burning roof, then off it, crashing to the ground beside the cells.

My cloak was on fire. I wormed out of it, tossing the smoldering garment aside. My skin held the fire's heat, but the burns were light, no worse than after the Culling.

Screams rolled across the village, and I raced up the nearest hill to get a better view. Women and children rushed in all directions as Dragonmen chased them. Sharp tongues of blue fire burst from the cottages beyond, towering above the rooftops.

My village was lost. I couldn't save it. But I could find Ishleen and get her to safety, helping as many others along the way as I could.

Staying low, hunching behind burning cottages, I crept deeper into the village, passing the corpses of our sentries. Torin had trusted Madoc and left Stony Harbor near defenseless. Dragonmen rounded up my people, binding them, beating them, but others joined the Westlanders—shorter, darker of skin and hair, in an odd assortment of outfits. Equally savage.

Glasnithian mercenaries.

Madoc had done this, brought the most vicious warriors of Iseneld and Glasnith together. How could we defeat the beasts of the Frozen Sun when it meant fighting our own people as well?

I'd nearly made it to Ishleen's cottage when I spotted the three Daughters of Aillira. Each one had a Dragonman guard at her side, holding out a torch, and the girls drew the fire onto their palms and hurled it onto the thatched-roof cottages. As the roofs began to burn, the girls raised their hands and the crackling orange flames burst into blue infernos, shooting toward the sky.

The fire-sweepers' eyes were unfocused, the three of them moving as if they were sleepwalking. They'd been marked by the Dragon, their minds trapped within his spell.

I squeezed the hilt of my knife. One Dragonman, I could handle, but three?

Down the hill was the sanctuary, a pack of Dragonmen prowling around its tower like wolves protecting their den. I spotted a girl with apricot hair being escorted inside it.

"Eathalin?" I whispered.

There were no structures to hide behind between here and the sanctuary. I sheathed my knife and shuffled as the fire-sweepers had, slow and deliberate, keeping my face slack and my eyes forward. The Dragonmen and mercenaries I passed glanced at me, assumed I was under Draki's control, and left me alone.

At the sanctuary, a Dragonman looked me over. "Lost your guard, *magiska*?" He ushered me into the tower. "The warlord won't want you wandering unprotected."

I was greeted by the shrill calls of the lammergeiers above, hunched deep in their nests, hiding from the storm. Women huddled together on the benches, holding on to one another, some weeping, some praying with Doyen, who stood beside the altar, calling out to the gods to save us. Dragonmen gathered at the sanctuary's entrance to keep us from escaping. They argued over what they would do to the women Draki didn't keep for himself.

If Sloane were here, he'd tell me I was a fool—I had no idea how to get back out of the sanctuary with so many Dragonmen surrounding it—but Sloane was dead, and if I left Eathalin behind, she would join him.

The spell-caster kneeled against one of the benches, and I hurried over to her. "Eathalin? Can you hear me?"

Eathalin remained silent, a vacant expression upon her face, just like the fire-sweepers. Gingerly I placed my finger behind her ear, searching until I found it: Draki's mark. I kept calling her name, as if it might wake her, but it wouldn't. Only one thing could.

I looked down at my scar of flame.

Reyker's *skoldar* protected me against Draki because we were both god-gifted—a connection steeped in blood magic. A mark that could only be made once. I could do the same for Eathalin.

Drawing the knife sheathed to my thigh, I pressed it to her wrist.

My hands shook as I cut a *skoldar* that matched my own into her skin. When I was done, I slashed my palm and smeared my blood over her wound. The connection was instant, a tightening in my veins, drawing me to Eathalin. Loosening the Dragon's hold.

"Eathalin." I shook her gently and she gasped, blinking back to life.

"Lira?" She clutched at me. I gave her time to collect herself, and then I prodded her to tell me what had happened. "The Dragon and his men were in the desert," she whispered. "After we left you and Reyker in the Tangled Forest, we headed back. We didn't know it, but they followed us. They took Ghost Village."

"What of the nomads? Zabelle and Mago? The prince?" Had Garreth been there when the camp fell? Had he been captured or killed?

Sobs racked Eathalin. "When they attacked, I was supposed to run, but they had Mago. They threatened to kill him if the nomads with gifts didn't come forward. I gave myself up, but they killed him anyway. The Dragon had captured and marked a pain-wielder, and they made me watch her flay Mago alive."

Sursha. In my dream, I had seen her with Draki at the temple. He must have gotten to her after she'd left Selkie's Quay. I hadn't known Mago well, but I ached for what had been done to him, and for Eathalin's loss.

"I don't know what happened to Zabelle or the others," she said. "After the Dragon marked me, he took me to Aillira's Temple. He compelled me to remove the veil that hid the temple, and then he captured them. All the Daughters of Aillira inside. It was my fault." Her words dissolved into whimpers.

I put my arms around her. "It wasn't. You had no choice. But I won't let them hurt you again." It was a promise. It was a lie. What could I do to stop it?

I locked eyes with Doyen, crossing the sanctuary, his intentions written across his face.

How could I protect Eathalin when I couldn't even protect myself?

"Beast-lover! Betrayer-whore!"

My knife was in my hand, and then it wasn't. Several of the other women came up behind me, grabbing my arms, my weapon, pulling me away from Eathalin. I tried to fight them, but I was still weak, recovering from my infected wounds.

"It's as I've said all along," Doyen told the women. "The soul-reader brought the beasts here. The gods won't hear our prayers and save us until we right her mother's wrong. The girl is a heretic, just like her namesake. She must be sacrificed."

"No." I squirmed, and the women's fingers dug harder into my skin. "Doyen, please. You're mistaken."

"We have carried forth through the ashes of your destruction long enough." He took out his dagger. "We must purge this blight so we will be forgiven."

The women dragged me onto the stone altar, holding me down. I heard Eathalin crying behind them. Rain hammered my face, nearly blinding me. Doyen raised his dagger over my heart, the jeweled hilt glinting.

Death had found me once more.

The dagger plunged. I pulled one of my arms free, grabbing the dagger's hilt, trying to push the blade away. The tip sank in just above my heart. With a cry, I shoved sideways and the blade raked across my chest, beneath my collarbone. My blood gushed across the altar.

"Stop," a hollow voice called from outside the tower.

At the sanctuary's archway, the Dragonmen yelled in alarm. "*Volva*," they said—*witch*—making gestures to ward against evil. They moved aside for someone.

The mystic entered the sanctuary, her creamy flesh studded with furious eyes. Away from the rotting Grove of the Fallen Ones, her beauty was restored. "I've come for the soul-reader. The girl does not belong to you, priest."

"Blasphemer," Doyen said. "I don't listen to the lowly servants of fallen gods." He lifted the dagger once more. I held my breath, awaiting its blow.

The mystic darted forward with extraordinary speed, grabbed the dagger's hilt, and twisted. The blade pierced Doyen's stomach. His eyes widened and the priest stumbled backward, into the fire pit, the torch setting his robes aflame. Doyen flopped to the ground, screaming, burning like an offering.

The other women backed away, shrieking, as the mystic snatched the dagger from the dying priest's guts and bent over the altar. Dozens of brightly colored eyes fixated on me.

"Mistress of souls. You are the chosen vessel of the Fallen Ones." The mystic sliced the dagger along the side of her own neck, releasing a flood of blue-black fluid thicker and darker than blood should be. It spilled onto my chest, the sludge from her torn throat flowing into my wound.

My chest caught fire.

White-hot pain poured into me, scorching me from the inside out, and my body stiffened from the shock. Darkness coursed through me, bonding with my own blood. It whispered, speaking with a thousand voices in a thousand languages, my skull pounding from the pressure. "No, I don't want it!" I clawed at the mystic, but she pinned me to the altar.

GIVE IN, the voices coaxed. WE WILL MAKE YOU STRONG.

I struggled harder, screamed louder.

ACCEPT US. WE WILL GIVE YOU SUCH POWER.

I had done this. I put my blood in the loch to save Reyker, gave a piece of myself to the fallen gods, and they had come for me.

YOU BELONG TO US.

My blood burned like fuel. My bones were stretched, on the verge of cracking. I felt my own fragility, how small and frail my life was in the shadow of their immortality. I was no match for the gods, and it hurt too much to fight them.

I gave in.

The agony dulled to a smoldering ache. Power surged through my veins, pumped through my heart, filling me. Oh gods, Torin had been right—I *liked* how it felt. As much as I'd fought it, I wanted this.

FREE US.

This voice, I knew.

ARISE, DAUGHTER, Veronis commanded.

The world spun, bobbing like the sea. I looked down at my chest, ran my fingers across the skin—beneath the smears of blood was a thin scar. The mystic's blood had healed my wound, just like the waters of the loch. She lay dead beside the altar, a shriveled, bloodless husk.

Was I a mystic now? Would my flesh sprout all-seeing eyes?

NO. WE HAVE A GREATER PURPOSE FOR YOU.

Doyen's body still burned on the floor. The women in the sanctuary gaped at me, as did the Dragonmen, crowding in the archway, watching. I slid from the altar, holding on to it to steady myself. "Let us go," I said in Iseneldish, retrieving my knife.

The Dragonmen glanced at one another warily. I took a step forward.

Out slipped their axes and swords.

These men attacked my people, burned my village, collected women in our holy sanctuary to enslave and abuse. Anger burned through me. Power spiked within my blood.

USE IT.

"Let us go!" All around me, the holy blood symbols painted on the sanctuary walls glowed like heated metal. The tower filled with bright red light. The lammergeiers screeched.

"*Volva*," the Dragonmen murmured.

In a burst of sparks, the symbols liquefied, bubbled, and melted. Blood streaked down the walls in long, thick trails, drenching the floor. The Dragonmen watched in awe, lifting their weapons higher.

UNLEASH IT.

I spoke a single word in the old tongue: "Destroy."

From above came a series of earsplitting shrieks. I had barely enough time to duck as a dark cloud rolled over me. The lammergeiers nesting at the top of the tower swooped down as one, diving at the Dragonmen. There were more than I'd realized, as many birds as invaders, each as large as a wolfhound. Their daggerlike beaks and talons tore at the men's skin, tangled in their long hair, pecked out their sapphire eyes and ripped open their throats.

The Dragonmen screamed and scattered. Some fell to the ground, clutching their wounds, while others ran, swatting desperately at the monstrous raptors.

I turned to the terrified women. Part of me wanted to leave them to Draki's mercy for what they'd tried to do to me, but to keep my promise to Eathalin, I needed them. "Can any of you sail?"

"I can," one woman said. "My husband taught me."

"Good. You can show the others what to do. Run to the harbor and take one of the fishing vessels. Head south to Selkie's Quay and warn them of what's happened here." I pointed to Eathalin. "Take her with you. Watch after her. She's a Daughter of Aillira, one of the last who remains free. Now go." No one moved. "Go!"

I herded them outside, where rain fell like rocks. The storm boiled into a wild vortex of wind and water. My senses assaulted me, every sight and sound amplified—colors pulsed with vivid radiance, trees and sky and fire glittered ethereally. This was the world as I'd never seen it.

I closed my eyes, pressed my hands over my ears.

When I opened them, the women were dodging past dead and injured Westlanders, rushing to the harbor as lammergeiers dove and screeched overhead. A Dragonman grabbed Eathalin by the ankle, and she kicked him in the head until he released her. I nearly laughed.

Howls echoed from the village. Warriors ran toward us, Dragonmen and mercenaries, trying to stop the women from escaping.

SUMMON THEM.

"Come forth," I commanded in the old tongue, spreading my arms to the weeping sky. A violent pulse of thunder answered.

They came.

Hooves pounded. The earth shook beneath my feet. Hulking shapes burst from the trees, baying with rage. They barreled into the men, trampling them, goring them. A herd of forest demons, with horns and tusks and fangs—they had once belonged to Veronis, god of all creatures, just like the lammergeiers, the Brine Beast, and every other animal on my island. The demons swerved around me and the other villagers, stomping on the fallen Dragonmen, stampeding into the village. The warriors screamed and fell beneath their hooves.

This time, I did laugh. Mangled bodies, death everywhere. Something deep within me, something that didn't feel like *me*, found it all quite amusing.

Someone laughed with me.

He stood twenty paces away. Ash-silver hair spilling down his back, bare from the waist up, ink spiraling across one side of his body. A shining golden god. "Good trick, little warrior."

His voice was a shard of obsidian. It was water hardening into ice. Not even the Fallen Ones' power could shield me from him. Would my *skoldar* still protect me now that Reyker was dead, or had its magic been severed?

"Draki." His name slipped off my tongue, a growl and a whimper. I snatched up one of the dead Dragonmen's daggers.

"Come to me," Draki said.

The scar behind my ear went cold. My legs began to move without my consent. "No." My *skoldar* warmed enough for me to stop, but Draki's face twisted into a beautiful, terrifying smile, and I nearly hit my knees. How could I ever hope to escape from him?

The sound of hooves made me turn.

A chestnut mare galloped toward me across the hills. "Victory?"

The mystic must have ridden her here. Rhys's horse came for me, to save me as I'd saved her. Maybe it was fate, or luck, or Veronis's influence—whatever it was, I would take it. Victory paused long enough for me to swing onto her back before running full speed to the shelter of the Tangled Forest. I didn't look back.

CHAPTER 48

We raced through the forest until it became a swamp. Even the thick canopy couldn't keep out the driving rains. Crystals gleamed in Victory's coat and mane; the rain had turned to ice, a translucent glaze falling across the earth. Gales battered us, but the forest stirred with more than wind. Draki was near. I felt him. Victory sensed it too, shifting her eyes with the fear of an animal stalked by predators. Distressed, the horse failed to notice the fallen tree blocking our path.

Her hooves skidded in the mud, her front legs crashing into the bulky trunk. Victory toppled over the tree, and I was thrown from her back into a deep puddle.

The water was as thick as quicksand. I struggled to my hands and knees, wading through the muck to get to Victory, who flailed on her side, unable to stand. I coaxed her, pushed her, but it did no good; I wasn't strong enough to help her up. I murmured, petting her muzzle, trying to soothe her. Around us, the trees shuddered. The Dragon was coming.

I stared into Victory's dark eyes. *Go,* they seemed to say.

"Damn you!" I screamed at the gods. "Why must I lose everything?"

The gods didn't answer; they wouldn't deign to explain themselves to mortals. I grabbed my dagger, kissed my brother's horse one last time, and left her behind.

Crawling through mud. Wading through puddles. "Show yourself," I said, envisioning the Grove of the Fallen Ones, the only place I might be able to hide from the Dragon. Before, the forest had transitioned from living to dying as I'd crossed from my world to the in-between space the grove occupied. This time, the grove sprang up around me—absent, then everywhere, all at once. Blackened trees stretching over me, rotting creatures scuttling about. The sickly loch, still and sinister, squatting in the center of everything.

I went to it, my toes poking over the edge of the bank. Outside the grove, I could hear the storm, but it didn't touch me here. No rain fell, no wind shook the decaying leaves and blighted branches. "What now?" I asked the loch, and the gods trapped beneath it. The water belched and bubbled, as if someone was speaking from deep in its depths. I crouched down, fingers hovering over the slimy surface. Words whispered through my head.

NOW, YOU CHOOSE.

The trees began to sway. The loch began to boil. And then the grove was gone, ripped away like a blindfold, rain and ice and wind pummeling me again. There was no loch, only muddy pools of rainwater.

"You hide, but I find you." Draki emerged from the forest, silver threads of wet hair clinging to the sharp planes of his face. The bare skin of his tattooed torso glistened. He tapped a finger behind his ear. "I always find you."

Blindly, I staggered backward, out of the cage of trees, onto a plot of flat green land that ended in a sheer drop-off. Beyond it, the Shattered Sea unfurled like an endless shroud. Far to the west lay the lands of the Frozen Sun. I'd made it to the northern bluffs.

The sky crackled with white veins of fire, and pearls of ice rained down on us. Draki seemed impervious to the glassy spheres bouncing off him. His eyes were radiant, full of expectation. I raised my dagger. "Stay away from me," I said in Iseneldish.

Draki switched to his native tongue, his words flowing smooth as silk.

"You cannot escape me. I have the blood of gods in my veins—my gods and yours. I was spawned from the womb of the serpent-goddess Ildja, the eater of souls."

I stared at his gold-green eyes. A serpent's eyes.

"I believe you know Ildja's brother." Draki paused, savoring my fear like the calm before a storm. "You call him Gwylor. The god of death."

"That's not possible." The Immortal Scriptures contained no mention of Ildja, or of Gwylor having a sister. But the Immortal Scriptures were a lie.

"It is"—Draki spread his arms wide—"because here I stand. I meant to feed you to Ildja, so she could taste all the souls you'd ever touched. She loves to eat the Daughters of Aillira, out of spite. You know, your people's scriptures are erroneous. It was my mother who started your Gods' War. Ildja was the one who told her brother to seduce Aillira and destroy Veronis."

Something clicked into place: Aillira, staring at the bog adder she used to kill herself. *I see you, goddess. Devour my soul if you dare.* Ildja. The serpent-goddess, eater of souls. That's who Aillira had seen in the adder's eyes.

Draki tried to circle me, but I shuffled my feet and moved with him, never letting him get closer. "I sense much power in you now," he said. "You would be wasted as a meal. I will keep you for myself. Would you like that? To be my devoted pet?"

I could feel him reaching out, stripping away my thoughts, my defenses. I lunged at him with the dagger, and Draki caught it with his bare hand, fingers jerking the blade forward, pulling me so I fell against him. He gripped my hair, sniffing at me, an animal memorizing my scent. The mark behind my ear turned to frost and images flickered through my mind.

Draki sits upon a throne—a monstrosity made of skeletons frozen in ice, matching the crown of ice and bone set atop his head. I kneel before him. His tattoos come alive, rippling across his skin, the ink dripping over me, staining me with its darkness. His muscles flex, his bones shift; glistening black wings burst from between his shoulders. "You are my savior," I tell him. "My master. My god." His wings encase me, swinging shut like a trap.

"Stop." I tore myself from the vision, but my will was disintegrating, my breath heavy in my lungs. I melted against him like wax under a flame, losing myself.

Draki leaned in, studying me, his lips nearly touching mine. "Make me, if you can."

Rhys. Reyker. I held them both in my mind like a talisman. The *skoldar* on my wrist smoldered, and the chains Draki had wrapped around my mind loosened. I stomped on his foot, pounded my fists against him, banged my knee into his groin.

He released me. "There you are, little warrior." An infuriating smile softened the harsh beauty of his face. "I see you. I know you."

I shuddered.

Draki glanced at the scar on my wrist. "When I rid you of that, you will be free. You will see the splendor of what we can accomplish together."

"You can't remove my *skoldar*. Not without killing me."

"A mortal would not survive." His gaze raked from my toes to my scalp. "But you have the power of gods in your veins too. You are not so easy to kill."

The healed wound on my chest gave credence to Draki's threat. I thought of Eathalin and the fire-sweepers, their eyes void of life—that was the fate awaiting me. Draki would drag me back to the village. And then what? Cut off Reyker's mark so he could take control of me? Use me as a weapon to hurt my own people?

I fumbled for whatever powers Veronis and the Fallen Ones had given me, desperate, but it was like groping for a lost weapon in the dark, knowing it was there yet finding nothing. I didn't know how to use those abilities, not without their coaxing, and for some reason their voices had gone silent. Did they not care if I succumbed to Draki's compulsion, or had he done something to quiet them, the same way he'd forced the grove to recede?

Foolishly, I stared at the forest. Searching. Waiting.

Where are you, Reyker? You promised you'd never leave me. You promised you wouldn't let Draki take me.

I reached for my medallion … finding nothing. Doyen's dagger must have sliced through the rope when he stabbed me. The last thing I had left of my mother, and of Reyker, was gone.

"Come, little warrior. I will take you home."

The wind howled. The sky ignited. The god of death's kin held out his hand to me.

I closed my eyes. Took a deep breath. Opened them. I knew what I had to do.

"My will is my own." I took several steps back, raising my dagger again. "Until the end."

I swung my arms hard, then let go, hurling the dagger at Draki. He laughed, reaching out to catch it, distracted. I turned and ran. My feet touched the ends of the earth. I kept going.

Off the edge.

Over the bluffs.

CHAPTER 49

What have I done?

It was mere seconds between the moment I leaped from the bluffs and the moment I was swallowed by the sea, mere seconds I spent plummeting through the space between land and water, but it felt like an endless journey, my resolve unspooling along the way.

Oh, gods, what have I done?

Time slowed down even as my life sped by me, all the things I'd lost, all the things I'd left behind, snapping around me like broken threads. I clawed the air, flailing, as if I could somehow climb my way back up and make a different choice.

I don't want to die.

The wind tore at my clothes, ripped at my hair. Below me, the gray waters churned and frothed, growing closer. I was falling, falling, yet it was as if I hung there, suspended. Mere seconds. An eternity.

The sea. It was so close.

Reyker. Amidst the grip of panic, I clung to thoughts of him. So little time we'd had. Not nearly enough.

Reyker's gods, his otherworlds, were different than mine. When I died, would I find him waiting beneath the waves, feasting with Rhys and Mother in the Eternal Palace? Or would he be with his own gods, his own people, in Fortune's Field? Would we wander through the hereafter, searching, never finding each other—separated evermore, like Aillira and Veronis?

The sea. It was here.

Blackness. Darkness. Endless.

I was reduced to nothing but a spark. The infinite cave of Death's mouth opened, teeth sinking into me. It was cold, dark, the blackest of winter nights. I was alone. But I didn't hurt. I wasn't afraid. I could stay here and sleep forever, no more pain or loss, just an icy oblivion.

I laid my head down, closed my eyes.

Something itched, scratching at the back of my mind. A voice, screaming my name. Haunting me. Waking me. Calling me back.

I sucked in a sharp breath. Choked on a mouthful of water.

My eyes flew open as something crashed into me, shredding my skin. My arms dug at the cold water until I'd pushed my way to the surface. I gulped air, but a wave knocked me back under. My body smacked into one of the jagged pillars of rock rising from the sea.

Once more, I splashed to the surface only to be thrust under, pounded against rocks again. I was trapped in the sloshing throes of the storm-ravaged sea. I would die here. The rocks would break me; the waves would drown me.

SING.

The thousand voices returned, Veronis's the strongest of them all. Without questioning, I did as the Fallen Ones bid me, opening my mouth to pour out all my pain.

The song—it was the same one I'd heard when I dove into the loch and Veronis first spoke to me; it was the same song he and Aillira had sung to each other, the same one she'd been humming when she planted the seed of the thorntree just before she ended her life. It was in the old language, and the words were different, but it was the song I'd sung to Reyker, the sea ballad my mother taught me as a child. I sang it now, and it rippled into the current.

How could my love be lost to me ...

I forced air from my lungs, throwing a torrent of vibrations into the water. I wanted to sing so loud none of the gods could ignore me.

His ship was swallowed by the sea ...

I harnessed the violet spark of my being, setting the verse aglow as it left my lips, hoping Rhys and Mother and Reyker might hear me, and know I was on my way to them.

I feel him close, but it's only his ghost ...

Delving into my head, into my blood, I sought every drop of power the mystic had given me, unleashing it, filling every word with its essence.

My love, my love, return—

A song answered mine, startling me. It was a wordless echo, mimicking the ballad's tune. Moments later, other songs joined it, harmonizing.

All around me, music swelled. It rose up from the floor of the sea, lulling and luminescent, a sweeping whirlpool of sound. The phantom choir crept out of the darkness below; I didn't see them until I was surrounded. They were as big as whales, but serpentine like eels.

The Brine Beasts. There wasn't one; there were many. A pod of them. A family.

And they still served Veronis, their fallen master.

One of the Beasts swam beneath me and surfaced, taking me with it. I took a gluttonous breath, and it dove down again. I clung to its slick scales as the creature slithered and glided, faster in liquid than any horse was on land. Its pod flanked us, moving as one, singing to one another. I should've been afraid—one of these Beasts killed my mother, my cousin. One devoured a boatful of Dragonmen. But it had also spared Reyker. It had spared me.

The Beast I held on to arced its body up, breaching long enough for me to gasp, then plunged. In this manner, we made our way swiftly along the coast, outrunning the storm.

—◆—

When the Beast finally slowed, grazing the air longer, I noticed the water was calmer. I wasn't sure how far we'd gone—at least ten leagues, if I'd had to guess. Far from Stony Harbor. The cliffs were smaller here, and a sloping shore edged the sea.

My ride was over. The giant eel shook and rolled, flinging me off like I was a parasite. All the Beasts were gone in an instant, darting into deeper waters.

I swam to shore, dragged myself onto the sand, and collapsed.

I slept, dreaming I was back on the bluffs with Draki, only I stood at the edge of them, staring down into the water. My chest throbbed as if my heart had shattered, the shards impaling me from within.

Fingers of sunlight brushed my skin, rousing me sometime later. I hauled myself up the rocky cliff, unsurprised to find the outskirts of the Green Desert on the other side.

I walked.

The day grew hot. The sun peaked and set.

The night grew cold. I didn't stop.

The sun burned the horizon once more. I pushed on, over hills, across the moorlands—thirsty, hungry, aching—until my legs gave out. I languished in the tall grass, waiting, unafraid.

This was where I was meant to be.

CHAPTER 50

REYKER

The horse wasn't fast enough.

Reyker put his heels to it, but it galloped no faster. The Tangled Forest sprawled around him, dark and dreary. The clouds dripped. His breath was tight, chest aching from the horse's concussive gait. Blood seeped around the priests' sutures, where the captain had stabbed him.

He should have gotten here sooner. The priests had lent him their small vessel, the one they'd been sailing when they had fished him from the sea, but it wasn't outfitted for ocean crossings; he'd been blown off course, landing farther south of Stony Harbor than he'd intended. And the stupid horse he'd stolen, despite its height and strength, ran as slow as an old man.

Thick plumes of smoke curled above the tree line. The raid had begun.

Finally they reached the village, the horse shying at the crush of heat and flame. Every cottage burned with unearthly blue fire. Draki must have commanded his god-gifted prisoners to do this. The Dragon meant to reduce Stony Harbor to rubble.

Screaming villagers ran from the hordes of Dragonmen. There were mercenaries too. Bog Men. The Ravenous, the clan that had attacked the cog. Others, who wore odd outfits like vests made of seaweed or armor made of skulls, carried strange weapons like spiked maces and tridents. It seemed Draki had forged his own alliances with the mercenaries.

No one paid Reyker heed as he rode through the turmoil. From afar, he was just another Dragonman.

Reyker closed his eyes, trying to hear the whisper in his blood that could lead him to Lira, but it was drowned out by the call of the black river, begging to be released. He felt the deep divide within him, blazing lights warring with suffocating darkness.

He steered the horse to Ishleen's cottage, where he'd last seen Lira, and saw a mob of Dragonmen cornering a small, brown-haired girl—Ishleen, screaming, swinging a short sword. She managed to stab one of the Dragonmen, but the others ripped the sword away, grabbing at her, tearing her dress.

Reyker dismounted. The black river stirred.

Let. Me. Out.

His blade split their flesh. He caught an axe as it dropped from one of their hands, making use of both weapons. He cleaved a skull, a chest. Every movement was fluid, the black river flowing through him. It felt like coming home.

When it was over, Reyker stood panting, exhilarated. Five men lay dead. His own men—beneath the glaze of blood were faces he knew.

Ishleen stared, terrified, until she recognized him. "*You?* What are you—"

"Where is Lira?" he shouted. The girl flinched. With effort, he lowered his voice. "She's in danger. I have to find her. Where is she?"

Ishleen pointed. "Lira went to the cells."

He'd dreamed of her there, in his old cell, calling out to him. He'd lain in the priests' sanctuary as the jagged hole in his chest slowly healed, holding fast to those dreams.

"Go," Reyker told the girl, nodding at the forest. He picked up her fallen sword, handing it to her. "Run and hide."

"My mother. An invader chased her. That way." Ishleen pointed in the opposite direction from the cells. "Please. Won't you help her?"

Reyker could not stop for everyone who needed saving. Not if he wanted to find Lira before Draki did. "Go!" he said, quelling her protests.

She ran. Reyker mounted and rode for the cells, watching over his shoulder to make sure Ishleen made it into the forest safely.

The horse climbed a slope and the cells came into view, bright with fire. He was off the horse before it halted, kicking in the door.

"Lira!" He felt his way to the bars through the smoke. The grates were locked. He knelt, searching the floor of each cell. She wasn't here. Rain leaked in through a hole in the roof.

Reyker stumbled outside, circling the building. Ashes of clothing smoldered in the grass. Small muddy footprints headed toward the village, and he climbed on his horse, following them.

Once more he closed his eyes and grappled for the cord of blood magic that connected them. This time he sensed it—a tug, a whisper.

It drew him toward the sanctuary. The tower was a gray smear in the swirling storm.

A sudden drumming rose above the thunder. Men screamed. Reyker's horse reared as dozens of creatures rushed at them, huge and horned, with coats like twilight, eyes like dusk.

Forest demons.

He jerked the horse's reins, dodging around the demons, but one blocked the way. The forest demon looked at Reyker, assessing. A moment later, it moved aside, bobbing its huge head. Judging him as one who meant no harm—someone who belonged here.

Reyker bowed back and rode on.

When he arrived at the sanctuary, it was surrounded by dead Dragonmen lying among a patchwork of blood and feathers. The men's throats were raggedly slashed, eyes torn and dangling from sockets, cheeks shredded so the white of teeth was visible through the holes. Giant raptors flitted about, picking at the remains.

In the distance, Reyker noticed a single fishing boat edging out of the harbor, tossed about, taking its chances on the rough seas.

He entered the sanctuary. It was empty but for a charred body and the corpse of a deformed woman, her body blotted by glassy eyes. Blood coated the altar, streaked down the walls. Something terrible had happened to Lira here. He felt it.

A silver disk stuck out of the mud beside the altar. Reyker picked it up, wiped it off. His own blood was still on the medallion, soaked into the carving. Was this her blood on the sliced rope necklace?

Reyker tucked the medallion under the tight leather of his jerkin and stepped back into the squall. His blood whispered, growing louder, more insistent. He let it lead him, chasing Lira's trail into the forest.

The trees were dense, the rain heavy.

The horse was still stubbornly slow. It stalled at a fallen tree, bucked when Reyker kicked it. The rain loosened his grip, and he was thrown through the air—he landed on the tree, rolled facedown into a puddle, and came up sputtering in time to watch the horse bolt.

"Now you find your speed, you stupid beast?" he called as it disappeared.

A snort made him jump. In the mud beside him was a chestnut-coated mare looking impatient. Like it was waiting for him.

This was Lira's horse. It had to be. She was close.

"Stuck, are you? Come on then." Reyker braced his feet against the fallen tree, his back against the mare, pushing with all his strength. The horse's body moved, just barely. "Are you even trying?" he grunted, muscles straining.

The horse rocked, and Reyker pushed until the animal staggered to all fours. He wasted no time climbing on, and the mare tore through the forest without prodding, as if it knew exactly where to go.

Reyker rode until the mud became too thick for the horse to wade through. "Stay here," he said, sliding off the mare. "I'll be back soon."

The horse whickered, watching him with doleful eyes.

Rain fell in chunks, white marbles of ice. He sloshed through puddles, mud sucking at his boots, slowing him. Ahead, the trees opened onto a glade. The northern bluffs—he had been here once before, with Lira.

The warlord's voice startled him. "Come, little warrior. I will take you home."

The black river stirred. Reyker sprinted for the clearing.

He caught a glimpse of violet hair, of green-fire eyes. "My will is my own," he heard her say. "Until the end."

Her words strengthened him, and he would have screamed her name if he'd had breath to spare. Between tree limbs, he saw a flash of silver—a blade. Draki laughed, reaching for it. Lira bounded forward. She leaped from the bluff and was gone.

Gone?

The air left Reyker's lungs in a rush.

He pushed his legs harder, aiming for the ledge she'd vanished over. *Not gone. Not yet.* He would follow. He could still save her. He was almost there.

An arm slammed into his chest.

Reyker sailed backward, crashing into a tree. He hit the ground and a hand closed around his throat, lifting him to his feet. "I see the rumors of your death were false. How fortunate."

No, no, no. He had to get to Lira soon or she would drown.

He struggled, but Draki's grip was unyielding.

"Where have you been all this time, Reyker?" Draki eyed his slave-brand, laughing darkly. "A captive? Such shame you've brought upon yourself. Tell me, did you find my fiery little warrior while you were imprisoned?"

Draki dragged him to the bluff's edge. Reyker stared, searching for Lira in the sea's mouth—white-tipped fangs snapping from powerful gray jaws. She wasn't there. Even if she survived the fall, the waves would have crushed her on the rocks.

Gone.

The fallen gods' prophecy rang through his head: YOU WILL CHASE WHAT YOU CANNOT CATCH. YOU WILL LOVE WHAT YOU CANNOT KEEP.

"She kept looking to the forest, awaiting a savior," Draki said. "She thought you dead, yet still believed you might come for her."

Prying Draki's fingers from his neck, Reyker roared at the sea as if she could hear him, as if it did any good. "Lira!"

He'd taken too long to get here. He'd failed her.

But it was Draki she'd run from, Draki she'd died to escape. Reyker turned on the warlord. "You could have stopped her."

"You hid from me, Reyker. You had to be punished."

A memory unearthed itself from the dark depths of Reyker's mind: his mother, screaming, her blood spreading across the floor beneath her. The knife in his own hand. She'd broken through Draki's control for a moment, begging him to free her by cutting Draki's mark from her flesh. He'd done as she asked, not knowing what would happen. When he realized she was dying, he'd run to Draki, pleaded with the warlord to save her. Draki had followed him to his mother's chamber, held him in place, and said, *For your defiance, you will watch the thing you love most in this world die.*

"You let Lira die to punish me?" Reyker unsheathed his sword and axe, the black river pounding through his veins. He welcomed it. "I will kill you for this."

"Go on then, little lordling." Draki drew his sword. "Do your worst."

Under the scour of rain and ice, their blades clashed. Reyker was pure rage, weaving one weapon over the other in furious strikes, anticipating Draki's movements before he made them.

Draki had taught him well.

Reyker's sword slipped past Draki's guard and struck the warlord's neck. Draki's head should have rolled.

It didn't.

The steel blade shattered like glass against the warlord's throat. Reyker dropped the useless hilt and swung the axe at Draki's heart; it crashed into his chest and disintegrated.

Draki's heel rammed into Reyker's stomach, sending him flying. He landed on his back and slid off the bluff's edge, but Draki caught his wrist, dangling him above the violent sea.

"You stupid, sniveling bastard. All this over a pretty bit of flesh?" Draki jerked Reyker's arm, hauling him back over the ledge and slamming a knee into his ribs. Reyker collapsed into the mud. "I tire of your outbursts, Reyker. Next time I might forget you are my brother and cut you into pieces so small not even the gods will recognize you."

Brother.

Reyker loathed that word, its hateful truth, the blood bond they shared that he wished he could break. "Aldrik was my brother. Not you."

"Aldrik." Draki flashed a pitying smile. "You think I've forgotten that boy who first trained you to hunt and fight? You live because I remember who I was. But Aldrik was weak. I became what he could never be. I became the leader Iseneld needed."

"I needed Aldrik. But he left me, and he came back a monster." Reyker tried to stand, but Draki shoved him back down. "You killed our father. You enslaved my mother, twisted her mind. She loved you like a son and you destroyed her."

"Your mortal ties only weaken you, Reyker. You could be a warlord, a king. Katrin and Lira made you weak. I'm trying to help you be strong."

"Do not dare speak their names!" Reyker threw himself into Draki's legs, taking him to the ground. He broke his knuckles punching Draki's grinning lips, as indestructible as the rest of him.

Draki's fist slammed into Reyker's jaw, knocking him sideways. "Who wielded the knife that killed Katrin? Not I." The warlord rose, snarling down at Reyker in disgust. "Katrin and Lira belonged to me. Their deaths were *your* fault—you killed them when you tried to take them from me. You should know by now that you can never take what is mine!"

Draki left him there and stalked into the forest, vanishing amidst the shuddering trees.

Reyker closed his eyes, lying on the bluff's rim, letting the storm maul him. Beneath the squall came another sound. What cruel madness was this? He *heard* Lira, singing from the bottom of the sea—the ballad she'd taught him that often drifted into his dreams, chasing away his nightmares. Always in her voice, sweet and clear, tinged with sorrow. As it was now.

He had only just lost her and already his mind was slipping. His blood whispered and tugged, drawing him to the sea. Reyker put a hand over the medallion. Loss tunneled deep through his chest, chilling the fires of his fury. He spoke to her, hoping she could hear him, making the same vow he'd made to his father. "I will avenge you."

Only one of the Dragon's own flesh can slay him, Reyker's father had said with his dying breaths. *It must be you.*

And the Fallen Ones' prophecy had confirmed it:

YOU WILL CHASE WHAT YOU CANNOT CATCH.

YOU WILL LOVE WHAT YOU CANNOT KEEP.

YOU WILL KILL WHAT CANNOT DIE.

Reyker would kill Draki, for his people, his parents. And for Lira. He would tear off the Dragon's head, carry it to the afterworlds, place it in her hands. He would comb every realm of the dead, searching for her.

No matter how long it took, no matter where she had gone, he would find her.

EPILOGUE

The sun was warm on my skin, the desert brush rough beneath me. I heard the horses coming, felt the beat of their hooves, from leagues away. They grew closer, closer, and then they were here. Voices trickled over me.

"Zabelle," I said, opening my eyes.

She lifted a waterskin to my lips, her gemstone eyes assessing me as I drank. "You found trouble once again, I see. Or it found you."

I gripped her arm. "The prince. Take me to him."

Nodding, she beckoned to her horse, and I knew it was Wraith even before I saw the smoke-gray stallion. Something in my blood had sensed him, as it sensed the other horses, and the crows flying overhead, the crickets chirping in the brush, the worms burrowing in the soil. I felt their energy, their minds. Their souls.

Zabelle climbed onto Wraith, and the other nomads helped me up behind her. My eyes drifted shut, my consciousness fraying once more.

I woke, sometime later, on a pallet inside a dark room. No, not a room, I realized—a cave, like the one where Ulver had held me hostage.

Garreth sat beside me, face drawn. He wore a glove on his right hand, and he practiced gripping the hilt of a sword.

"Lira?" When he saw I was awake, he put the sword down.

He seemed different—older, harder. "Prince of Ghosts, I presume?"

"So the nomads call me." Garreth smiled faintly. "I came as soon as I got Zabelle's message."

The weight of everything that had happened crashed down on me all at once. I sat up, speaking in a rush. "Garreth, Stony Harbor lies in ruin. Ishleen, Olwen, the Sons of Stone—they may all be dead. Everything is gone."

I wept then, releasing tears I'd held back since Madoc set the cells aflame. *Reyker*, my heart sobbed. *My wolf is dead.*

"Not everything." Garreth's arms came around me, and the layers peeled away—the exiled warrior, the nomad's prince. He was simply my brother. "You and I are still here."

"Yes," I whispered, holding him tightly, trying to shut out the feeling of the bats on the cave ceiling, the rats and scorpions skittering inside the rock walls, the disturbing connections forged between myself and every beast of Glasnith by a god whose essence now inhabited my body. "We are."

And I feared I'd only just begun to understand why.

ACKNOWLEDGMENTS

Getting this book into your hands was a long, hard journey, and I'm so lucky to have had help and support along the way. First and foremost, I have to thank two amazing women at Writers House to whom I'm eternally grateful: Genevieve Gagne-Hawkes, who picked my messy manuscript out of a slush pile and put me on this path, and Beth Miller, who patiently read revision after revision and walked through submission hell with me (twice!) until we made it to the other side. I would never have gotten this far without the both of you.

Thank you to everyone who had a hand in the revising of this book. To my talented editor, Madeline Hopkins, who pointed out what was missing and helped me fix what was broken, polishing this manuscript until it shined. To Jocelyn Davies, who took the time to share her ideas with me, and whose advice helped shape this book in the best possible ways. To the diligent Writers House interns who read through versions of this book, catching errors and offering suggestions that helped make it better: Ilana Masad, Eleanor Embry, Melissa Nezhnik, Stacy Shirk, Erica Buchman, and Sara Stricker.

Thank you to my awesome publishing team at Blackstone. To Rick Bleiweiss, who picked my book and made my dream come true. To Kurt

Jones, whose work never fails to impress me, for creating a gorgeous cover that exceeded all my expectations and designing the perfect warrior-mark graphics for Reyker and clan Stone. To Mandy Earles, who patiently taught me how to navigate the rocky terrain of social media. To Ember Hood, for her insightful and diligent copyedits and for helping me through my colon and semicolon addiction. To Sean Thomas, for my amazing book trailer. To all the other fantastic people at Blackstone who worked so hard to get this book out and make it a success: Jeff Yama-guchi, Lauren Maturo, Greg Boguslawski, Josie Woodbridge, Stephanie Stanton, Ananda Finwall, Tom Williamson, Kathryn English, Keith McFarland, and all the unsung-hero copyeditors and proofreaders who caught and fixed my mistakes.

Thank you to the following people for your influence and expertise. To Erin Beaty and Jessica Leake who generously read an early, unedited draft of this book (over the holidays) and offered kind and thoughtful blurbs that made me feel like a real author. To Juliet Marillier, Jaque-line Carey, and George R. R. Martin, whose brilliant books inspired my own. To Mallory Lass, who wrote a rejection letter so kind and supportive it gave me the strength to keep going. To Hafsah Faizal of Icey Design, who helped create my badass author website. To Mindy McGinnis, who forced me to become a better writer than I ever realized I could be. And to the creative writing professors at UCF who taught me so much: Susan Hubbard, Terry Thaxton, Lisa Roney, and Jocelyn Bartkevicius.

A heartfelt thank-you to my various friends and family who have encouraged me all along. To my parents, for reading to me as a child and letting me read as much as I wanted, even at the dinner table. To my sister, Julie, for not getting too mad when I borrowed her books and not telling Mom and Dad when I read books I wasn't supposed to. To Katla, for pulling me away from the computer and reminding me of all the joy life has to offer.

Thank you to Brock, for making all of this possible—for keeping me well fed and sane, for doing far more than your share of chores and child-watching, for arguing with me about grammar rules, for believing in me despite my empty-glass attitude. For being a good father, a good husband, and a good man. No amount of thanks will ever be enough.

And finally to you, dear reader, for picking up this book and giving it a chance, for being part of my journey—thank you.